The Kitchen Isn't Where You Cook

Candace Johnson

Published by Candace Johnson, 2024.

The Kitchen Isn't Where You Cook
Candace Johnson
Copyright 2024

THE KITCHEN ISN'T WHERE YOU COOK

First edition. December 3, 2024.

Copyright © 2024 Candace Johnson.

ISBN: 979-8230832928

Written by Candace Johnson.

To my late parents, Joseph and Betty McCrary, for letting me believe I could be anything I wanted to be.

To Stephanie and Amy: Two childhood friends who have remained "real ones" and who I turned to first for feedback on this book. Your support and encouragement mean the world to me.

To my sister, Nikki, for giving me your leftover school notebooks so I could write, for teaching me how to type and for buying me my first typewriter when I went to college.

To my husband, Donald, and my children, Kristina and Derek: Thanks for leaving me alone when I got into my "writing zone." I love you beyond measure.

BOOK ONE
"I Want to Be Farrah Fawcett"
1978-1987

December 1978
Petersville, Michigan

CHAPTER 1

It sounded kind of silly to say she first fell in love in the fourth grade, but that's when it happened for Marisa Logan.

Sure, she'd known her neighbor Barry Montgomery for as long as she could remember and she'd always had a crush on him, but it was during the last-day-of-school-before-holiday-break Christmas party in Mrs. Bailey's fourth grade class that she fell in love with him. Hard.

It was during the gift exchange, when she'd had to exchange gifts with that grody Timmy Franklin because she'd drawn his name in the hat. He, apparently, also drew hers because he gave her a bag of rubber bands. What kind of gift was that, anyway? Sure, his family was poor and his mother a well-known drunk, but ... rubber bands?

As she put Timmy's gift in her desk, Barry came toward her with a package in his hands. She felt her pulse race – as it always did when he was around – and smiled at him.

"Hey Marisa," he grinned and flopped down at the desk in front of her. "Merry Christmas." He set the gift-wrapped package on her desk.

"You didn't draw my name," she said in surprise. "I thought you had Lindsay."

"I did. But I saw this in the store and knew I had to get it for you."

Her heart fluttered again, and she felt herself blush. It was obvious that he'd wrapped the skinny rectangle box himself because it was kind of wrinkled with too much tape on it. Biting her lower lip, she glanced around the class to see if anyone was watching. Everyone was. Jen, Tara, Timmy, Kristin...even Mrs. Bailey kept glancing over at them. And why not? Barry was by far the most popular – and cutest—boy in the fourth grade. And the smartest. Marisa was just as smart and they loved competing against each other. But with everyone's eyes on them, she began to get embarrassed. She wished he'd given her the present later, after school or anytime over the break. He did live just across the street, after all.

But no, here he was, staring at her eagerly with that endearing smile on his full lips, his dark blonde hair tousled over his forehead as always. "G'wan. Open it!"

With a giggle, she slowly ripped open the gift and smiled at what lay inside. It was a bottle of Hawaiian perfume.

"Remember when you got in trouble for using some of your mother's perfume when you went to your cousin's wedding that time?" Barry was saying. "So I figured you should have your own bottle."

Smiling widely, she opened the box, removed the cap and took a sniff. It was heavenly.

"Thank you." She finally lifted her eyes to meet his. "I love it." They sat in silence, shyly smiling at each other before she interrupted the awkwardness. "I have a gift for you, but it's at home. I figured I'd give it to you later."

"OK." He smiled again and was about to rise when Timmy Franklin interrupted.

"You gave her a present? What is she, your girlfriend?" He guffawed loudly. "You want a burnt girlfriend?"

At that, Marisa's joyful mood disappeared. Leave it to that dummy Timmy to remind everyone that she was black. Barry didn't care. Her friends and teachers didn't care. But idiot Timmy had to bring it up, to Marisa's mortification.

"Shut up, Timmy!" Barry said menacingly.

"You shut up. You really want a girlfriend who was left in the oven too long?" He laughed again and began to walk away, but Barry rose and pushed him in the chest, knocking him into Kristin's desk.

"I said shut up! You don't talk about Marisa like that!"

And that's when it happened. Marisa fell in love.

THE KITCHEN ISN'T WHERE YOU COOK

***

On her way home that afternoon, Marisa slowed her steps and listened to the *crunch, squeak, crunch, squeak* of her Rainbow Moon boots on the packed snow, littered with the footprints of her classmates rushing home to start their Christmas vacations. She usually walked home with Barry, but Mrs. Bailey made him stay after school and clean the blackboards since he'd pushed Timmy. Timmy had gotten detention. She couldn't believe Barry stood up for her like that. On one hand, she could stand up for herself. She had two older brothers, after all. But on the other hand, it was so cool that he did that. It reminded her of how Bobby Ewing stood up for his new wife, Pamela, against his evil brother, J.R.

Marisa ran across Main Street and slowed when she came to her two-story house. She admired the Christmas lights that she and her two older brothers had strung across the wraparound porch and stood at the door for a moment smiling at the wreath her grandmother had made. Grandmama could make most anything, but Marisa wished she'd stop knitting her sweaters. She'd rather have a V-neck from the store. But she couldn't tell her grandmother that, she enjoyed knitting too much.

The house was warm and glowing when she entered. Grandmama had lit a fire, and the Christmas tree lights were already on. The Mississippi Mass Choir was singing "Joy to the World" on the record player and Marisa could smell molasses cookies. That was another thing about Grandmama. She never left the kitchen before seven o'clock at night. They had three cookie jars on the counter because of all of her baking.

Marisa tromped halfway through the living room before she realized she hadn't removed her boots. Uh-oh, Grandmama would get on her about that, for sure. But maybe she wouldn't notice. After all, it wasn't mud, it was just a little snow that could easily melt and dry before she came out of the kitchen.

"Baby?" No such luck.

"Hi, Grandmama." Marisa sat on the floor in the foyer, pulling and tugging at her boots.

"Don't pull off your boots yet, baby." Grandmama glanced at the wet carpet in the living room as she came out of the kitchen. "Chile, what is all this? Now you know better than to go traipsing through the house with them wet boots on! I just vacuumed."

To hear Grandmama tell it, she had always just vacuumed or just made the bed or just ironed. But she couldn't argue with her, so she just nodded and said, "Sorry, I forgot."

"You forgot?" Grandmama put her hands on her wide hips and shook her head. "Well, anyway, I need you to go to the store for me. I need some more corn meal for the fish. You know where it is?"

"Yes, ma'am." Marisa stood and yanked her hat back on over her two long black braids.

"Now here's the money. That's the exact amount so I don't expect no change back. You sure you know where it is?" She peered sharply at Marisa, as if her errand was a matter of world peace.

"I know where it is. It's by the flour and stuff." She'd only been going to Food Market her whole life. She knew where everything was.

"All right, now, go on. I been waiting on you for a while. Did you stop at the store yet to say hi to your Mama and Daddy?" Grandmama handed her two molasses cookies – still warm –then tightened her blue, checkered apron.

"No. I will, though." Her parents owned Logan's Hardware, which was right in front of their house. The store was kitty corner from O'Neill's Hardware, but Ernest O'Neill's store was always messy and he was always grouchy with the customers. Her daddy was always smiling, knew everything about the hardware business and kept the store bright and decorated. People in town loved her daddy's store.

"All right, but you hurry home, now. I gotta get the fish on." Grandmama had moved in with Marisa and her family three years ago, after Grandaddy died. Marisa loved having her around. She spoiled her and called her "sugar" and she loved the way she scratched and greased her hair every Sunday night. Grandmama's skin color was like lightly browned toast, with hardly a wrinkle in sight. In that respect, she and Marisa favored. Marisa didn't think she looked "burnt," no matter what that dumb Timmy Franklin said.

"Guess what, Grandmama? I got a Christmas present." She pulled out her perfume, debated telling her about Timmy and Barry getting into a fight and decided not to. Grandmama didn't need to know all her business.

"Oooh, 'Reflections.'" Grandmama looked up and down the box with a curious gaze. "It sure is big enough! Who gave this to you?"

"Barry." She said it proudly, but secretly hoped Grandmama wouldn't say anything to tease her. Grandmama didn't like white people too much and wouldn't like the fact that her granddaughter liked a white boy. It didn't matter that the Montgomerys had lived across the street most of her life and that Barry came over to play almost every weekend, he was still white. And blond, at that. For some reason, blond, white people were worse than the others.

"Oh, now, isn't that nice?" Grandmama took a sniff of the perfume and bucked her eyes at the too-sweet scent. "I'll keep this right here for you until you get back. Now go on."

Marisa was at the corner when she realized she'd forgotten her scarf. It was lying in a heap in the entryway, wet from the snow she'd tracked into the house. Oh well, she'd run to the store and run back to say hi to her parents. It wasn't like Petersville was that big. According to the atlas her daddy had, Petersville had eight-hundred people living in it. That wasn't a lot, especially when she looked at how many Kalamazoo had. Over a thousand! But Marisa liked Petersville. She knew everybody, everybody knew her, there was no crime, no noise and no traffic jams. She wished they had a Burger Chef or a movie theater, though. But maybe they'd have one by the time she reached high school. That would be cool, then she and her friends could hang out there after school the way Archie, Betty, Veronica and Reggie hung out at Pop Tate's. She loved reading Archie comic books. So far she had fifty of them and she planned on collecting them until she had more than a hundred. She liked to think that Riverdale was a lot like Petersville. Just a nice small town with no stop lights and one grocery store.

That grocery store, McCallum's Food Market, had recently been renovated. It now had five checkout lines instead of the usual two that had been there for as long as she could remember. It was about time, too, because with eight-hundred people in town the store could get pretty crowded.

She wandered down every aisle singing "Joy to the World" in a soft voice, even though she knew exactly where the corn meal was. She liked to pretend she was really shopping, and she'd buy all of the things her mother never did, like Spaghetti-O's. Mama didn't really like things in a can. She said it wasn't as healthy as homemade stuff. But how do you make Spaghetti-O's from scratch? Neither Mama nor Grandmama had mastered that feat yet. She'd also buy some cereal besides Corn Flakes or Cheerios. Yuck. Marisa hated Cheerios. They tasted like cardboard. If she were shopping, she'd buy Frosted Flakes or Alpha Bits.

She entered the aisle where the corn meal was and picked up the box, never breaking stride. In the potato chip aisle, she lingered at the Jay's Hot Stuff and stared longingly at the barbecue pork rinds. Daddy loved those, but every time he bought a bag, Marisa and her brothers would eat them up. So she suspected that he only ate them at work now, while they were in school.

"Marisa!"

She stopped singing mid-verse and saw Jennifer Van Sikkema pushing a cart behind her mother. Marisa noticed that their cart had a box of Cap'n Crunch in it. She promised herself to tell her mother that. If the Van Sikkemas, the only doctors in town, bought sweetened cereal for their family, couldn't Mama buy it, too?

"Hi Jen."

"Hello, Marisa. How are you today?" Dr. Lorraine Van Sikkema smiled down at Marisa with that fake doctor-smile of hers. She was the town's dentist while her husband was the town family doctor. They shared an office building right on Main Street, only four buildings down from Logan's Hardware, but for some reason, Marisa and her family didn't go to them. Their doctor and dentist were both in South Haven, fifteen miles south of Petersville, right on Lake Michigan. For that reason, Marisa always felt weird talking to Jen's parents. It seemed like everyone but her family went to the Van Sikkema's.

"I'm fine." She answered politely before Jen spoke again.

"What's that?" She pointed to the corn meal.

"It's corn meal. My grandmother is frying fish."

Jen turned up a pointed ski-jump nose. "Fish? Eww, is she frying that catfish we had at your house that one time? That is so gross."

"Jennifer, that's rude," her mother admonished.

Marisa hoped it was catfish. It was the only seafood she liked, but she didn't tell Jen that.

"Guess what? Mom, can I tell her?" Jen leaned toward her mother with wide eyes while her long blonde hair fell over her shoulder.

"Go ahead. Here, you take the cart and come find me when you're done talking. Goodbye, Marisa. Tell your folks I said Merry Christmas." Dr. Van Sikkema's tall, thin frame strode away in long steps, her ivory wool coat swaying with each move.

"Guess what?" Jen grabbed Marisa's arm with a black suede glove. "What?"

"I'm having a slumber party! On Friday. You'll come, won't you? You are my best friend."

Sometimes Marisa believed it when Jen said that, other times she wasn't so sure. Jen could be snooty and mean. But she'd learned not to cross Marisa and not to talk down to her the way she could Kristin, and especially Tara. Marisa didn't stand for it. Although she was only nine-years-old, she knew a few cuss words and she'd used them on Jennifer. "I have to ask my mom first."

"You have to come! Kristin and Tara are both going to be there!" Jen's blue eyes widened with worry. "Why wouldn't your mom let you come?"

"Well, I have to ask her first!" Marisa knew her parents really didn't care for Jen. They said she wasn't a good friend to her. But she'd known her since the first day of kindergarten. That was the day she'd met Kristin and Tara, too. Ever since, the four had been inseparable.

Jen's mother stopped at the end of the aisle and told her to bring the cart because she had a handful of things to put down. "Call me tonight and tell me, OK? We're gonna have fun! We'll watch all our shows then maybe pop popcorn or roast marshmallows in the fireplace, OK?"

"OK." Marisa watched as her friend ran down the aisle with the cart, narrowly missing Bruce McKay, the town mechanic/tow truck driver.

She followed him to the checkout line and was glad to see that Cora's line was empty. Cora was nice, she always winked at Marisa whenever she came through.

"Well, hi there!" Wink. "Have you been good for Santa?"

"Yes." Marisa smiled, thinking about her presents. She'd asked for a Tyco race track and a Lite Brite.

"That comes to sixty-four cents."

Marisa pulled out the two quarters her grandmother had given her. That was only fifty cents. "Sixty-four cents?"

Cora glanced at the register. "Yep. Is that all you have?" When Marisa nodded, Cora scratched her dyed-red Toni Tennille head. "Well, you want to go home and get some more money? I'll hold it right here for you."

Grandmama would be mad. She didn't get the prices mixed up often. It must be because of this inflation thing she heard her parents complaining about all the time. "OK. But she wanted it soon so she could fry the fish."

Cora smiled and looked at the woman standing in line behind Marisa. "I know, but if you hurry, you'll be right back and—-"

"Wait a minute, Cora." The older woman started digging in her purse with a sigh. "Here's fifteen cents. That should cover it."

Marisa stared at the woman. She didn't know her name. She must not come into the hardware store very often. She seemed mad. But if she was mad, why did she offer the money? "Thank you."

The woman smiled thinly and glanced at Cora out of the corner of her eye. "You're welcome."

Marisa took the bag, said Merry Christmas to Cora and was putting her mitten back on when she heard the woman mutter, "The poor thing..."

Outside, Marisa walked with her head down. She didn't think she was poor. Her family had a nice house, two cars and went on vacation every year. This past summer they even went to Disney World. That wasn't poor. Poor was the Franklins, who lived in a trailer on the outskirts of town.

Inside Logan's Hardware, Marisa waved at her father, who was helping Mr. Nelson pick out a toolbox for his father-in-law. In the back, she saw her brothers sweeping the floor and stocking shelves and her mother behind the counter, ringing up Mrs. VandenKamper.

Marisa went behind the counter in the middle of the store and sat on a tall stool while she waited for her mother.

When Mrs. VandenKamper finally stopping talking about all the snow they were supposed to get this weekend, she inched her way out of the store and into the cold. Victoria Logan turned to her only daughter.

"Your grandmama is looking for you. Said she sent you to the store thirty minutes ago and that the fish is waiting." She swiped at the counter with a rag. "What were you doing?"

"I saw Jen. She asked me to go to her slumber party Friday. Can I?"

"Friday is just two days before Christmas Eve. You should be with your family."

Marisa rolled her eyes. "But Friday's not Christmas Eve. Pl-e-e-a-s-s-e-, Mama? Everyone is going to be there."

Her mother glared at her with a raised eyebrow. She hated whining, but it usually got Marisa what she wanted. Anything to shut her up. "We'll see."

"What does that mean?" Marisa started swinging her legs on the stool and beating her thick boots against the steel legs. The sound reverberated through the store and she saw her father glance up. She stopped swinging.

"It means we'll see. Now you better get home before Grandmama comes after you with a switch."

So Marisa trudged home over the icy sidewalk and back up the front porch. By now the porch light was on and the Christmas lights were illuminated better. Down the street at Barry's house the lights were the blinking kind that Marisa and her brothers had wanted but her father nixed. For no good reason, either. He just said no. And no was no as far as Daddy was concerned.

This time she remembered to take her boots off before treading across the carpet, and she went into the kitchen still wearing the brown earth shoes she'd worn under her boots. "Here, Grandmama." She lay the bag with the corn meal on the counter.

"And what took you so long, little girl?" Grandmama was at the sink cleaning the fish. Marisa tried looking over her shoulder to see if it was catfish, then realized she didn't know what catfish looked like.

"I saw Jen in the store. She invited me to a slumber party Friday." Marisa sat at the kitchen table and played with the plastic yellow placemat.

"That'll be nice."

"But when I asked Mama if I could go, she just said 'we'll see.' Will you tell her?"

Grandmama turned around and smiled. "Tell her what, chile? I don't tell your mama how to raise you-all. She's grown."

Marisa groaned. She just had to go to the party! If Grandmama didn't help her, she didn't know who would. If she asked Daddy, he'd either say no or "ask your mama."

"Now are you gonna help with dinner or are you gonna sit there pouting?"

Marisa didn't feel like helping. Besides, "The Brady Bunch" was coming on soon. "Help with what?"

"You wanna clean the fish?" Grandmama laughed at Marisa's turned-up nose. "Go on in the living room, then. I know your show is about to come on."

"OK." Marisa swiped a handful of molasses cookies out of the jar. "Is that catfish?"

"Mm-mm."

Marisa went into the living room content, thinking Jen was crazy not to like catfish.

Five o'clock came and with it the afternoon talk shows. Her grandmother hollered from the kitchen to turn up "The Mike Douglas Show" so she could hear it in the other room. She did and took her bookbag up to her bedroom.

She adored her room. It had three huge windows, including one with a window seat that looked out over the side yard. She could sit there and watch the baby robins in their nests and she also had a clear view of Barry's house. His house was similar to Marisa's, but wasn't as big and didn't have the huge wraparound porch. But it was still nice.

She sat on the blue-covered bed and unloaded her bookbag. The perfume fell out first and she smiled again. Marisa Montgomery ...the name had a nice ring to it. Her parents wouldn't want her to marry a white boy, but she really, really liked him. Had ever since kindergarten. He was the epitome boy-next-door, even though he technically lived across the street. Maybe he would want to go sledding tomorrow. If she told him her brothers were coming, then she knew he'd jump at the offer. He worshipped Marisa's brothers, even though she thought they were both idiots.

That night, they joined her in watching some Christmas cartoons. "The Year Without a Santa Claus" came on, complete with Heat Miser and Mother Nature, and afterward, Mama told Marisa to go to bed.

"But it's only nine o'clock!"

"And that's your bedtime."

"But there's no school tomorrow!" She looked at her father, pleadingly.

"Oh, Victoria, let her stay up. It's vacation." Daddy winked at Marisa, who smiled at him gratefully.

"OK, but only thirty more minutes. If you're gonna be staying up at Jennifer's place on Friday, you'll need your sleep now."

Marisa didn't ask if that meant she could go to the slumber party. She assumed it did. She went over to her father and sat on his lap. She loved her daddy. He was tall, like Robert Jr. was going to be, and big. He was like a big teddy bear, with light brown skin and deep voice. She leaned against him like a pillow and watched the Christmas lights on the tree reflect off each other. Then she counted the presents under the tree. If she went outside to the northwest part of the porch, she could see Petersville's city tree glowing next to the post office. Marisa and Barry and Kristin had gone to the tree lighting earlier this month, then they'd come over for hot chocolate and molasses cookies afterward. That was fun. She hoped they'd all stay friends forever and ever ...

"Come on, baby, it's time for bed." Her father nudged her, then picked her up. "Want me to carry you up like when you were little?"

She giggled as he swung her up the stairs and continued smiling as he tucked her in and kissed her on the forehead. Her mother came in next, smelling like lavender. "Mama?"

"Mmm?"

"Did you see the present I got today?"

"What present?"

She pointed to the dresser. "Over there. The perfume."

"Oh." Mama went over and smelled it. "Well, that's really nice. Who gave that to you? Jennifer?"

"No."

"Then who?" She sat on the side of the bed and brushed back a strand of Marisa's hair.

"Barry." Marisa said it shyly.

"Oh." She could see her mother trying not to smile. "That was sweet of him. Did you thank him?"

"Yes." She was glad her mother didn't ask her a bunch of questions. "Did you know they changed the price of corn meal?"

Mama laughed. "No, I didn't know that, but thanks for telling me."

"It comes to sixty-four cents instead of fifty cents. This lady behind me gave me fifteen cents so I'd have enough."

"Well, everyone is in the holiday spirit, huh?" She kissed her on the cheek. "Good night now, baby."

"Mama?"

She paused at the door. "What is it?"

"Are we poor?"

"Are we poor? Why do you ask that?"

"After the lady gave me the money I heard her say to Cora, 'poor thing.' I didn't think we were poor. Are we?"

She could see Mama's lips curl in the doorway. "No, we are certainly not poor. I don't know what that lady was talking about, but don't you listen to her. We're certainly not rich but we're sure not poor, either. Now go to sleep."

That was a relief. She suspected the woman said that because she was black. Everyone thought black people were poor. Well, she wasn't like other black people. She wasn't poor or on food stamps, like the people she saw when she went to visit her Aunt Shirley in Gary, Indiana. Now that was poor.

***

Friday night her mother picked up Kristin from her house near the school and took them both to Jennifer's house on Peters Lake. All the rich people lived up there. The Van Sikkema's house had a perfect view of the lake and Jen's father even had a speedboat that he practically lived on during the summer.

Jen opened the door before they could ring the bell and the three stepped into the lavishly decorated foyer. A white, tabletop Christmas tree sat in the center while mistletoe hung from the wide entryway.

"Why do you have mistletoe up?" Kristin asked in a whisper. Jen's house demanded hushed tones. It was too perfect to go around screaming or laughing in.

"Yeah, who are you gonna kiss?" Marisa and Kristin giggled together while Jen rolled her eyes and led them up the curving staircase.

"My parents put that up for their party tomorrow night. Grown-ups don't care who they kiss once they have enough eggnog."

She led her friends down the wide hallway and into the corner room that housed a spectacular view of Peters Lake. Large windows dominated the room and Jen even had two window seats, both filled with stuffed animals and pillows. Her pink canopy bed sat in the center of the room looking out to the TV and stereo.

"I thought Tara was going to be here," Kristin remarked as she threw her bag on the floor.

"She got in trouble so now she's begging her mother to let her come," Jen said with a snort.

"What'd she do?" Marisa asked.

"Oh, she didn't feed a calf or a goat or something when she was supposed to. I don't know how she can live on a farm!" Jen flounced dramatically on her bed, leaving Marisa and Kristin to share a window seat.

"They don't have any goats," Marisa explained. "Only cows and sheep and chickens."

"Whatever. It still stinks, just like that perfume Barry gave you." She raised up on one elbow and smirked at her friend over one shoulder.

"It does not stink! You're just jealous."

"Yeah, Jen," Kristin piped up. "Did any boys give you a Christmas present?"

The blonde girl let out a laugh. "Like I really like any of these boys around here." Jen liked to think she was too good for Petersville. Her parents had family in Holland and Grand Rapids and she pretended that her "real" friends and soon-to-be boyfriends lived there. Whoop-dee-doo. What was so great about Holland or Grand Rapids? Marisa preferred Kalamazoo or Chicago.

"Anyway," Jen was saying as she stood up. "My mom says we can have whatever we want for dinner. What do you want to eat? We have—-"

"Tacos!" Kristin and Marisa shouted in unison, then collapsed in giggles. Jen even joined them, for she knew her father made the best tacos in the world. He was already downstairs making them and the trio ventured into the large kitchen to help. Marisa was shredding the cheese when Jen's mother ushered Tara in.

"Look who made it!"

"Hi, Tara. Did you bring your goat along?" Jen said with a smirk.

"Ha, ha, Jen." Tara hopped up on a kitchen stool and swiped a diced tomato. "That's so funny I forgot to laugh." Tara was good with the comebacks, almost as good as Marisa. She was a born comedian, with bright red hair and tons and tons of freckles. She helped with dinner and afterward they all sat in the den watching their three favorite shows, "The Incredible Hulk," "The Dukes of Hazzard" and "Dallas."

By eleven o'clock, they were gathered in Jen's room in their pajamas, with Jen pretending she was Sue Ellen Ewing.

"Ah swea-ah, J.R.! Ah hate you!" Jen's eyebrows raised dramatically just like Sue Ellen's. The other girls cracked up, then Marisa stood and pretended to be J.R.

"Sue Ellen, you're nothing but a tramp and a drunk. You've embarrassed ole J.R. for the last time. The sooner I'm rid of you, the better." She then picked up one of Jen's hats like it was a Stetson and walked out the door. She came back in to see her friends on the floor, laughing hysterically.

"You do that so good, Maris," Kristin was saying. "You act just like J.R. You should be an actress when you grow up."

"Yeah," Tara chimed in. "You're pretty enough."

Marisa flopped down on a large pillow and drew her legs up under her. "I don't know. I never thought about acting."

"You should," Tara said, wide-eyed. "If you could choose to be any actress, who would it be? I'd be Lindsay Wagner."

"I'd be Valerie Bertinelli," Kristin offered.

"I'd be..." Marisa thought a moment. "I'd be Farrah Fawcett."

"Farrah Fawcett?" Jen spoke up. She had been lying on her bed on her stomach watching her friends on the floor like they were her servants. "You can't be Farrah Fawcett!"

Marisa turned to her. "Why not?"

"Because you're black! You have to be that girl from 'Good Times.' What's the daughter's name?"

"Thelma," Tara answered, all the while keeping one eye on Marisa and what her reaction would be to Jen's declaration.

"Yeah. Thelma. She's the only pretty black girl on TV, anyway. You be Thelma." Jen told her in a patronizing tone.

If Marisa were white, she would have turned bright red in embarrassment and anger. Embarrassment because she hated it when people pointed out that she was different. She knew she was black. But she wanted to be treated and respected like everyone else. Half the time she knew her friends forgot she was black and that was the way she liked it. She was angry because who was Jen to tell her what she could be and not be? She was going to say something when Kristin suggested playing truth or dare. It was one of Marisa's favorite games.

The girls caught Jen in a lie about whether she still wore an undershirt and they made Tara run down the hall like an Indian until Jen's parents told them to be quiet. When they asked Marisa what boy she would most like to kiss, she told them Barry.

"Barry?" Jen smiled, but it wasn't the same smile Tara and Kristin were wearing. It was like the cat in "Alice in Wonderland."

"Yes, Barry. He gave me perfume for Christmas." Marisa grinned, just thinking about it. He was so cute. Every girl in the fourth grade liked him, but he gave her a present. She knew he liked her. This proved it.

"You can like Barry all you want, Marisa. But you can't marry him."

Marisa tensed up again. She knew what Jen was about to say. "Why not?"

Jen's stringy blonde hair was flung over one shoulder. "Because he's white and you're black. It just doesn't happen that way."

Before Marisa could say anything, Kristin jumped up. "That's not true, Jennifer! Color doesn't matter!"

Jen looked annoyed. "Yes, it does. No one will want to be your friends and your kids will be all screwed up."

"They will not! It shouldn't matter what color you are, as long as you love each other." Marisa was surprisingly calm. She knew Kristin and Tara agreed with her and were sick of Jen's know-it-all attitude.

"Yeah, Jen. It shouldn't matter. You'll be lucky if you get anyone to marry you," Tara said with a laugh. "You're such a baby, no one would want to put up with your whining."

"You just shut up, Tara!" Jen scowled and stomped to her bed. "I'm going to sleep. You guys can go home for all I care." The others watched as she threw the covers over her head and punched a fist into her pillow. They turned off the lights and lined their sleeping bags next to each other across the room.

"Jen's so stupid sometimes," Tara whispered, giggling. "She thinks she knows everything."

"I know," Kristin agreed.

Marisa was quiet while Tara and Kris continued to talk about Jen. Sometimes she hated being different. She wished sometimes for an easier life. And to her fourth-grade mind, life would be so much easier in Petersville if she was white like everybody else.

***

Christmas Day. After opening her gifts and playing with her Lite Brite for hours, Marisa joined her grandmother on the porch, where she was breaking string beans for Christmas dinner.

"You enjoying your Christmas, baby?" Grandmama asked. She was wrapped in one of Daddy's old coats and had her new fluffy house shoes on her feet.

"Yes, ma'am. Thank you for the sweater." Grandmama had knitted her another sweater, but at least this one was a V-neck, like Marisa wanted.

Marisa sat next to her grandmother and the two sat in silence for a while, the only sound the sharp snap of the beans. When Marisa's fingers got cold, she took a break and stuffed them in her pocket.

A few minutes later, Marisa saw movement at Barry's house and realized it was him, coming down the street with a bright orange toboggan dragging behind him. Marisa felt her pulse race and tried to hide her grin from her grandmother, who was watching her out of the corner of her eye. Barry reached the walkway and stopped.

"Well, Merry Christmas, Barry!" Her grandmother greeted.

"Merry Christmas," he said with a shy grin. He was wearing a snowmobile suit and his favorite blue Dallas Cowboys hat. Marisa smiled at the way his usually tan cheeks turned red when cold. She tried to figure out what was cutest about him and decided for now, with him all wrapped up, it was his dark eyebrows. His hair was a dark blond, but his eyebrows and eyes were dark, which made a nice contrast. Those attractive eyebrows frowned as he watched Marisa and her grandmother. "What are you doing?"

"Snapping string beans." Marisa spoke up.

"Why?"

"For dinner," she laughed at him, more out of joy at seeing him than from the conversation they were having.

"But it's cold out. Why are you sitting on the porch?"

Marisa didn't have an answer for that and looked to her grandmother.

"Because I'm a Southern girl. And in the South, people have porches. And you sit on those porches. Whether it's cold or not." She continued to snap and rock and started humming "Going Up Yonder."

"Oh." Barry continued to stand on the sidewalk. He looked back at his house, up to Marisa's porch, then down at his feet. Scratching his head, he asked, "Can you go sledding?"

"I'll go ask." Marisa jumped up and ran into the house, where her mother told her she could go once she finished snapping the green beans. Moaning, she ran back outside.

"I can't go until the green beans are all done." She looked to her grandmother and half expected her to tell her to go on anyway. But she knew better than that. Grandmama didn't interfere once her parents told her something.

"Oh." Barry scratched his head again.

"Can you go later? We're almost done." Marisa didn't want him to leave. It was apparent he got the toboggan for Christmas and wanted to try it out.

"Yeah, I can wait. Can I help? Then we can get done faster."

Thrilled that he was being so nice and helpful, Marisa's "yes" was so soft that he didn't hear her. In a louder voice, she repeated it and pulled a chair over so he could join the circle. He was pretty efficient at snapping beans, even though he'd never done it before. He didn't even like green beans, he announced. He and Marisa ran down their Christmas lists and he said he wanted to come over tomorrow to see her race track. What a holiday this was turning out to be. First a bottle of perfume from the cutest guy in her class, then a slumber party, then an afternoon of sledding with said cute boy. And tomorrow they were going to play with her race track. In the midst of all of this excitement, she forgot that she had a present for him, too. Her mother told her it was appropriate since he gave her one.

Before they went sledding with her brothers, who rudely invited themselves along, she presented him with a Tony Dorsett football. He went crazy over it and thanked her over and over, making her grandmother laugh.

When they finally started walking to Junior High Hill, Marisa and Barry kept stride together, which to Marisa meant they were destined to be boyfriend and girlfriend, no matter what Jen said. Looking over Petersville's holiday decorations and the quiet, serene streets, she realized not even Santa could have brought her a better Christmas.

CHAPTER 2

October 1981

"Mama, can Barry come over?" Marisa was helping her mother fold clothes on a crisp fall Sunday when the phone rang. It was Barry, asking if they could practice their seventh-grade English presentation in front of her father. Barry loved her daddy. His own father was a truck driver and hardly ever home. Barry and his mother were usually home alone except on the rare occasions when his sister visited from Plainwell with her husband and baby boy. She was only eighteen and had married this biker guy after only two months. The Montgomery family was mortified when they found out she "had" to get married. Now Barry was an uncle. He hardly ever talked about it, though. He said all the baby did was cry and spit up.

"Come over for what?" Her mother was asking her.

"We want to practice our verses. He wants to know what Daddy thinks." Barry and Marisa, the two smartest kids in the seventh grade, were picked to present a special project on Geoffrey Chaucer's "Canterbury Tales." They'd decided to recite the Olde English version of the prologue and had spent the past week memorizing and translating it.

"OK. But he can't stay too long. Dinner is almost ready."

"OK." She ran to the phone and gave Barry the green light. Once she hung up, she made a beeline for the kitchen door.

"Hold it!" Her mother called from the laundry room.

"What?"

"Don't what me. Where do you think you're going? We have a lot of laundry to finish."

"Mama! I have to go get ready." Marisa was impatience personified, fidgeting from one foot to the other and tapping her fingers on the counter.

"Get ready? For what?"

"I ..." She didn't want to tell her mother that she wanted to change out of her sweats and sweatshirt and into some jeans and a sweater. She'd tell her not to. Those clothes were for school. "I have to get my books and stuff together."

"Is he coming over now?"

"Yes, Mother. I told you that." Gosh, was her mother deaf?

"Girl, I'd watch my tone if I were you. Go on, but he's not staying long! You have more chores to finish. Plus, I have to grease your hair tonight."

"OK." She ran out of the kitchen before her mother finished speaking. She ignored her brothers in the living room watching football with their father. Funny how they could sit around all day doing nothing while she was stuck in the kitchen doing chores. What a bunch of lazy bums.

Upstairs, she brushed her wavy hair from her forehead and threw on a red headband. She dug her Gitano jeans from her laundry basket and wiggled into them, newly tight and warm from the dryer. She rummaged through her dresser and found her red pullover sweater. No, too dressy. Instead, she threw on a red Mickey Mouse sweatshirt that she got at Disney World during the summer.

She barely had time to gather her books before she heard Robert yelling, "Marisa! Barry's here!"

Although she wanted to run down the stairs, she took a deep breath inside her room before walking swiftly downstairs.

"Hi." She greeted him in what she hoped was a nonchalant voice.

"Hi, Marisa." He was standing in the doorway with his hands in his pockets wearing a gray hooded sweatshirt.

"Do you want to go on the porch and practice?"

"Sure." He began to follow her when Matthew called out. "Hey, Marisa! You weren't wearing that a minute ago."

She wanted to die. Barry stopped and looked her up and down. "Shut up, stupid."

"Marisa, don't call your brother stupid."

Marisa shook her head in exasperation and led Barry outside where they sat on the porch steps together.

"Oh yeah, I meant to tell you, I like your pumpkins. Did you carve this?" He pointed to the one sitting next to him.

"No. Matthew did that one. I did this." She gestured to the pumpkin on the bottom step, the one with the happy face.

"Figures yours would be happy and not scary, like Matthew's."

"Yeah, well, Matthew is disturbed. We're trying to get him admitted."

"So are you ready? Do you want to practice before we do it in front of your dad?"

"Sure, if you want to."

They ran through the verses without hesitation, then Marisa went to the door to call her father.

"Are you two ready?" He came to the door with a grin. "Are you sure you've practiced enough? I'm a hard critic."

They looked at each other and grinned in confidence. "We're ready." They answered in unison.

"All right." He sat in the rocking chair. "Go to it."

When they finished, her father clapped and stood. "Perfect. Even though I don't know what you were saying, it sounded good. I don't know why you say you needed practice. You got it down pat to me."

"Well, we just wanted to be sure." Barry smiled at her father, who patted him on the back before retreating to the house.

"Your dad's so cool." He joined her on the steps again. "Hey, do you think he'll hire me in the store when I'm older?"

"Sure. You know the store just as well as I do." That would be really neat, having Barry working for her father. She'd see him all the time.

A comfortable silence engulfed them while Barry picked at a fallen leaf and Marisa tapped her outstretched feet together. This was what she loved about being with him. Yeah, she liked him and all, but they were still friends and could hang out together just like she did with Kristin or Jen or Tara.

"So are you going to the dance on Friday?"

"Of course. I'm helping organize." She was on the Student Council, which was sponsoring the annual Halloween dance. It would be her first time attending a dance and she was beyond excited.

"Are you dressing up?"

"You mean like in costume? We don't have to, you know."

"Yeah, I know. Are you?"

"No."

Another few seconds of silence ticked by. "So are you going with anybody?"

The comfort level they had been sharing immediately disappeared. Was he asking her out? To the dance? Her pulse began to race and she could feel her face flush. "Uh...no...I mean, unless Kris and I go. Or Jen or somebody."

"But you're not going with a ...date?" His voice broke as it did sometimes, and she wanted to laugh. It was so cute.

"No." All this time, neither one looked at each other. He had ripped the leaf to shreds and her foot had fallen asleep. But she was scared to move. To do so might ruin the moment. "Are you?" He had been going with Amanda Littlefield for a while, but that only lasted the first two weeks of school.

"No...I mean, unless you want to go with me."

Yes! She was so thrilled she could barely speak. Finally! "Uh, sure. That'd be nice."

"OK. That's cool. I mean...that's cool." He tossed the leaf aside and finally turned to look at her. She smiled shyly and he returned it with a mischievous look on his face. But then again, he usually looked mischievous. "So we're not dressing up, right?"

"Right. Just normal, dance-type clothes."

"OK. Hey, Dennis is going to ask Kristin to the dance. Do you want to go with them?"

Omigosh! Her first double-date. "Sure. That'd be fun."

Barry looked relieved. His shoulders rested against the porch step railing as he turned to her. "I wonder who got stuck taking Jen?"

She laughed, then sobered quickly. "I shouldn't talk about her. She's one of my best friends."

"Why? She's a doofus. And a snob. Why do you hang around with her?"

She wondered that herself sometimes. But Jen was OK, most of the time. She just needed to be brought back a peg or two. Before she could explain it to him, Matthew came charging out of the door.

"Mama says to set the table. It's dinnertime. Your boyfriend has to go home now."

"Why don't you just shut up?" she screamed at him.

"Ooh, did I hit a nerve? Huh?" He pushed at her and she almost fell off the steps.

"You idiot! Leave me alone!" She scrambled up and pushed him back, but he dodged her, laughing the whole time.

"Marisa, I'll see you tomorrow. Bye, Matthew." Barry trudged down the steps, shaking his head as the two continued to fight.

Robert came to the door and broke them up. "Boy, will you leave her alone? One of these days she's going to haul off and dough-pop you."

Marisa followed her brothers into the house and raced upstairs to change back into her sweats before her mother saw that she'd put on her school clothes. She quickly set the table, gulped down her food then scraped the plates for Matthew to wash. She had to call Kristin. The news of her date with Barry was too good to save for school.

But her mother had other plans. "Marisa, it's time for your bath."

"I have to call Kristin first, OK?"

"No, it's not OK. You two will be talking forever. Take your bath first."

Marisa rolled her eyes and made a "tsk" sound.

"What did you say?"

"Nothing." Her family was driving her nuts. Why couldn't they just leave her alone?

She splashed around in the bathtub for five minutes, then plodded to her room in her robe. Once there, she smoothed on some Love's Baby Soft lotion, then threw on her pajamas. She felt comfy and soft. Wandering downstairs warily, she searched for her mother. If only she could get to the den and the phone without anyone seeing her...

"Come on, Marisa, I have to grease your hair." Mama walked past with the Ultra Sheen, a black comb and the bag of rollers.

"Let me call Kristin first, OK? Please? It's really important."

Sighing, her mother put a hand on her hip. "What's so important that it can't wait for school tomorrow?"

"Puh-leeze, Mama?"

"Don't whine, chile! You know how I hate that. If you're not off the phone in five minutes, I'm hanging it up for you."

"OK." She dialed while her mother left the room, muttering to herself.

Kristin answered on the first ring.

"Kris. Guess what?"

"What?"

"Barry asked me to the dance." She could barely contain her excitement. But she didn't have to. Kristin's scream was loud enough for both of them.

"What?! Really? When? Today?"

"Yeah. He came over so we could practice for English, then he asked me right before he left." She couldn't wipe the big smile off her face.

"That is so awesome! What are you going to wear? We already decided we're not wearing costumes."

"Right. I don't know. You think my mother will let me get something new?" She doubted it. Her mother was rather cheap.

"Maybe. My mother said I could. I've already outgrown two of my skirts that I bought for school."

"Yeah. My mother wants me to wear more skirts anyway. Maybe if I told her I wanted a dress or something she'd get it for me."

"You? Wear a dress? This, I've got to see."

"Listen, I can't talk long, my mom is being a pain. Do you want to get our dresses together? Do you want to go on Friday? Then we can get dressed over here and you can spend the night."

"OK. Will you French braid my hair?" Kristin's hair was long and shiny and thick. Not as thick as Marisa's, but still.

"Yeah. Oh, and one more thing. Dennis is going to ask you."

"Ask me what? To the dance?" Another squeal. "How do you know?"

"Barry told me. He wants us to double-date." It sounded so grown up. "Won't that be cool?"

"I can't wait until Friday! I gotta go now, Dennis might be trying to call. I'll see you tomorrow, OK?"

Marisa fairly skipped into the living room and plopped down at her mother's feet. "Are you done? That must be a record."

"I had to tell her something. That's all." Marisa winced as her mother pulled on her hair. She wasn't tenderheaded, her mother was just too rough. She could pull the mane off a lion if she wanted to. "Scratch here." It was easier to have her mother scratch her head than actually try and comb it. She pulled at the kinks too hard. But when she scratched, Marisa could easily go to sleep.

"What was so important that it couldn't wait until tomorrow?"

"The dance."

"The Halloween dance? Are you going as a gypsy again?" Her father asked.

"Nooo, Daddy. I'm not dressing up. That's kid stuff."

"You are a kid!" He teased.

She rolled her eyes. "You know what I mean."

"Oh. I see. So you had to tell Kristin not to come as a witch, huh?"

"No, I had something else to tell her." She was dying to spill her secret but knew her family would get all hyper about it.

"What?"

She bit her lip with a small smile. They'd find out sooner or later anyway. "Barry asked me."

"Asked you what? If you were dressing up?" Her mother parted her hair and forced her head to the side.

"Nooo. He asked me to the dance."

Her father stopped watching "60 Minutes" and her mother stopped scratching. Out of the corner of her eye, she could see them exchange glances. "You mean a date?"

"No. Well, yeah, kinda. We're going with Kristin and Dennis."

"I didn't think this was a dating-type dance. I thought you kids just went to ..."

"To do what, Daddy? All the eighth-graders are bringing dates. Why shouldn't we?"

Her mother resumed scratching. "No reason you shouldn't. You and Barry have been friends for years. Of course you can go with him." Her words and tone were directed at her husband, who recognized both as a sign that they'd talk about it later.

"Can I get a new outfit?" Marisa asked.

"We'll see."

"What does that mean? Kristin's getting one."

"I don't care what Kristin is doing. If she was jumping off a bridge, would you want to jump, too?"

Marisa hated it when her mother said stuff like that. Like Kristin would really jump off a bridge. And like Marisa would be dumb enough to follow her. She was only buying an outfit. And if Kristin got one, she wanted one, too.

"Can I?"

"I said we'll see, now! And that's that."

***

She ended up buying a red peasant skirt and white, puffy-sleeved blouse with a skinny red bow tie. It was pretty, and she did look cute in it, although it wasn't her first choice. She'd wanted a different dress but her mother said it was too "grown-looking" and too expensive.

At home, she and Kristin began to get dressed for their big night. First Kristin showered, then Marisa. They shared Marisa's Love's Baby Soft lotion and powder, then Kristin sat on the floor so Marisa could French-braid her hair. While Kristin was slipping on her dress, Marisa plugged in her hot comb.

"What's that?" Kristin came over for a closer look.

"Uh, it's a hot comb."

"A hot comb? What's it do?" She reached to touch it, but Marisa slapped her hand.

"No, don't! It gets hot really fast." Her mother had bought her one of the new electric ones, the kind you didn't have to put on the stovetop.

"But what's it do?" She kept staring at the comb's shiny gold teeth.

"You comb your hair with it. It makes it straight." But only for a while. Marisa's hair was so soft and thick that by the end of the night her hair would curl up again. She hated it. She wished she had hair like Kristin's – straight and not too thick. The kind you could just wash and let air-dry.

"Wow. Lemme see." Kristin stood next to the mirror and watched in unbridled fascination as Marisa carefully hot-combed her hair, adding grease before each comb. "Why do you put that in your hair?" She turned her nose up. "Ewww! It's all ikky."

"It's grease. It helps not make your hair dry."

"But doesn't it get greasy?" She reached out and touched Marisa's hair, then recoiled upon contact. "Gross! It *is* greasy!"

"Kristin, black people use this all the time." She felt funny having to explain it, like she was from another planet or something. "Your hair is different from mine. My scalp is dry. Yours isn't. That's why you wash it every day, to keep it from getting too oily."

Her friend's eyes bucked. "You mean you don't wash your hair every day?"

Embarrassed, Marisa turned away, bending to plug in her curling iron. "No. I'd have an Afro if I did that."

"Ewww! When do you wash it?"

"About every other day or so." It was a lie. Her mother washed her hair every other Sunday. And even that was a chore because she had soooo much hair.

"Oh." Kris looked relieved. "That's different. I forget to wash mine sometimes, too. Hey, look. It's all straight and shiny now."

Yes, it was straight and shiny and styled like Janet Jackson's character Charlene on "Diff'rent Strokes." Or as close as Marisa could get to Charlene's. The feathered side wasn't as pretty, it was just kind of curly, but that was OK. She looked nice.

Which is what Barry told her when he rang the doorbell forty-five minutes later. She returned the compliment and knew he was floored by the change in her looks. He'd never seen her in a dress or skirt in all the years he'd known her. She looked like a new person. She was even wearing lip gloss. Barry was wearing gray slacks and a gray sweater with his name embroidered over his left breast. He had a black Izod shirt underneath with the collar tilted up and Marisa thought she'd never seen him look so good. He was soooo cute. And her was *her* date.

Not that anyone at the dance would know that, however. Upon entering, the girls hightailed it to the other side of the gym with the other girls while Barry and Dennis ventured to the refreshment table with the rest of the boys. After about ten minutes, the girls decided to dance together. Marisa and her friends formed a tight circle and started fast-dancing. She knew she was the best dancer in the seventh grade. No one else seemed to have any rhythm at all. They just bent their knees up and down and twisted their bodies back and forth off-beat. Marisa tried to imitate the dancers she saw on "Soul Train" every Saturday, but it was hard. Those girls were good. "Let's Get Serious" by Jermaine Jackson came on and everyone tried imitating Marisa doing the Rock. She complimented them, but they looked pretty goofy. "Jessie's Girl" by Rick Springfield came on, causing most of the girls to scream. They loved Rick Springfield. Marisa thought he was a better actor than singer, but he was cute, regardless.

After his song, the deejay finally switched to a slow song. "For Your Eyes Only" by Sheena Easton blasted over the speakers and Marisa waited by the bleachers for Barry to ask her to dance. When he did, she took his hand and practically floated on to the dance floor. It felt almost natural to move closer to him so her chest was against his and to wrap her arms around his shoulders a little tighter. They danced for two more songs before the deejay switched to Hall & Oates' "Private Eyes." Marisa stayed on the dance floor almost the entire time. She finally took a break toward the end of the night to get some punch and to cool off for the last dance, which was always a slow one. She wanted to make it special with Barry. She downed the punch and waited expectantly while the deejay warned the students to make the last dance "count." When the strains of "Endless Love" floated over the gym, she wanted to melt. She loved that song! She searched the crowd for Barry but couldn't see him. She saw Dennis and Kristin. And Tara and Paul. And Jen and ... Jen and Barry? What were they doing dancing? Marisa felt hot all over, wondering if she was seeing things. She looked again and sure enough, they were dancing. Not as close as she and Barry, but still...Marisa stood rooted to the spot, wondering what to do. Should she cut in, like they did on TV? Leave? No, she couldn't do either. So she stood there, alone, while all of her friends danced. She glanced around the gym and noticed the only people not dancing were the geeks. The Franklin boys. Debbie Hatchett. Nerds. And she was on the sidelines with them. Yuck. She felt grody and out of place. For a moment she wondered if she would be in this position if there were more black boys at school. She didn't know. All she knew was she felt conspicuous and embarrassed standing there alone, especially when she was supposed to have a "date."

When the song ended, Barry immediately came over to her. "Marisa, how come you weren't dancing?"

"I, uh..." She looked away, shrugging with an airy attitude. "I didn't really feel like it. I was dancing all night. I'm tired."

"Oh." He searched her face in the darkness. "I wanted to dance this last dance with you but Jen...she said you were dancing with Mitch Lawson."

"Mitch?" Mitch was an eighth grader who was pretty friendly. Marisa thought he was cool. "He gave me some punch. But then he danced with Caitlin Cooper."

"Oh. Well, gee, that sucks. Jen told me you were already on the dance floor, then she asked me to dance. I'm sorry. She thought you were already out there."

"I'm sure." She narrowed her eyes and shot Jen a dirty look. Jen pretended not to see it as she threw on her coat.

THE KITCHEN ISN'T WHERE YOU COOK

"Let's go get our coats, OK? Are you ready to go?" Barry steered Marisa into the hallway, into the band room and to the percussion room in the back. Not too many people knew how to unlock it, but he did. After all, he was the band's star percussionist. They were the only ones who put their coats in there and Marisa felt like they shared a great secret. She reached up to turn the light on, but he caught her hand. "Wait."

Turning to him in the dark, she felt him move closer to her. He nudged the door shut with a hip and held her hand in both of his. "You look really pretty, Marisa."

She had to gulp, had to do something to loosen the lump that had suddenly formed in her throat. But she couldn't gulp. He'd hear her! So she stammered, "Thank you."

In the dim light from the hall, she saw him smile nervously. He gripped her hand tighter and asked in a soft voice. "Can I kiss you?"

She was afraid to answer. Afraid she couldn't answer. How many times had she dreamed about such a thing? And it was finally here! What had she said in her daydreams? She couldn't remember. She looked up at him and felt reassured at his warm smile. He was waiting for an answer. She nodded slowly, her mouth already parted for her first kiss. He tilted his head to the side as she stood frozen to the floor. As he leaned in, she grabbed his other hand just to have something to hold on to. His lips met hers in a soft, quick kiss. Then it was over. Their eyes met and she suddenly realized the lump in her throat was gone. Matching grins met each other and when he leaned in for a second kiss, she willingly obliged. That one was over just as quickly.

"Will you go with me?" he asked.

The lump was back. "Uh-huh." She didn't trust herself to speak. Wait until she told Kristin!

She was unable to look him directly in the eye on the way home and once there, ushered Kristin into her room after the cursory good night to her parents. "Kris! Eeeee! Guess what?" She pulled her onto her bed.

"What? What?" Her friend was wide-eyed and excited, even though she had no idea why.

"Barry asked me to go with him!" She squealed the words out and buried her face in her pillow so she could scream in delight without causing the whole house to come running.

"What? Omigod! How awesome!"

"I know. And guess what else?" Marisa rested the pillow on her lap. "He kissed me!"

"No way!"

"Yes! It was so nice. He is such a good kisser." Marisa acted like she had someone to compare him to, but Kristin was too excited to notice.

"That is soooo cool. You guys make such a cute couple." Marisa's mother yelled at them to get to bed and once the lights were off and they were under the covers, Marisa told her about Jen and her schemes.

"That is so bogue," Kris said. "Jen is a liar to the max. I can't believe she'd do that."

"I do. She's just so jealous. She thinks she's so great. Hey, let's not talk to her on Monday, 'kay?"

"'Kay. At least Barry can see through her. He obviously wasn't too impressed or he wouldn't have kissed you or asked you to go with him." Kristin got excited all over again. "I can't believe this! You're going with Barry. Finally."

"I know."

Silence followed while both reflected on the romance that had occurred that night. "You think you'd want to marry him, Maris?"

"I don't know." She really didn't. She figured she'd have to marry a black guy, but where would she find one around here? She'd have to leave Petersville to date any black guys and why would she want to leave? Petersville was her home. All of her friends were here. Her family was here. It was pretty and peaceful. Unless a black family moved to town, she figured she'd have no choice but to marry Barry. And for her, that didn't sound bad at all.

CHAPTER 3

May 1985

"Hey, Marisa, what did you get for number eight?" Barry ran to catch up to her in the hallway after geometry class.

"Why, what did you get?" She glanced sideways at him warily. Barry always did this. They were ranked first and second in the sophomore class and although he was first – for now, anyway – he was always trying to challenge Marisa during and after class. Like now. He had to know that they both got the same answer. He was just needling her.

"I asked you first."

"Forget it, Barry. You know we both got an A. I don't know why you do this." She tried to walk faster than him so she could get away, but he being taller had no problem keeping pace.

"Do what? I just want to know what you got." He grinned down at her, and as always, the sight of his smile and mischievous gleam in his eyes filled her with warmth. They were still great friends, even though she still liked him. But she doubted they would ever get back together. They'd "dated" through most of seventh grade, teaching each other how to kiss and being regarded as the supercouple of Petersville Middle School. But when spring came, so did wandering eyes, and they'd broken up right before Mother's Day. Marisa was crushed and steered clear of him through most of the summer, but by Labor Day they were hanging out again. She figured he'd always be one of her best friends and that suited her fine. Now if only he'd get rid of this competitive streak he had.

"Forget it! We'll get our tests back tomorrow." Marisa smiled at a freshman girl who complimented her on her pink Forenza sweater.

"All right, all right." Barry stopped her in the middle of the hallway. Students had to walk around them to get to class, but Barry didn't seem to care. He was already one of the most popular kids in school. He started as running back for the junior varsity football team and was a small forward on the varsity basketball team, leading the Panthers to their first district championship since Marisa's brother Robert played for them, back in 1982. As for Marisa, she didn't care about popularity so much, it just seemed to follow her, especially considering her brothers' accomplishments. Robert was in college at the University of Chicago and Matthew was finishing his freshman year at Howard University in Washington. Howard was like the black Harvard, is how she explained it to her friends who had never heard of it. With her brothers gone, Marisa worked in the hardware store on weekends. That is, when she didn't have a track meet or a game to cheer for, Student Council business or a parade to march in. She knew she and her friends were envied by others, but she couldn't help that. She just did the things she enjoyed.

"Barry, I have to get to typing class." She started to walk away, but he stopped her again.

"Wait a minute. What do you want for your birthday?" Her sixteenth birthday was coming up. Finally. All of her friends were already driving and here she was, putting around with her learner's permit.

"Uh...I don't know." She smiled and shifted her books from one arm to the other. "You don't have to get me anything."

"I know that." He playfully punched her on the arm. "But I want to."

Marisa could tell he was getting distracted by the number of people yelling greetings at him. Mitch stopped by and asked him about the Motley Crue concert they were going to Saturday in Detroit, and Barry told him he'd call him later.

"Your parents are letting you drive all the way to Detroit?" Marisa was surprised. Detroit was at least a three-hour drive from Petersville and Marisa had never even been there. She preferred Chicago anyway.

"Yeah. Well, I'm not driving. Mitch is. Did you see the new car he got?" When Marisa shook her head, he let out a whistle. "It's a silver Grand Prix. It's nice."

"So you're going to see Motley Crue? Man, I'm jealous. I love Tommy Lee." Most of the guys in school were impressed that she liked heavy metal. Her favorite groups included Van Halen, Scorpions and Triumph. Especially Triumph. She liked other music, too, like Michael Jackson, Madonna, Prince and British bands like ABC and Duran Duran. But as far as black music, there was no way she could listen to any. The local NBC station in Grand Rapids had stopped showing "Soul Train" and there were no R&B stations that reached down to Petersville, so she had no choice but to watch "Friday Night Videos" and listen to Top 40 and heavy metal stations.

"That's right. I forgot you like him." He suddenly grinned at her as if a thought had come to him. "OK. Well, I'll see you later. I've got physical science to get to."

"OK." She was puzzled at his sudden departure, then it dawned on her. He was buying her a Motley Crue shirt from the concert for her birthday. A private grin lit her face as she walked to typing class. No one knew Barry better than she did. She could read his mind like a book.

That afternoon after track practice, she was surprised to find a package on her bed. Dropping her duffel bag, she inspected the box and found that it had come from Robert in Chicago. Cool! Must be her birthday present. She flopped on the bed and ripped the box open, finding a card with twenty bucks in it and a cassette tape. When he was home for spring break, she'd made him promise to tape record some of the black radio stations in Chicago. That way she'd have at least an inkling of what some of the hot songs were nowadays.

"Marisa," her mother called from the hallway. "I need you to fix some dinner. Your grandmother's not feeling too well. I have to go to a Chamber of Commerce meeting until eight." Fixing her necklace, her mother peered into her daughter's room. "Do you have much homework?"

"No." She did, but she didn't tell her mother that. Marisa usually stayed up until around midnight doing her homework, unbeknownst to her parents. She thought better late at night and if she looked out the window, she could see Barry's bedroom light on, too. So if he was studying that hard, she knew she had to, too.

"Warm up some of that beef stew for your grandmama."

"What's wrong with her? Is she OK?" Her grandmother had slowed down in recent years, leaving the gardening to Marisa and more of the cooking to Mama. She usually spent her days watching "The Young and the Restless" and reading the Bible. She napped more, too. Marisa worried about her sometimes, but every time she voiced her concern, her parents would reassure her, telling her it's only natural that Grandmama didn't have the same energy she had when Marisa was a child. But that didn't mean she was about to die, they said.

"She's just tired. Her arthritis is acting up." Her mother paused at the door. "Will you make sure she takes her medicine? And if she needs it, will you rub Ben-Gay on her calves for her? It's getting hard for her to climb those stairs."

"OK." Marisa waved at her mother while pondering her grandmother's situation. She was seventy-three now, definitely old, as far as Marisa was concerned. It was probably a given that she'd never be the same spritely woman from Marisa's childhood. Arthritis had put an end to the braiding she used to do for Marisa and to the knitting that she so loved. It had been about two years since Marisa had gotten a homemade sweater for Christmas. The thought saddened her. She wanted her lively grandmother back.

Her thoughts were interrupted by the phone. "Hello?"

"Marisa." It was Barry.

"Hi." What a surprise! She thought he was going over to Jen's house that evening. They'd only been dating for about a month, but Jen tried her darndest to keep him on a short lease. As for Barry, he no longer considered Jen a "doofus." Her long blonde hair and willowy figure – not to mention her incessant flirting – had changed his mind about her. "What's up?"

"Hey, did you get your invitation? I'm sure you did. Aren't you excited?" Barry's voice was enthused.

"Whoa. What are you talking about? What invitation?"

"You know. The thing for the National Honor Society. The induction ceremony is on the 30th. I wonder who else from our class got in. There's usually only three or four sophomores."

As Marisa vainly tried to listen to him babble, her heart sank. She had applied for induction into the National Honor Society last fall, getting recommendations from two of her teachers and writing what she considered a sterling essay. She wanted nothing more than to get in as a sophomore. Neither of her brothers made it until their senior years and she was determined to beat them in. But if Barry got his acceptance letter today, then where was hers?

"Marisa? Are you there?"

"Uh...yeah. Uh...congratulations, Barry. That's great." She really was happy for him. He definitely deserved it.

"Thanks. Congrats to you, too."

"Uh...I didn't get mine."

Awkward silence filled the phone line. "You mean you didn't get yours yet. Did you check the mail?"

"No. But the mail is already here. I got a birthday card from Robert today." Was it just late? But Barry lived right across the street. Why would he get it sooner than her?

"Oh. Well, maybe it'll come tomorrow."

"Maybe." Doubt started to fill her mind. Robert was smart as hell. So was Matthew. Why didn't they get in as sophomores or juniors?

"Hey, don't be like that." Barry's voice was soothing, reassuring. "I'm sure you'll get in. You're the smartest girl in our class! Don't worry, OK?"

"OK." She sighed, worrying anyway. "Uh, I have to fix dinner now. I'll talk to you tomorrow, OK?"

"OK." His voice took on a tone of pity and it made her angry.

"Bye, Barry. And congratulations." She hung up before he could answer. Self-doubt, an emotion she rarely dealt with when it came to academics, began to set in. Maybe her essay sucked. Maybe her 3.9 GPA wasn't good enough. Maybe....maybe she should stop worrying and get dinner ready.

She forced a smile on her face as she entered the den, where her grandmother was rocking in the recliner, a gold afghan thrown over her knees. She'd crocheted it herself, right before Marisa was born. "Hi Grandmama." She kissed her cheek and kneeled next to her. "How are you feeling?"

"I'm just fine, baby. How are you?" Grandmama smiled at her and caressed her hair, which was still messy in the ponytail she'd thrown together during track practice.

"I'm fine." She took a close look at her grandmother's face, looking for signs of exhaustion or old age. Nope, she looked the same as always, just a little tired. "Did you take your medicine?"

"Yes, Marisa, I took my medicine." She smiled. "Your mother told you to ask that, didn't she?"

"Yes." Sometimes her mother treated Grandmama like a baby. Marisa could relate to that. "I'm going to warm up some of that beef stew, OK? Do you want something to drink in the meantime?"

"Could you bring me some hot tea? It's a little chilly today."

"For sure."

THE KITCHEN ISN'T WHERE YOU COOK

"I thought that Valley Girl talk was out-of-style," she teased.

Marisa laughed as she walked into the kitchen. "It is. But it's hard to get rid of completely." After delivering the tea, she stood at the microwave, warming up a bowl of beef stew and thinking about the National Honor Society. Who else got their letters today? Barry did. Dennis probably did. He was third in the class rankings. Marisa hoped Jen didn't. That would really suck, if Jen got in before her.

"Here you go." She set the tray of beef stew, biscuits and applesauce on the table next to the recliner. "Anything else?"

"Oh, no. This looks fine, baby. Where's yours?"

"Oh, uh, I'm going to eat later." She was lying. She wasn't hungry. She wanted to lose a few pounds before summer and eating her mother's heavy beef stew wouldn't help her cause at all. Maybe she'd nibble on some Ritz crackers later, but nothing more. She was already a size seven and was determined to stay that way.

"Grandmama?"

"Hmmm?"

"Barry got his letter for the National Honor Society. Did you get all the mail today?"

"I didn't go to the post office. Your daddy went and he put all the mail on the table. You got your package from Robert, didn't you?" She blew on her beef stew, which was still steaming. Marisa had kept the microwave on too long.

"Yeah." She'd already checked the hallway table. No letter.

"Don't worry. I'm sure it'll come tomorrow."

***

The next morning, Mr. Steinga, the economics teacher and faculty adviser for the National Honor Society, stopped her in the hallway before first hour.

"I wanted to talk to you about NHS," he said in a low voice.

"OK." She breathed a sigh of relief. He was about to congratulate her. Thank goodness!

"I just wanted to tell you that we, the selection committee that is, think you are one of the brightest students we've ever had in this school." When she laughed, he patted her on the arm. "I mean that, Marisa. You are truly gifted."

"Thank you." She wished he would get on with it. She had to figure out what she was going to wear to the induction ceremony.

"You're welcome. Your essay was brilliant, your teachers love you, but – "

But?

"...your community service work was a bit lacking. That was one of the reasons we didn't select you this year. Give you some time to work on that. Maybe this summer you can volunteer at the Migrant Program."

"Uh-huh." A protective shield went up around her as she listened to him drone. How could she not get in? She was brilliant, just as he said. Her face turned red as she stood there, wondering who was overhearing this conversation. How could she face Barry, who would probably get an innate thrill at beating her at something? And what about Jen? She'd gloat like there was no tomorrow. How could this happen? She'd worked so hard.

"So just keep up the good work, Marisa, and maybe next year will be your year." He patted her on the arm again and walked away, leaving her shocked and embarrassed in the hallway.

She adopted a haughty air as she walked into English, which she shared with all of her friends. Barry was there, talking to Dennis about his acceptance letter; Jen was there, fawning over Barry as usual. Tara was scrambling to finish her reading and Kristin was looking over her homework. She walked past all of them without a word, but knew it would only be a matter of time before Barry approached her.

"Hey." As he took a seat on her desk, she pretended to be busy. "I saw Mr. Steinga talking to you in the hall. Did he say why you didn't get your letter yet?"

She opened her book with a thud and kept her eyes downcast, fearful that tears would sprout if she looked at him and the pity that she knew he was about to display. "Yes."

"Well, why? Dennis got his. So did Lisa Curry."

"I didn't get mine because..." She didn't want to tell him. Didn't want to look like a failure. Didn't want to look like she even cared. But she did. Deeply. "I didn't make it." She abruptly raised her eyes to his in defiance. He wouldn't know how hurt she was.

"What?" His tan face turned a shade paler at the shock. "You're kidding."

"Nope." She tapped her pencil on the desk, looking around to see who was listening. So far no one. But Jen was keeping an eye on them from across the room.

"But why? I don't get it."

"Me either." She shrugged, still nonchalant. "But I'll make it next year. It's no big deal. As long as I can put it on my college applications, right?"

"Yeah, I guess so." To his credit, Barry didn't look at her in pity, just in surprise. "You're right. I don't know why they even let sophomores in anyway. What good does it do us this early?"

His attitude made her feel a little better. He always could brighten her day. With a wan smile, she reached out and took his hand. "Thank you, Barry. Please don't say anything. People will find out soon enough."

"No prob." He squeezed her hand and climbed down from the desk.

Her parents, though, were less calm when she broke the news to them that night.

"I can't believe this! You're the smartest student in the tenth grade!" Her mother shrieked.

"Well, actually, Barry..." Marisa began.

"You get better grades than anybody! What is he talking about, community service? You volunteered to make those lunches for the Adopt-a-Grandparent program! What about that?"

"Well, actually, that was through the Student Council..."

"So? You did it." Her parents were pacing around their bedroom while Marisa sat perched on the edge of their bed, still reeling from the news herself.

"Don't tell me this is a coincidence," her father said through clenched teeth. "It's awfully funny that first Robert, then Matthew, now Marisa, have to wait until they're almost out of school to get into the Honor Society. What good does it do them a month before they graduate?"

Her mother nodded vigorously. "I know. I thought the same thing. Don't tell me this is a coincidence."

What were they talking about? "Mama, it has to be. Robert's community service was bad, too, because of all the sports he was in. Matthew's teachers badmouthed him because of his smart mouth. Of course it's a coincidence."

"Marisa." Her mother looked at her in pity. "Baby, I'm sure you'd like to think so, and I wish it was just a coincidence, I really do. But that's not how the world works. You're old enough to know about prejudice. That's what we're dealing with here."

Marisa rolled her eyes. Not this again. "Mama, please. It is not." Where did her parents get such notions?

"Well, explain why Matthew didn't get one of the ten scholarships the school gave out last year?" Her father stopped pacing and faced her. "Those were based only on academic achievement, not teacher recommendation, not community service. Why didn't he get one?" Marisa couldn't answer, for she was shocked herself when Matthew's name wasn't called at graduation as a scholarship recipient. People who were so-so students got them over him. At the time, her parents wanted to talk to the principal about it, but Matthew and Marisa stopped them. Marisa said she'd be too embarrassed, and Matthew said it didn't matter. He was still going to Howard, no matter how much the folks in Petersville tried to deter him. So they'd let the matter drop. But Marisa knew it still weighed heavily on her parents' minds.

"I don't know..."

"Of course you don't. Because you all didn't want us to find out. Now maybe you'll let me talk to Mr. Steinga."

"Daddy, no!" Marisa jumped up and tugged on her father's arm. "Puh-leeeze don't! I'll get in next year! It's no big deal!"

"Of course it is!"

"Daddy...pleeeeeeeease don't say anything." God, how embarrassing would that be? Her daddy fighting her battles for her. "Why do we want to let them think they can hurt us?"

"That's what I mean. They need to know that they *can't* hurt us. That we won't stand for it anymore."

"Please, Daddy. I have to have him for econ senior year. I don't want him to have this grudge against me."

"What? He better not..."

"Robert, just let it go." It was her mother, speaking from the vanity chair, where she'd been staring at herself in the mirror.

"What?"

"We'll let it go this year." She turned around. "But next year, if you still don't get in, we are definitely going to talk to someone. Agreed?"

"OK." She sighed. That was a close call. She didn't want her parents causing a fuss, making it seem like she was a whiner or something. "Thank you. Oh yeah, can I go to Holland?"

"What? Holland? Tonight?" Her father began massaging his wife's shoulders and Marisa warmed at the sight. What a pretty couple they were.

"Yeah. With Tara and Caitlin."

"For what?" Her parents got tired of her always going to Holland. They wondered why her friends never wanted to go to Kalamazoo, where there were some black kids. But who were they fooling? They'd never let her go all the way to Kalamazoo anyway. Holland was only a twenty-minute drive and the traffic was easier than in Kalamazoo.

"We're going out for pizza."

"Marisa, your track meet is tomorrow. What time are you all leaving?"

"I have to be at the school at seven-thirty. I'll be back by eleven. Maybe even earlier. We're just getting some pizza."

"Just you three?" Her mother raised an eyebrow. She was immediately worried if more than two kids rode in a car together.

"Uh-huh." Marisa didn't say that they were meeting everyone else at the pizza parlor and that she might come home with someone else besides Caitlin, who was hoping to go to a party with some kids she knew from Holland High School.

"All right, then. Go on. But you be home by eleven!" Marisa ran out of the room. "You hear?"

"Yeah!" She'd try to make it home by then, but then again, it depended on what the night would bring.

***

For Marisa, the night in Holland brought little excitement. Caitlin, however, indeed got invited to the party hosted by kids from Holland High and although she invited both Tara and Marisa along, they'd declined. Caitlin was seventeen, a junior. She had more freedom than they did, and they envied her. At first, she acted like she didn't want to go without them and she even pointed to a black boy in the crowd who was checking Marisa out at the pizza place.

"Look, Marisa, see?" She raised her pinky finger in the direction of the Holland kids and the lone black guy. He was wearing a red varsity jacket and kept glancing in their direction. "He keeps looking over here. He likes you."

"Shut up." Marisa was embarrassed. Yes, he was looking at her, but she wasn't interested. He was ugly. He was really tall and skinny, probably a basketball player, no doubt, and really dark, like Eddie Murphy. And his hair. It was all nappy-looking. Yuck. Why did her friends think she'd automatically like any black boy she saw?

"Go for it, Marisa! Come on! His name is Joe." Caitlin waved at him and he laughed, then whispered conspiratorially to his friends.

"Will you stop it? I don't want to talk to him!" Marisa was ready to leave. How embarrassing. Her friends were so stupid sometimes.

"Come on, Maris. He's cute. He looks like Eddie Murphy without the mustache," Tara noted.

"So? Eddie Murphy's not cute!" She took a long sip of her Coke and stared out the window with her nose in the air. What was wrong with them? Didn't they know she still liked Barry? Why would she want to date someone from Holland? Especially some tall, gawky basketball player who probably couldn't speak correct English?

En route to the track meet Saturday morning, after Caitlin filled them in on her escapades from the night before, she turned to Marisa. "Joe asked about you."

"So?" She faced the window with her knees propped on the seat in front of her, which Caitlin was leaning over.

"He said you're pretty and wants to know if you have a boyfriend."

"I hope you told him yes."

"No way! I told him I'd ask you, but that you were really into your studies and stuff." She gathered her frizzy permed hair into a ponytail while she talked. "Is that good?"

"That's perfect." Whew. At least she didn't have to deal with him.

"But why didn't you like him? He's cute. And he's really nice."

"He is not cute. Now Prince? He's cute." Caitlin nodded in agreement, as did Tara, who was sitting next to Marisa.

"You know who else is cute?" Caitlin raised an eyebrow and grinned. "Your brother."

Marisa's head popped around. "Whose brother?"

"Yours. I had the biggest crush on Matthew last year." Caitlin fanned herself with a hand dramatically.

"Ewww! That's gross. Matthew's not cute. He's an idiot." Marisa played it off, although she knew both of her brothers were good-looking.

"No, he's not. He's really cute. He doesn't look black, though." Caitlin said it in wonder, her eyes staring into the distance.

"What does that mean?" Of course they were black. Sometimes she thought her friends forgot about that.

"I mean he doesn't look like Joe, for instance. Actually, no one in your family looks like any black people I ever see. You guys are all good-looking." Caitlin smiled as Marisa pondered her comment.

"Thanks." She was warmed at the compliment, but she already knew that. Their hair was nice, their faces kind of light, and Marisa was proud of her high cheekbones. Yes, she knew the Logans were better-looking than most black people. It wasn't her fault that people like Caitlin noticed, too.

Marisa only had one event to run at the meet, and she finished fourth in her heat in the 220, leaving her with nothing to do for much of the afternoon. While Caitlin was running the mile, Marisa decided to walk around the stadium. Near the end of the bleachers, across the field from the Petersville team, she noticed a group of black kids lounging and laughing while a boom box played an unfamiliar song. She stopped suddenly and decided to sit near them, but far enough away that they wouldn't notice her. Maybe she could find out the name of the song and buy the .45 at the music store. While sitting there, she couldn't help noticing how much fun they were having. They were dancing and laughing and burning each other with jokes. They seemed so at ease. The girls and the guys acted like they'd known each other forever. With that thought in her mind, Marisa's gaze drifted across the field to where her teammates were. They were sitting or lying on the bleachers, talking. Quietly. No one was hollering and if someone did laugh, it was restrained. Their body language looked stiff compared to the black kids, who weren't afraid to let out a loud laugh, straight from the belly. One guy was laughing so hard that he began flopping around and hollering, "Girl, you a trip! You crazy!" Marisa didn't know what was so funny, but she smiled to herself anyway. Their laughter was infectious. Soon she was tapping her feet to the music, which she figured out was called "Cutie Pie." "Cutie pie, you're the reason why, I love you so, I don't want you to go..." She had to remember that so she could buy it later.

"Hey Maris!" She turned at the sound of Tara's voice. She was practically skipping toward her, followed by a panting Caitlin.

"What are you doing over here?" Tara stood over her, glancing around like she was about to be mugged. "I'm keeping Caitlin company on her cool-down. Want to come?"

Marisa glanced from Caitlin to the black kids, who barely gave the trio a second glance. "No. You guys go on."

"Well, why are you over here? You should sit with your team." Tara glanced behind her again, then turned her back when one of the boys looked at her. "Mitch is about to run the hurdles. We have to cheer him on."

"I'll be over in a minute." Marisa was irritated. Why didn't they just go away? They acted like they had to protect her or something.

"OK. But hurry up. Mitch needs our help." Tara climbed back up the stairs slowly, with several glances behind her. Once she and Caitlin were out of earshot, she heard a black girl ask, "What the hell was she looking at?" Her friends shrugged and dismissed the question as another song was played. Marisa hung her head, embarrassed that her friends were so...so rude. And even more embarrassed that she was with them.

Maybe her parents were right. Maybe folks in Petersville were a little prejudiced. She stretched her legs out on the bleachers and daydreamed about attending an all-black school. What fun she'd have. She'd have people to talk to about her hair and make-up, they'd like the same music, and the guys! The guys would love her, she knew it. But no, she was stuck in Petersville, where it was becoming more and more evident that she was very different from her friends. A difference that would never change.

***

"Happy birthday, Marisa!" The greetings came from all sides as she walked down the hallway Wednesday. She was finally sixteen. Her parents gave her a new outfit and promised that she'd get the bigger present that night when they cut her birthday cake.

At her locker, streamers were flowing from the vents and someone had taped up a narrow banner that read "Happy Birthday." Dozens of signatures were on it as well, everyone from freshmen to seniors wishing her a happy sweet sixteen. "Who did this?" She asked with a wide smile as her friends gathered around her locker.

"Don't anyone tell!" Jen warned. "It doesn't matter who did it. You're the last one to turn sixteen so we had to do something special to welcome you into the club." She gave Marisa an enthusiastic hug.

"Thank you, you guys. You're sweet." She was touched. What a great bunch of friends she had. She just hoped they'd be able to stay friends forever, just as they'd written in their yearbooks.

Barry stepped forward with a large square box wrapped in blue. "Here, Marisa. Happy birthday."

"Barry! We were going to wait until lunch to give her our presents!" Jen hit him on the arm.

"I never said that. You guys made up that rule. Besides, she's going to like my present best anyway." He laughed and winked at Marisa, who was tearing open the box. Inside was a Motley Crue jersey shirt with black sleeves and a picture of the group on a white background, just as she'd figured.

"Barry! Thank you! How cool!" She smiled at him warmly, the grin anchored by a bite on her lower lip.

"You're welcome." He claimed her in a tight hug, whispering in her ear. "Happy birthday, sweetie."

Ooooh, what he did to her. He smelled like Polo cologne and was wearing a light blue button-down shirt tucked into Levi's. He seemed to get better looking as each day passed. "Thank you, Barry." She kept her gaze downcast, so no one could notice the gooey expression on her face.

The festivities carried over into first-period English. A balloon bouquet was delivered to class courtesy of Matthew. Then, during morning announcements, the principal read the results of the elections for the class of '87, Marisa's class. She was running for vice president against Dennis. She was hardly surprised when her name was read. Practically everyone she knew told her they'd voted for her. Dennis was too much of a class clown to be taken seriously. Lisa Curry was re-elected president.

"Wow, Marisa, can this birthday get any better?" Jen asked as the class congratulated her.

It did. She aced her geometry quiz and breezed through cheerleading tryouts. When Caitlin dropped her off at home that afternoon, she was surprised that her father's car was gone. They were supposed to be home, getting ready to eat her birthday dinner and cut her cake. And, most importantly, give her the rest of her presents. "I wonder where he went?" she mused as she got out of the car.

"Don't worry. He probably had to run to the store or something," Caitlin offered. "Anyway, happy birthday, Maris! I'll call you later."

"OK! Thanks!" She stumbled up the porch steps with her balloons, duffel bag, backpack and numerous gift boxes. Before she got to the door, it swung open. Barry's mother stood there.

"Oh, Mrs. Montgomery...hi." Marisa tossed her head back in a vain attempt to get her hair out of her face.

"Hello, Marisa. Here, let me help you." Barry's petite, dirty-blonde mother stepped forward, took the balloons and presents and carried them into the house, which was eerily quiet for six o'clock in the evening.

"Where is everybody?" she asked. She didn't smell any pork chops, her favorite dish. She didn't smell any cake. Were they trying to surprise her in some way?

"Uh, that's why I'm here, dear." Mrs. Montgomery tied the balloons to the stairwell, placed the presents on the table and took Marisa by the arm, leading her into the living room. "Your father called around two-thirty today. He asked me to come over and wait for you."

"But where is he?" Marisa was getting worried. Her parents never took off like this. Especially not on her birthday. Something was definitely wrong.

"He's at the hospital." Marisa felt her pulse beat faster and she stared at Barry's mother, who began speaking very slowly. "Your grandmother has had a stroke."

"What?" The word was a mere breath, coming without thought from deep within. "What?"

Mrs. Montgomery hugged her, patting her on the back consolingly. "It's OK, Marisa. Your mother was with her. She was able to call an ambulance rather quickly. At least your grandmother wasn't here alone, my goodness…"

"Is she OK?" She pulled away, a look of horror on her face. Grandmama had to be OK. She just had to be.

"She's in Holland Hospital. They want me to bring you up there." She was still talking slowly, too slowly for Marisa's taste.

"Why didn't they call me at school? Or come get me today?" Man. She was prancing around all afternoon basking in birthday wishes and athletic and scholastic accomplishments when all along her grandmother was …omigosh…she had to get up there.

"There wasn't time, dear. Your mother rode in the ambulance and your father followed. He didn't call me until he got to the hospital." Barry's mother shook her head. "Such a shame."

"Can we go now?" Marisa headed to the door, leaving Mrs. Montgomery flustered.

"Uh, no, we have to wait for Barry. Do you know if he's on his way home?" She followed Marisa onto the porch, where she was pacing back and forth.

"I don't know. Uh, baseball practice was over at about the same time…oh wait, there he is." She ran down the stairs as Barry cruised down the street in his used Nova, blasting Triumph's "Fight the Good Fight."

"Come on, Marisa, I'll tell Barry where we're going. You can wait in the car if you want." Marisa followed Mrs. Montgomery across the street, where she was talking to Barry as he stood in his open car door.

"…there's some casserole in the refrigerator. Warm that up, OK? I should be home by eight or nine. Do you have much home – " Mrs. Montgomery's words drifted as her son stepped away from her and toward Marisa, who was heading toward his mother's Skylark parked on the street.

"Marisa…" His arm stopped her from getting in the car. "I'm so sorry. Are you OK?"

Nodding, she glanced at their reflections in the car windows. He, tall and athletic with his baseball cap and a University of Michigan T-shirt; she, withdrawn and frowning, still in her PHS cheerleading T-shirt and sweatpants. "I'm fine."

"Barry, get in the house. I'll call you when we get there." His mother came around the car and opened the driver's side door. "Don't stay on the phone, either."

"Wait! I'm coming, too." He ran back to his car, shut and locked the door, then hurried back to the Skylark. "I'm coming, too. Get in, Marisa." His hand at the small of her back ushered her into the back seat. She obliged without argument. Anything to speed them on their trip. He climbed in beside her and ordered his surprised mother to get going. She, too, obliged. If Marisa wasn't so shocked and worried, she'd have laughed at Barry's brazenness. As it was, all she could think about was her grandmother. Over and over, she was praying. "Please, God, don't let her die. Let her be OK. Please God. Please." So fervent was her prayer that she barely noticed Barry take her hand. He held it throughout the entire trip while his mother commented on the slow drivers on the scenic road leading to Holland.

Twenty minutes later, Mrs. Montgomery pulled into the emergency parking lot. "Here, Marisa. I'll let you out here while I find a parking space. Ask the nurse where you should go."

"OK. Thank you." She climbed out, ran around the car and ran into Barry on the sidewalk. "Where are you going?"

"I'm coming with you." He took her hand and led her into the hospital, where he asked a nurse where Dorothy Caldwell was.

"Dorothy Caldwell. Oh yes, she's in ICU. Go down this hall, turn left and through the double doors. You'll see it on your right."

En route, Marisa suddenly slowed her steps. What would she find through those doors? What if her whole world was about to come crashing down on her? She tugged on Barry's hand, causing him to turn around. "What's wrong?"

She shook her head, her eyes welling with tears. "I'm scared." She whispered the words, for if she said them any louder they would be a scream.

"Aww, I know you are." He hugged her tight and she took a deep breath against him. "It'll be all right. Everything will be fine." Patting her back, he rocked her back and forth slightly, then pulled away, a reassuring small smile on his face. "It'll be OK. Come on." He led her into the ICU, where she saw her father leaning against the wall, a cup of machine coffee in his hands.

"Daddy?" His pose scared her. He looked beaten, uncertain.

"Marisa. Hi, baby." He put an arm around her and kissed the top of her head.

"How is she?"

With a sigh, he jostled her shoulder. "She'll be OK. We're just thankful that your mother was able to get help so soon."

"Are you sure she's OK?" She looked up into his face, feeling like a little girl again, waiting for him to tell her the boogie man in her closet didn't exist.

"Yes, honey. But she has a long road to recovery." For the first time, he noticed Barry, who was leaning against the opposite wall. "Barry. Hi. Thanks for bringing her. Where's your mother?"

"She's parking the car. I'm glad Mrs. Caldwell is going to be OK." His hands were stuffed in his jeans pockets nervously and it dawned on Marisa that he was worried about her grandmother, too. After all, she had taught him to snap string beans, taught him to love biscuits and syrup, even taught him how to knit a little. Her heart swelled with relief that her grandmother wasn't dead and gratitude that she had a great friend like Barry.

"Can I see her?"

"No, they don't let anyone in under sixteen ...wait a minute. You are sixteen now, aren't you?" He smiled slightly and jostled her shoulders again. "I'm sorry about your cake and everything, baby."

"Oh, Daddy..." Like she really cared about that. She just wanted to see her grandmother. But when they asked the nurse, she said only two people were allowed in at a time.

"You go on, Marisa. Tell your mama I'll be in in a minute." He kissed her on the cheek. "Don't be too long. I'll be out here with Barry, OK?"

"OK." She followed the nurse into the care unit and saw her mother at the far end of the room, leaning over a bed with a frail hand clasped in hers. "Mama?"

Her mother looked up, tears streaming down her face. "Marisa..." But she didn't move from her stance. Marisa walked around the bed and stood beside her mother, her arm around her shoulders.

"Daddy says she's going to be fine." Her voice sounded more sure than it had all evening. But her mother looked so upset, Marisa had to say something to make her feel better.

"Yeah, she'll be fine." She smoothed back a lock of Grandmama's hair with a wan smile. "She'll be fine."

For the first time since entering the room, Marisa looked closely at her grandmother. The sight made her feel oddly relieved. She looked the same as always, except for the I.V. and the tube in her nose. Other than that, she looked like she was sleeping. Marisa kissed her mother's cheek, feeling a sense of responsibility now. Almost like she was the mother and her mother was the daughter. "Do you need anything?"

"No, baby...I'm fine. Tell Barry's mother thank you for everything. She was a big help."

"OK." Marisa wanted to stay and go all at the same time. She wanted to be of support to her mother, but she didn't want to see her mother upset. She didn't know what to do. Fortunately, her mother read her mind.

"You can't stay here all night, Marisa. Tell your daddy to come back in here."

"Are you sure?"

"Yes. I'll stay up here tonight. He'll take you home later. You can come back up tomorrow morning if you want. OK?"

"OK." She hugged her mother again, then sought out her father, who was shaking hands with Barry. "Daddy? Mama wants you." When he disappeared, she turned to Barry. "What was that all about?"

He sighed, a look of surprise on his face. "Uh, he …wait a minute. How's your grandmother?"

"She's OK. She looks like she's sleeping." They sat on the hard, orange seats in the waiting room, where a TV brought soundless repeats of "The Andy Griffith Show." "What were you and Daddy talking about?"

He leaned forward, rested his arms on his thighs and rubbed his hands together. "He asked me to work in the store."

"Really?" Marisa smiled. "But I figured he'd hire you this summer, anyway. At least that's what my mother told me."

"Yeah, but since your grandmother's sick, your mother's hours are going to be cut back. He's giving them to me."

"That's great, Barry. You're going to be making a lot of money this summer." And he'd be working with her. What a funny way for things to work out.

"Yeah. Hey, I'm going to get something to eat. Wanna come? My mother is already in the cafeteria."

"No, I'm OK." She settled against the uncomfortable seat and picked up a gardening magazine. Even though it was three months old, she still found a few useful tips to help her keep Grandmama's garden in tiptop shape. That was the least she could do. That way

Grandmama could sit on the porch and smell the lilacs and hydrangeas. Before she was halfway through the magazine, Barry was back, hiding something behind his back.

"I told you I'm not hungry." She threw the magazine on the table. "What is that?"

Without a word, he brought out a package of Hostess Cupcakes. "Thanks, Barry, but I ..." Her words drifted when he tore open the package, placed the cupcakes on the table with its cardboard liner and proceeded to place a birthday candle on each cupcake. "What are you...?" Her mouth hung open in delighted surprise as he lit the candles with a lighter – where'd he get a lighter? – then kneeled down next to the table with a small smile. "Now, make a wish."

"Barry..." She was touched beyond words. What would she have done without him today? "I can't believe you!"

"Make a wish."

Laughing, she glanced at the nurses, who were grinning and pointing at them. What a spectacle he'd made. "OK." With her eyes closed, she made her wish, leaned close, then blew out the candles. While she was still bent over the table, she leaned forward and kissed him. He was so surprised that he couldn't even kiss her back. "Thank you, Barry. You're a great friend."

In spite of himself, he blushed. "Same to ya. Happy birthday, Marisa." Then, in an effort to lighten the mood, asked, "So what did you wish for?"

She giggled quietly. It was just like the final scene in "Sixteen Candles" except they weren't sitting on a table, she wasn't in a bridesmaid gown and he looked nothing like Jake Ryan. "None of your business." She didn't need to tell him. She was certain it was going to come true.

CHAPTER 4

Summer 1985

Marisa's grandmother was released from the hospital after a one-week stay and things around the house changed drastically upon her return. Marisa's mother stayed home during the day, caring for Grandmama, while her father worked extra hours to take up the slack in his wife's absence. However, his workload eased once summer began and Barry started in the store.

He was a good worker, always on time, courteous to the customers, doing extra work without anyone telling him to. In fact, Marisa's father even commented over dinner one night that he wished Marisa worked like Barry. In response, she rolled her eyes. She was tired of watching Barry become Mr. Hardware Man. Why did he enjoy it so much? She hated working all day. She was sixteen! She wanted to hang out at the beach or mall like Jen and Kristin. She wanted to go cruising in her car on hot summer evenings. But wait, she didn't have a car. Robert and Matthew's old Grand Prix was sitting on blocks behind their house because the transmission was out of whack. Her father debated whether it was even worth getting fixed. Marisa said no, just get me another one. Unfortunately, her parents ignored her.

Even if she did have a car, she couldn't go anywhere in the evenings anyway. She had to help around the house. Her mother couldn't keep up with the housework and tend to Grandmama too well, so the cleaning and laundry and sometimes cooking were left to Marisa. She didn't mind the cooking too much. She was actually pretty good at it and found it relaxing.

Late one Saturday afternoon, she was wiping off the store counter as the clock ticked to closing time. It had been an extremely busy day, less than a week before the Fourth of July, and she was tired. Tired, cranky and bored. She hadn't been able to hang out with her friends at all this summer. She hadn't spoken to Jen since early June, when she'd called in tears because Barry had broken up with her. But she didn't really care that Barry was free now. Well, she did, but she saw too much of him now anyway. To see him outside of work would have been torture. He always seemed to be sucking up to her father, asking all kinds of questions about the business and stuff. He claimed he wanted to major in marketing in college, but gee whiz, that was two years away. Why couldn't he just regard the job for what it was? A temporary, summer job.

"Marisa, can you give Mr. Jenkins a refund?" He came behind the counter with a can of paint. "This color was mixed wrong somehow. He wants his money back."

Stifling a sigh, she smiled thinly at Mr. Jenkins, who was never satisfied with anything, anyway. After she gave him his money back and shooed him out of the store, she called to her father, "I'm closing up now, Daddy! It's six o'clock!" Without waiting for an answer, she turned the store sign to "Closed," then went outside to retrieve the bikes, kiddie pools and barbecue grills. For once, Barry helped her.

"Hey, what are you doing tonight?" he asked while pushing a ten-speed inside. "Want to catch a movie?"

"No." She huffed past him with a riding lawn mower.

"Let me get that. That's too heavy for you." He parked the bike and reached for the mower's handles, but she slapped his hand away.

"I've got it! I've been doing this all my life, you know. I'm not a weakling." What did he think, that they couldn't manage at the store without him around? Get real.

She missed the look of confusion that crossed his face. "What's wrong with you?"

"Nothing." She busied herself in the corner so she wouldn't have to face him, because if she did, her anger would fade. But why was she angry? She didn't even know herself.

"I only offered to help. You didn't have to bite my head off." His retreating footsteps made her feel ashamed. Ashamed that she'd been so mean to him when he was one of the best friends she had. But she didn't feel like hanging out tonight. She was tired, she was hot, she was sick of seeing the same people in the store every day. And if she admitted it to herself, she was sick of the air of depression and doom that floated over her house since Grandmama came home. She was recovering slowly but still had little use of her left arm and had to use a cane to support her weak left leg. Her speech, although clear most of the time, slurred at the end of the day or when she was tired. And this seemed to be all the time. Marisa didn't know how much more of it she could take. And she knew that a few hours at the movies wouldn't make it any easier. She'd just have to come back home.

"Marisa?" It was her father, standing behind her.

"Yes?" She turned to face him and was struck by how weary he looked. The past few weeks hadn't been easy on him, either, she realized. While trying to run a business, he was also trying to be a supportive husband to a wife who was edgy, tired and worried. On top of that, he had a sullen daughter to deal with. "Yes, Daddy?" She tried to lighten her tone.

"Why don't you go to the movies with Barry tonight?" He spoke in a low tone so Barry, who was in the storeroom, couldn't hear him.

"I don't feel like it."

"What's there to feel like? He's driving. All you have to do is sit there and enjoy the movie."

"Yeah, but..." She shrugged and glanced out the window, where Petersville's Main Street was already empty and quiet. "I just don't feel like it."

"Marisa, you've been working hard all summer. Go out and have some fun."

Sighing, she weighed her options. Go to a movie with Barry and escape to a world of make-believe, or go home, wash dishes, do laundry, maybe read a little, then go to bed. When she thought about it that way, she felt dumb. "But I was so mean to him. He probably doesn't even want to go now."

"I'll explain it to him. You've been working here and at home for weeks. You're on edge, that's all." He kissed her forehead. "I'll straighten everything out."

Whatever he said must have worked, because a few minutes later, Barry emerged with the Holland newspaper. "I'm not taking 'no' for an answer. You're going to hang out tonight. No one has seen you for weeks. Everybody's wondering what happened to you."

She smiled and leaned over the counter, where he'd spread the newspaper. "OK, OK, I'll go. I'm sorry I was such a grouch."

"No problem. You're always a grouch." He laughed at his own joke while scanning the paper and she playfully bopped him on the head. A night out. It sounded like the perfect remedy for whatever ailed her.

However, when she returned home just before midnight, she felt her dark mood returning. Sure, she'd had fun. They'd skipped the movie and instead went go-karting in Saugatuck with Kristin and Dennis. Caitlin and Mitch were there, too. Afterward, they all went downtown for some ice cream, where they harassed Tara on her job. They ate their cones on sidewalk benches, watching the tourists from Chicago and Indiana and trying to figure out who was gay and who was not. Saugatuck was a hot vacation spot for gay couples, and it wasn't unusual to see some men holding hands while they walked. Mitch called them "faggots" and Barry and Dennis laughed. They then watched the sunset on the beach with Barry putting his arm around Marisa while she tiredly leaned her head against his shoulder. She was surprised to find it comforting and friendly, but not romantic. It was exactly what she needed at that moment. When they said good night to their friends, Marisa climbed into the Montgomery's Skylark and rested her head against the seatback, enjoying the feel of the warm night air hitting her face while the radio played "Crazy for You" by Madonna. For those few moments, she could pretend she had no cares, no worries about tomorrow.

But upon entering her house, she was hit with a feeling of dread. She could see the piles of laundry in the laundry room, waiting for her. The breakfast dishes would be stacked in the sink when she woke up while her father did yard work or repaired something, and her mother washed and braided Grandmama's hair. Maybe if she slept in she could buy herself more time.

The next morning, the telephone woke her from a deep sleep. Before she could answer, she heard her father's surprised shout of greeting and figured it was one of his old Army buddies or one of his cronies from his wild childhood in Louisville. She turned over and buried herself under her sheet, pleased that they were in the middle of a summer storm, and fell back to sleep.

When she finally arose and ventured downstairs, it was past ten o'clock and she followed laughter and raised voices into the kitchen. Her parents and grandmother were sitting around the table, talking excitedly.

"What?" she asked, suddenly wide awake. They hadn't had this much noise in the house in weeks.

Her father clapped his hands together. "Your Aunt Liza and Uncle Gene are coming to visit."

"Really?" Aunt Liza was her father's younger sister. Her husband Gene was retired from the Air Force and they lived in Hampton, Virginia. Marisa had been down there once, when she was about six and barely remembered it. The last time she'd seen Aunt Liza was at the huge Logan family reunion in Louisville two summers ago. "When?"

"They'll be here on Saturday. And they're bringing Matthew back."

"Really?"

"Yep. And they're bringing your cousins, too. Janine is going to be a senior this fall. And Terry is … I think Terry is a year younger than you. Yeah, he's fifteen." Her father stared into space as he spoke. "Wow, you kids are growing up fast."

"Are they staying here?" Marisa asked. She hoped she didn't have to share her room with Janine. The last time she saw her, all she did was tease her because Marisa didn't know that the "kitchen" referred to the nappy hair at the base of her neck. Marisa thought she was referring to the place where they cooked and ate.

"Of course they are." Her mother set a plate of French toast in front of her daughter.

"How long are they staying?"

"About a week."

As Marisa and her parents talked about getting the house ready, she decided the visit may not be such a bad thing. It would at least bring some excitement to what was already becoming a boring summer.

***

Saturday morning, Marisa worked at the store only half a day so she could help her mother prepare the house for their guests. Barry said he hadn't seen her in such a good mood in weeks and he wanted to meet her family. Maybe they could all go out for pizza or something. She shrugged, wondering what her Southern cousins would think of small Petersville.

When they arrived later that evening, Marisa followed her family outside to greet them. Matthew jumped out of the blue van and ran straight to his parents. He then turned to Marisa, who he surprised with a big bear hug. "Hey, girl. Long time no see."

She laughed, buoyed at seeing him. Since he left for college, their relationship had improved. He no longer teased her and occasionally even listened to what she had to say and gave her advice about certain things. He released her and ran to the porch to greet his grandmother, who was leaning on her cane in front of the screen door with a big smile on her face.

Marisa turned back to the van, where her father and mother were exclaiming over how good everyone looked. Aunt Liza was tall, like her brother, and had lost a few pounds. Uncle Gene was tall, too, with a small pot belly and salt-and-pepper hair. Their kids looked like twins. Janine and Terry were tall and big-boned with the same caramel complexions and hook noses. They all came toward Marisa, who greeted them by welcoming them to Michigan.

After enduring Aunt Liza and Uncle Gene's exclamations of how pretty and grown-up she looked, she followed them into the house, where the adults sat in the kitchen while Marisa served iced tea. While Uncle Gene bragged about the great time he'd made on the trip – "woulda been faster if Liza hadn't had to go to the bathroom all the damn time" – Marisa and Janine stood awkwardly in the doorway, summing each other up. Janine's hair was cut in a cute, feathered style and she wore gold hoop earrings and a Hampton University T-shirt. Next to her tall cousin, Marisa felt short and country in her blue jean shorts and orange tank top. Her hair was pulled back in a simple ponytail and she wore no jewelry.

"Marisa." It was her mother. "Why don't you take Janine's things upstairs? Maybe she'd like to freshen up."

"OK." She turned to her cousin shyly. "Follow me." In her room, Janine spoke for the first time.

"Dang! You got a nice room! I wish mah room was this be-ugh." Marisa wanted to laugh at her Southern accent, but figured that would be rude.

"Thanks. Uh, I cleared a drawer for your things and there's room in the closet if you want to hang something up." She rested against the window seat while Janine surveyed her surroundings.

"This room is huge. You got all these windows..." she looked out one of them. "This is so cool. You're lucky."

"Thanks." The conversation ceased while Janine looked over Marisa's bookshelf and gazed at the pictures on her dresser and in her mirror.

"Who are all these white kids?" She was looking at a picture from last year's Homecoming where she and all of her friends were posing before the sophomore float.

"My friends. Uh, that was during Homecoming."

"Oh." Her eyes skimmed pictures of her friends before stopping at a snapshot of Marisa and Barry, taken over Christmas break when a bunch of them had gone cross-country skiing. His arms were wrapped around her from behind and she was leaning against his chest with a red ski suit on. It was her favorite picture. She looked really pretty and happy, and Barry, in his bright blue suit and hat, was laughing while he bent his face next to hers. "Don't tell me. This must be Barry."

Marisa jumped from the window seat and stood behind her cousin. "How did you know?"

"Matthew told me all about him on the way up here. He said you two have been best friends for years and you've liked him for about that long, too. He lives across the street, right?" She walked to the window seat Marisa had just vacated and pointed. "Is that his house? The one that looks like yours?"

Nodding, Marisa looked at the snapshot again. They looked perfect together. Anyone could see that. "Do you have a boyfriend?"

"Me?" Janine sat down. "Girl, you should see him. His name is Lorenzo, right, and he is fi-i-i-i-ne! He's a senior, too, and he plays basketball."

Marisa was impressed. Sounded like her dream guy. "How long have you been going together?"

"Since before prom. I liked him for awhile, right, but he had to get rid of his fast girlfriend. Then he asked me out."

"Sounds nice." Marisa smiled as Janine babbled on and on about Lorenzo and how she was going to miss him "something fierce" while she was away and what would be a good gift to bring him from Michigan? By the time she took a breath, Marisa was thoroughly amazed. Her cousin was too cool.

"Can I get something to eat? Girl, I am starving."

"Sure. Come on." She led her into the kitchen, where her mother, aunt and grandmother were sitting at the table, yakking over some sweet iced tea. She heard her father and uncle in the garage and suddenly felt happy. It was great having some life in the house again.

That evening, Janine offered to do Marisa's hair. "It's so pretty. It's all thick and wavy and stuff. Why do you wear it in a ponytail all the time?"

"I get hot with it down. All this hair feels like a rug on my head sometimes." She was sitting on a chair before her bureau while Janine fluffed her hair out with her fingers.

"I'm pretty good at this. I'ma hook you up," Janine said, while frowning at the curling iron on the dresser. "You use this on your hair?"

"Yeah, why?"

"This thing doesn't get hot enough! You get this at the drugstore or something?" At Marisa's embarrassed nod, Janine rummaged through her open suitcase and pulled out a large black and gold curling iron. "Your hair is pretty and all, but you can't be using the same stuff on it that these white girls do. You need to get one that gets really hot. Your curl will hold longer."

When they were getting ready for bed, Marisa snapped her fingers as she remembered her plans for the next day. "My hair is going to get messed up tomorrow. We're going to the beach."

"That's OK. I'll just wash and blow dry it. I like doing hair." And Marisa liked having her here. She was learning a lot, from the latest slang to the latest styles to the popular songs. Janine talked about Hampton so much that Marisa almost wanted to go back with her.

The next day, Marisa drove her mother's Regal to Saugatuck, where she, Janine and Terry lounged on the beach all morning, laughing and pointing at people in ill-fitting suits. Although none of them were strong swimmers, they still had fun splashing around in the water. By early afternoon, as they were contemplating what to eat for lunch, Marisa heard someone call her name. Shading her eyes with a hand, she saw Jen and Tara coming toward her.

"You know those girls?" Janine asked.

"Yeah, they're friends of mine." Marisa waved, silently hoping they'd keep walking. They didn't.

"Hi, stranger!" Jen hit her on the shoulder. "Where ya been all summer?"

"I've been around. Working a lot."

"Oh. How's Barry?" The question was asked with a sneer. Apparently, Jen wasn't grieving over their break-up any longer. She'd moved on to the anger phase.

"He's fine. Working a lot, too." Silence fell while everyone waited for Marisa to make introductions. "Oh. You guys, these are my cousins, Janine and Terry. They're visiting from Virginia. Guys, this is Jen. And that's Tara."

Terry waved a hand lazily and closed his eyes in an attempt to go to sleep.

"Nice to meet you." Jen smiled brightly at Janine. "You're from Virginia? What part?"

"Hampton."

"Hampton..." Jen put a finger to her mouth. "Mmm. I don't think I know where that is."

"It's near Virginia Beach and Williamsburg." While Janine spoke politely, Marisa knew she was sizing up Jen and not liking what she saw.

"Oh. My parents have friends in Culpeper. They have a huge horse ranch. Do you know where that is?"

"I've heard of it."

"Oh. Good."

Silence again before Tara broke the awkwardness. "Are you going to Mitch's party on Saturday? It's at his parents' beach house in Holland."

"No. This is the first I've heard about it," Marisa answered, wishing they'd go away, because Jen and Janine were sizing each other up. It was only a matter of time before someone said something stupid.

It ended up being Jen. She was complimenting Janine on her black maillot when her voice suddenly changed. "I'll bet those dudes be checkin' you out down in Virginia, right? If I were you, I'd say, 'Yo! You can look but you cain't touch!' "

Marisa was mortified. Jen sounded so stupid. She was trying to talk black but ended up sounding condescending and offensive. The comments made Terry sit up with a frown. Even Tara looked at Jen like she'd lost her mind.

"Why are you talking like that?" Janine rose and stood before Jen with her hands on her hips.

"Like what?" Jen's face, which was pink from too much sun, carried a smirk.

"You know what I'm talking about. You know damn well you don't walk around here saying 'yo.' Who are you trying to imitate? Me? My brother? Marisa?"

"Noooo. Marisa doesn't talk like that." Jen laughed but stopped when Janine got in her face.

"And neither do you. Which leads me to believe that you're making fun of me or my brother."

Jen was smart enough to realize how pissed off Janine was and backed away. "Nooo, I didn't mean..."

"Oh, so you're just imitating black people in general, is that it?" Janine stepped to her again, her taller figure making Jen cower.

"No. I wasn't trying to...make fun of anybody." She looked to Marisa to defend her, but she just shook her head in disgust. Jen was too dumb.

"Sure you weren't." Janine glanced at Marisa, looking for confirmation to continue or to hold back. Marisa just shrugged. Jen deserved whatever was coming her way.

Janine decided to hold back. But just a little. "So uh, I think you were leaving right about now, weren't you?" At that, Jen turned and hurried down the beach, sand kicking up behind her in her haste.

Tara picked up the beach bag her friend left behind with downcast eyes. "I'm sorry for ... what Jen did. It was nice meeting you. See you, Marisa." She hurried after Jen.

"Girl! How can you call that girl your friend?" Janine was still ranting. "She is prejudiced! Don't you see that?"

Shrugging, Marisa picked at the loose hairs on her Mickey Mouse beach blanket. "I know she can be a pain, but we've been friends since kindergarten. We all have. We're cheerleaders together and everything."

"But she's a damn racist! I'm from Virginia, so I can spot 'em a mile away, girl!" Janine plopped back down on her blanket, her thick eyebrows furrowed.

"She dated Barry last year, too."

Janine's nostrils flared as she stared at Marisa. "What? She knew you liked him and she still went out with him?" At Marisa's nod, Janine let out a low whistle. "Girl, I'm just tellin' you. Watch your back. You can't trust her. She'll be smilin' all up in your face then turn around and stab you in the back."

"I know. I don't think I've ever trusted Jen. We just kind of hang together out of, I don't know...habit, I guess. And we have a bunch of mutual friends."

"I can understand that, but just...watch your back."

"I will." Then in an effort to lighten the conversation, she added, "What can you expect from someone who likes Menudo?"

"Menudo?" Janine cracked up. "Girl, no she don't like Menudo! I knew that girl had problems..."

By the end of the week, Marisa felt as if she had a sister in Janine. They stayed up late talking – well, Janine did most of the talking, but Marisa loved hearing her stories. She was shocked when she admitted that she'd had sex with Lorenzo. "It hurt like hell, girl, and I bled, too. But it got better the second and third time, though."

"Are you...I mean, you might get pregnant or VD or something!" Marisa was dumbfounded. Janine talked about sex so casually. No one she knew had had sex yet. And if they had, they kept it secret.

"Nooo, he wears a rubber." Janine didn't notice Marisa turn red at the blunt conversation. "Anyway, maybe you'll meet him if you ever come down. I know! You come down for my graduation in June, then maybe you can stay a few weeks and meet all my friends and stuff. There will be parties galore, girl!"

"That sounds fun. I'll ask my mom and dad." Marisa was excited. She'd always wanted to go away for the summer, and now that she and Janine got along, it was only fitting for her to visit her in Virginia.

Her parents loved the idea. As they stood outside bidding Aunt Liza and her family farewell, her mother promised to make arrangements for Marisa's month-long visit next summer. "It'll do her good to get around some black kids. I tell you, Liza, some of these girls she hangs around with just get on my last nerve!"

Marisa, overhearing the remark, was surprised. All of her friends loved her mother. If they only knew that she didn't return the compliment. Oh well, Marisa would have a bunch of black friends before she knew it. Then her family would be proud of her.

CHAPTER 5

Fall 1985-Spring 1986

"Hey! Watch where you're swinging that thing!" Jen yelled at Paul Bankhead, who was carrying a tube of chicken wire for the junior class Homecoming float, under construction at Tara's family farm.

"What time is it, anyway? I have to get home. Trevor may be trying to call." Jen looked around in near panic. "What time is it, Marisa?"

"It's only eight-thirty. We have another thirty minutes to go, Jen, so relax. Trevor can always call you back." Jen was dating some blonde, ultra-preppy guy from Saugatuck and was becoming more obnoxious as the relationship flourished.

"Hey, Marisa, congratulations!" Amanda Littlefield walked past with a wave and a smile.

"Thanks." Marisa smiled to herself and continued painting the mock ladder on the float. She, Lisa, Barry and Dennis were all on the junior class Homecoming court and tomorrow at the pep rally they would find out who was Man and Maid of Honor. Marisa was so glad she'd made it. Both of her brothers had been Homecoming kings and she didn't want to be the only one in the family not to be crowned. If she won, she'd be Petersville's first black Homecoming Maid of Honor. And next year – dare she dream? – its first black Homecoming queen.

"Hey, Barry! I'm running out of paint! Got anymore?" she yelled.

"You're out already?" She watched as he ran over to her, clad in an old U of M sweatshirt and worn, faded jeans with his hair mussed from the work he was doing. She didn't remember ever seeing him look so sexy. Even Tara and Kris had commented on it, whispering to her with giggles as he spoke to them at the start of the evening in his official role as chair of the float committee. Marisa felt a twinge of jealousy. Why were they looking at him that way? They knew she still liked him. And that meant hands off.

"You didn't give me a whole can in the first place." She tilted the almost-empty can so he could see.

"Yes, I did. Jen was supposed to give it to you. It wasn't even open." He searched the barn for Jennifer, who was working on signs for the Friday pep rally. "Jen! Where's the paint I told you to give to Marisa?"

"It's right here!" She held up a huge posterboard that read "Class of '87 Rules."

With a disgusted sigh, he shook his head and turned back to Marisa, who dropped to a sitting position on the side of the float. "She gave you the wrong can. God, she's so stupid." Leaning against the floor of the float, Barry shook his head again. "Hey, I didn't get a chance to congratulate you. Are you excited?"

She shrugged with a slight smile. "A little. Are you?"

"Nah. You girls get into this more than we do."

"Yeah, right. Besides, you've been on the court every year since we were freshmen. This is my first time."

"Well, you'll enjoy it, then. Riding in the parade and all. Will you save me a dance?" He had the nerve to grin at her with that...grin of his and wink. Wink! She wanted to melt on the spot.

"I think I can spare one or two for you." She giggled and blushed slightly. Who else did he think she wanted to dance with, anyway?

"Just one or two, huh?" He laughed, straightened, then stared hard at her.

"What?"

"You have some paint on your nose." With a gentle smile, he reached up and rubbed her nose with a thumb. "It's starting to dry. Hold on." He stepped closer, cupped her chin in his hand and rubbed the paint off.

"Ouch." Laughing, she touched her nose gingerly. "That hurt."

"Sorry." He didn't move from his oh-so-near stance and didn't seem to notice others glancing at them. "Want me to kiss it and make it better?"

Did she ever! But not in front of everyone. How embarrassing would that be? No, if he wanted to kiss her, he'd have to wait for another time. Instead, she pushed him away in mock irritation. "Such a flirt. Don't you have some work to do?"

He walked away laughing while Marisa sat on the float shaking her head. Ever since school started, he'd been acting like he wanted to get back together with her. They'd worked together all summer and hung out sometimes, but always with a group of friends. But once school started, he'd offered to give her a ride to school every day. And he even told her to wait for him after football practice so he could take her home, too. They were together almost all day long. They had all of their classes together – a first – and they usually ended up going out for pizza with their friends on Friday nights. Saturdays were reserved for video parties at various friends' houses or movies in Holland. From all appearances, they were dating. But he hadn't kissed her or asked her to go with him. So what was the deal? She was getting tired of waiting and debated whether she should make the first move. But no, the rejection would be too painful to take.

Friday finally came and with it the big pep rally. As it came to a close, Caitlin, as president of the Student Council, took the microphone to present the Homecoming court and to announce the royalty. Marisa joined Barry, Lisa and Dennis on the floor and waited nervously while Caitlin announced the winners. Marisa tried to appear regal, like Princess Diana, but didn't think she succeeded.

"And now, the 1985 Homecoming Man and Maid of Honor are…" Caitlin opened the envelope while Marisa held her breath. "Barry Montgomery and Marisa Logan!"

She screamed and hid her face in her hands in pure joy. She did it! She was Maid of Honor! And with Barry! Lisa was hugging her and Dennis was patting her on the back. Then there was Barry, removing her hands from her face to gather her in a warm hug. "Congratulations," he said in her ear, then kissed her on the cheek.

"You too." She smiled and clasped his hand while the crowd grew quiet and waited for the announcement of the king and queen. But Marisa barely paid attention as Mitch and Diana Carrillo's names were read. She was the first black Maid of Honor in Petersville's history. Her family would be so proud. She knew PHS was not racist, no matter what her parents said.

At the dance Saturday, Marisa got more than her usual share of compliments on her appearance, and it was no wonder. She was radiant. Her red dress complemented her light caramel skin and she had finally perfected the hairstyle her cousin Janine had shown her over the summer. She had lost about five pounds since July and was wearing her mother's Halston perfume, a scent that sparked Barry's attention en route to the dance.

"You smell good. What is that?" He leaned over and sniffed her neck, making her recoil and laugh.

"Stop! That tickles. It's Halston."

"Oooh...fancy." Smiling, he met her eyes across the seat. "You look beautiful, Marisa."

She was almost speechless. What was coming over him lately? "Thank you."

"But then again, you usually do." He said it matter-of-factly, like one speaks of the weather. Once they arrived, he refused to fast dance with her, as usual, so she took to the floor with her girlfriends and Mitch, who thought he could dance but usually just bounced around with an imaginary guitar in his hands.

On the first few slow dances, Paul Bankhead claimed her before Barry could get to her, so she made small talk with Paul while keeping an eye on Barry, who was dancing with Amanda. Soon after, the Homecoming court was told to line up for the crowning, so Marisa once again was paired with Barry while they walked under the trellis arm-in-arm. After Mitch and Diana were crowned king and queen, the deejay switched on Whitney Houston's "Saving All My Love For You," and Marisa stepped into Barry's embrace. They'd danced many times before, but this one felt different. He held her closer than he had before, with his head buried in her hair and her head resting on his shoulder. With her eyes closed, she imagined she was in the crowd with her classmates, watching as they moved in slow, syncopated circles. And for the umpteenth time since the fourth grade, she thought, "I love Barry Montgomery." Who cared that he was white? He obviously didn't care that she was black, hadn't since the first grade, when they'd been sitting on her porch playing cars and trucks and he'd leaned in to tell her a secret.

"Guess what?" he'd whispered.

"What?" she'd answered, wide-eyed.

"You're brown," he informed her as if she didn't know. That was the last time either of them had mentioned the difference in their races in more than a passing conversation. It obviously didn't matter.

As the song came to a close, she opened her eyes to see Jen watching them with a scowl on her face. Oh well, she'd have to get over it. She couldn't have Barry back. She was about to turn away from Jen when she saw her lean over and whisper something to Adrienne Gates, a petite, pretty sophomore with light blonde hair. Adrienne was nice, but Marisa didn't know her too well. She didn't associate much with the underclassmen.

When the song ended, the deejay switched on Madonna's "Dress You Up" and the dance floor filled up again. Barry held her hand and was about to lead them to the corner bleachers when Jen suddenly appeared before them with a bright smile and a camera. "Smile!"

Before they could blink, she snapped the picture, causing them to rub their eyes from the flash.

"Jen, why didn't you wait until we were ready? I don't even have my flowers," Marisa said in annoyance.

"Oh, that's right. Let's get another one of you with your flowers. By yourself, though." She pulled Marisa by the arm to the side of the gym, where she went through a huge picture-taking production, pulling Kristin, then Tara, then herself into the photos. By the time Marisa turned around to find Barry, he was standing by the refreshment table talking to Adrienne Gates. The same Adrienne Gates Jen had been whispering to so furiously a few moments before. Doubt filled Marisa as she wondered whether to approach him or not. Adrienne was giggling and smiling during their conversation and whenever she spoke, Barry had to lean down to hear her because she was so short. Marisa stood by her friends' table, waiting for Barry to look up and search the gym for her. But he continued talking and laughing with Adrienne. Soon Survivor's "The Search Is Over" came on and she saw Adrienne whisper something in Barry's ear. Nodding, he laid his scepter aside and led her to dance floor where they slow danced much the same as he and Marisa had only moments before.

The radiance that had lit her face most of the night suddenly disappeared as she watched them dance. Mortified, she picked up her bouquet of roses and nonchalantly walked to the exit without a second glance. All of her friends were on the dance floor so no one saw her leave. No one saw her feign illness to Mr. Simpson, the biology teacher and chaperone, who, alarmed at the tears in her eyes, offered to take her home. He didn't know that while the illness was fake, the tears were very real.

At home, she lay in bed for hours, waiting for the phone to ring, for Barry to ask what had happened to her, why she'd left so suddenly, was she OK. At twelve-thirty, ninety minutes after the dance ended, she finally let the sobs come and realized she'd let her imagination run wild again. Barry didn't want her. He was just playing with her. And even if he had wanted her, he'd wised up when a pretty, blonde girl like Adrienne showed interest. Why would he want Marisa when he could have someone like Adrienne? And for what must have been the millionth time in her life, she wondered if she would be feeling so unworthy and ugly if she went to a black high school. For some reason, she had a feeling the answer would be no.

***

By Wednesday, Barry and Adrienne were going together, and at every opportunity, Jen chirped to Marisa, "Aren't they a cute couple? They just look so good together." As a result, Marisa started to retreat into a protective shell, shunning parties and dances to stay home and read with her grandmother, to practice cooking and to study. By January, she had overtaken Barry in the class rankings and increased her grade-point average to 3.98. Everyone wondered why she was studying all the time and why she didn't seem to want to do anything anymore. She said she wanted to make sure her grades were good enough to get into any college she wanted. But for now, she didn't know what she wanted. Matthew was trying to talk her into Howard, but she didn't want to follow him. And while she liked Chicago, she didn't really want to go to Northwestern. Their sports teams sucked. She was considering Spelman, but figured she wouldn't like the South. She didn't even consider nearby Hope College, Grand Valley State or Western Michigan. They were all too close. Her counselor then recommended the University of Michigan or Michigan State. Barry liked U of M. He was a fanatic. But Marisa had never considered either one. She always figured she'd go out of state for college, like her brothers did. So she continued to search.

In February, temperatures dropped to below freezing and southwestern Michigan was hit with more than a foot of snow. During snow days at home, Marisa would sit before the fire with a

Danielle Steel book and remember snow days when she was little. She and her brothers would lounge around in their pajamas all morning, eating pancakes and watching "The Electric Company." By lunchtime, Barry would come over and they'd all play in the snow or go sledding. Afterward, they'd sit at the table and chomp on Grandmama's hot biscuits and syrup or molasses cookies. She missed those days. She missed her brothers. She missed Barry.

Since he began dating Adrienne, she rarely saw him. She drove to school herself now, in her mother's old Regal, relegated to her when her parents bought a new Buick. Barry still worked weekends in the store, but Marisa rarely joked with him like she used to. He didn't even seem to notice her mood change. He was too busy trying to save up enough money to give Adrienne a great gift for Valentine's Day.

One night, while the winter winds howled outside, and Marisa and her family were watching "The Cosby Show," her mother piped up. "How come your school doesn't do anything for Black History Month?"

"Huh?" Marisa, who was buried under an afghan on the couch, frowned in confusion.

"Black History Month. You do know February is Black History Month, don't you?"

"Of course, Mother." Did her mom think she was stupid? She read Ebony and Jet, after all. And her parents reminded them every year anyway.

"So did your history teacher mention it at all?"

Marisa pictured Mrs. Mead, a sixty-something U.S. history teacher with bad eyes and a cranky disposition. She doubted Mrs. Mead even knew there was a Black History Month.

"No. We talked about slavery and Harriet Tubman back in the fall, though." She remembered the looks she got from her classmates whenever slavery was discussed. Some of them blatantly stared at her, like they expected an angry outburst. Others glanced at her out of the corner of their eyes. She didn't remember ever feeling so conspicuous in school. During those discussions, she either kept her eyes on her textbook or focused on the chalkboard.

"That's all you ever talk about is slavery and Harriet Tubman. For all white folks know, we were slaves, Abe Lincoln set us free then Martin Luther King led us to the promised land. Now everything is all right?" Her mother shook her head. "What about all the positive things black people have done in history? You never hear about that."

Marisa, who hadn't moved from her cocoon on the couch, stared at the television while she pondered her mother's comments. True, most of America watched Bill Cosby every Thursday night, but surely they knew there was more to black America than what was on TV. But maybe not. Maybe they needed someone to tell them.

The next day, she approached Mr. Walzer, the librarian, and asked him if she could decorate the display case in the hallway for Black History Month. Mr. Walzer, a former hippie, thought it was a great idea. "But it's already decorated for Valentine's Day, Marisa. We can't just take that down. Paul and Amanda worked hard on it."

"I know." Marisa had already thought it out. "Can I put it up after Valentine's Day? I mean, it doesn't make much sense for us to keep it up after the 14th, does it?"

"You're right." He clapped his hands and peered at her over his horn-rimmed glasses. "You can put your display up right after Valentine's Day."

She went home that night and told her mother the good news. "What kind of stuff should I put up? Martin Luther King?"

"No. We just celebrated his birthday last month." Mama smiled in excitement and sat at the kitchen table with her daughter, who was twirling her hair around a finger nervously. She hadn't told any of her friends what she was doing and was wondering how they'd react.

"Then who?" She herself knew little about black history, except for slavery, Dr. King and Shirley Chisholm.

"Let's put up a map of Washington, D.C. Yeah, that's a good idea," her mother was flipping through the February issue of Ebony magazine. "No, no, wait. Pictures of D.C. would be even better."

"What about D.C.?" Marisa was confused.

"Washington was designed by a black man. Benjamin Banneker." She looked at her daughter with a smirk. "You didn't know that, did you?"

"No." She wanted to add that he must have been drunk when he did it, because to her, D.C. was a mess. Her father got lost every time they went up there to drop off or pick up Matthew.

"Yes, we'll put up pictures of D.C., we'll add pictures of Harold Washington, too. The first black mayor of Chicago." Marisa sat back and watched as her mother planned the whole display case. She didn't mind. Mama knew more about black history than she did, anyway. If she was going to do it, it may as well be done right.

The next week, she came to school early to take down the Valentine's Day display and began arranging her Black History Month window. She stapled cut-out letters to the back of the display case explaining what the month was and was setting up a miniature stop light when the first students began arriving. Some of them yelled greetings at her and kept going, while others stopped, read the words, then continued without comment. As she was stapling a picture of Langston Hughes, Mitch stopped next to her.

"What are you doing?"

"I'm putting up a display for Black History Month." She didn't look him in the eye and continued her work.

"But you're not a library aide. Are you?"

"No. Mr. Walzer said I could do it." By this time, Caitlin and Jen had stopped, too.

"I thought only library aides could come up with display case ideas." He turned to Jen, who had wandered over. "Isn't that right?"

"Usually. Why'd you take down the Valentine's Day stuff? It was pretty." Jen stared at Marisa with bug eyes.

"News flash, Jen. Valentine's Day is over. And so is this conversation." She'd told herself she wasn't going to get angry, but so far she felt like cussing out her friends.

"Sor-ree. Come on, Caitlin." Jen pulled her friend by the arm and they disappeared into the bathroom for their morning hair-teasing ritual.

"So when is White History Month, Marisa?" Mitch laughed at his own ignorant joke. Trouble was, some other kids in earshot laughed, too.

"It's the other eleven months of the year. That's when." She shoved him with an elbow. "Now move. I have to finish before first hour." He finally got the hint and took off down the hall in a jog, leaving her face red with anger and shame. Anger because her friends were so ignorant and shame because she still called them her friends. How could she hang around with such boneheads?

"Hi Marisa." A quiet voice greeted her from behind. It was Kristin. "What are you doing?"

"It's a display for Black History Month." She stepped back and surveyed her work. It looked great, even if she said so herself. The bright colors coupled with the props and pictures were definitely eye-catching.

"It looks cool. Was this your idea?"

Marisa glanced at Kristin out of the corner of her eye. Her friend was nodding her head in approval with her books crushed to her chest. "Uh, yeah. My mom gave me the idea, though. And she helped a lot, too."

"That's great. Do you need any help?" She turned to her with a catching grin.

"Uh, no, not really. I'm done. But uh, you can help me clean up if you want." She was surprised at Kris' interest. But then again, maybe not. Kris had always been the most considerate and levelheaded of all of her friends. She grew up in a stable, church-going family and hardly said anything bad about anyone. She was intelligent and thoughtful as well. "Thanks, Kris."

"You're welcome. So explain some of this to me. What's this stoplight for? And why do you have pictures of Washington, D.C.? And who is Langston Hughes?"

***

In April, Marisa, as class vice president, started to focus on the junior-senior prom. She and Lisa did most of the work, calling around for locations, calling engravers, deejays and decorators. They finally settled on a lodge on Holland's lakeshore, tucked in the woods near the beach. Now all they had to do was find a theme song. That job was left to Marisa.

She was sitting in her room one rainy Wednesday evening listening to the radio for potential songs when she heard her father stomp up the stairs and wander into her room.

"How you doing, baby girl?" He tugged on her ponytail. "How was school?"

"Fine. I'm still trying to find a song for the prom." She was leaning toward "Tender Love" by Force MDs, but knew her friends and classmates probably wouldn't like it. But she'd try to pitch it anyway. Wouldn't hurt.

"So who are you going with, anyway? Shouldn't you be looking for a dress?" Her father reached inside his pocket for his reading glasses and didn't notice Marisa turning crimson.

"Oh, I don't know..." her voice trailed. She always figured she'd go to prom. Everyone went. It was the premier event of high school. But no one had asked her. Not yet, anyway. She didn't know if anyone would.

"All this work you're doing on it and you don't have a date yet?" Daddy peered at her in surprise. "Who's Barry taking? That little blonde girl?"

"Adrienne. Yes, he's taking her." That "little blonde girl" had already gotten her dress, as had Jen, Kristin and Caitlin. Tara didn't have a date yet, either, but she'd told Marisa today that she was going to ask Paul to go. That left Marisa as the only one of her friends without a date. They all told her to go stag or to ride along with one of them, but she'd never be a third wheel. How awkward! And they were only saying it out of pity, anyway. They didn't want her to tag along without a date, no matter what they said.

"Well, what about Dennis? Or Mitch? You can go as friends," her dad offered helpfully.

"They all have dates already." She tried not to sound worried or lonely, but she was. She didn't want to be left out on prom night. The night she'd helped create. She was the one who had found the lodge in Holland. She was the one who'd called and hired the deejay. And now she was the one searching for the perfect song. Her dad was right. It'd be totally unfair if she didn't go.

But the next day, as she sat in the cafeteria, she scanned the room searching for someone she'd actually want to spend an evening with. Someone she'd actually want to get dressed up for, go to dinner with. Time and time again, her eyes rested on Barry, who was standing in line with his hands on Adrienne's tiny waist. She needed to face reality. If she couldn't go with Barry, she just wouldn't go. She broke the news to her friends that afternoon before the junior class meeting in the auditorium.

"What do you mean you're not going?" Jen asked, horrified. "Marisa, you have to go! Prom won't be the same without you!"

"Yeah, Maris. You can still go. You don't have to have a date," Kristin added.

Marisa, who was sitting on the edge of the stage, averted her eyes. "Yeah, right, like I'm gonna be the only one there without a date. I'm sure."

"But you can hang out with us. We told you that!" Jen looked to Tara and Kristin for help, who both nodded.

"I'm not going!" Marisa felt a lump well in her throat as she tried desperately to sound nonchalant. She was failing miserably. "It's no big deal. I'm not going to die if I don't go to prom."

"But Marisa! You have to go!" They were still trying to convince her when Barry walked into the auditorium.

"Yak, yak, yak! I can hear you girls all the way in the hallway." He jumped next to Marisa on stage. "What's the fuss about? Is the meeting cancelled?"

"No. We were just..." Marisa was about to change the subject, but Jen interrupted.

"Marisa says she's not going to prom."

Marisa bit her lip while Barry turned to her in surprise. "What? How come you're not going, Marisa?"

"It's no big deal..."

"She doesn't have a date so she thinks she can't go," Jen finished for her. "Will you tell her it doesn't matter? She'll listen to you."

"You don't have to have a date." Barry hardly seemed surprised that no one had asked her. "Besides, as a class officer, aren't you required to go?"

The room fell silent. No one had thought of that. "Ye-e-a-ah..." Jen clapped her hands. "That's right! You have to go now!"

"That's not a rule..." Marisa began, worried that she might be wrong.

"I don't know. I think it might be." Barry jumped off the stage and playfully untied her shoe. "Anyway, you can always go with Adrienne and me."

"Yeah, right." She couldn't hold back the sarcastic snort. "That'll be the day." He turned around with a look of confusion on his face, eyebrows furrowed, lips drawn like he wanted to continue the conversation, but just then the rest of the class started pouring in.

During the meeting, the class nixed Marisa's idea of "Tender Love" but pounced on Lisa's suggestion of "These Dreams" by Heart. Marisa liked that song, too, so she wasn't too bummed about being overruled. After the meeting, she dodged questions about the prom, saying she hadn't made up her mind. In truth, she wanted to find out if she was required to go. When Mr. Steinga, one of the class advisers, told her no, she knew the matter was settled. Forget what her friends said. They could go to prom and enjoy the fruits of her labor, but she'd be home. Alone. Probably studying while they were out having the best time of their lives.

The week before prom, Marisa's mother cornered her in the kitchen with a smile and a folder in her hands. "I have a surprise for you."

"What?" She chomped on Combos while her mother sat at the table.

"How would you like to spend next weekend in Chicago?"

"Chicago?" Marisa smiled, ignoring the crumbs that fell from her mouth. "But we were just there, for Robert's graduation."

"I know. But this time it'll be just you and me. We'll stay in a hotel and go shopping. Maybe get our hair done. Would you like that?"

Was she kidding? She loved Chicago. And a shopping spree, too? "Of course! But what about Robert? And Grandmama?"

"Your Aunt Shirley is going to come up for the weekend to tend to Grandmama while your daddy is at the store. And we'll see Robert. But with his student-teaching, we won't get to spend much time with him."

"Oh. That sounds cool, Mama. Whose idea was this?" Marisa stopped eating. If she was going to get new clothes, she needed to look good.

"Mine. You've done so good in school this year and you got into the National Honor Society, and you've helped around the house so much. Just consider this your birthday present and vacation all rolled up in one."

Marisa couldn't stop grinning. "But I thought my trip to Virginia next month was going to be my vacation."

"Well, it is. We're just going to find you a few clothes for you to take to Hampton, OK?"

"OK." She stared into space, already picturing how good she was going to look at Janine's graduation. Then she snapped back to reality. "Wait a minute. Next weekend? Prom weekend? Is that why we're going?"

Her mother busily brushed some crumbs off the table. "Well...partly. I just didn't want you sitting home while your friends were out all night."

"Oh." She smiled wistfully. What a nice thing to do. "Shoot, I'll probably have more fun than all of them now. It's no big deal, Mama. I'll go to prom next year."

Her mother brushed the bangs off her daughter's forehead. "Of course you will. I just wish...I just wish there were some black boys around here. They'd love to take you. You're so pretty and smart."

Laughing, Marisa hugged her. "I know, Mama. I know. So hey, can we go to Marshall Field's?"

"Sure."

"And to Carson Pirie Scott?"

"OK. But don't push it. I'm not rich, you know."

"I know. And Mama, don't worry about me." She stood and walked to the door before turning around. "I really am fine about prom. Even though I don't have a boyfriend or a prom date, doesn't mean I have low self-esteem or anything. I know I'm pretty. And I don't really think I'm fat. It's just a little harder for me at school than it is for my friends." She smiled, suddenly proud of how grown she sounded. "That's all. But like Grandmama always says, 'This, too, shall pass.'"

CHAPTER 6

Summer 1986

"I hope you have fun in Virginia," Barry said as he watched Marisa load the family car with suitcases. "It's going to be weird here without you or your dad in the store."

"Yeah, well, it's about time he took a vacation," Marisa said with her head inside the trunk. "He needs it."

"You'll have fun. Tell your cousins I said hi." He leaned an arm on top of the raised trunk and hooked a finger through his belt loop. "Do you think they remember me?"

She raised her head and grinned, squinting her eyes against the early morning sun. "Of course they do. Janine still asks about you."

"Really?" Smiling, he chuckled. "What does she say?"

With a smirk, Marisa punched him lightly on the arm. "Never mind that. Besides, what would Adrienne think if she knew you were asking about another girl?"

His smile faded and he looked away. "She can't say too much. We broke up last night."

"What?" The news made Marisa gasp. They'd been inseparable for months. So much so that everyone in school started to complain about how sickening they were to watch. "What happened?"

"She was getting too possessive, you know?" He shook his head and gazed down the street, the light summer wind ruffling his golden hair. "She didn't want me hanging out with Mitch or Dennis or anybody without her. Remember when we went to the Tigers game last week?" At Marisa's nod, he continued. "Well, she was mad about that. She wanted to go."

"With all of you guys?"

"Yeah. And she doesn't even like baseball!"

"Oh." Marisa didn't know what to say. Barry didn't seem too upset about the break-up so any comforting words that came to mind seemed futile. "I'm sorry."

"Hey, don't be sorry. At least now I'm free for the summer. Man, you don't know how good it's going to feel to go where I want to go without worrying about calling her and stuff. She wanted to do *everything* with me!"

With a shrug, Marisa tried to pretend that she was sympathizing with him, but in reality, she wanted to laugh. That's what he got for going with such a young girl. Someone whom Jen pushed on him. Oh yes, although she had no proof, she knew that Jen had urged Adrienne to ask Barry to dance way back during Homecoming. She saw how close she and Barry were getting and wanted to push them apart, so she sicced Adrienne on him. And things hadn't been the same since.

"You know, she was even jealous of you," Barry was saying.

Marisa shook her head to clear her thoughts. "Huh? Me?"

"Yeah."

"Jealous of me? For what?" She wanted to laugh. How ironic is that? Marisa had been jealous of Adrienne for months and now she discovered that the feeling was mutual.

"She was jealous of our friendship. She said I seemed different around you, like I could talk to you more than her or something. I'm telling you, she was really, really possessive." He glanced down at her and laughed loudly at her expression. "Close your mouth! Why are you looking like that?"

"Because I'm shocked, that's why. Adrienne, jealous of me? I mean, you and I have barely hung out or anything this year. Why be jealous of me?"

"Yeah, speaking of which," he tugged on her ponytail. "Why haven't we done anything besides work together this year? What happened to us hanging out and riding to school together and stuff?"

"Well, I – I started driving my mother's car..." she began.

"Yeah, but that's not all. We barely seemed to do much of anything. Was it because of Adrienne?"

She looked up at him and almost sighed at the earnest expression on his tanned face. He seemed so hurt and confused. "It wasn't just because of Adrienne..."

"But she had something to do with it, right?"

"Barry, it wasn't just her. I mean, she didn't hold a gun to your head, you know. You were pretty involved with her. You didn't have room for anyone else." She tried to stop the words from sounding bitter, but knew she failed when he let out a mumbled curse.

"God, you're right. You're right. Dennis and Mitch said the same thing. But I never thought I'd ever treat you like that. I mean, sometimes I need a break from those guys, you know? But not from you. Never from you." His dark eyes stared into hers unblinkingly and Marisa felt her throat constrict. Why was he telling her all of this now, when she was about to leave for four weeks?

"It's OK, Barry. I didn't take it personally or anything."

"But still, I'm sorry. That wasn't right. Do you forgive me?"

She smiled. "Of course I do. But it's no big deal." She yelped when he grabbed her and lifted her off the ground in a big hug. "Barry! Stop it!"

"Man, I'm going to miss you. Promise you'll send me a postcard, OK?"

He set her down but kept his arms around her waist loosely. She busily straightened her hair and tried to ignore how good it felt to be in his arms. "I will. For sure."

"Promise?" He touched his forehead with hers, causing her to take a quick breath.

"I promise." She whispered.

"Good." He stared at her for a quick second, then lightly brushed his lips on her forehead. "I've gotta go. Have fun, OK? And bring me back something cool."

"I will. Stay out of trouble." She waved as he ran across the street.

"Always. Bye, Mr. Logan!" He waved to Marisa's father, who had materialized out of nowhere on the side porch. "Have a safe trip!"

"Thanks Barry!" Her father waved, then slowly joined Marisa next to the car. "So what was that all about?"

"What?" Marisa busily re-arranged the suitcases in the trunk in a futile effort to ignore her father's curious gaze.

"That goodbye I just saw. He kissed you. What happened to that little blonde girl he was dating?"

"They broke up. And her name is Adrienne."

"Oh. So what's he trying to do? Date you next?'

"Daddy!" She looked behind her to make sure Barry was out of earshot. Thankfully, he was nowhere in sight. "Don't you like Barry?"

"You know I do, but I don't know if I want him playing around with you the way he did Jennifer and that little blonde girl, uh, Adrienne." Her father closed the trunk, dusted off his hands, then rested them on her shoulders. "You deserve someone who knows he wants to be with you. Not someone who goes from girl to girl."

Marisa shook her head with a small smile. Her daddy was so old-fashioned. "Yes, Daddy, I know. But Barry and I are just friends. He was just apologizing to me for being such a butthole the whole time he was dating Adrienne. That's all. Nothing else." She feigned indifference, but inside she was wondering if he really was interested in her again. The thought stayed with her through most of the trip, but once they reached the Virginia state line, she started to put Michigan and Barry behind her. She was on her way to an exciting summer with her cool cousin. Barry and his problems could wait.

***

THE KITCHEN ISN'T WHERE YOU COOK

"They're here! They're here!" Janine screamed as she raced down the front steps to the Logan's car. "Ter-ree! Mama! They're here!" Janine jumped up and down by the car and banged on the window excitedly while waiting for Marisa to get out. When she did, she hugged her cousin tightly around the neck, causing Marisa to choke.

"Janine!" Marisa laughed as she pulled away. "I can't breathe!"

"I don't care, girl! I'm just so glad to see you!" She hugged her again, and Marisa, realizing she was facing a losing battle, returned the embrace.

"Hey! Don't I get a hug?" Her father came around to the girls and grabbed his niece in a tight embrace. "Look at you! Graduating from high school already!"

"Yeah. Did Mama tell you I finished eighth in my class?" Janine grinned smugly.

"She did. We're all real proud of you, baby. Where is that sister of mine?" He looked up at the sound of the front door slamming. "There she is!" While her father greeted Aunt Liza, Marisa leaned against the car and surveyed her cousin.

"Your hair is cute. What did you do to it?" Marisa was jealous. It was cut in an asymmetrical style with golden highlights in it.

"Girl, I had this cut for a couple of weeks. You like it?" She twirled around.

"Yes. Do you think Mama will let me cut it like that?"

"Don't you dare! Your hair is so pretty! Don't you cut it!" Janine peered at her. "But you do need to get it out of that ponytail."

"I will." Marisa was suddenly self-conscious. "I just did this for the trip down here. I'm gonna curl it the way you showed me."

"Naw, girl, I'll do it for you. Come on in. Welcome to Virginia." She pulled her cousin into her brick ranch house and whisked Marisa through greetings with the family and back to her room before she could blink.

"Are you tired? Wanna take a shower?" Janine threw a robe at her before Marisa could answer. "I have to go back to school in an hour or so to practice for graduation. You want to come?"

While Marisa was curious to tour Bethel High School, she was suddenly shy. She didn't know if she was ready to be paraded around so quickly. "Uh, no. You go on. I want to rest for a while. And I am kinda hungry."

"OK. But I told all of my friends that you were coming. And I told them about Petersville, too. They can't wait to meet you. They want to know what my small-town cousin is like." She giggled and didn't notice Marisa frown. What did that mean? Were they expecting some kind of country bumpkin? And why did Janine have to say something like that, anyway? Now she'd feel all self-conscious and stuff.

"Tonight we're all going to the movies, OK?" Janine started combing her hair with a rake-like comb that Marisa had never seen before.

"OK. Who's we?" She hadn't moved from her perch on the bed. Her legs felt kind of wobbly. She never had been much of a party girl and wanted to prepare herself for the evening ahead.

"Just a few people. Me, you, Katrina, April and Bonita."

"Oh." Marisa felt a little better. Just the girls. That would be OK.

"We're supposed to meet Lorenzo, Marcus and Keith in the lobby at eight. Bring a sweater or something 'cause the movie theater gets real cold inside, OK?" Janine stopped raking her hair and turned to Marisa with a smile. "I'm so excited! We're gonna have so much fun!"

"Yeah." Marisa smiled wanly. She wanted to have fun, but she knew she'd feel awkward around all of Janine's friends. "If I'm not too tired."

"Too tired? You can't be too tired! You can rest while I'm at practice, OK? Here, lay down." She fluffed the pillows and threw an afghan over Marisa's legs. "I'll close the door and tell everyone you're taking a nap. Then you'll be ready for tonight. OK?" At Marisa's nod, Janine grinned again. "Cool. I'll see you later." She closed the door but opened it a minute later. "Oh, and go ahead and use my make-up and stuff if you want. I don't care."

Marisa turned on her side and sighed deeply. Man, her cousin was tiring. She sure could talk fast. Now that she was gone, Marisa took the quiet moments to survey her cousin's room. Rising from the bed, she walked across the room and gazed at the bulletin board, automatically comparing the photos of Janine's friends to her own back in Petersville. There all of her pictures were of white people. Here, Janine had nothing but pictures of black kids. Curious, she took down each one and read the messages on the backs. They pretty much all sounded the same.

Moving to the mirror, she pulled out a picture of a brown-skinned guy with a mischievous grin. It had to be Lorenzo. Turning the picture over, she shook her head at his short message: "Love you, girl! L." What a doofus, Marisa thought. He could have at least said "good luck in the future" the way everyone else did. The guy below Lorenzo caught her eye. He was light brown with a friendly smile and small dimple. His message read: "Janine, I just want to say that I'm glad we're friends, even though you're just a little nuts." Marisa giggled. "Actually, a LOT nuts." She laughed. "But for real, you really are a piece of sunshine and I'm going to miss you and your big smile next year. Keep in touch and take care. Love, Keith." Keith. He was cute, Marisa decided. Studying the picture closer, she nodded. Very cute. And he was going to be at the movies tonight. Uh-oh. She began to panic. What did she know about flirting? Especially with a black guy? Looking in the mirror, she frowned at her reflection. She looked so ugly! Her hair was sticking out in different directions, her T-shirt and shorts were wrinkled and her face was shiny from the heat. Mentally, she reviewed all of the clothes she'd brought with her. What could she wear tonight? Nothing. None of her clothes were right. Her hair wasn't right. She wasn't right. What was she doing here, anyway?

Lying back down, she felt like crying. Why did she ever agree to stay here all month? She'd never fit in. In a panic, she debated asking her parents to take her back to Michigan with them after graduation. But Janine would be so upset. And her parents would never do that, anyway. They thought this visit would be good for her. Hmph. What did they know? If they wanted her to be around some black kids and soak up black culture, then they never should have moved to Petersville! Dang!

With a deep sigh, she tucked the pillow under her chin securely. Maybe she could get out of going to the movies tonight. She didn't think she would be good company, anyway. She could always say she was too tired, too sleepy or too hot. After all, she did just spend twelve hours in a car. Yeah, that's it. She was too tired to go to the movies, which is what she told her mother when she poked her head in the door a few minutes later.

"Too tired? I thought you were taking a nap so you'd be refreshed for tonight?" Her mother came in and sat on the edge of the bed, smoothing Marisa's bangs from her forehead. "Do you feel OK?"

With downcast eyes, she decided to confide in her mom. "I don't know. I just...I won't know how to act."

"What do you mean you won't know how to act?" Her mom frowned in puzzlement.

"I mean around Janine's friends. They're all sophisticated and stuff. And here I am, some dumb country bumpkin who acts and talks white. They're gonna say I'm an Oreo or something."

"Marisa!" Her mother's surprised gasp brought tears to Marisa's eyes. "Of course they won't think that! What makes you say such a thing?"

"Mama, you don't understand!" Sitting up, she pointed to Janine's bulletin board. "Look at them! And look at all of Janine's clothes. I won't fit in. I'm just like a white girl."

"Marisa, listen to yourself. You are not a white girl, so I want you to stop saying foolish things like that, y'hear?" Her voice rose, then got quiet again. "Now. We all know you haven't been around a lot of black people, but that doesn't mean they're aliens. Janine's friends know where you come from. And if they're her true friends, they'll accept you for who you are. Now I want you to stop it. You've been looking forward to this trip for months. You got all of those nice clothes from Chicago in your bag and you say you don't have anything to wear? Shoot, I'll bet half of these girls here have never even been to Chicago."

That made Marisa feel better. She did get some nice things on Michigan Avenue.

"Now I want you to get up and take a shower. That'll make you feel better. Then pick out an outfit to wear tonight – maybe that pink shorts suit – and wait for Janine to get back to do your hair." She pinched Marisa's cheek. "OK?"

"OK." She stood. "But it's so hot, Mama. Can you French braid my hair instead?" Janine was jealous that Marisa's hair was long enough to be French-braided, so she figured others might be impressed, too.

"OK. Come get me when you're ready. I'll be in the kitchen."

By the time Janine returned home, Marisa was in the mirror applying her new makeup that she'd bought at Carson Pirie Scott. Her hair was shiny and swept back in a thick French braid and the hot pink shorts set accented her copper skin.

"Wow, girl! You look good! Where'd you get that sharp outfit?" Janine screeched, circling Marisa with her mouth hanging open. "I'm scared o' you."

"I got it in Chicago. Mama took me shopping there a few weeks ago." Marisa grinned. Looked like her mother was right for once.

"Uh-oh. Check you out. You got your hair all French-braided and stuff. Girl, you look fly! I'm jealous. Now what am I going to wear?" She flew to her closet and stood there muttering while Marisa glowed with confidence from the compliments.

"Hey, why don't you wear this sundress?" Marisa fingered a black dress with tiny yellow flowers. "It's so pretty."

"Nope, that's the dress I'm wearing to Keith's graduation party. I can't wear that. I think I'll just wear my blue jean shorts and this blouse."

While Janine changed and rattled on and on about Bethel High School gossip, Marisa wondered about Keith. So he was having a graduation party. She wondered if he was dating anyone. "So when is this party you're going to?" She asked, hoping her tone was nonchalant.

"You mean Keith's?" Janine sprayed some "Forever Krystle" perfume and inspected herself in the mirror. "It's Saturday night. The day after graduation. Keith has some of the best parties, girl! We're gonna have so much fun. See, this is him here." She pointed to the picture Marisa had inspected earlier. "He real cool."

Marisa wanted to say he was cute but didn't want Janine to start playing matchmaker. How embarrassing. "Have you guys ever dated?"

"Me and Keith? Nah. I liked him once in junior high, but that was only for about a week. He was dating this girl DeeDee this past winter, but he quit her. She was all siddity and stuff. None of us liked her."

"Siddity?" Marisa giggled. "What does that mean?"

Her cousin shook her head. "Girl, you ain't never heard siddity before? That's like someone who's all stuck-up and stuff. That was DeeDee."

"Oh." She glanced at Keith's picture again. So he didn't like stuck-up girls. That meant she would have to be friendly and get over this shyness thing. She knew people mistook her shyness for snobiness, but she couldn't help that. Once people got to know her, they knew the truth.

"You ready?" Janine looked cute. Her gold chain and big hoop earrings accented her orange shirt and golden skin.

"I think so." Marisa glanced in the full-length mirror again. "Are you sure I look OK?"

"Girl, you look fine! Really pretty." She stood behind her cousin and dropped her tone. "You're not nervous, are you?"

Biting her lip, Marisa lifted one shoulder in a small shrug. "A little. You know I've never hung out with black people before. What if they make fun of the way I talk?"

"If they do, I'ma beat they head in."

"You used to." Marisa didn't say it to be confrontational, she just wanted Janine to remember how funny she used to sound to her.

"I know I did and I'm sorry. I was stupid. But these are some of my best friends. If they treat you wrong, then they treat me wrong, you know what I'm saying? And I don't think any of them will do that." She yanked on Marisa's braid. "You ready?"

Picking up her purse, she followed Janine out of the room, trying to ignore the butterflies in her stomach.

At the theater, dozens of kids were milling around in the parking lot, some hanging out of open car doors, others sitting on short concrete walls. Walking by, Marisa felt several guys' eyes following her, but she kept her eyes straight ahead. Inside, the lobby was packed with even more people, standing in line for tickets.

"I don't see them yet. Let's wait over here." Janine led Marisa and her friend Bonita to an empty space near the wishing well. "Trina better not be all late and shit. You know how she gets."

"Yeah," said Bonita. "And April would wait for her, too. Not like you, who'd leave her in a minute."

"Sure would, girl. Hey, there's Marcus!" Waving, Janine motioned Marcus over to the fountains.

"Hey. Where's Lorenzo and Keith?" Janine asked.

"They're playing video games." Marcus spoke to Janine but kept his eyes on Marisa. "You must be Janine's cousin we've heard so much about."

She nodded with a small smile while Janine did the introductions. Marcus was short and well-built with a small mustache that gave him a mysterious aura. He wasn't exactly good-looking in Marisa's view, but not ugly. And definitely friendly. "Welcome to Virginia."

"Thanks." She kept her arms folded in front of her self-consciously, for Marcus gave her a quick, but obvious, once-over.

"Where your girls at?" he asked Janine.

"They'll be here. Someday. Y'all wanna go get Keith and Lorenzo?" Without waiting for an answer, Janine headed to the arcade area, where several boys were hunched over the pinball machine, Pac-Man and Dungeons and Dragons. Marisa immediately recognized Lorenzo, who was watching someone on Dungeons and Dragons. She assumed it was Keith, but wasn't sure.

"What are y'all doing over here? We have to get in line for the movie." Janine commandeered Lorenzo's hand possessively.

"Hey. We will. We just wanted to get a game in." He gazed at Janine with lazy eyes and Marisa felt embarrassed just watching them. It was such an intimate exchange.

"Lorenzo, this is Marisa. Marisa, Lorenzo." Janine was grinning like a schoolgirl and Marisa giggled to herself.

"Hi."

"How you doin'? Hey, man, quit that game and meet J's cousin." He kicked Keith in the heel. "You ain't gonna beat my score anyway."

"Aw, man, see what you did? I got distracted." Keith was saying as the screen flashed "Game Over." Turning around, Keith's eyes zeroed in on Marisa, who struggled to stifle a gasp. He was gorgeous. Even more handsome than his picture. "Hey, Marisa. It's nice to meet you." He flashed a warm smile her way and extended his hand.

"You too." She shook his hand and felt herself get all flustered from the touch. His hands were big and soft and warm.

"You just get in?"

"I'm sorry?" She didn't know he was still talking to her, so engrossed was she in his looks.

"Did you just get into town today?"

"Oh. Yes. We arrived a few hours ago." Man, she sounded snooty.

Keith smiled again. "Well. Welcome to Virginia, Marisa." If she didn't know better, she'd have assumed he was flirting with her. Maybe he acted that way with everyone he met. She glanced at Janine and was shocked to discover her cousin and Lorenzo grinning at the two of them. Uh-oh. Maybe he *was* flirting. What should I do next, she wondered. Flirt back? But she didn't even know where to begin.

"Hey, let's get in line," Marcus was saying. "We'll save two seats for Trina and April, OK? I don't feel like waiting on them anymore."

The six of them stood in the ticket line and talked about the graduation rehearsal they'd been through earlier in the day. Marisa listened quietly, laughing when necessary and smiling the rest of the time. During a lull in the conversation, Keith turned to her. "What are you smiling about?"

"What?" She was caught off guard.

"You're just standing there all quiet, smiling that pretty smile of yours. What's up?" He stuffed his hands in his khaki shorts and grinned.

"Nothing. I'm just...smiling. No reason." She laughed shyly.

"No reason, huh?" He touched her shoulder briefly. "Janine, I see your cousin didn't inherit your mood swings."

While Janine attempted to defend herself, Marisa tried to control her racing heart. *He said I had a pretty smile,* she thought to herself. *He touched me on the shoulder.* She wondered if he'd try to sit next to her in the movie and how she'd react if he did.

He did. She was sandwiched between Janine and Keith, who saved the seats next to him for April and Katrina. "Do you want some popcorn?" Keith asked once they had claimed their seats.

"No, thank you."

"Are you sure? It's no trouble."

She shook her head again. It was all she could do to just sit next to him. To eat in front of him would have been torture.

"How about a soda?"

Her mouth did feel a little dry. "OK."

He stood there a minute, as if expecting her to continue. "What kind?" He asked with a small smile.

"Oh. Uh, a Coke?"

"One Coke coming up." Keith joined Lorenzo and Marcus in the aisle and the girls watched them walk away.

"Girl, Keith likes you!" Janine giggled loudly.

"He does not." Marisa kept her gaze averted.

"Yes, he does! Don't he, Bonita?"

"He's sure acting like it. What's the matter, don't you think he's cute?"

"He's cute." Marisa admitted. She was afraid to go into further detail because she was embarrassed. "You guys, please don't make a big deal out of this, OK?"

"OK. But he does like you. Just relax and be yourself, OK? You're doing fine. Just don't get all nervous." Janine advised.

"I won't. That is, if you guys leave me alone and don't like act you're trying to fix us up."

"We won't!" Janine acted hurt. "We won't. You can trust us."

When Keith and his friends returned to their seats, they had Katrina and April with them. Janine did quick introductions, but Marisa couldn't speak long because the lights dimmed and the movie previews soon splashed across the screen. In an effort to control her nerves, she took a deliberate sip of her drink then carefully set it back on the floor, where she noticed that Keith was wearing a new pair of Adidas. So not only was he cute and nice, he knew how to dress as well. Very impressive.

At that moment, Keith slouched lower in his seat and spread his legs a little wider. In doing so, his thigh brushed Marisa's, causing her to jump. With a quick glance at her, he whispered, "Are you OK?"

"Uh-huh." She nodded and kept her eyes glued to the screen, grateful that he couldn't see how red she was turning. Man! He must think I'm a total dweeb, she thought. Calm down, Marisa. You act like you've never been around guys before! "But I haven't been around black guys," she silently reminded herself. And from what she could see so far, they were a totally different breed from the white boys in southwestern Michigan.

Glancing at the screen, she saw that Tom Cruise and Kelly McGillis were about to kiss for the first time and the audience began erupting in loud comments.

"Yeah, man, g'wan and get that!" One guy yelled from the back.

"Oohoo! I told you home girl was a freak, man! I told you!" Another yelled from the side.

While the rest of the group laughed and made their own comments, Marisa was looking around in surprise. Why were they so loud? Back home, if anyone even whispered too loudly, they were shot dirty looks. Here, people had been talking at the screen throughout the entire movie. And no one seemed to care. Too weird.

After the movie, Marisa followed Janine and her friends outside, where they contemplated their next move.

"What do y'all want to do?" Marcus asked, looking around to see who he knew in the crowd.

"I don't care. Are you hungry, Lo?" Janine was holding Lorenzo's hand and gazed up at him with a loving grin.

"Yeah, I could eat. Wanna head over to Mickey D's?"

"Sounds good," Keith agreed. "Marisa?"

All eyes turned to her. "Huh?" She was suddenly self-conscious again.

"Does that sound good to you? You're the guest here. Where do you want to go?"

"I don't care. McDonald's is fine."

"McDonald's it is." Keith clapped his hands together. "Trina, April, y'all in?"

"I guess so. As long as they don't start shooting or nothing over there," Trina said with a grimace.

"Shooting?" Marisa let the word slip before she could stop it.

"Yeah, shooting." Trina turned to her, looking her up and down. "This ain't small-town Michigan no more. They be shooting and fighting around here all the time."

"Trina, they do not! Stop scaring her!" Keith protested with a soothing hand on Marisa's arm. "Why you gotta say something like that?"

"Because it's true, that's why." Trina turned her nose up at Keith, then glared at Marisa again, who visibly blanched under the hateful gaze. "What, you gonna try and pretend this is farm country when it ain't?"

"Katrina!" That was Janine. "What is your problem?"

"What? I'm just saying, why lie to the girl? You know there's been fights and stuff at that McDonald's. Don't pretend there ain't." Her hand was on her hips and she was popping her gum loudly. Marisa decided she didn't like her. At all.

"We know that, Ka-*trina*. But what's with the attitude?"

"No attitude. I'm ready to go. I'm hungry. Are y'all gonna meet us there or what?" She started to walk off and in doing so, stepped on Marisa's toe. Marisa jumped back, shocked, and looked around to see who else noticed. Apparently no one had, so she didn't say anything. April followed Trina, issuing last-minute instructions to the group to meet them at the restaurant in ten minutes. Suddenly that was the last thing Marisa wanted to do. She didn't want to be around Trina a moment longer and she certainly didn't want to be anywhere where there'd been a shooting.

"Uh, you know what, guys?" She interrupted with a fake yawn. "I'm really tired. Why don't you drop me off at home and go on without me?"

"No!" Janine protested. "You're coming with us."

"Janine..." she faltered. How could she explain that she felt like crying and never coming back to Virginia again? How could she tell her that even though they were all the same age and the same race, she felt like an alien among them?

"Marisa, is it because of what Trina said? About the shooting?" Keith stepped in front of her and rested his hands on her shoulders, causing Marisa's mind to go blank.

"The shootings? Well, kinda..." That was part of the reason. She couldn't explain the other part so the shootings were just as good of a reason as any.

"I thought so. Tell you what, let's just go someplace else. OK?" His brown eyes bore into hers warmly and she felt oddly protected and instantly speechless.

"That's a good idea. Forget Trina. Let's go to Denny's." Janine suggested.

"You got Denny's money?" Bonita asked loudly.

"I ain't trying to eat a full meal, girl. Maybe just some fries or something. I got you, though. Marisa, you got enough money?"

"Yeah." The group started walking to their cars and when she looked up she caught Keith smiling at her pensively. She smiled back then quickly averted her gaze to the ground shyly.

"Hey, Lo, why don't you ride with Janine? I'll drive Marisa over there." Keith offered.

"All right." Lorenzo opened the Mustang's passenger door. "Marcus, you got Bonita?"

"Yup. I'll see y'all over there." Bonita and Marcus took off, leaving Marisa standing next to Janine, who was grinning so wide Marisa thought her cheeks must hurt.

"Are you OK?" she mouthed.

Nodding shyly, Marisa followed Keith to a blue, two-door Cavalier. He unlocked the passenger side for her and she got in quickly, uttering a quiet "thank-you" before he shut her in. Oh my God, what was she supposed to talk about? She never had been very good at small talk. And with a cute, black guy she'd only just met? Her tongue was figuratively tied.

"So if you were home in...Michigan," he swung his car out of the parking lot, "what would you be doing tonight?"

"Tonight?" She kept her eyes straight ahead, because he kept looking at her. The glances made her self-conscious and flattered at the same time. "Uh...today is Wednesday. I'd probably be working in my dad's store until six. Then I'd either go home or go cruising with a friend or something."

"Cruising? That's all? No boyfriend?"

Her pulse quickened. Surely Janine had told him how boring Petersville was. "No."

"I find that hard to believe," he said lightly.

"Why?" Marisa looked at him for the first time since they got in his car.

"A pretty girl like you? Shoot, I'll bet the boys at your school fight over you."

At that, Marisa let out a laugh. "That's funny."

He joined her laughter. "Why's that funny? You don't think you're pretty?"

"No, that's not it."

"Oh, so you *do* think you're pretty," he teased.

"Nooo...I mean..." Flustered, she instinctively hit him on the arm in mock consternation. "I mean the boys don't fight over me at school."

"How come? Are they blind?"

"They're all white," she said by way of explanation.

"So? Are white guys not supposed to admire a pretty girl when they see one?"

"No, I mean..." How could she explain it? "I think they think I'm pretty, but they think I'm pretty for a black girl. You know?"

Nodding, his carefree expression quickly turned serious. "Yeah, I know what you mean. And that's stupid. Black women are gorgeous. And you're one of the prettiest I've ever seen."

She wished he'd stop it. His comments made her feel weird. Part of her liked them, but the other part wanted him to just be her friend. Not make her feel like he was going to jump her the first chance he got.

"You don't like it when I compliment you, do you?"

Surprised, she caught his eye. "How'd you know?"

"I can tell. You get really embarrassed. I'm not telling you just to butter you up or flirt with you or anything. I just wanted you to know that I think you're very pretty. That doesn't mean that I'm going to try anything, OK?"

At Denny's, she couldn't suppress a thrilled grin. He liked her! He actually liked her! And he said she was pretty! For the first time all day, she was glad she'd come to Virginia.

***

"Are you almost ready, girl?" Janine was standing in front of the mirror putting the final touches on her make-up. It was Saturday night, the day after graduation, and Marisa and Janine were about to leave for Keith's mega-party. Marisa's parents had left that morning, with last-minute instructions to Marisa to behave, mind her aunt and uncle and to have fun.

"Are you sure you'll be OK?" Her mother whispered to her in the driveway before they took off.

"Yeah." Marisa smiled. Now that it came time for them to leave, her mother seemed to be the one having second thoughts. Marisa, on the other hand, was having a ball. Keith had called her every day since Wednesday and had come over Thursday night to take her for a walk. Her parents instantly approved, too. Said he was polite and well-mannered.

"What do you mean, am I ready? I've been waiting for you for fifteen minutes!" Marisa said from Janine's easy chair. She was flipping through the latest issue of "Right On!" and impatiently checking her watch. Janine was so slow.

"All right! I'm coming. I know you can't wait to see Keith, but hold on. He ain't going nowhere." Janine clicked her purse shut and turned to her cousin with a mischievous grin. "So, did he kiss you yet?"

"What?" Marisa turned red. She didn't want to talk about that!

"You heard me. Did he kiss you yet?"

"No." She wanted to go on and explain that it wasn't a big deal, but she'd be lying if she did. She really wanted him to kiss her and so far he'd made no move. None.

"Don't worry. It'll happen tonight. Big Cuz is deejaying and he always plays the best slow jams," Janine was saying as they bid her parents goodbye and climbed into her Mustang.

"Who is Big Cuz?" Marisa asked.

"This guy who graduated last year. He's at HU now working at their radio station. Or should I say 'our' radio station." Janine was enrolling at Hampton University in the fall.

"Oh. But you know I don't know any of the latest dances or anything." Marisa was more nervous about this party than she let on. She knew black parties were nothing like the ones her friends had in Petersville. There everyone stood around drinking or playing kissing games or watching videos. Keith's party would be just like a nightclub. Lots of dancing. He even hired a deejay!

"You worry too much. Just watch me. Or watch the other girls on the floor. Ain't nothin' to it. I know you got rhythm."

But what if she didn't? What if she got on the dance floor and started to move all stiff like a white girl? She knew everyone would laugh at her and Keith would probably wonder what he ever saw in her in the first place. And Janine! Janine would be embarrassed beyond reason. No, the best thing for her to do was to stay off the dance floor.

When they arrived, they trailed a group of girls into the house and followed the music to the vast living room. What greeted them made Marisa stiffen with semi-dread. Dozens of young black kids were dancing and joking and eating. She recognized some of them from Janine's graduation open house, meaning she was one of the few – if not the only – stranger in there. She stuck close behind Janine while they threaded their way through the dancers and into the sunroom, where Bonita and April were talking to a group of guys.

"Hey, y'all! This party is bangin'!" Janine yelled above the music.

"Sure is. Hey, Marisa." Bonita greeted.

"Hi." She smiled wanly, still nervous, and noticed the guys in the group halt their conversation.

"Marisa? Is this your cousin, J?" A burly, dark-skinned boy named Carl asked.

"Yup." Janine then introduced her to the three guys, who looked her up and down curiously.

"So this is Marisa," Carl grinned. "What'd you do to my boy Keith? He can't stop talking about you."

Joy – and embarrassment – flooded Marisa while she smiled at Janine. "Really?"

"Really," Carl laughed. "And it's no wonder. You all sweet and stuff. Janine, are you sure you're related?"

"Shut up. Have you seen Lorenzo? He's supposed to be here by now." She was scanning the crowd anxiously.

"Uh yeah. He's here. I saw him outside a while ago." He paused. "Talking to LaTonya Pierce."

"What?" Janine waved a hand dismissively. "Oh no she didn't. Guys, I'll be back." And before Marisa could say anything, Janine disappeared into the crowd, leaving her cousin standing awkwardly with a group of strangers. Bonita and April went back to their conversation with the guys, and after a few minutes of trying to look interested, Marisa turned away and inspected the food table. She piled her plate with some goodies, then searched the room for a place to sit. The only available chair was a fold-away in the corner. Thank God. A sanctuary. A place where she could discreetly disappear without anyone trying to goad her into conversation or ask her to dance. By hiding in the corner, she could watch everyone else without being put on the spot.

Nibbling at her food, she marveled at the easy way the guys and girls talked to each other. The guys weren't being obnoxious or crude the way Barry and Mitch could be sometimes. Instead, they were smooth, looking the girls in the eye and caressing their hands before the girls snatched them away. And the girls! The girls sailed through small talk like it was nothing. Watching the exchange saddened her. It would take forever for her to feel that comfortable around black guys. Every time one spoke to her she felt tongue-tied and self-conscious because she talked white. And no matter what her mother or Janine said, people noticed. They probably thought she was a wannabe. And a snob. And sitting in the corner didn't help matters. She couldn't help it, though. She didn't know anyone here – Janine had disappeared – and she didn't know the first thing about mingling. She didn't have to mingle in Petersville. She knew everyone in town!

"Hey! There you are!" Looking up, she was startled to see Keith's smiling face. "I've been looking all over for you!" He kneeled in front of her with a hand on her knee, which seemed to burn straight through to her soul. "Are you OK?"

"Uh-huh." She nodded, weakened by his beauty and the cologne he wore. She had no idea what it was, but he smelled divine.

"Are you sure?" Another dumb nod. "Why are you in the corner? Where's Janine?"

"Uh, she went to look for Lorenzo, I think."

"So she just left you? Come on." He tugged at her hand, but she resisted.

"No, that's OK. I'm fine. You go tend to your guests." She was sure he wanted to dance with her, but she couldn't. Fast-dancing in Petersville was one thing, but here? No way.

"What? No. You're my special guest, so you're coming with me." He pulled her out of the chair and led her through the sunroom and toward the dance floor.

"Keith, no, I don't want to dance." She began to panic. The deejay was playing some rap song she'd never heard of, and although it sounded good, she couldn't dance the way the others were. She didn't know how.

"Shhh. Just wait. Follow me." Keith took her hand and led her toward the kitchen.

"I need some help in here. Do you mind? I need to get more sandwiches and drinks."

"No, I'm glad to help." Breathing easier, she was grateful to be away from the thumping music and the curious eyes in the sunroom. The kitchen was big and cozy, with lots of wood paneling and a huge counter with a couple of stools. "What do you need me to do?"

"How 'bout," Keith spoke from the refrigerator, where he was withdrawing some condiments and a big sandwich platter. "How 'bout you sit there and keep me company?"

"Keith..." she smiled playfully. "I really can help. Do you want me to chop some tomatoes or something? Make some Kool-Aid?"

He laughed heartily as he dropped his bounty on the island counter. "Kool-Aid, huh? What kind? Red?"

"No, I was thinking green." She giggled.

"Green? Uh, no. How 'bout we stick to the soda and punch?"

"OK." She leaned her arm on the counter and rested her chin on her hand. It was so much easier to talk to him without a bunch of people around. At least he liked the way she talked.

They chatted about the graduation ceremony, the gifts he received from his family and his summer job at a local sneaker store before he grabbed some Sprite and Hawaiian punch from the refrigerator. "Can you carry the sandwich tray for me?" He nodded toward the counter and picked up a bag of chips with his teeth. "C'mon."

Back in the sunroom, she followed him, aware of several pairs of eyes watching their every move. She deposited the tray on the table then volunteered to take the empty tray back into the kitchen, anything to stay away from the dance floor, which was even more crowded now, with dozens of people dancing to some rap song about "a funky beat." It sounded good. Everyone looked good. And a fair share of them were looking her way, which is why she made a quick exit back to the kitchen.

She took her time washing the sandwich tray, until Keith came back with some trash, Carl following.

"Why are you washing dishes? Put that down," Keith ordered.

"I'm done now." She wiped her hands on the dish towel, avoiding Carl's curious stare.

"Yes, you are. Now it's time for you to enjoy yourself." Keith shut off the overhead lights, leaving only the soft glow from above the stove. He took Marisa's hand and followed Carl into the other room, where she saw Janine wrapped in Lorenzo's arms while a slow song began. This was obviously the time for all the couples to pair up. But she and Keith weren't a couple.

"Dance?" He squeezed her hand and spoke quietly in her ear. She jumped instinctively, then forced herself to calm down. Did she like him or not? Yes. So get over your nerves and dance with the boy, she scolded to herself.

At her nod, he led her to the center of the floor, where he took her in his arms. The song, like all the others, was foreign to her, but when it came on, everyone else kind of moaned and got excited, so she figured it must be pretty popular. It would probably reach Petersville around Thanksgiving, she thought ruefully.

"What's this song?" She asked Keith, partly to ease her curiosity and partly to ease the thickness in the air. He smelled so good, and he was holding her so seductively. She was starting to feel really weird.

"This is Stephanie Mills. You never heard this before?"

Shaking her head, Marisa readjusted her arms around his broad back. Man, he had some strong shoulders. "We don't get any good radio stations in Petersville."

"Mmm. That's rough."

Keith's tone told her that he didn't feel like talking, so she shut up and eyed the rest of the room. No one was paying them any mind; they were all caught up in their own romances. Lorenzo and Janine were in full make-out mode in the corner, and Bonita and Carl were dancing pretty closely. So far so good, Marisa thought. At least this slow dance thing wasn't too difficult, although they did dance differently here than they did back home. There, the guys and girls were basically wrapped in a great big hug swaying back and forth stiffly. Here, guys were caressing the girls on their backs and grinding their hips back and forth, around and around. It looked pretty sexy to Marisa, and she wondered if she was the only virgin in the room. Probably. The rest of them looked very experienced.

The song ended and another slow one came on, one Marisa recognized. It was "Funny How Time Flies" by Janet Jackson. Very seductive. By now Keith had pulled her closer and she didn't resist. It felt good. Very good. With a deep breath, she closed her eyes and gently laid her head on his right shoulder. Keith immediately drew her closer and lightly ran his hand up and down her back, causing her knees to turn to Jell-O.

"Will you come with me?" Keith whispered in her ear, rousing her from her near-delirium.

"Mmm? Where?" She wanted to keep dancing.

"Outside. It's a nice night out. We can keep dancing out there."

"OK." She didn't care, as long as she was able to get back in his arms. She couldn't believe how good he felt.

Taking her hand, he led her through the dancing crowd, into the sunroom and onto the patio. There, he slowed his steps until he was at the side of the house, away from the sliding glass doors.

"Can you still hear the music?" He asked while reaching for her at the same time.

"Uh-huh." She smiled softly as they continued their dance, this time under a canopy of stars and a hood of moonlight.

"Marisa?"

"Hmmm?" She kept her head on his shoulder, blissfully comfortable.

"Can I kiss you?" He felt her stiffen and drew away so he could see her face. "I'm sorry. I didn't mean to…"

"No…I mean, uh…" Darn it! Why was she so stupid? Now he probably thought she didn't want him to kiss her.

"I didn't mean to scare you." He was saying, his eyebrows furrowed with concern. "I don't want you to think…"

"No. No, Keith, it's OK." With a deep breath, she admitted. "It's OK."

"It's OK? It's OK, what?" He teased with a soft smile. "It's OK that I asked or it's OK if I kiss you?"

"The last part." She said with a shy smile.

With strong arms, he drew her closer and kissed her briefly, with full lips that were soft and supple. Marisa instinctively caressed his shoulder and he hugged her tighter. A second kiss followed, this one longer and deeper. My …God. She'd never been kissed like this before, she thought through a pleasant fog. She couldn't believe it was really happening to her. Her first kiss with a black guy.

He pulled away slightly and Marisa was greeted by moist lips formed in a cute smile. "You do that pretty well."

"Do what?" She whispered. Her fog hadn't completely cleared.

"Kiss." He chuckled. "You kiss pretty well."

"I do?" She was dumbfounded. In her whole life, she'd only kissed Barry. And the last time that had happened was last year in the hospital when her grandmother had had a stroke. And that wasn't a real kiss. It was really just a kiss of gratitude because he'd been so nice about her birthday.

"Do you think I can take you home? Do you think Janine would mind?" He was holding both of her hands in his and his forehead was resting on hers.

"I don't think so. She probably wants to be with Lorenzo anyway."

With her hand in his, he led her back into the house, where they found her cousin and Lorenzo still swaying even though the deejay had already started packing up his equipment.

"Hey, girl, you ready?" Janine asked, looking relaxed and happy.

"Um, Keith is giving me a ride home. Is that OK?"

A big grin lit her cousin's face. "Is that OK!?" She hit Marisa on the arm lightly. "G'wan, gurhhl!"

Groaning, Marisa shushed her. "Be quiet! What time is curfew?"

"Curfew? Mama don't care. She said as long as I don't keep you out 'all hours of the night,' whatever that means. She wants you to have fun. But I wouldn't push it past one."

After helping Keith clean up, they sat in the darkened sunroom where he kissed her again. And again. Then tentatively touched her tongue with his. At first she was shocked and recoiled in surprise, but when he tried it again, she returned the exploration. She was seventeen. It was about time she learned how to French kiss.

"I really like you, Marisa," he said later that night as they sat in his parked car outside of her aunt and uncle's house. "You're so sweet. I'm glad you came to Virginia."

Those were the words she carried with her for the next few weeks, while they continued to see each other, at the movies, at Busch Gardens, at the beach. All the while they continued to kiss and make out. Marisa even let him unbutton her shirt and touch her breasts, but only with her bra on. She was tempted to let him take it off once, but knew it was too risky.

When it came time for her to return to Michigan, Keith wasn't at the house to say goodbye. He was in Charlottesville at orientation for the University of Virginia. They'd said their goodbyes two days earlier.

"I'll write you," he said.

"Me too."

"Call me when you get home, OK?"

"I will. Maybe I can come back for Thanksgiving."

He'd smiled. "That would be great. I'll miss you."

"I'll miss you, too," she whispered. Saying such intimate things had become easier for her over the past few weeks. She was still surprised at how open she'd become around him.

"Take care of yourself, OK? And stay sweet." Then he'd kissed her and all she had to take with her to Petersville were a few pictures, a couple of seashells and memories of her first summer love.

CHAPTER 7

August-December 1986

"Why don't you want to go camping, Marisa? You went to Girl Scout camp when we were kids," Jen was saying over the phone. "Come on. It'll be fun. Our last get-together before school starts."

"I don't like camping," Marisa said for the third time. She'd been home from Virginia for about six weeks and for the first time started noticing how small and backwards Petersville was. They had to drive at least an hour to get to the mall in Kalamazoo or Grand Rapids and at least thirty minutes to see a few black folks in South Haven. In Hampton, everything she wanted was right at her fingertips. The mall, radio stations, black folks, hairdressers. On top of that, she'd started noticing the differences between her and her friends. Sure, they couldn't relate to her hair or dry skin regimens, but there were other things...cultural things. This camping thing for one...

"Marisa, *everybody* is going," Jen was saying. "You'll be the only one in town."

"Who cares? I'll be working anyway. That way I can save more money." She started swinging the cabinet door from her perch on the kitchen counter.

"You hardly need the money. Come *on*! We're going to swim and hike and roast marshmallows, and the guys are going to fish."

"Yuck! You know I can't swim that well. And sleeping outside is not my idea of fun. I'd rather stay in a hotel."

"That defeats the entire purpose, Maris! And I know you like roasting marshmallows. I remember how much you like s'mores."

That was true. During Girl Scout camp one summer, Marisa had eaten so many s'mores she'd gotten sick. But she'd also gotten eaten alive by mosquitoes and was forced to get up at 6 a.m. to go "polar bear" swimming in the freezing lake. She'd hated every minute of it.

"Jen, I am not going camping, period. You guys have fun." She was ready to get off the phone. Jen was getting on her nerves, as usual.

"Fine." Jen sucked her teeth in disgust. "Y'know, you are absolutely no fun since you got back from Virginia. You don't want to do anything. Well, I'm sorry we're not good enough for you anymore."

"What does that mean?" Marisa frowned.

"I mean, I know we're not as exciting as your cousin or her friends, but give us a break! We've known you since we were kids. Why don't you want to hang out anymore?"

"What are you talking about? I don't want to go camping. That doesn't mean I don't want to hang out anymore. Who else am I going to hang out with?" That much was true. Caitlin was off at Ferris State and Mitch had enlisted in the Army.

"I still wish you were going. Maybe Barry can talk you into it."

Barry. Ha. Since returning to Michigan, Marisa had hardly thought about Barry. Sure, they worked together and occasionally hung out with their friends, but she was too busy thinking about Keith to worry about Barry anymore. Why would she want Barry when she had good-looking, sexy Keith in Virginia writing her nice letters and calling her just before he left for U.Va.? "Look, I gotta go. Daddy is barbecuing. I think he's going to burn the house down."

Hanging up, Marisa sat on the counter for a few minutes, thinking about her conversation. So her friends noticed her acting differently, huh? Good. It was about time they realized she was not like them and for once didn't want to be.

***

Classes that year were the hardest of Marisa's entire academic career. She, Barry and Kristin all had study hour during third period, but the last thing they did was study. If they weren't in the library doing homework they were cruising around Petersville or hanging out at Kristin's house.

"Watch," Barry pointed to the TV screen one September afternoon at Kristin's house. He and Marisa sat at the counter chomping on Doritos and watching "The Price Is Right" while Kristin made grilled cheese sandwiches. "She's the one that's going to play for the car."

"How do you know?" Marisa asked.

"Trust me." He swigged a mouthful of cherry Coke.

"You don't know," Marisa said scornfully. "I'm not even listening to you." Instead, she flipped open Kristin's copy of Seventeen magazine, wondering silently why there were no black girls in it. Not one.

"Hey, Maris, are you going to go for early admission?" Kristin asked from the stove.

"I don't know. Probably."

"Where to?"

She was quiet for a minute. She didn't really know where she wanted to go to college. Now that she was a senior, she guessed it was time for her to decide. "Definitely Howard. Maybe Hampton." That way, she could hang out with Janine and see Keith sometimes.

"What about the University of Virginia?" Kristin giggled as she set the plate down in front of her guests.

"Ha, ha..." Marisa was embarrassed. Truth was, she had thought of U.Va., but didn't want it to look like she was following Keith. He wasn't her boyfriend, and he'd never once told her to apply there. In fact, since school started, she'd only gotten one letter from him, explaining how his roommate got drunk every weekend and how pretty the campus was.

"So when are you going to see this Keith again?" Barry, who'd been inhaling his food, spoke up. "Are you going down there for his Homecoming?"

"No." Her answer was evasive. "I don't know. Maybe Christmas. It's so far."

"Yeah. Are you sure you want a long-distance relationship?"

"What do you mean?"

He finally turned to look at her and she was mad at herself for noticing how his summer tan made his face and hair look golden. Almost like a sun god. "I mean, is it worth it? You never get to see each other. If I were you, I'd rather be with someone I can at least talk to every day. And hold. And kiss." His eyes dropped to her lips. "Wouldn't you?"

"Uh..." She couldn't think of a reply. Darn him for being so cute! And darn him for zooming in on her just when she was wondering if Keith would ever write her again. "I don't know. We'll just have to see what happens, won't we?"

***

By Homecoming, she still hadn't heard from Keith, although she'd written him two letters since September. Janine said he was probably still adjusting to college – "U.Va. ain't no joke" – and to give him a little more time. So she did. She threw herself into Homecoming activities, her studies and researching colleges.

One Sunday afternoon, while helping her mother peel potatoes for dinner, Marisa confessed that she was thinking of applying to Michigan State, merely as a financial back-up.

"Michigan State? Isn't that a party school?" Her mother asked.

"Not really. Well, yeah, but that's not why I want to go there. They have a good engineering program." She'd decided to major in some kind of engineering but was still undecided as to which one. Chemical? Civil? Mechanical? She figured she had plenty of time to figure it out. "And tuition would be a lot cheaper because it's in-state."

"Don't worry about money. You just worry about your education. Now, I won't lie and say I'm not happy that you'd be close to home, but what about Hampton? I thought you were sold on that after your trip down there this summer?"

"I was."

"So what happened?"

What did happen? "Nothing. I'm just keeping all of my options open, that's all."

By mid-November, she was anxiously waiting to see where she was accepted. She'd applied to Howard, Hampton and Michigan State. And the more she read about the latter, the more she liked it. Barry had gone to Boys State up there over the summer and told her how big and pretty the campus was. "It's like its own little city!" he said. And although she was anxious to get around some black people, she didn't know if it was smart to totally immerse herself around them so soon after leaving Petersville. She'd have a huge culture shock, she was sure of it. But MSU had some black students, too. Around eight percent. Didn't sound like a lot, but considering the school had more than thirty-five thousand students, that eight percent sounded OK.

***

"Congratulations. You are a Spartan." Her mother read the letter to her over the phone in early December. Marisa was still at school, waiting to board the bus for an away basketball game when she'd called home on a whim, wondering if her acceptance letter came. Hampton and Howard – the "HU's" as her father called them – had already told her yes. Now she was just waiting on MSU.

"Yes!" She pumped her fist. "I got in!" She yelled at Barry, who was fooling around with the other basketball players near the trophy case. She laughed while they cheered and hooted for her. "Mama? What else did they say? Any word on scholarships?"

"Uh, let me see. Here it is. Yep, they're going to give you – uh, wow...quite a bit of money. They really like you, sweetie."

Hanging up, she let out a rebel yell and laughed when Barry picked her up in a huge bear hug.

" 'With a rebel yell, she cried more, more, more...' " He sang. "Congrats, dude. That's cool. So which is it gonna be?"

"Michigan State. They're offering the most money, plus it's closer, it's cheaper, and they have a great sports program."

"Ha. Not like U of M, though."

She groaned. "You know, we're not gonna be able to be friends anymore. I'm going to be a Spartan and you insist on rooting for those Wolverines, even though you're not even going there! Don't understand!"

"Doesn't matter. Wolverines rule! You'll see next year when they beat you guys in football. And basketball."

"Uh-huh. Yeah, right. I still don't understand your logic. But wait! Could it be – Satan?" She mocked the famous catch-phrase from "Saturday Night Live."

"Ha ha. Really, though. I'm happy for you, Marisa. That's cool."

"Thanks. Now there's only one problem. How am I going to tell my father?"

"What, he doesn't like Michigan State?" He grabbed his duffel bag and followed her out the door to the waiting bus.

"He likes it fine, he just likes Howard and Hampton better. Howard because that's where Matthew is and Hampton because that's where his sister is. There's no one to keep an eye on me at Michigan State."

"Well, you know I like your dad and stuff, but it's your life."

That's what she kept telling herself the next morning as she stood in her room, practicing how she was going to break the news. Expelling a deep breath, she ran downstairs and skidded to the kitchen table, where her father was filling his Thermos with coffee to take to the store. "Good morning."

"Well, good morning, Miss Collegiate. Looks like we're hot property, huh? Got in to all three choices." Her father grinned. "So which one will it be? Which HU will be the lucky one?"

Here goes. "Well," she stuffed a forkful of French toast in her mouth. "I don't think it'll be either one."

"Don't talk with your mouth full," her mother scolded automatically. "We can't understand you. What'd you say?"

Swallowing, she cast a wary eye to her father, who was leaning against the kitchen counter expectantly. "I said, I don't think it'll be either one. I want to go to Michigan State."

"Really?" Her mother smiled. "You'll only be two hours away! You can come home on weekends." Yeah, right. She'd be too busy having fun to come home to boring Petersville.

"Michigan State? But I thought you were all set on Howard. Or Hampton," her father said.

"I was. But MSU is offering me the most money. And it's closer, like Mama said. It's a good school, Daddy." She gulped her juice quickly, for her mouth had suddenly turned dry.

"I know it's a good school, but it's also a party school."

"That's blown way out of proportion. I'm not going to do anything stupid. Don't you trust me?"

"Robert, Marisa is a very responsible girl. She knows academics come first." Leaning over, her mother kissed her on the forehead. "I'm very proud of you, sweetie."

"Thanks." She peeked at her father, who'd returned to the table.

"But Marisa, you see how much Matthew likes Howard. And Janine and you get along so well. You could even room together."

"I don't want to follow in anyone else's shadow. I want to go to Michigan State. It just feels like someplace I belong. Like I can call it home." She already liked the idea of being a Spartan. Like she was in an elite family. "Besides, if my education is really what you're concerned about, you should be happy I'm going to State. Their engineering program is better."

"Who told you that?"

"Mr. Reilly." He was the school's guidance counselor. "He said neither Hampton nor Howard had a good program." She added more syrup to her plate, unaware of her father's face turning red.

"You mean you'd rather listen to a white man advise you about your future instead of your own family?" He yelled.

"Daddy..." She was startled. Since when had this turned into a discussion about race?

"That man wouldn't know a good school if it bit him in the ass."

"Robert!"

"I don't care, Victoria. She's going to sit here and tell me that she let some white man talk her out of attending a black school because he thinks it's not good enough?"

"He didn't talk me out of it!" Marisa rolled her eyes and stood up. "I was interested in Michigan State since the fall! And why are you going ballistic?"

"You better watch who you're talking to!" He pointed a finger in her face. She was rarely on the receiving end of his wrath. That was usually reserved for her brothers. "Hampton and Howard are good schools! Just because they're black doesn't mean they're not as good as any other school out there!"

"I never said they weren't! Why do you think I applied in the first place? It's my life anyway. Why don't you just stay out of it?" She bolted from the room before her dad could react because she'd never spoken to him like that before. She had no idea what he would do once her words sunk in so it was best to hightail it out of there.

She heard him leave for work shortly after and silently hoped he wouldn't snap at Barry, who she knew was going to mention the MSU letter. Why was he being so irrational?

Later that evening, when Marisa was getting ready to go out for pizza with her friends, her father knocked on the door.

"Truce?" He asked quietly.

She stood at the mirror, picking imaginary hairs from her brush. "Sure."

"I didn't mean to upset you. I'm proud of you, you know that. I just...turn that down." She was listening to Chaka Khan. Instead of turning it down, she turned it off. It was time to leave anyway. "I just don't want you to think that anything black is inferior. And that's what some of these teachers might be trying to tell you."

"Daddy, I know better than that. I know how good those schools are. I mean, look at Matthew and Janine. I just think I'll like MSU better, that's all. It's not a knock against the other two."

"OK. But I do admit that I'm still a little disappointed. At least in Hampton you'd have your Aunt Liza to look out for you. And Matthew in D.C."

"I knew it. I told Barry that's why you really wanted me to go there," she teased.

"Well...maybe just a little." He crossed the room and hugged her. "As long as you get a good education, that's all I want."

A few weeks later, she relayed the conversation to Robert, who'd come home for Christmas with his wife of one month, Monica. They'd eloped without warning one day before Thanksgiving. "We didn't want a big fuss," he'd explained over the phone to her shocked family. "We just knew we wanted to be married." Marisa had wondered if Monica was pregnant, but her mother quickly assured her that that wasn't the case. She'd apparently wondered the same thing herself. Monica was a brown-skinned, tall girl who'd gone to Notre Dame and worked at the Chicago Board of Trade. She was really smart, Robert said, and very ambitious. "She can tell you about grad school if you want."

"I'm not even in college yet! Why would I even worry about grad school already?" He and Marisa were in the family room, rearranging the gifts under the tree and sharing a bowl of walnuts and almonds.

"It's never too early," he said. "Well, at least Daddy got over it. MSU is a good school. Just don't get too caught up in the party scene."

"Yes, Robert," she said automatically. She'd heard the same thing from everybody.

"So where are all of your friends going? Where's Barry going?"

"Grand Valley. He's hoping to walk on to their football team. Jen is going to Hope, of course. And Kristin really wants to go to Northwestern for journalism."

"Really? That's a good school. If she goes, tell her she can stop by anytime."

"I will." They were silent for a moment, listening to the crackle of the fireplace and the hum of voices from the kitchen.

"So are you and Barry an item again?"

"Huh?" Her eyes bucked. "Where did that come from?"

"Well, you're wearing that pin." He nodded toward the gold Christmas tree pinned to her cardigan. "You said it was a gift from Barry."

"Yeah, so? We always exchange gifts." She thought back to the Hawaiian perfume he gave her in the fourth grade.

"True, but I saw the way he looked at you when he was over here yesterday. He acts like he likes you."

Biting her lip, she wanted to drown out the words. She didn't want Barry to like her. She still liked Keith. She'd sent him a Christmas card, but hadn't heard a word from him since September. She felt foolish, but part of her liked to build up their relationship into a bigger deal than it was. In reality, it was just a summer fling featuring a cute boy teaching a pretty, shy girl how to French kiss. Nothing more.

"Barry doesn't like me. We're just friends." She said automatically.

"I don't believe you. You guys have always been more than just friends."

That was true. She knew Robert was right, but she remembered last year when he started showing an interest in her then completely burned her for Adrienne. She refused to go through something like that again. "Well, he *has* been acting differently ever since I got back from Virginia. What do you think that means?"

"It means," Robert got up and bopped her on the head. "He's interested in you again. And in case you didn't know, he always has been."

CHAPTER 8

January 1987

"I hate January. Ugh! It's so cold and dreary," Marisa complained while wiping the counter in the store one Saturday evening. The temperature that day was about four degrees and the Petersville streets were covered in dirty, old piles of snow. Spring, sunshine and – most importantly – graduation seemed light years away.

"Well, at least exams are over," Barry said while dusting off a snowblower. "I can't believe you aced that calculus final. You didn't even miss one!"

"I can't believe it, either. It was hard." She smiled to herself. She was almost guaranteed to be valedictorian in June and although she almost felt sorry for Barry, it was a good feeling to be the best.

"So what are you doing tonight?" He leaned against the counter.

Shrugging, she tucked a thick strand of hair behind her ear. "I don't know. What are you doing?"

"Nothing. My parents are at my grandmother's tonight. She's not feeling well."

"Oh. Sorry." Marisa tried to sound compassionate, but she didn't really mean it. She didn't like his grandmother. She was a snob and was always staring at Marisa like she was an alien. Her mother called her a "racist hag," and Marisa began to wonder if she was right.

"Wanna come over and watch some videos?" Barry was asking.

"I guess so. Whatcha got?"

"Nothing yet. We can go to the video store and pick out something."

"OK. I'll call Kristin and them." She reached for the phone.

"No." His warm hand covered hers. "I don't want a lot of people in my house."

"It's just Kristin. And maybe Dennis and Tara."

"Nah… I just…" he faltered for a moment, then looked her in the eye. "I don't want anyone else. Just me and you."

His hand on hers started to feel even warmer and she lost her train of thought while staring into his brown eyes. "OK." Suddenly shy, she turned away and grabbed her coat. "Let me go tell my dad."

Five minutes later, they were in the music/video store with several other people browsing through the movie collection. "I guess everyone had the same idea," Barry said.

"I guess." Marisa wandered to the new releases and grabbed a copy of "Peggy Sue Got Married." She'd wanted to see it in the theater but didn't have a chance because of work, cheerleading and college applications. Turning the box over, she began reading the plot when she felt someone behind her. It was Barry, reading over her shoulder and making her pulse pound with his nearness.

"Oh yeah! I haven't seen that. Have you?"

"Uh, no. You wanna get it?"

"Sure. Do you want anything else? They don't have a lot of new releases left."

"Uh, no, this should be fine. Besides, don't you want to watch 'Hunter' tonight?" The show was one of his favorites.

"I think it's a repeat, but yeah, we can watch that, too."

Once they were at Barry's house, Marisa paused while gathering cups and plates for the pizza, thinking how weird it would be not to rummage through his kitchen next year. Sure, they'd see each other over Christmas and summer breaks, but it wouldn't be the same. She followed him into the living room, where he threw his coat and the video bag onto the armchair.

"Hey! That's my favorite chair. Why are you putting all your junk on it?" she protested.

"Just sit on the couch. With me." He said this while setting their drinks on the coffee table and didn't notice Marisa looking at him with a frown. What did that mean? Did he want her to sit next to him? Or was it just an offhand comment, not meant for her to analyze the way she always did? Shaking her head, she promised herself that she would relax and forget about Barry's subtle flirting. They were just friends. That's all.

Once the pizza was done, he put in the video and joined her on the couch, where she sat cross-legged with her shoes off, balancing a plate on her knees. After two large pieces of pizza, she sighed. "OK, I'm full. I'm ready to just kick back." Grabbing a throw pillow, she leaned away from Barry and onto the opposite arm of the couch. A few minutes later, she felt something on the bottom of her feet. She jerked away. "Stop it." The tickling continued. "Stop it!" Unable to stop herself, she began to giggle. "Barry, would you *stop*? I'm trying to watch the movie!"

"I'm trying to watch the movie!" he mocked. Grinning evilly, he took hold of her ankle and vigorously tickled her foot until she rolled off the couch, laughing hysterically.

"You know that tickling is a form of torture, don't you?" she sputtered.

"Oh yeah? Well, it's torture time!" He sprang from his perch on the couch and began tickling her ribs this time. She screamed, she laughed, she pleaded, she squirmed, but she could not get away. His strong legs held her own down in a tight lock.

"Say uncle! Say uncle and I'll let you go."

"Stop it! Barry! Stop! I'm gonna get you! Quit it!" When she could take it no more, she stammered, "OK, OK! Uncle! Uncle!"

With one last tickle for good measure, he stopped and rested his arms on either side of her head. They were both out of breath and giggling quietly. Marisa's eyes were trained on the ceiling fan, which she noticed was quite dusty. Leave it to Mrs. Montgomery. She never was a very good housekeeper. "You bum. I'm gonna get you."

"Oh yeah? What are you going to do?" His face was next to her cheek so that his words were a breath on her face.

"I'm not telling. You'll see. I'll get you when you least expect it."

She turned her face to his with a warm smile that faded when she saw how close he was. The expression on his face caused her to take a quick breath. He was looking at her intently, staring at her as if for the first time. She couldn't bring herself to turn away or lighten the mood; then again, she didn't want to. With a quick tilt of the head, he kissed her. Briefly and lightly. For a moment, she wondered if it had really happened. Realizing it had, she rose up slightly and kissed him back. They looked at each other for a moment, then it was his turn again. This time, the kiss was longer, slower and sweeter. He shifted his body so he was holding her instead of holding her down and she wrapped her arms around his back. All kinds of thoughts ran through her mind, from, "Finally! I'm finally kissing Barry again!" to "Man, this feels good!" to "Whoa, where'd he learn *that*?" He'd become more experienced since the seventh grade and she hoped she had, too. His kisses were full and soft and moist.

The movie droned on, forgotten, and still the kisses continued. Marisa ran her fingers through his dark golden hair and he caressed her cheek. When she released a small, satisfied sigh, he touched her tongue with his. Startled, she opened her eyes.

"Barry, wait," she whispered. "Get up."

"What's wrong?" He held her face and kissed her cheek and nibbled on her ear.

"Oh man, that feels…good," she murmured. She hadn't had feelings like that since Keith had touched her for the first time at his party.

"Barry, please. Wait. I …I have to go to the bathroom." Yeah, that was a good excuse.

Releasing a breath, he rolled off her and gazed at her with half-closed eyes. "You're coming back, aren't you?"

Damn, he looked good! His lips were red and moist and puffy and formed a crooked, cocky smile on his flushed face. "Yes, I'll be back," she answered.

In the blue and white bathroom, Marisa stared at herself in the mirror, bewildered at the turn of events. After all the times she'd been to his house, after all the years hanging out and teasing each other and arguing and calling and competing, he decided to make a move now? Mere months before graduation? What the heck was the holdup? She leaned close to the mirror, still dotted with white specks of toothpaste, and surveyed herself. She was pretty, there was no denying that. But what about their friendship? Would it be ruined now? Would she feel funny around him? And what exactly did he want from her, anyway?

She splashed her face with water, smoothed down her hair and straightened out the pink argyle sweater her mother had bought her for Christmas. She'd paired it with gray corduroy slacks and suddenly remembered the first time she'd worn it to school. Barry had been at his locker and did a double-take when he saw her. "You look really good in pink." That was all he said, but from then on, she decided it was her favorite color.

In the living room, Barry was sitting on the floor with his back propped against the couch, nibbling on a pizza crust and watching Kathleen Turner make out with Nicolas Cage. "Hey, you're back. Do you want to rewind this so we can see it from the beginning?"

Still standing in the hallway, she frowned. Why was he acting like nothing had happened? "Uh, no. Um, I think...I think I'm gonna go home." Twirling on her feet, she hurried to grab her coat from the piano bench. But before she could shrug into it, he grabbed her arm.

"Wait." She yanked away. "Marisa, wait. Please."

With her back to him, she paused. Please say something, she thought. Explain what just happened. Explain what's going to happen. Please.

"I'm sorry. I didn't mean to...freak you out or anything." She heard a slight tremor in his voice and was oddly touched. He sounded nervous. "Marisa, I...I like you. I've always liked you, you know that."

"What?" Turning, she gaped at him. "What?"

With a full-fledged blush, he averted his gaze. "C'mon. Don't act all surprised."

"I am surprised! We've been friends forever. That's all I thought we ever would be."

"We haven't just been friends forever. We went out in the seventh grade. Remember?"

"That was seventh grade, Barry. It hardly counts."

"It counted for me." His voice got soft. "Marisa, you had to know that I always looked at you as more than a friend, but I didn't want to...didn't want to ruin that by doing something stupid."

She was speechless, so she continued to stare at him with her mouth hanging open. "Our friendship is too important to me to mess up. I mean, what if we started dating, then I did something stupid like I always do and we broke up? Then you'd hate me. And I don't think I could live with that."

"I could never hate you." She almost felt like crying. It was such a relief to hear the words coming from his mouth, because for years she'd wondered what was wrong with her that he couldn't see how much she liked him.

At that, he touched her cheek again, staring at her. "You're so beautiful. And you're smart and funny and kind and classy." Then he shrugged. "You're perfect."

To say she was startled was an understatement. Not even one of her Danielle Steel novels could have written the script better.

Taking her hand, he led her back to the living room, where he sat on the couch, pulling her next to him so their knees were touching. "Tell me now if you don't want to do this."

"Do what?" she asked warily. Surely, he wasn't talking about – no, not that.

"Go with me."

"Go with you? You mean go out with you?"

"Well, yeah, but I mean go with me go with me. Like be my girlfriend."

"But...but what about..." she racked her brain, trying to think of someone he'd dated in the past year. But there was no one.

"Do you really think I'd have kissed you if I didn't want you to be my girlfriend? I never would have let that happen."

She knew she had to say something before she burst. "Barry...I, you...you have no idea how long I've waited to hear you say that."

"Uh uh!" With an endearing grin, he laughed. "Really?"

"Really." Smiling, she took his other hand. "I've liked you for as long as I can remember. True, I valued our friendship, but I always thought there was no one cuter and no one who knew me better. I just figured you didn't like me."

"That's crazy! You're so pretty..."

"So you've said." Unable to wipe the smile from her face, she felt tears well in her eyes. She literally felt like she was floating, she was so happy.

"C'mere." He grabbed her around the neck and kissed her loudly. "There! No more wondering. No more staring and being nervous. I like you. A lot."

"I like you, too. A lot." Giggling with joy, she let herself be pulled into another embrace. "But wait. What will everyone say?"

"I guess they'll say it's about time!"

"No, not everyone." She was thinking of Jen. "Some people might have a problem with us dating."

"Why?"

She wished he would stop staring at her like that, it was distracting. "Because I'm black and you're white."

He stopped his caresses and stared at her again, this time with a different expression on his face. It was one of puzzlement and borderline anger. "So?"

"Don't be naïve. Some people at school – while not saying it out loud – think I should only date black guys. The fact that there are none in Petersville doesn't matter. You're a golden boy. You're white. You belong to them, not to someone like me." She said it sadly but matter-of-factly.

"That's their problem! I don't care what anyone thinks!" He tilted her chin to meet his gaze. "Do you?"

She was silent for several moments. This was the guy she'd grown up with, fought with, cried with, studied with, partied with, worked with. He was real. He was here and he was offering her what she'd dreamed of for years. "No, I don't care what anyone else thinks."

"Good. Now, can we pick up where we left off?" And the last thing she saw before he covered his lips with hers was a big smile.

***

That night, she went to bed but didn't go to sleep right away. She was too wound up, too excited to sleep. After their talk, they had rewound the movie and sat cuddled on the couch together, his arm around her and her head nestled on his shoulder. He'd played with her hair – marveling at how thick it was – kissed her on the top of her head and rested his own head against hers when the hour got late. When the credits began rolling, she began anticipating another make-out session until she heard the side door open. His parents were home. Instinctively, she'd jumped up and made sure her hair and clothes were straightened. After bidding his parents good night, she threw her coat on and was on the porch when she heard Barry behind her. "Wait! I'll walk you home."

"Barry, it's freezing. Go back inside."

THE KITCHEN ISN'T WHERE YOU COOK

"Will you just come on?" Grabbing her hand, they ran across the street and stood on her side porch, away from his house and prying eyes. "I'll see you tomorrow, OK?"

"OK." She hadn't stopped smiling for what seemed like hours.

They stared at each other, their cold breath co-mingling in the frigid night air. Still-warm lips met hers and he ushered her inside with a tiny wave. "Bye."

Rolling over in her bed, Marisa snuggled under her thick comforter, warmed by her thoughts and cozy in her bed. The winter winds were howling tonight, which only made it colder outside. But suddenly, January didn't seem so dreary anymore.

***

They decided not to share the news right away, but it was hard not to show their feelings for each other at school. Although they'd ride to school together, eat lunch together and walk to class together, no one thought anything about it because they'd been doing those things for years. But now she'd feel his eyes on her more and she'd feel his hand on her leg under the table during class before quickly moving it away. He seemed to enjoy this game of cat-and-mouse but Marisa was perfectly paranoid about it.

By Wednesday, they were alone in study hour while Kristin was at a dentist appointment. Marisa was sitting on the floor in the back corner reading about Robespierre for her French paper when she felt Barry slip his arms around her from behind. A series of kisses followed on her cheek before Marisa freaked.

"Stop it! Someone will see us!" she whispered furiously.

"No, they won't. We're the only ones in here."

"Are you sure? What about Mrs.—" His kiss silenced her.

"She went to the teacher's lounge for a pop. No one is in here and if someone does come in, we'll hear them before they get back here."

Against her judgment, she relented. He wrapped his arms around her and kissed her while she tried keeping the book from sliding off her lap. Just when she was about to give up, she heard the door open. "Someone's coming!"

But instead of standing, he just inched away and stayed on the floor next to her. Looking back guiltily, Marisa saw Kristin throwing her books on their usual table by the window.

"Hey! What are you doing?"

"Nothing." Marisa said it too quickly. "Uh...what are you doing back?"

"It was just a cleaning. You know how fast Dr. Van Sikkema is." Kristin left the table to stand over the two of them. "So what are you doing?"

Marisa glanced at Barry, who looked like he wanted to laugh. Anyone looking at them could tell they were sitting too close to be "just friends." And they looked guilty, like they'd just been caught playing "doctor."

"We're not doing anything, Kris," Barry answered as he stood. "Hey, I have to run out to my car. I left my basketball shoes out there. I'll see you in class, Maris."

"OK." She tried burying her nose in her book again, but Kristin kept staring at her. When he was out of earshot, she took his spot on the floor.

"Marisa!"

Oh Lord, here it comes.

"What?"

"What is going on with you two?" Kristin's eyes were wide and her just-cleaned teeth sparkled in a wide, amazed smile.

"Noth—" Marisa was about say "nothing" when she remembered who she was talking to. Kristin was one of her best friends and an understanding one, at that. She'd rooted for Marisa and Barry since grade school. "Well, OK. But promise not to tell anyone?"

"Tell anyone what?" Kris' grin got wider.

"We're going together." Marisa giggled, relieved that she was finally telling someone.

"Are you serious? When did this happen?"

"Saturday night. He invited me to his house to watch videos and for some reason didn't want me to call you or anybody else."

"He wanted you all to himself!" Kris giggled, one hand covering her mouth.

"Stop!" Marisa's ever-present smile turned reflective. "Anyway, I went over there and he started tickling me. Then I fell on the floor and he tickled me some more. Then he just...just kissed me."

Kristin was shaking her head, her newly permed hair swaying with each move. "That is sooooo sweet! I'm telling you, you guys belong together! They say friends make the best couples and you guys have been friends for like forever!"

"I know. But no one else knows, so don't say anything, OK?" Marisa looked around furtively, making sure no one was eavesdropping.

"Why don't you want people to know? You act like you're ashamed or embarrassed. I think people would be happy for you. Everybody likes you two. You're the most popular kids in school."

"After you, of course, Miss Homecoming Queen," Marisa playfully shoved her then turned reflective again. Looking toward the door and toward the empty hallway about to be overrun by her classmates, she shrugged. "I don't know. I just want to hold this close to me. Call me paranoid, but I think some people might try to sabotage us if they knew."

"But why?"

"Because." She didn't know how to explain it to Kris, who was as colorblind as anyone she knew. "They might not like interracial couples."

Kris' heart-shaped mouth dropped open slightly, her expression one of confusion. Mere seconds later, it closed again, this time in a firm, straight line. "Then that's their problem! You guys are best friends. Who cares what other people think? Don't let that bother you. Don't you want to hold hands in the hallway and tell us about all the sweet things he tells you? I mean, don't you want to burst with excitement?"

Marisa's wan smile belied the lump in her throat. "You sound just like a writer."

"Don't change the subject. Answer me."

Sighing, Marisa snapped her book shut. "Of course I want to do all of those things. It's killing me to act like nothing is happening. I see him looking at me all day and I just want to hug him. But...I don't know. I just need to keep it private for as long as I can. I don't like people gossiping about me."

Leaning forward for a supportive hug, Kristin sighed. "Well, congratulations anyway. But you know it's going to get out, don't you?"

As the bell rang and Marisa followed her friend out the door, she knew with a sinking heart that she was right.

***

"Barry! Come here!"

He turned from the water fountain after school the next week and saw Jennifer standing near the trophy case. He had just finished basketball practice and was anxious to see Marisa, who had stayed home from school that day with a head cold. "What?"

"I have to ask you something." Jennifer was still in her sweats from cheerleading practice and was wearing her boyfriend's letter jacket from Saugatuck. Taking his arm, she led him down an empty hallway near the woodshop classrooms.

"What is it, Jen? Hurry up."

Turning to face him in the darkened hallway, she narrowed her eyes and put one hand on her hip. "Is it true?"

"Is what true?"

"Are you going with Marisa?"

Startled, Barry was speechless for a few seconds. During that lapse, he thought about lying, thought better of it then decided to drill the skinny blonde girl standing before him looking insulted.

"Who told you that?"

"Does it matter?"

"Who told you?" His voice was low, threatening.

"Adrienne said she saw you take Marisa home yesterday during third hour and when you got in the parking lot you were holding her hand."

Damn that prissy Adrienne. "So what? She was sick."

"Yeah, but her mother or father could have gotten her. Or Kristin could have taken her home. She has study hour then, too."

"You know, Jen, you must not have much of a life if you're this concerned with me and Marisa." He started to walk away when her next comment stopped him.

"How could you, Barry? She's black!" The word was whispered furiously, like it was profanity.

"What the hell..." He stormed back to her and stood toe-to-toe with her. "I always knew you were a bitch, but now I see you're a racist, too."

"I am not...I'm just saying..." Her duffel bag and purse tumbled from her arms while he leaned close to her face.

"Listen to me. Marisa has been nothing but a friend to you and this is how you repay her? All these years, you were hating her just because of the color of her skin? What kind of ignorant slut are you?" Jennifer had the grace to actually turn red in shame, but Barry wasn't finished.

"Oh yeah, one last thing. Yes, it's true. Marisa and I are dating and it's about time. And you can tell Adrienne or anyone else who has a problem with that to go somewhere. Because you're all just ignorant nosy bitches."

Striding down the hall, he ignored the calls from his buddies and stormed to his car. Inside, he was still fuming. What was wrong with people? Couldn't they see the beauty in Marisa that he did? He thought her light brown skin was radiant, not ugly. Her shiny, thick black hair was amazing, not weird. Her wide brown eyes mesmerizing, not different. And her personality! And intellect! Those were the most beautiful of all.

He was still fuming ninety minutes later when he rang the doorbell at the Logan's home.

"Hi Barry, come on in." Mr. Logan stepped back into the dimly lit foyer and ushered Barry in. "I assume you're here to see our patient."

"Yes, sir."

An amused grin lit Robert Logan's face. "Sir? Are you getting sick, too, Barry?"

"No. No..." He couldn't explain why he felt the need to be more respectful to Mr. Logan. Jennifer's comments really messed him up. "Is she feeling better?"

"Maybe just a little. She's been sleeping most of the day and just came downstairs. Go on in, she's in the living room. We're having some pound cake and coffee in the kitchen if you want some."

"Maybe later. Thanks."

Barry walked into the familiar living room and was surprised at how fast his pulse started to race. Marisa was propped on the couch under a thick quilt with pink flannel pajamas on. Upon closer inspection, he noticed that they had little yellow flowers sprinkled on it. Very cute. Very Marisa.

"Hey. How do you feel?" Leaning down, he kissed her before she could protest.

"You shouldn't do that," she began, but stopped when he sat on the edge of the couch and kissed her again.

"Why not?"

"You...uh, you might catch what I have." His attitude confused her. He seemed bolder today, almost defiant. Not like the easygoing Barry she knew.

"I don't care." He touched her forehead. "So how are you? Is the fever gone?"

With a quick glance at the doorway, she nodded. "Yes, the fever broke this afternoon. My throat still hurts, though."

"Yeah, you still sound stuffy and stuff." He continued to look at her, debating whether to tell her about Jen. Decided not to.

"So, what happened in school today?" She didn't really feel like talking but was warmed by his visit and his apparent concern for her.

"Oh, nothing. Nothing. I was going to bring you your homework, but figured you'd be too sick to do it."

"I might do some studying tonight. I'll be back in school tomorrow. Mama's been feeding me chicken soup and ice cream. And Grandmama even made me a hot toddy."

For the first time all afternoon, he smiled. "A hot toddy? I remember the last time she made that for you. You said you felt drunk."

"I know," she smiled and burrowed deeper under the covers, suddenly tired. "This time it just put me to sleep. And when I woke up, my congestion wasn't as bad."

A lull followed while Barry surveyed the room he'd been in countless times. "Jeopardy" was on television and Cosmopolitan and Essence magazines were splayed on the floor at his feet. Glancing at the covers, he couldn't help comparing the two cover models. One was tall, blonde and thin while the other was chocolate-colored with striking cheekbones. Which one was prettier? He honestly didn't know. Girls were girls as far as he was concerned. He turned back to Marisa to catch her staring at him. Forcing his tone to be light, he kissed her on the forehead, which was still slightly warm. "Well, you seem tired. I'm gonna get going."

"Wait." She grabbed his hand. "What's wrong?"

"Nothing. I'm just tired from practice. That's all." He could tell she didn't believe him, so he stood and averted his gaze. "So I'll pick you up in the morning?"

"Uh...OK." She trained her gaze on the TV screen.

"Call me if you're not gonna go, OK?"

On his way to the foyer, he suddenly turned and walked into the kitchen, where Marisa's parents and grandmother were reading the paper and drinking coffee, empty cake plates before them.

"So Barry, changed your mind, huh? Couldn't resist the pound cake, right?" Mr. Logan laughed and put down the sports section.

Barry laughed with him. "Actually, sir, I uh, I was wondering if I could talk to you."

The adults glanced at each other in surprise. He sounded so serious. "Sure, Barry. Let's uh, let's go in the garage. I think you wanted to borrow my new drill, didn't you?"

"Uh, yeah. Yeah."

In the garage, the pair sidestepped the two vehicles and stood before Mr. Logan's tool chest. "So what's on your mind, Barry? Is it work?"

"No." He turned the drill over in his gloved hand. "It's Marisa."

Frowning, Mr. Logan folded his arms in front of him. "What about her?"

"Well..." Barry looked down, suddenly having second thoughts. "I uh...well, you know how much I respect you. And your wife. Shoot, your family practically raised me. And Marisa has been my best friend for years."

The older man cocked his head to one side, raising an eyebrow. "Yeah?"

"Well, I thought you should know...I thought you should know that Marisa and ...Marisa and I are...we're ..." his voice broke before he hastily cleared his throat. "We're dating."

His boss, neighbor and mentor said nothing. He just stood there with his arms folded across his Negro League baseball sweatshirt and said nothing. After several seconds of scrutinization, he cleared his throat. "You're dating."

"Yes, sir." Barry finally looked him in the eye.

"OK. And you're telling me this because...?"

"Well, because I didn't want to hide it anymore. I didn't want you to think I was ashamed of Marisa...or anything."

"Are you? Ashamed of her, that is?"

"No! No way! I love...I mean, she's my best friend."

"So you've said."

"I mean, I would never want to hurt her. Your daughter is beautiful, Mr. Logan. Inside and out. And I really care for her."

"I see. Didn't you also care for that little blonde girl?"

"Adrienne?" Saying her name was like bile on his tongue. The nosy little bitch.

"I did at the time, but not like I care for Marisa. She knows me better than anybody. I'd do anything for her."

For the first time, Mr. Logan cracked a semblance of a smile. "Well, that's nice to know. And you know I've always liked you, Barry. You're like one of my own. But no father wants to see their little girl with a broken heart. She values your friendship, you see. And I hope you value it, too."

"Yes, sir. More than you know." He released a pent-up breath.

"And how long have you two been...dating?"

"Only for a couple of weeks. We didn't know how you guys would take it."

"I see. And does Marisa know you're out here talking to me?"

At that, Barry's face turned pale. She'd kill him. "No, she doesn't. She'd probably want to hit me."

A hearty laugh lifted the mood. Mr. Logan grinned and slapped Barry on the shoulder. "Yep, that's my girl, all right." With one hand on his back, he led Barry to the side garage door. "Well, I won't tell her you told me. But I will tell my wife. It's up to you if you want to tell Marisa about this conversation. She won't hear it from us. I'm sure she'd be very embarrassed."

"Probably." Outside, Barry turned to the older man. "Thanks, Mr. Logan. I'll return your drill as soon as I can."

"Keep it as long as you need to, Barry." With a smile, he closed the door. His daughter. His beautiful, strong-willed, kindhearted daughter. Dating a blonde, white boy. If it were anyone but Barry, he might have been upset. But it *was* Barry, a boy who'd ached for a father figure for years. Who used to follow him around his hardware store asking questions all day. Who asked for advice on cars and sports and grilling. And somehow, it was all right with him.

CHAPTER 9

Winter-Spring 1987

Marisa used to hate Valentine's Day. Well, that wasn't exactly true. She used to feel sorry for herself on Valentine's Day because she'd see all of her friends get flowers, candy and cards and she'd get nothing.

This year was different.

When Barry picked her up for school that day, he presented her with a big box of chocolates. She, in turn, gave him a card.

"You'll get your real present later," she promised as she tore into the box and bit into an almond cluster.

"Oh yeah? Can't wait for *that*!" Leering at her, he laughed softly.

It took her a minute to catch on. "I don't mean that!" With a slap on his arm, she blushed. No matter how much she thought about Barry, wrote his name on her notebook or yearned for him, she wasn't ready for ...that. To her, sex in high school was useless. They didn't have any privacy, couldn't check into hotels and were relegated to "doing it" either in cars or on basement sofas or on tiny beds with the fear of discovery looming. Not very romantic, if you asked her.

To be honest, she'd gone farther with Keith than she had with Barry. She and Barry only kissed, held hands and hugged. Not once had he tried to feel her breast or anywhere else. That was OK by her. No use in tempting him for nothing.

She floated through the day, offering her candy to Kris, Tara and Jen, who'd declined. That was OK by her, too. Lately Jen had been avoiding her. She figured it was because of her relationship with Barry, but Marisa didn't care. She always knew that once they graduated, their friendship would be over, so if it ended a few months earlier, then all the better.

That night, she joined Barry at his house for a Valentine's Day meal.

"Did you really make this all yourself?"

"Well, my grandmother showed me how to do the Cornish hens. And the scalloped potatoes are from a box. The green beans my mother made. Oh shoot! I forgot the drinks." Scooting his chair back, he ran into the kitchen then returned with a bottle of sparkling cider.

"Barry." She took his hand, her expression serious. "Thank you. This is so sweet."

He kissed her and smiled. "No, you're sweet. Now let's eat. Tell me how you like my masterpiece."

Taking a bite of the meat, she nodded. "It's not bad. Not bad at all." In truth, it was rather dry and underseasoned, but she wasn't going to tell him that. The recipe came from his grandmother, after all. His old, wrinkled, rich, prejudiced grandmother. Marisa had never liked her.

"Uh, did your grandmother ask why you wanted to know how to make this?" she asked casually.

"Well, yeah. I just told her I was going to make it for Mom's birthday. But that's, like, not until next month." He took a deep swig of his cider.

"So...you didn't tell her it was for me?" She didn't want to feel hurt, but for some reason, she did. She wanted him to confront his grandmother more than anyone else. Just because she was such an old biddy.

"No." Looking up, he caught her disappointed expression. "Was that wrong?"

"No, no. I don't know. Forget it." She stabbed at her green beans, which tasted nothing like the kind her grandmother cooked after she made Marisa snap them with her.

"What is it? Did I do something wrong?"

"No, of course not. We agreed that we weren't going to spring this on people, right?"

"Right. Even though everyone at school knows and my mother knows."

"She does?" Marisa grimaced. Great. Now Mrs. Montgomery would be scrutinizing her and treating her differently from now on.

"Yeah, but she doesn't care. She's too concerned with my dad now. Some stuff is going on at his job."

Barry's father was a truck driver for a local fruit canning company, which kept him on the road a lot. "What's wrong?"

Barry sat with his head down, like he was embarrassed. Then he shrugged with one shoulder and said quietly, "I guess he got into some trouble or something…I don't know."

"Oh." He didn't need to say anymore. Marisa guessed that his father had either shown up to work drunk or was pulled over for drinking and driving. Instant termination. His only hope was his union stepping in.

"My mom and grandmother are all freaked because I'm about to go to college, and graduation and prom are coming up. They think I'm going to have to miss out on something because the family budget is tight. And you know he hates asking Grandma for help." He played with his food, then set his fork down with a clank. "But I told him that I already have a pretty good savings account from working for your dad."

"Yeah?" Marisa felt a glow of pride. Her good ole' daddy.

"Yep. But still, I guess losing your job is hard, no matter what."

Marisa wished she could help him, but didn't know what to say. Her family had never been through any financial hardships. And if they had, she'd been kept in the dark. Business was always booming, as far as she could tell. How else could they afford to send Robert and Matthew and now her to college?

The rest of the evening, as the next few months, passed by peacefully. No one at school gave them any problems except for a few glares from Jen and others of her ilk. By early April, the news came that Mr. Montgomery was indeed fired, despite the union's efforts to save his job. That meant no unemployment benefits, so Barry asked Marisa's father for extra hours and he got them. He'd leave baseball practice then stock shelves in the store until eight every night, except for game nights. Marisa went to every one of his games and swooned at how cute he looked in his hat and uniform. She finally confided to her parents that he was her boyfriend, and the news was met with scoffs and chuckles.

"Oh yeah? What a surprise!" Her mother laughed.

"You mean you knew?" Marisa flung herself across their king-sized bed, where her mother was knitting and her father was watching the NBA.

"Of course. We're not blind. And you know we like Barry. He's like one of the family."

"Yeah." Marisa rolled her head to look at her father. "You, too, Daddy?"

"Hmmm." The Pistons were playing the Celtics, so Marisa knew that was the only response she'd get from him all night.

"Anyway, we're fine with you and Barry dating. He's a nice boy." Her mother put down her knitting. "So I guess that means you'll be going to the prom this year?"

"Well, yeah, I guess so." She didn't tell her mother that Barry hadn't asked her yet. Hadn't even mentioned it. But she had been thinking about it. A lot.

"You guess? Well, he's asked you, hasn't he?"

"Not exactly." With her eyes averted, she played with the edge of her mother's yarn ball. "Maybe he's just assuming we'll go."

"He shouldn't assume. He should ask you, like a gentleman would." Mrs. Logan ignored the dirty look her husband shot her. The conversation was interfering with his game.

"I know. I'm sure he'll ask. He's just distracted with his father being home all day and stuff. It's weird over there." As a result, Barry was spending more time at Marisa's house or at the store than at his own home. He said his father always made a big mess in the house and drank too much beer. In public, Mr. Montgomery was a pillar of Petersville society, but behind closed doors, Marisa suspected he was a borderline alcoholic.

"I understand. Well, you should know something soon, though. We have to get you a dress."

The next afternoon, Marisa met Barry in the park to commiserate on their physics project and to enjoy the suddenly warm spring air.

"I was talking to Tara last night," she began. They were sitting on the swings and she began moving in a circle so the chains above her became twisted. "She said Walter Hoag asked her to prom."

"Walter?" Barry laughed. Walter was short – about five-six – wore glasses and was the quietest person in their class. "I can't believe he had the nerve."

"Me neither."

"What did she tell him?"

She glanced at him with a small grin, noting with admiration the way the late afternoon sun played with the golden highlights in his hair. "She told him she had a date already."

"That's a nice way to let him down." Barry was straddling the swing like a horse. That way, he was face-to-face with Marisa, who was now tangled up in the twisted swing. "Who is she going with?"

"Um, she's going with John Strouse. I guess she doesn't care that he's a junior." She hoped this line of conversation would lead him to think about his own prom date. She was tired of waiting.

"So what's our plan? What color is your dress? What color should I wear? My mother was bugging me about it last night."

"What?" She stopped twisting, suddenly dizzy as she looked at him.

"Your prom dress. What color should I wear?"

"Uh...are we going?" She knew she must sound stupid, but she had to have some things spelled out for her so she wouldn't jump to conclusions.

"What do you mean, are we going? Of course we're going. Don't you want to?" He nudged her foot in the dirt with his own.

"Sure. It's just that...you never asked me or anything." Looking toward the softball field, she felt his eyes on her.

"Oh...well, I just figured we'd go. I thought it was just a given." He leaned forward and turned her chin to meet his warm brown eyes. "I'm sorry. I didn't mean for you to wonder or anything."

"I wasn't." She suddenly felt silly. Of course they were going together. They were the supercouple of Petersville High! Like Luke and Laura.

"I'm sorry." He dropped his voice while staring into her eyes. "Marisa, will you go to the prom with me?"

Smiling, she nodded. "Yes, Barry. I would love to go." She felt excitement building as he kissed her shortly. Thoughts instantly flew to the wonderful night she knew they'd have together. She'd be beautiful in her dress; he'd be handsome in his black tuxedo. They'd take her father's car, then go to dinner at some fancy, waterfront restaurant in Holland or Saugatuck. Then it was off to the prom at the West Ottawa Golf and Country Club. There they'd mingle, dance, take pictures and remember the night as one of the best of their high school years. Afterward there would be parties and the beach and moonlight then breakfast then...sleep. She had it all planned.

***

It was early May, less than two weeks before prom. Marisa and her friends were counting the days, dieting, exercising and keeping their nails strong and protected. The white girls were, of course, tanning. She heard through the grapevine that Jennifer and her stupid boyfriend were both going to wear tuxedos. "Tuxedos? If I were that girl's mama, I'd beat her tail." Mrs. Logan sniffed. "What's she trying to look like a boy for?"

While sitting at lunch with Kris one day, Paulina Lowe approached their table. She was the junior class vice-president. "Hi guys. Is that all you're eating?" She motioned to the small salads with no dressing.

"Gotta get ready for prom," Kris laughed while Marisa nodded.

"That's what I'm here for. Marisa, I just wanted to remind you that the deadline to buy tickets is Friday. And you're going to have to sign up then if you want formal pictures taken."

Marisa frowned. "Barry is taking care of the tickets."

Paulina's freckled face registered surprise with a slight lift of her eyebrows. "He is? He hasn't bought any yet. I've tried to tell him about it but he's always brushing me off. So I figured I'd tell you."

"Oh." Marisa felt an unsettling flutter in her stomach. "Well, you know how guys are."

"Yeah, I know. Well, I just wanted to let you know. It'll be too late after Friday."

"OK. Thanks, Paulina."

Turning back to Kris, Marisa sipped her drink slowly. "I wonder why he hasn't bought the tickets yet."

"Has he mentioned it to you?"

Shaking her head, Marisa didn't confess that Barry had hardly mentioned anything lately. After baseball practice, he'd work late then go straight home to study. No more stopping by her house for her notes or just to hang out. His car had recently died, so he'd been hitching a ride with different buddies every day. She'd offered to drive him in her car, but he'd declined for some reason. At the time, she thought it was odd, but dropped it. She was so busy preparing for prom, the district track meet and graduation that it didn't weigh on her too much. And at school...come to think of it, he'd been avoiding her at school, too. During study hour, he'd either have his head in a book at the library or he'd volunteer to help the baseball coach/gym teacher over at the middle school. At lunch, he was either not hungry or already eating with his friends.

"You know, he's been acting kind of funny lately," she said absently. "Really elusive and stuff."

"Really? Maybe it's the stuff with his dad. You said he was having a tough time."

"Yeah, but he was always able to escape it at school or at my house. Now he's just...I don't know." She pushed her salad bowl away. "Do you think I should offer to pay?"

"I don't know. How would he take that? Would he be insulted?" Kristin stood up as the warning bell rang.

"Maybe. I guess." As they stacked their trays, Marisa grabbed Kris' arm. "Can you do me a favor? Can you talk to him? Ask him nonchalantly if he's bought the tickets yet and what dinner plans he has for us. Act like you're just being my nosy friend."

"OK. I can do that." Kris nodded, then hooked her arm through Marisa's. "Don't worry. I'm sure it's just end-of-school stress. We can all relate to that."

That evening, while Marisa was studying her physics with one eye on "Cheers," the phone rang. It was Kristin.

"Hey Kris." She leaned against the couch from her perch on the floor. "Are you watching 'Cheers'?"

"Uh no. My dad's watching the Tigers."

Her sudden silence and subdued tone of voice made Marisa's pulse quicken. "So did you talk to Barry?"

More silence. "Kris?"

"I'm here. Yes, I talked to him." Her usually sunny voice was subdued.

"And?" Marisa inexplicably started to worry. Why did Kristin sound so odd? And angry? What on earth did Barry say to her?

"And he's...he's going through some stuff right now."

"I know. His father, right?" Frowning, she gripped the phone tighter.

"Yes, that. And..."

"Kris, just tell me. What did you say to him, anyway? Did you do what I told you?"

"Yes, yes. I asked had he bought the tickets yet..."

"OK. So what did he say?" Marisa urged.

"He said no. Then it seemed like he didn't know whether to brush me off or keep talking. He decided to keep talking."

Sighing in frustration, Marisa practically yelled into the receiver. "Will you just tell me already?"

Silence again and Marisa heard Kris gulp. When she began again, her voice was shaking. "He said he didn't buy the tickets yet because he wasn't the one paying for prom. His parents took all of his money out of his bank account. Apparently, they needed that money to pay some bills. You know, the tickets, the tux, pictures and dinner add up to a lot of money. So his grandmother offered to pay for prom. Kind of like an early graduation gift."

As soon as she said the word "grandmother," Marisa knew the rest wouldn't be good. "Go on."

"So when she asked who Barry was taking, she...she changed her mind." Kris' voice got softer and softer as the story went on.

With a big gulp of her own, Marisa shook her head in amazement. That old bigoted bitch! "Don't tell me. She doesn't want Barry going with a black girl."

"Marisa, I'm sorry..." Kris sounded like she was going to cry.

"Don't be sorry. You're not the prejudiced one. She is. She's got some nerve!" Sighing, she forced herself to calm down. "So what did Barry say? He told her to forget the whole thing?"

"No...see, that's where the problem comes. Barry seemed scared to defy her. He doesn't know what to do. He doesn't have the money any other way."

"What?" This news shocked Marisa even more. Her best friend? One of the most colorblind people she knew?

"It's his grandmother. She's old. She's set in her ways and he knows he can't change her mind."

"Wait a minute..." Anger and resentment started to build inside her in the shape of labored breathing and flared nostrils. "You know, Kris, I shouldn't even be talking to you about it. I should be talking to him. Why didn't he tell me any of this?"

"He didn't know how. I swear, he sounded really torn up. You should go over there."

With pursed lips, Marisa nodded then realized Kris couldn't see her. "You're right. I'm going right now. Thanks, Kris. Thanks for everything."

"You're welcome. Call me when you get back, OK?"

It took a few minutes of pleading to persuade her parents to let her go to Barry's at almost ten o'clock at night. But when they saw the semi-crazed look on her face, they relented. "Back by ten-thirty, you hear? And just across the street. Nowhere else."

"Daddy, there's nowhere to go in this stupid town."

She ran across the darkened street and her mood was somewhat calmed by the cool spring air and the light scent of lilacs. Slowing her steps, she stood on the Montgomery's walkway and stared up at their house. So identical to hers, yet so different. One car in the driveway and almost every light on. To her, it meant that everyone in the family was in different rooms. Not together, the way a family should be.

On the porch, she took a deep breath then knocked softly. She saw Mrs. Montgomery peek through the front curtain, then heard her shushed whisper to someone inside. Seconds later, Barry opened the door.

"Hi," she said. He didn't look directly at her, instead he glanced behind him, said something to his mother, then stepped onto the porch, closing the door tightly behind him.

"Hi." He walked to the steps and sat morosely on the bottom. She followed, sitting next to him uneasily. She nervously began playing with her hair.

"So...how are you?"

"Fine," he muttered, staring straight ahead.

She followed his gaze and noticed the large crack in the walkway that had been there since she was about seven years old. "So...do you want to talk?"

He frowned, grabbed a leaf off the nearby lilac bush and tore it to shreds. "I take it you talked to Kristin?"

Hesitation, then: "Yes."

He still didn't look at her and by now was on his second leaf-shredding mission.

"Barry, let's talk about this." She placed a hand on his shoulder. "You can't let your grandmother do this to you. I can pay for the tickets, we can have dinner at my house and we can take our own pictures. All you have to do is get the tux."

He sat motionless for several seconds, then ran his hands through his already-tousled hair. "I knew you'd say that. I can't let you pay for everything. I asked you. I should pay. That's how it works."

"But Barry, it's no big deal. Who's gonna know?" She scooted closer and put her arm around him.

"Me, that's who! And your parents. And my parents and probably all of your friends." She was surprised by his angry tone. Barry was usually one of the most easygoing people she'd ever known.

"Who cares if they know? It's no...big...deal." She was about to kiss him on the cheek when he suddenly jumped up and began pacing around the front lawn.

"Look, you don't understand. Things around here are...they're really bad. My grandmother is basically keeping us off food stamps and she's...well, she basically runs this family, you know that. Whatever she wants, she gets. She's all alone, she's old, she doesn't know what to do with herself except meddle in everyone's business."

"Yes, I know that. Otherwise we wouldn't be having this conversation." Her tone became harder, edgier. Why was he fighting her on this? He either wanted to go to the prom with her at any cost or not. It was that simple.

"OK, let me break it down like this. You want to go to prom with me, right? And you don't want to hurt your grandmother. The only way to do that is to let me pay for it."

He stopped pacing long enough to finally look at her. Silently, he stared for what seemed an eternity. When he spoke, his voice was calm and clear. "Marisa, I can't. I can't go to the prom with you."

Form her perch on the steps, her mouth – and stomach – dropped. Surely she heard wrong. "What?"

"I ... I can't go to the prom with you. My grandmother really wants me to go and she really wants to pay for it. It would make her so happy. I can't disappoint her, I can't."

"So you can disappoint me, is that it?" Unable to move, she sat frozen on the penultimate step.

"I don't want to, you know I don't. But it's my grandmother! She grew up back in the days when there were no black people in Petersville or anywhere around here. She didn't even speak to one until like, 1970. To her, it's just wrong."

With her mouth still hanging open, Marisa struggled to regain some composure. In a clipped, tight voice, she avoided his gaze, for to look at him would hurt too much. He couldn't be serious. "Stop sugarcoating it. Your grandmother is prejudiced, Barry! Racist! She doesn't want me going with you because I'm black. And you don't see anything wrong with that?"

"Of course I do! But how can I defy my grandmother? She told my parents that if they allow it, she'd cut them off. And then where would we be? She said we could be friends, but..." His voice trailed off and he finally had the grace to look embarrassed.

"But what?"

"We could be friends, but I couldn't date someone...'like that.'"

The phrase hit Marisa in the gut. She felt ugly and dirty and stupid and unworthy. Her skin actually felt like it was crawling, as if she'd stepped into a hole full of snakes and spiders. *Someone like that.* *"Like that."* After all the times Barry had made her feel pretty and loved and special, his two little words made her feel like a pickaninny. Suddenly her hair felt too coarse and thick, her skin too dry and dark, her lips too large, her hips too wide and curvy. *"Someone like that."* She felt the tears building and forced herself to hold them at bay. No way in hell was he going to see her cry. She thought he was different. That he didn't care about skin color. That he liked her for her. And that he'd do anything for her. Ha. He was just like Jennifer. Janine was right. You couldn't trust any of them.

Rising, she dusted off her jeans and began stalking back to her house. When she reached the street, she heard him behind her, felt his hand reaching out to grab her arm. "Marisa, I'm sor—" The last syllable never left his mouth because she slapped him. Hard. Right across his tan, startled, *white* face. "Go. To. Hell. Don't ever speak to me again, you fucking coward."

She knew he was shocked at her words and at her slap. She left him standing in the middle of the empty street with a hand to his face and his mouth hanging open. And for the first time in her life, she hated – literally hated – Barry Montgomery.

***

At home, she stood in the darkened kitchen, unsure of what to do. Her parents were upstairs, still knitting and watching television. Her grandmother had been asleep since eight o'clock. Kristin was probably waiting for her to call back, but she didn't feel like talking to her. She was white. She was probably just like the rest of them. Oh sure, she put on a great show of friendship and tolerance, but when it came down to the nitty-gritty, Marisa just wasn't good enough in their eyes. No matter that she was smarter than almost everyone else in school and that her father owned one of the most successful businesses in town. They still couldn't see past color. To them, she was just a little black girl. A nigger.

Walking up the stairs, she paused as she considered whether to tell her parents or not. If she could tell them without crying. Deciding she could, she knocked softly on their door.

"You're back. Right on time." Her father was flipping through the channels during commercials of "L.A. Law." "Your homework all done?"

She opened her mouth to speak but found she couldn't say anything. So she nodded. That's when her mother looked up from her knitting.

"Marisa? Sweetie? What's wrong?"

Swallowing a huge lump that had suddenly formed in her throat, she stayed outlined in the doorway. "I just came to tell you to cancel my hair appointment in Grand Rapids. I'm not going to prom."

The words, once they were spoken, made her want to cry. After all the planning and wishing and money. No prom night. No dancing. No pictures, no dinner, no moonlight, no after-parties. Just – nothing.

"What?" Her father asked while her mother queried simultaneously. "What do you mean?"

Marisa looked away. Her parents looked so alarmed. She wanted to make it seem like it wasn't a big deal. She didn't want them to see how much she hurt. "Barry can't afford to buy the tickets or rent a tux or take me to dinner."

"Oh, is that all? Well, don't worry. We'll pay for it. And he can rent two tuxedos for what he's making in the store."

Shaking her head, Marisa shifted from one foot to the other. She had to explain. Everything. "No, that's not it. His family needs the money he makes to pay some bills and he doesn't want my help in paying for it. But that's not it, either."

"Well, what is it then?" Her mother looked flabbergasted in her white cotton, comfy nightgown.

"I...he...his grandmother agreed to pay for his expenses but changed her mind when she found out he was taking me." With a sigh of resignation, she dropped the bomb. "She doesn't want him taking a black girl."

As she knew they would, her parents' expressions hardened. She imagined they were thinking back to their own racist experiences in the sixties. And how could they not? It would stay with them forever.

"Oh, Marisa, come here." Her mother jumped out of bed and rushed to put her arms around her daughter. "Surely Barry doesn't feel that way. He's been your friend for years! Maybe your father can talk to him." With wide eyes, she turned to her husband. "Robert?"

Her husband was standing at the foot of the bed with a hand on his hip. "What did Barry say about this?"

"He...he said he couldn't disappoint his grandmother. That she said it was OK to be friends with a black girl but he couldn't date...couldn't date... 'someone like that.'" The words still stung.

Her father nodded. "Uh huh. And did he argue with her? Did he say anything at all?"

With a shake of her head, Marisa felt her tears build. "No. He didn't. All he kept saying was how he couldn't disappoint his grandmother. How she was the head of the family. He didn't say anything." With tear-filled eyes, she glanced up at her mother. "He couldn't even look at me, Mama. He couldn't even look me in the face."

"Oh, shh. It's OK, baby, it's OK." In a tight embrace, she held Marisa and rocked her back and forth. "It's OK. Shhh. Hush now." Marisa was so engulfed in her mother's arms that she didn't hear the phone ring. She heard her father's voice and raised her head. He caught her gaze and mouthed the words, "It's Kristin." With a shake of her head, she declined the call. Nodding, he spoke low into the phone. "She can't come to the phone right now. She'll talk to you another time, OK? OK. Goodbye."

Sniffling, Marisa let her mother lead her to the bed. There, she handed her a blue Kleenex. "It'll be OK, Marisa. It will. Here, dry your eyes."

Blowing her nose sadly, she spoke to the floor. "And the worst part is, he didn't even have the decency to tell me. He was avoiding me all week and today someone told me that he hadn't bought the tickets yet so I got worried. I asked Kris to talk to him and he told her. He told her everything but he couldn't tell me." It was still hard to believe.

"Is that why you went over there tonight?" Her mother continued to rock her back and forth.

"Yes. I had to tell him not to worry. I figured he'd just let me pay so he wouldn't have to do what his grandmother said. But he refused. To me, that was proof that he agreed with her. He didn't even stand up to her! He just her talk about me like I was some runaway slave."

She felt her parents glancing at each other in indignation and realized they were hurt, too. They'd treated Barry like one of the family for years. They'd watched him grow up, they'd rooted and cheered for him, gave him advice, trusted him with their daughter. Betrayal from a supposed friend hurt. Especially when it was someone you trusted. It was a blatant slap in the face and a kick in the gut.

"Marisa," her father sat on the opposite side of her. "I know you're upset now, but trust me...one, two years from now you won't even be thinking about this or about Barry. You're starting a new life at Michigan State soon and you're going to fly higher than any of these hicks around here." She smiled wanly. "You'll realize that all of this is just a small speck on the wonderful life you're going to have."

"I know, I know." Twisting the Kleenex in her hand, she tried to stop the tears. "It just hurts. He was...m-my b-best friend." And now he was nothing. How could they go back to where they were? He'd just thrown away almost fifteen years of friendship over what? A bitter old lady? A few dollars? It made no sense.

"It's going to hurt, baby." Her mother was saying. "Life does hurt. I'm not gonna lie. And you'll probably be hurt even more before you're called into heaven. But you're strong. You're stronger than any of these people around here and you know why?" Marisa glanced up at her and felt her tears dry up at the resolve and confidence on her mother's face. "Because we have to be. We always have. Don't let them break you. That's what they want. Don't let them."

Her parents continued with the pep talk for another few minutes before she announced she wanted to be alone. They told her she could stay home from school the next day but she had to go back to school on Monday with her head held high.

The next morning, she stayed in bed until ten o'clock, not sleeping, not crying. She just stared at the ceiling. It was a beautiful day outside, seventy-eight degrees, brilliantly sunny and breezy. But she felt no desire to go out. Instead, she was reliving the years she'd spent laughing with Barry. Studying with him. Going sledding, snapping green beans, watching football, competing in class, rocking to Motley Crue. Not once had she ever thought him capable of hurting her like this. Not once. Jennifer, yes. Of course. But Barry?

Never. He had an almost naïve quality about him that made it almost impossible for him to be prejudiced. She'd never heard him utter disparaging remarks about Hispanics in school the way some of the other boys did. He never talked about gays, either. Well, OK, he laughed when Dennis or Mitch would call each other "faggot," but they all laughed. And not once had he let the word "nigger" fly from his lips. Timmy Franklin had called her that in the sixth grade once, and Barry had pushed him against the lockers and made him apologize. And when Dennis made a crack last year over lunch that the Petersville basketball team didn't stand a chance "against those colored boys in Covert," Barry had taken him to task before Marisa could utter a word. "It's black, Dennis. Not colored. It's not 1960, anymore, stupid. Now apologize."

"For what?" Dennis hadn't seen anything wrong with his comment.

"For being an asshole! Apologize to Marisa."

Dennis had become flustered. "I wasn't talking about her. She's not like the others."

She'd wanted to ask what he meant. What are "the others" like, anyway? Drippy Jheri curls? Ignorant language and criminal backgrounds? But she'd said nothing. It wasn't the first time she'd heard comments like that, either. "You're different. You're not like the others." Or "You're not really black." Or "You don't look black." What did they mean? Did they really think they were complimenting her?

A glance at her bulletin board made her get out of bed. Several of her friends smiled at her from their senior pictures. Barry had even given her two – one in his baseball uniform, the other in a gray sweater and matching slacks while he leaned against a tree with his arms folded. She took them both down and studied them closely. She was startled to discover that she didn't feel anything for him but contempt. And to be honest, a little regret. Maybe she was too hard on him. Maybe it was unfair of her to ask him to defy his grandmother. But as soon as the thought came to her, she squashed it. That's bull. He was a coward. He didn't want to show his children his prom pictures with a black girl. He didn't want to stand up for her. He didn't have the backbone to tell his grandmother and everyone else who had a problem with them dating that it was none of their business. And for that, she couldn't forgive him. Couldn't even look at him.

Tossing his pictures in her desk drawer, she glanced around her room quickly. Before she could stop herself, she'd taken down everyone's photos from her bulletin board – except for Janine's and Keith's – and stashed them in an envelope in her drawer. Then she tore down her Petersville High banner, her Homecoming Maid of Honor sash, her crown, the Valentine's Day card Barry'd given her and her pom-poms and stuffed them all in a box. Closing the lid quickly, she pushed the box into the back of her closet. There. Although graduation was still a month away, she was ready to say goodbye to Petersville. And everybody in it. Even Kristin, who had stopped by just a few minutes earlier. Her mother shooed her away and left Marisa alone. Good. She didn't want to talk to Kris, who was obviously curious enough to hear what had happened that she'd come over during her study hour.

She replaced the PHS banner with an MSU one and stuck a Spartans pin on her bulletin board. Her new life was just a few months away. No more close-minded, small-town white folks to deal with. She'd finally be around some black people. She'd make friends for life. The people she'd grown up with here in Petersville – Jennifer, Tara, Kristin, Barry – meant nothing to her anymore. They were white. She was black. And no amount of Motley Crue, Valley Girl talk or Seventeen magazines would change that fact.

***

Robert Logan looked up when he heard the front door of the store jingle. It was five-thirty. Barry was right on time.

He usually spoke when he came to work, but this time, he walked right past Marisa's father like he didn't even see him. He averted his eyes as he disappeared into the back room to put down his books and pick up his name tag. Mr. Logan followed him.

"Barry," he closed the door so the customers and sales clerk wouldn't hear him. "I need to talk to you."

With satisfaction, he watched as Barry turned pale and took a step back. "Yes, sir?"

You'd better call me sir, Mr. Logan thought. "I was doing some of our books just now and I decided that I need to cut back on some expenses. I'm cutting the number of lawn mowers and edgers this year because we weren't able to move all of them last year, remember?"

Visibly relaxing, Barry nodded. "I remember."

"But those are just some of the cutbacks." With a steady gaze, Mr. Logan stepped closer to the teenager. "I'm going to have to let you go."

Barry's mouth dropped open. His eyelids blinked rapidly – three, no, four times. "I...what do you mean?"

"I mean that your services are no longer needed here. Marisa will be taking over your hours." He watched while Barry's face turned a bright red at the mention of his daughter's name.

"But...Mr. Logan, I – I need this job."

"I know you do." That single sentence, uttered without feeling and without regret, informed Barry of the real reason behind his firing.

"If this is about Marisa, I can explain – "

"No, no. I told you. It's a cost-cutting measure." Mr. Logan stood tall and never let his steady gaze leave Barry's, causing him to fidget and stammer.

"But you said I was your best worker! What if I take a cut in hours? You're going to be so busy this summer...you're always busy in the summer."

"No, Barry. We don't need you here anymore." He walked to his desk, opened a drawer and handed the startled young man an envelope. "Here's your last check. Oh, and I need your name tag."

For a second, he thought Barry was going to cry. Good. Let him cry the way my daughter was crying, he thought. But inside, he was hurting, too. He'd looked after this boy for years. He'd bragged about him to all of his customers, trusted him with inventory and the store. His money. To let him go like this wasn't fun. But it was definitely necessary. No way was this kid going to hurt his daughter and smile in his face like he'd done nothing. No, if his daughter wasn't good enough for him, then neither was this job.

Slowly, Barry dislodged the name tag from his T-shirt. With his head down, he traded the tag for the envelope. An awkward silence enveloped the room while both tried to keep their emotions in check. Finally, Mr. Logan spoke. His voice was soft, but firm. "You disappoint me, Barry."

Without looking up, Barry trudged to the door. Before stepping out, he spoke over his shoulder. "I'm sorry. I'm so sorry."

***

Marisa heard what her father had done over dinner.

"You fired him?"

"Yep. If you want his hours, they're yours." Her father took a long sip of his lemonade.

"But Daddy..." At first she was going to protest. It didn't seem fair. This fight was between her and Barry, and he did need the money, after all. But on second thought, if he continued to work there she'd have to see him all summer. She didn't think she could stand that. "OK. I'll take his hours. I can save more money for school."

"That-a girl."

After dinner, while picking out her best outfit for school on Monday – no sense in walking in there like she was in mourning – she wondered how Barry was feeling now. She hoped he found another job. But she hoped he also started to realize how it felt to be discriminated against. For once, a black man had authority over a white person and could do whatever he wanted. The same way they'd been treating her people for years. Served him right.

On Monday, she walked into school with her head held high, her bright pink sundress a flattering contrast to her smooth brown skin. Before she could open her locker, she was assaulted by Kristin.

"Marisa! I've been so worried about you! You didn't call me back..." Her voice trailed off when she noticed the cold, dismissive stare Marisa shot her.

"I was busy, Kristin. My life doesn't revolve around calling you."

She heard Kris gulp and knew she was being unfair and mean. Kris hadn't done anything to her. Yet, she reminded herself. Better not to let her guard down.

"How are you? I talked to Barry yesterday. He...he told me what happened. Are you OK?" Kris put a hand on her arm.

"I'm fine, Kris. What, did you think I was going to die because I'm not going to prom? Who cares? I didn't go last year, remember? And I survived."

Kristin took a step backward, confused at her friend's attitude. "I know. So...what are you two going to do instead? Just hang out?"

"What?" Marisa grabbed her economics book and slammed her locker door. "What are you talking about? There is no 'you two.' We broke up."

Kris' eyes bugged. "What? Why? I mean, I guess I know why, but is that necessary? I mean, just because you're not going to prom..."

"Kris, grow up. If I'm not good enough for prom, I'm not good enough to date. Got it? Now I gotta go."

She didn't see Barry all morning. Good. He was probably at home, embarrassed because he'd been fired. She wanted to laugh. He didn't know who he was messing with. Her daddy could be ruthless when he wanted to.

During her free hour, which she spent in a corner in the library, her name was called on the intercom. "Marisa Logan, please report to the office."

Perplexed, she gathered her books and strolled to the office, hoping she wasn't in trouble for some reason. Once there, the secretary pointed her to the principal's office. Inside stood Mr. Amos, the principal, and the senior class advisor, Mrs. Gooding.

"Have a seat, Marisa," Mr. Amos said. "We have good news for you. We were just going over the transcripts for the senior class and you have been named the valedictorian."

Although she'd been expecting it, she was still excited. Valedictorian. The best. The smartest. Ha. Better than Barry. "Thank you. It's a great honor."

"Well, you've earned it. You've been an exceptional student and leader in this school."

"Thank you." Grinning, she thought about how proud her parents would be. And especially Grandmama. She couldn't wait to tell them. This news almost made up for the prom mess with Barry.

After being lectured about what she could and could not say in her speech and the deadline for approval on her final draft, she was dismissed. While walking out the office door, she came face-to-face with Barry.

She froze, not knowing what to do. She'd still had a smile on her face from the news, but it disappeared quickly when she saw him. He averted his eyes but held the door open for her. "Excuse me," she muttered, then swiftly walked out without a second glance.

Through the grapevine that afternoon, she heard that he'd been named salutatorian. Second best. Several of her classmates congratulated her throughout the day and she politely smiled and nodded and agreed on how exciting it was. Truthfully, she couldn't wait until graduation. It would be the last time she'd have to see any of these people. It was an odd thought, one she never thought she'd express. Years ago, she never wanted to leave Petersville. Now she was counting the days and weeks until she was gone.

She saw glimpses of Barry after school. While walking to track practice, she caught him gathering baseball bats outside the locker room. While running her warm-up around the school grounds, she noticed him catching balls on the baseball field. She knew the exact moment he saw her, too, for he stopped in mid-throw, dropped his arm and stared at her before lowering his head. For a split second, she felt a lump in her throat. Barry was her buddy! Her boy! And he looked so sad. One kind word from her would lift his spirits, she knew. But she couldn't. Instead, she just kept running.

***

They were trying too hard. Her parents. Robert and Monica. Even Matthew, out in D.C. They were all trying to distract her from the looming prom with offers of trips to Chicago, to Washington, even to Virginia to visit Janine. They were all tempting, but Marisa didn't feel like running away. Why? She had nothing to be ashamed of. She did nothing wrong. The incident and subsequent breakup circulated around school like wildfire. Some people apologized to her, saying they were sorry it happened. She just glared at them. The ones who were talking about her behind her back would openly stare at her in the hallways then turn away guiltily when she caught them. Then there were people like Kristin, who looked like they wanted to say something but didn't know what. Barry, she'd heard, was going to prom with DeAnna Lukic, a junior who'd moved to Petersville two years ago. She'd asked him. Marisa wondered if that meant she was buying the tickets. Wondered if his grandmother would take pictures of them before the dance. If he'd dance with her all night. If he'd kiss her afterward.

OK, she had to stop this. She had to stop torturing herself. Janine, during a phone conversation a week before prom, forced her to look on the bright side.

"Girl, you are going to meet so many men at Michigan!"

"State, Janine, Michigan *State*!" She had to correct her all the time. She kept forgetting they were two different schools.

"Oh yeah. At Michigan State. Barry and his stringy blonde hair will be just a memory. Remember how all the guys down here were all in to you?"

Marisa smiled at the memory. "They were not!"

"Girl, you know they were. They were like, 'J, your cousin is fine.' And 'J, your cousin is sweet and so pretty!' And they all thought you had the nicest grade of hair. Trust me, those guys from Detroit will be all over you at college. You'll forget all about Barry."

But she didn't know if she could forget him. Or even wanted to. He was a vital part of her childhood and teenage years. How could she reminisce about anything without thinking about him? And when would the thoughts of him stop hurting?

Prom came and Marisa worked in the store until six-thirty. Afterward, her father grilled some steaks and vegetables and the whole family ate on the newly built wooden deck. Even her grandmother came outside and pointed a shaky finger at her garden while patting Marisa's hand in approval. It didn't look as vibrant as if she'd gone out there herself, but Marisa was doing an OK job.

That night, Marisa couldn't help sitting on her window seat to watch Barry's house. He was out with DeAnna and all of her classmates celebrating their last big night together before graduation.

DeAnna didn't belong there. She did. They were *her* friends. Her lifelong friends. They should have been celebrating this together.

A low rumble vibrated through the quiet air and she was startled to see the Montgomery's sedan swing into the driveway. Barry stepped out, his black tuxedo jacket slung over his shoulder. It was only eleven-thirty. No after-party? No beach? No hanging out until dawn? She watched as he slumped into the house with his head down and closed the door. That pose, that dejected walk. Seeing it suddenly erased all bitterness from her. She didn't want him to be sad forever. And truthfully, she was sick of being mad. Tired of always fighting. There were only two more weeks until the seniors' last day. And only three weeks until graduation. She wanted to have fun.

***

Slowly, she was able to start mingling with Kristin and Tara again. Jen, she only spoke to when she had to. The three of them planned the senior dinner, senior breakfast and baccalaureate. They were together when it came time to pick up their caps and gowns. They were together when they studied for their final final exams. They cried together when listening to the class song, "The Greatest Love of All."

On the last day of school, she was cleaning out her locker during free hour when she felt someone behind her. It was Barry.

"Hi." His hands were stuck in his faded blue jean pockets and he fidgeted from one foot to the other.

"Hi." Throwing an old trig paper in the open trash bin, she paused in her work.

"A lot of crap to clean out, huh?" Barry had always teased her about her messy locker. The comment made her smile wanly.

"Yeah, I should have kept it cleaner. But whatever." She forced herself to look at the mess instead of at him.

"I know you told me not to talk to you again, but I had to. I had to explain."

She held up a hand. "Stop. I'm fine. I don't want to talk about it."

Sighing, he bit his lip. "But I – "

"No, Barry, please. I'm fine. I'm over it."

"Well, can I at least apologize?" The question was spoken so sincerely, so earnestly that she almost wanted to cry all over again.

"Marisa, I...I'm sorry I hurt you. I hate myself for hurting you. I literally wanted to beat myself up. I wanted you to beat me up. Or your dad. Or your brothers. I deserved it. I was a chicken and stupid and a wimp. I know that. And...I know I don't deserve your forgiveness. I know our friendship will never be the way it was..." At that, his voice shook and a lump formed in Marisa's throat. "But I...I'm so sorry. I know you hate me, but I had to say how sorry I am."

"I don't hate you, Barry." She finally looked up at him. "It takes too much energy to hate you."

A small smile, then sobering. "I can't believe I did this to you. I just...you'll always be my best friend. Do you know that? No matter what. Even though I don't deserve a friend like you."

Marisa caught his gaze and for a moment, all of their years together flashed before her eyes. But just like a movie spinning on its last reel, it stopped abruptly. She knew this was the end. "Thank you, Barry."

"Uh, I guess we're not...we're not still walking together at graduation?" They'd made plans to walk together early last fall when they knew they'd be first and second in the class. Graduation without him on her arm just wouldn't seem right.

"No. We're not walking together. I'm walking alone." She'd made the decision last week and gotten Mr. Amos' approval. She was the valedictorian. She was the only black. She wanted to walk in with her head high. Alone.

"OK. So uh, if I don't see you before then, good luck on your speech."

"Thanks. You too." They stared at each other another few seconds before Marisa stepped forward. Stiffly, they embraced each other. Then it turned into a full-fledged, heartfelt hug. Marisa was glad. It took too much energy to hate him. And besides, who was she going to brag to when Michigan State beat Michigan this fall?

Book Two
"Fight the Power"
1987-1991

185

CHAPTER 10

September 1987

It was too quiet and starting to get dark outside.

Marisa sighed, then backed into her dorm room, softly closing the door. "Whatever you do, leave your dorm door open as much as possible," Matthew had told her. "It's the best way to meet people." But how could she meet people if there were no people out there to meet?

"Where is everyone?" her mother asked when they dropped her off for the last time two hours ago. "Where is Charla?" The first roommate she'd met was out. She was from some suburb of Detroit, which meant she knew a bunch of people on campus. Marisa, however, knew no one. No one from her senior class – except her – went to MSU. No one from the class before her went. So Charla was probably out having fun on this Saturday night. Marisa didn't care for her too much – she already took up half of the closet space – but at least she was someone to talk to. Her other two roommates hadn't arrived yet. The resident assistant (R.A., she reminded her mom) told her she had the most coveted room in the building: the first-floor quad, a huge corner room with four girls.

Marisa eyed her newly made bed – thanks Mama – and debated curling into a ball and crying into her pillow but didn't want to seem like an immature small-town girl, so she decided to arrange her toiletries in her shower caddy. That took all of two minutes. What next? Posters! Yes, she would turn on her new boombox and put up the posters around her bed. She snapped Bon Jovi's cassette tape into the boombox then paused before hitting play. What if the black girls on her floor heard her listening to Bon Jovi? No, that wouldn't do. Whitney Houston? No, too mellow. The house mix tape from Chicago that Robert gave her? No, it would seem pathetic to listen to that if there wasn't a party going on. Instead, she clicked the dial to "radio" and turned to the AM R&B station. How cool that she could finally listen to the latest R&B and rap songs? She would finally know what the latest hits were without having to scan the charts in the back of each week's Jet magazine.

Standing on her bed, she taped up her new Chicago Bears posters. There, that was a little better. She walked to her desk and eyed it with a discerning scowl. No high school photos, Janine had said. You want to leave all that behind. Instead, she put up a framed photo of her and her goofy cousin, one of her by herself at the beach with a fabulous sunset behind her and one of her entire family at Robert's post-elopement dinner. Unlike Charla, who had photos of her ugly cat all over the desk, Marisa had no pet photos. No boyfriend photos, either. Seeing the picture of her family made her suddenly homesick and she gave in to the urge to pick up the phone.

Her mother breathlessly answered on the third ring.

"It's me." Marisa tried to swallow the lump in her throat at the sound of her mother's voice.

"Marisa? What's wrong?"

"Nothing," her voice trailed as she perched herself on her desk. "I just wanted to make sure you made it home OK."

Her mother sighed. "Yes, yes, we're just walking in the door." She spoke away from the receiver. "It's Marisa . . . Yes, I know. Marisa, are you all right?"

"Uh..." She was about to tell her how she was homesick already and that it was lonely and too quiet and too dark and couldn't they just stay the weekend, just one more night, when a knock sounded on the door. "Uh, hold on, Mama. Someone's at the door."

She cracked it open to find a heavy, light-skinned black girl standing there. "Hi. Oh, sorry, I didn't know you were on the phone." She was about to walk away when Marisa told her to wait.

"Mama, I'll call you tomorrow. . . Yeah. No, it's a girl from . . . down the hall?" She looked at the girl for confirmation and she smiled and nodded.

After bidding her parents goodbye, Marisa hung up the phone and shrugged. "Sorry about that."

"No problem. I'm Nikki, your neighbor. I live right there." She pointed to the room to her right. "Are you a freshman?"

"Yeah. Uh, I'm Marisa."

"Melissa?"

"No, Marisa."

"Oh." Nikki looked at the door, which had welcome signs with everyone's names on them. "I thought you'd be Charla."

"Me? Charla?" Marisa smirked. "No, that's my roommate."

"The blonde girl with the short hair?"

"Yeah, that's her."

"Huh." Nikki laughed. "Charla sure sounds like a black girl and she's as far from black as you can get."

Marisa laughed. She just made her first MSU friend! She liked her. "Are you a freshman, too?"

"No, I'm a sophomore." Nikki strolled into the room. "You must be from Chicago," she said, eyeing the Bears posters.

"No, my brother lives there, though. I just really like the Bears."

"Obviously." Nikki was surveying the room. "So where are you from?"

"Uh, a small town you probably never heard of." Marisa resumed her perch on her desk, trying to figure out a way to describe Petersville.

Nikki laughed. "A small town? Where is it? In Michigan?"

"Yeah, it's over near Holland." Marisa waved her hand dismissively.

"Holly?"

"No, *Holland.*" She'd never heard of Holland? Or maybe she was just hard of hearing. She looked at her closer, expecting to see a hearing aid or something, but all she saw was dyed brownish hair in a cute asymmetrical cut and big gold earrings. She reminded Marisa of Stacy Lattisaw.

"Oh, that place with all the tulips and the windmills?" Marisa nodded. "Yeah, I think I heard of that. I'm from Detroit." She said proudly, although Marisa didn't know why people were so proud of Detroit. She preferred Chicago. By far.

"Cool."

She didn't know what else to say, especially since Nikki was a sophomore. She already knew people and knew her way around campus, so maybe she could offer her tips on adjusting.

"Where are your other roommates? Not here yet?" She returned to the door and read their names. "Jacqui and Courtney. Maybe Jacqui is black. Not sure about Courtney, though."

"Why do you think Jacqui is black?"

"Cause of the way she spells her name, look." Nikki finally stopped her pacing and stood facing Marisa. "Well, welcome to MSU and Brody and Emmons Hall. You'll like it here. We have a Black Student Alliance and we do lots of stuff together. You should join."

"Um...OK."

"You got a boyfriend back in Holland?" She leaned next to Marisa to peer at her photos.

"No, no boyfriend." She was about to tell her that she wasn't exactly *from* Holland, but decided to drop it. "You?"

"No, I don't have a boyfriend. I did last year, but . . ." her voice trailed off and she shook her head. "He wasn't saved."

"Oh." Marisa didn't know why that mattered. Being saved meant you were a holy roller. One of Grandmama's sisters was in a Pentecostal church and they spoke in tongues and cried and "carried on," as her dad said. She decided to change the subject. "What are you majoring in?"

"Business. What about you?"

"Engineering." Charla was an advertising major but was already thinking about changing majors.

Nikki smiled. "You must be smart then."

How to answer that? Marisa just smiled and shrugged. "Where is everybody tonight? I thought it'd be really busy with people moving in and stuff."

"They're at the bar or at the club." Nikki shook her head. "I don't drink or do any of that. Do you?"

Marisa shook her head. "I'm not even legal yet, so no, I don't drink."

Nikki tilted her head and looked at her, smiling yet puzzled. "You're not legal? Girl, you think that matters to anybody here? They barely even card you at these places around here." She raised an eyebrow at Marisa's expression. "Yes, girl … just you wait."

An awkward silence followed but before Marisa could ask another question, Nikki invited her over to her room.

Nikki's room exhibited the difference between freshman and sophomore style. Marisa gaped at the L-shaped loft, brown papasan chair, throw pillows and stereo.

"Wow…" she breathed. "Your room is amazing." She pictured herself hanging out here with all of the other black girls, watching "21 Jump Street" or "A Different World." Maybe it wasn't such a daydream after all.

"I know, right?" Nikki plopped on the papasan chair. "Sit down. These rap posters belong to my roommate, Trish. I don't listen to secular music. That's my poster." She pointed to a poster of a group called Take 6.

Marisa knew she'd get a funny look, but she had to know. "Who is Take 6? I've never heard of them."

"You never heard of them? They're a gospel group." Nikki tucked her legs underneath her and for the first time, Marisa noticed the Bible on the floor next to her and the inspirational quotes and Scriptures on her desk. Wow. She was really into religion.

"We didn't have any black radio stations over in my neck of the woods," Marisa explained, hoping to alleviate the weird looks she would certainly get when it was revealed that she knew next to nothing about the hottest songs, dances, slang, fashion or hairstyles. "Only Casey Kasem."

Nikki laughed, not really in a mocking way but in an "I understand" way. "Well, they don't have any up here, either."

"They have a black radio station," Marisa interjected.

"Girl, one radio station. And an AM station, too? Please." She shook her head. "We about lost our minds up here last year."

"At least we got one." Marisa felt the need to defend it. It was all she'd ever had and she was enjoying it so far. She even had plans to put a blank cassette tape in her boombox and tape the weekly countdown so she'd have something to listen to when she went home for the holidays.

She still hadn't taken a seat and just as she was about to flop onto one of the floor pillows, she heard a deep voice behind her. "What's up, girl?"

Turning, she saw a light-skinned, thin guy with glasses bop into the room. He was wearing gray sweatpants and a red Adidas T-shirt.

"Heeeeeey! Mike!" Nikki unfolded herself from the papasan chair to rise and hug him. "How you doing? When'dyougethere?" Marisa noticed how Nikki's voice had changed all of a sudden and she wondered if she was trying to talk white just because Marisa did.

"I just came in today. What about you?" Mike glanced at Marisa and then tried to pretend he hadn't.

"Yesterday. Hey, meet Marisa. She's a freshman next door in the quad. Marisa, this is Mike. He lives upstairs." Nikki didn't act like she liked him; Marisa assumed they were just friends.

"Hi." She said softly.

Mike smiled and looked Marisa directly in the eye. "How you doing?" Apparently that was the de facto version of "hi" in black college culture.

"Good." Suddenly self-conscious, she started to back away. "Well, I'll let you two catch up."

"Where you from, Marisa?" Mike asked.

Not this again. "Uh….over near Kalamazoo and Grand Rapids."

"I thought you said Holly," Nikki piped up.

"Holland," she corrected. Good God, was this going to happen every time she met someone?

"I heard of Holland," said Mike. Grinning slyly, he licked his lips in a wanna-be LL Cool J way. "Not many sistas over there, huh?"

Shaking her head, Marisa agreed. There was an awkward silence while he continued to stare at her. Here it comes. Marisa always figured that if she was ever around any black guys they would flock to her, flirt with her and basically harass her all the time. Not that she was conceited, but she *was* pretty. With great hair. And to hear Mama tell it, big legs that black men would love. And she just knew that being from Petersville, she was different. And different equaled exotic.

"Well, it was nice meeting you, Mike. Nikki, I'll see you later."

Ducking into the security of her room, Marisa sighed with relief. She'd survived it. Her first introduction to black college life.

***

Around midnight she heard her roommate Charla tiptoe into the room, but what good was tiptoeing if you turned on the desk light, the closet light and knocked over a stack of books?

Rising on her elbows, Marisa raised an eyebrow at her. "Hi."

"Oh, I'm so sorry!" Charla's face was flushed and she giggled. "I didn't mean to wake you up!"

"That's OK. Where were you?" Marisa sat up, suddenly in the mood for girl talk.

She listened with envy as Charla recapped the club she'd gone to with friends from across campus. When she finally stopped talking, Marisa asked her about lunch tomorrow. It was going to be her first time eating in the cafeteria and she didn't want to eat alone. Nikki would be at church so Charla was it.

"Yeah, let's head over around 11," Charla agreed. "I didn't want to eat alone, either."

Others on the floor felt the same way, because when Marisa and Charla left their room the next morning they ran into red-headed Molly and tall brunette Sharon, who were also heading to lunch. The four of them made the trek across the courtyard to the cafeteria, where other half-sleepy yet terrified freshmen lined up for their first college meal. Marisa watched what the others were doing, showed her ID with her meal plan-colored stickers, then ventured to the right where the other girls were in line.

Once at a table, Marisa looked around and was surprised at how few black students she saw. Nikki made it seem like Emmons and Brody were teeming with black students but she was the only one. Again. Disappointed, she turned her attention to the table, where the girls were making plans to go out tonight.

"There's a place over on M.A.C. where you only have to be 18 to get in," Sharon was saying. Her sister was a senior at MSU so she knew more than everyone else at the table. "They still won't serve you but at least we can hang out and dance. How about it?"

Everyone, including Marisa, nodded. Going out with them was better than sitting in the dark in her room again. Besides, she liked Molly and Sharon. They were high school friends from Jackson and already told Marisa not to make jokes about the state prison being there because they'd already heard them all.

Later that afternoon, Marisa's other roommate appeared. Her black hair was teased four inches high and she had on heavy black eyeliner and blue eyeshadow. She was wearing tight jeans and a Metallica T-shirt.

To everyone's surprise, she was also from Jackson and immediately hugged Sharon and Molly with a squeal.

"Are you on this floor?"

"Yes, I'm right here, two doors down from you!" Sharon turned to Marisa, "Courtney, this is your roommate, Marisa. Marisa, this is Courtney. We know her from Jackson, although she went to a different school."

"Hi."

"Hey, Marisa. Nice to meet you. This is my boyfriend, Jamie. He dropped me off." Wow. Her boyfriend, and not her parents, brought her to college? On closer inspection, Marisa realized that Jamie was gorgeous. Underneath all of that hair was a strong jaw, tanned skin and green, sleepy eyes.

The entire group walked into Marisa's room and settled down to chat. Marisa learned that Courtney went to the Catholic high school in Jackson after being kicked out of the public school for smoking and skipping class one too many times as a freshman. Her parents hated Jamie but the only way Courtney would go to college was to continue seeing him, so they relented. Marisa figured they'd last until Thanksgiving before breaking up.

The conversation was fun, fast and lighthearted. Courtney was cool. Jamie, who would probably be on campus every weekend, was cool, too. Molly and Sharon were cool. Charla, on the other hand, not cool. When she returned to the room, she took one look at Courtney and Jamie and turned her nose up. She then immediately inspected her desk – and her precious computer – to make sure nothing had been touched. Courtney caught Marisa's eye and she shook her head, silently agreeing that Charla was their common enemy. Just her luck that she'd be stuck with a roommate who reminded her of Jen.

As the group continued to laugh and talk, Marisa noticed a few black girls peek in while walking down the hall. She caught their eye and smiled tentatively, but they didn't smile back. They just looked at her and kept walking. Marisa knew what they were thinking: Look at the Oreo. She'd rather be with the white girls than with us. That wasn't true at all, but Marisa had to make friends somewhere, somehow and these girls here were the friendliest by far. So she continued to hang with them. They hung out at the bar that night, they hung out in the cafeteria –where she was still puzzled at the lack of black people she saw – they hung out in her room, the biggest on the floor.

By Friday, after making it through her first three days of classes, she returned to her dorm and was walking past the bathroom when a head popped out of the room across the hall. "Hi!"

Marisa jumped. "God, you scared me."

Laughing, the girl pushed her glasses up. "I've been watching you. You're a Gemini, aren't you?"

"What?" Marisa was stunned. "How did you know that?"

The girl continued to laugh. "I knew it. I'm really into astrology and you seem like a Gemini."

Marisa shook her head, still stunned. "But you don't even know me."

"Yes, I do."

"No, you don't!"

"You're Marisa. You live down in the quad with those two white girls. One of them is a punk rocker. She cool, though."

Trying to wrap her brain around this bizarre conversation, Marisa came closer. "Yeah, that's Courtney. Who are you?"

"Shawnda. I'm a Libra."

"How nice for you." Marisa didn't care if she was rude. The girl was a lunatic.

Shawnda didn't seem to mind. "You're not into astrology?"

"No, not really."

"You should try it." They stared at each other. Shawnda had a big butt, glasses and a shoulder-length bob. "I heard you like the Bears. I'm from Chicago."

"How do you know so much about me?" Marisa frowned.

"You can't miss those Bears posters on the wall! Your door is open all the time and they're pretty hard to miss." Shawnda shook her head. "What, you think I'm stalking you or something?"

"You basically attack me in the hallway then tell me you've been—" air quotes – "watching me. What am I supposed to think?"

Instead of being offended, Shawnda laughed. "Girl, you crazy. There are seven black girls on this floor. We all know each other. You're the only one who don't hang out with us."

Marisa felt her face grow hot. Seven black girls? She only knew Nikki and now this crazy girl. "No one has invited me anywhere. How am I supposed to hang out?"

"You don't need an invitation! Look, next time we're hanging out I'll come get you, OK?"

"OK." Lingering, Marisa peeked into her room and saw a standard dorm room with very few decorations. It was, however, spotless. "You haven't unpacked yet?"

"Yeah," Shawnda glanced behind her. "You talking about our room? I'm kind of a neat freak. I don't like a lot of clutter."

"Yeah, but posters on the wall wouldn't be clutter."

"True, but I don't know what posters I want up. I was going to bring some that I ripped out of *Playgirl*, but I figured I couldn't put up any naked men," Shawnda laughed.

Marisa tried to hide her shock and failed. "You were really going to put up pictures from *Playgirl*?"

"Girl, yes. I have a subscription. Have you seen the latest issue?" She went into her closet and rummaged around in a duffel bag, pulling out a magazine. "Here...."

"Uh, no thanks." Marisa grimaced.

"Just look," Shawnda turned to the centerfold, where a tanned, blonde man lay back against a bearskin rug with his legs open, one arm above his head and one hand on his chiseled, shiny chest. His penis stood erect, like it was pointing directly at Marisa. She turned away. "Eww."

"Eww? Girl.....come on. Look at that!" Shawnda continued to stare at the man. "Mmmm-mmm....That is one good-looking white boy."

Shaking her head, Marisa inched toward the door. No one she knew had ever read *Playgirl*, although Tara and Jen had tried to peek at it once during a trip to Grand Rapids, before being discovered by the salesclerk.

"You got a boyfriend? You do, don't you?" Shawnda wrinkled her cheeks to push her glasses up. "Is he hung like this?"

"Hung?"

"Hung!" She tapped the centerfold. "Do his dick look like this?"

"Oh my God..." What kind of girl was this? Who talked to a complete stranger like this? Lowering her head, she trained her eyes on the blue carpet. "No, I do not have a boyfriend."

"No? You look the type." Throwing the magazine onto her bed, Shawnda hoisted her ample lower half onto the top of her desk.

"And what type is that?" Even though she'd wanted to leave, something kept her hanging around. Maybe it was Shawnda's complete lack of guile, her openness, her humor . . . whatever it was, she was the total opposite of Marisa and somehow she was mesmerized by it.

"You're pretty, you got nice hair, you speak good…"

"Well," Marisa corrected before she could stop herself.

Shawnda shook her head, staring at her. "See? If you don't have a boyfriend now, you will soon."

"Who cares? I'm here for school, not a boyfriend." She recited her mother's classic reminder from the summer, especially when she'd see Barry around town and come home in a funk.

"Don't matter. Someone's gonna snatch you up." Giggling, Shawnda glanced out the door at two black guys walking by. "Like them," she pointed. Doing so caused the guys to stop at the door.

"What?" One of them asked.

"Nothing," Shawnda smiled and batted her eyes. "I thought you were someone else."

Smirking, the dark-skinned guy asked, "Oh yeah? Who?"

"Nobody! Dang, ain't nobody trying to talk to you!" Shawnda chirped with a yes-I'm-trying-to-talk-to-you laugh. "Marisa, are you trying to talk to them?"

Marisa shook her head, not trusting herself to speak. She was never good at flirting and flirting with black guys would have been absolutely impossible. Better to stand back and watch the expert do it.

"See, we didn't mean to call you in here. Sorry to take up your time." With a sideways smile, Shawnda waved at the guys.

"Alright, then. Later." The guys walked off without even looking Marisa's way.

"You. Are. Crazy." Marisa couldn't help giggling in admiration.

"I know, right? I don't care." She went to her dresser and began combing her hair. "What time you going to dinner? You want to go with us?"

Swallowing, Marisa didn't know how to explain that she had plans to go to dinner at the Union with Molly and Sharon because there was going to be a pep rally nearby before tomorrow's game against Florida State, the sixth-ranked team in the country. It was going to be her first big-time college football game and she was so excited she could barely sleep. "Aren't you going to the pep rally?"

"Pep rally?" Shawnda acted like she'd never heard the word.

"Yeah," Marisa couldn't contain her enthusiasm. Her voice got louder and her eyes got bigger the more she spoke about the pep rally, dinner and the game tomorrow. Shawnda's hand paused while gripping the black comb as she surveyed Marisa.

"Girl, you are too happy for me." Shaking her head, she sprayed a smelly, white cloud of hair spray all over her hair, causing Marisa to cough.

"So are you going?" she sputtered.

"To a football game? Hell no."

"No? We're going to be good this year."

Shawnda just shook her head and continued her beauty routine, moving on to lip gloss. "Girl, I don't care about all that. You have fun, though. Who you going with?"

"Uh, Molly and Sharon. Do you know them?" Her voice lost some of its spark as she realized – yet again – that she was choosing white girls over black ones. But dang, who in their right mind wouldn't want to go to a Big Ten football game?

"Yeah, I met Molly. Redhead, right?" Shawnda seemed to be bored with the conversation as she continued to analyze herself in the mirror.

"That's her. Well, I gotta go. Nice meeting you, Shawnda." She rapidly walked out of the room, not looking back while trying to figure out what exactly just happened. Either Shawnda liked her and wanted to be her friend or she was just talking to her to find out why she was so different and standoffish. And why she was the only black girl on the floor who didn't "hang."

***

THE KITCHEN ISN'T WHERE YOU COOK

Marisa's third and final roommate arrived on Sunday morning, a full week after everyone else had moved in. Jacqui was an unsmiling, dark-skinned black girl who'd asked Marisa within five minutes of entering the room with her parents and boyfriend if they'd left her any closet space or if she was "supposed to live out of her suitcase for the whole year?"

"Oh, don't worry," Marisa scurried over, kicking some of her things out of the way. "We'll make room for your stuff. You were so late getting here that we didn't know if you were coming at all, so our stuff just kind of . . ." her voice trailed.

"Well, I'm here now. Did you leave me any drawers?" Jacqui stepped around Marisa and stood looking at the nearby dresser.

"Uh, yeah, we have plenty of drawer space. Courtney and Charla took that dresser over there and this one is mine. . . and now yours." Everyone stood without a word, while Marisa wondered what the heck was wrong with all of them. And why on Earth was she a week late to college? Who does that? "So where . . . " She was about to ask, "Where were you," but caught herself just in time. "Where are you from?"

"Fort Wayne." Jacqui threw the words over her shoulder while she walked back to her boyfriend who was staring at the posters and pictures on the walls. She took his hand and possessively caressed his arm through his brown leather jacket. Great. Another roommate who was obsessed with her high school boyfriend.

Quiet greetings circled the room before Marisa excused herself to take a shower, where she came face-to-face with Shawnda.

"Hey girl..."

"Hey." Marisa tried not to laugh at the large pink shower cap on her head. It was two sizes too big. She decided to confide in Shawnda about her new roommate. Maybe she could read the stars to find out why she was so rude.

"Your new roommate is just now movin' in?" Shawnda asked incredulously. "But classes already started!"

"I know."

"Where she been?"

Shrugging, Marisa shifted her powder blue shower caddy to her other hand. "I have no idea. I was afraid to ask because she's not very . . . talkative."

"What, she shy or sumthin'?"

"No, just not very . . . happy."

Shawnda grunted. "Girl, everybody can't be as happy as you! You be skipping around here like you in heaven!"

"What?" Marisa couldn't help laughing and Shawnda giggled along with her, straightening the shower cap.

"You so happy to be in college and to be going to football games and shit. You be like some Cathy Co-ed or something. Ha!" Laughing at her own joke, Shawnda disappeared into the shower area. Marisa followed and took the stall next to her.

"Anyway," she drawled, trying to sound like her cousin Janine, "they're still in my room, so I need someplace to change after I get out of the shower. Can I change in your room?" she heard herself asking before she could overthink it.

"Yeah, girl, I don't care."

In Shawnda's room, they continued to talk about Jacqui. "Why do you think she's so late?" Shawnda asked.

"When I was talking to her mother just now, she said Jacqui needed some time to 'sort through some things' before coming to school," Marisa said, watching as Shawnda slathered her arms with lotion. "That's why she was late."

"What sorta things?"

"She didn't say. Her boyfriend? Maybe she didn't want to leave him." Marisa took out her Jergen's lotion and started in on her legs and feet.

"Girl, ain't no nigga worth missing a whole week of college." Shawnda disappeared into the closet and pulled down a pair of jeans and a red pullover sweater.

"I know," said Marisa, adding, "and he's not even that cute."

"Tsk." Shawnda shook her head as she pulled on her jeans while Marisa tried not to look. Once they were on – snugly – she threw her sweater on and watched as Marisa easily put on some jeans and a thin long-sleeved shirt. "Did you play sports or something? You're so fit."

Shrugging, Marisa inwardly glowed at the compliment. She'd never been called fit or skinny before, not in Petersville, where everyone looked like "sticks," according to Mama. "I ran track and I was a cheerleader. Can't you tell from my big legs?"

"Girl, I would die for those legs! I don't know how these chicken calves hold up all of this ass I got," she smirked. "But men don't mind! They love all this meat!" Cackling, she brushed her hair quickly, smeared on some lipstick and disappeared into the closet again for her shoes. "You ready?"

Startled, Marisa froze. "Ready for what?"

"Lunch! What, did you get up early and eat breakfast or something?"

"No, I didn't eat yet." Marisa paused. She didn't know when Molly or Sharon or the rest of the girls were going to lunch but she didn't want to eat alone in case she'd missed them.

In the cafeteria, Marisa automatically moved in line to the right. Shawnda, however, moved to the left. "Where you going?" they asked in unison.

"I always go in this line," she explained.

"Get over here," Shawnda said. "You don't want to sit over there."

Confused, Marisa moved behind Shawnda. "Sit over where?"

"On that side. We all sit over here."

Marisa didn't know who "we" were, but once she'd gotten her food and followed Shawnda, she realized who "they" were.

Unbeknownst to her, there was a second dining room. This dining room was smaller and decorated more sparsely, but it cleared up something that had been confusing her all week. It was where the black students ate.

"I didn't know this was over here!" she said as she followed Shawnda to the beverage station.

"Girl, where did you think that other line was going?"

Shrugging, Marisa felt stupid. "I don't know....uh, I thought it curved around...over there..." her voice trailed.

Shawnda shook her head. "Whatever, girl. Only the white kids eat over there. No wonder I never saw you at dinner!"

Amazed, Marisa glanced around the room. Yep, there was Nikki, her friend Mike and several other black students she'd seen around Emmons. Mystery solved! Now that she was eating in the "black" dining room, maybe they'd stop looking at her like she was a traitor.

Shawnda took a seat at an empty table next to Nikki, Mike and several others, but they were packing up their trays to leave. They all greeted each other and Marisa noticed a few girls giving her extra glances. Or was it just her imagination?

"What'd you do last night? I knocked on your door and no one answered." Shawnda was buttering her roll while keeping an eye on the room, presumably for cute guys.

"Well, after the game a bunch of us hung out..." Marisa didn't go into detail. She assumed Shawnda wouldn't be interested.

"So you like hanging out with white people, huh?"

"No. I mean....it's just what I'm used to. And Molly and Sharon are nice."

"If you say so...." Shawnda dug into her meat loaf, made a face, shrugged and kept eating. "It's just so weird being here with all of them!"

"All of who?" The meatloaf wasn't too bad; it wasn't as good as Grandmama's, but Marisa was starving so it would do.

"All these white people! I never seen this many white people in my life."

"Really?" Shocked, Marisa stared at her then glanced around at the random white students still huddled together in this smaller dining hall. "How can that be?"

"I grew up on the South Side of Chicago. We had no white people in my neighborhood! And my school had maybe – " she put her fork down to count on her fingers – "ten or eleven, tops."

"That's it?" Marisa was amazed.

"Yep. They were cool, though. They may as well have been black, they talked like us and liked our music and shit. But these motherfuckers..." she looked around the room. "They walk around like they ain't got a care in the world."

Nodding, Marisa didn't know how to answer. She knew Shawnda thought the same thing about her. But hopefully, now that she finally had a black friend, a black roommate and knew where she needed to eat from now on, maybe she would start to fit in for once. For even though she'd loved Petersville, was popular and had a bunch of friends, she always remembered that she was different. A difference that she couldn't change. It slapped her in the face with a fury during the whole Barry/prom fiasco, but now....maybe.....she would start to feel complete.

CHAPTER 11

October-November 1987

September turned into October quickly, and the campus became awash in shades of orange, red and yellow. Sometimes Marisa would walk home from class and stop on a bridge or next to the river and just stare. The campus was beautiful, and she still couldn't believe she was here, walking along with the other students like she knew what she was doing. She and Shawnda were becoming fast friends and even Jacqui started to warm up to her more.

One night, while Marisa was washing her face in the bathroom, she heard the conversation in Shawnda's room between Jacqui, Shawnda and another girl named Janet. Jacqui was slowly coming out of her defensive shell, and Shawnda's room had become the gathering spot for the black girls in the dorm due to her big color TV. Stepping out of the bathroom, Marisa leaned against the dorm room door and listened. They were talking about guys and as usual, Shawnda was center stage, talking about her sex life and how she needed to "get some" soon. The other girls nodded in agreement then looked up at Marisa.

"Hey girl," Shawnda greeted.

"Hey," Marisa began to back away. She had nothing to contribute to this conversation so better to disappear before she became embarrassed. But Shawnda called her back.

"You seen any guys you like around here?"

"Me?" Marisa paused. She hadn't. "Actually, no."

"That's just what we were saying! Where all the fine men at? These dudes look like nerds around here."

"I heard they're all on east campus, around Akers or Hubbard," said Janet.

"No, I bet they be over by the football building. What are those dorms over there? Wilson? Case? That's where all the football players live," Shawnda declared. Hmm, meeting a football player would be cool, Marisa thought. Especially Lorenzo White, the team's star player.

"We should go over there for dinner one day," Janet said. "Marisa, you in?"

Laughing softly, she straightened and turned away. "Sure, I'm in. But I'm here to learn, not to love." She smiled as she heard the girls laugh and scoff.

"You just wait! Wait until some guy scoops you up! You'll be learning something totally different!"

***

"Sorry," Marisa muttered automatically after bumping into a guy in the lobby while getting the mail. She'd been looking at a postcard from Janine, who had detailed Hampton's Homecoming weekend. She was smiling at the postcard and Janine's familiar large, circular writing and didn't see the tall guy striding through the lobby.

"You're all right," he said, and his deep – really deep – voice made her look up. He smiled at her. "Must be reading some good news."

"Oh," she smiled again, looking down at the postcard. "Just a note from my goofy cousin."

"Oh." He kept smiling at her.

"Sorry, I just didn't see you," she said, wondering how on Earth she could have missed him, though. He was as wide as a refrigerator, as tall as the vending machine and the color of creamy coffee. The analogies made her stomach growl. She couldn't seem to move her feet as she stared at his wide shoulders stretching out his soft brown leather jacket.

He seemed to read her mind and chuckled. "You didn't see *me*? That's a first."

Laughing with him, she continued to stare. Damn, his smile was gorgeous. His hair was cut in the latest short fade and his black backpack was slung over his right shoulder casually. She didn't remember ever seeing him before. "I'm Marisa," she said, shocked that she was taking the first move.

"Kyle." He nodded at her and she flushed when he looked her up and down. Thankfully, she was dressed cute today, in a plaid skirt with green tights and dark blue cardigan sweater. She looked like a private school girl, but she'd gotten plenty of compliments on the outfit. Sensing his approval, she purposely tucked her hair – her best feature – over her right ear. She might actually be getting the hang of this flirting thing.

"Nice to meet you." She couldn't think of anything else to say and an awkward silence followed. So much for this flirting thing.

"You, too." His gaze held hers for several seconds before he started backing away. "Well, I'll see you around. Marisa." He turned and strode away as her gaze fell from his shoulders to his butt.

"Damn...." She muttered. Walking away, she floated back to her room, fanning herself with the postcard.

But she didn't see him around. Not that week, not the next nor the next. She figured he didn't live in Brody and was just visiting someone that day she'd met him. Hopefully it wasn't a girlfriend. She'd spent as much time in the lobby as she could without making it weird in the hopes that they'd run into each other again. Mostly she used the TV as an excuse because her roommates never did like to watch "Knots Landing" or "Monday Night Football" with her. Unfortunately, watching "MNF" in the lobby came with the company of a bunch of white guys who thought she was the "coolest chick ever" because she liked – and knew a lot about – football.

November came and with it, thoughts of the Rose Bowl. With a pivotal game against Indiana looming, Marisa became obsessed with the football team's chances of going to Pasadena. On a particularly cloudy and blustery day, she was sitting in the lobby of the Union reading the sports section of The State News when she saw a pair of dark blue denim legs standing before her. Looking up, she saw that it was him. Kyle. Looking as yummy as ever in his leather jacket, this time buttressed with a brown and red plaid scarf.

"Hey!" He sat down next to her. "How are you doing?"

She folded the paper and set it beside her, mad at herself for throwing her hair back into a banana-clip ponytail. Instead of a cute skirt, she was in stone-washed jeans and a pink Guess sweatshirt underneath a heavy fall jacket. "Hi. I'm good." She paused, wondering if he could hear her heart pounding in her chest. "How are you?" No, dummy, too formal, she thought to herself. You should have said, "How you doin'?" That sounded more casual.

"All right. You reading the sports section?" He leaned over her to grab it. Good God, he smelled like Drakkar Noir, her favorite cologne. She thought she was going to melt right then and there.

"Yeah, I'm so psyched about this game against Indiana," she blurted out. Talking about sports put her at ease. "We have got to win this! Can you imagine how cool it would be to go to the Rose Bowl? Especially my first year here?"

He glanced at her, his smile turning into a laugh. "That would be very cool." He paused as he continued to gaze at her. Looking down at the paper, he asked, "So, you're a freshman?"

"Yes." She tried not to stare at his broad shoulders, so she kept her eyes trained on the hallway, where a group of students rushed in for coverage against the cold. "How about you?"

"Me too."

She was surprised. "You are?"

Glancing at her again, he grinned. "Yeah. Why? Are you surprised?"

"No," she lied. "You just look...."

"Old?" He teased.

Blushing, she playfully hit him on the shoulder then immediately regretted it. Good God, his arm was as solid as a rock. "No, you just look like you know what you're doing around here."

"Oh. And you don't?"

"I'm learning," she admitted.

"As am I," Kyle said.

Wanting to talk to him longer, she blurted, "Where do you live? I haven't seen you around Emmons at all." Shoot. Why did she say that? That let him know she'd been looking for him.

He knew it, too, as he leaned back and tried not to smile. "I live in Shaw." She'd never met anyone who lived in Shaw so she couldn't come up with an excuse to go stalk him in the lobby.

"Oh." Wanting – needing – to know more about him, she asked, "Where are you from?"

"Philly."

She did a double take. "Philly?" He nodded. "Philadelphia?"

Laughing, he leaned back against the seat and rubbed his palms on his knees. "Yes, Philadelphia. I know, I know. What am I doing here, right?"

"Yeah." She was perplexed. She'd never met anyone from Philly. She'd never even been to Philly. The only thing she knew about Philly was that "Rocky" took place there.

"My moms went here. My pop, too. They met here. He played football here back in the day."

She loved the way his deep voice said "moms and pop." "Really? That's cool." So that's why he was so built. "You don't play, do you?"

He shook his head. "Nah. I played in high school and I was recruited by some small schools, but my parents didn't want me to play college ball."

"Really? Why not?"

He pointed to his temple and looked her in the eye. "Up here. They wanted me to concentrate on my studies. And honestly, I just wasn't feeling it anymore. It would have been like having a job or something."

"Oh." She didn't know if she agreed with that, because she thought there would be nothing cooler than to be on the MSU team this year when they had a great chance to go to the Rose Bowl. "So what are you majoring in that's so important?" Then she paused, realizing that she sounded too nosy. "I'm sorry. I'm asking you too many questions. You don't have to answer any more..."

"No, it's all right," he shifted in his seat and his shoulder bumped hers for a second. During that second, Marisa caught her breath. She didn't remember even Keith making her feel this way. Back then she was just nervous and shy and self-conscious. Not sure why Kyle brought out a more talkative side in her. "I'm a physics major."

"Oh my God..." she let her words hang in the air. "You must be a genius."

He laughed again. "No, I'm just good at what I like." Pausing, he glanced at her again, letting his eyes roam over her hair. "What about you?"

"What about me?" She asked dumbly.

"What are you majoring in?"

"Oh. Engineering." It used to sound impressive, until he said "physics."

"What kind of engineering?"

She'd been asked that question a lot lately and she had no idea. "I'm not sure yet. Maybe civil or mechanical." She shrugged. "I don't know. I have a couple of years to figure it out."

"Well, you must be pretty smart yourself if you're majoring in engineering." He turned his head away, averting his gaze, which she found odd.

"I guess." Silence wafted down upon them and she unfurled her legs from her Indian pose, checking her watch dramatically. "Well, I guess I better go. . ." In truth, her next class didn't start until one-thirty and it was only noon. She'd come to the Union to grab lunch but got distracted by the sports section she spotted on the way in.

"Which way are you going?" He asked, suddenly looking at her once again.

"I'm just going to go grab some lunch over here. My next class is in Olds Hall."

"Oh. Want some company?"

Blushing, she caught his gaze and was rendered speechless for a second. "Sure."

He kept staring at her then seemed to talk to himself. "Nah, maybe I better not."

"Excuse me?" He was really starting to act weird.

"You are beautiful." He blurted out, staring at her once again.

"Uh...thanks." She smiled, heartened by the fact that he thought she was pretty. Was she supposed to say that he was handsome? Because he definitely – definitely – was.

"You must have a boyfriend, though," he began, then his eyes got big as she shook her head. "No boyfriend? At all? Not at home?" She continued to shake her head. "Not here?"

"Nope."

"What the ...How did the dudes in Emmons not snatch you up already?"

"Snatch me up?" She scoffed. "That's the second time I've heard someone say that to me. I'm not someone to be 'snatched' up. I'm here to learn, not for a boyfriend."

"OK, OK, I hear you."

Dang it! Maybe her saying that caused him to think she didn't want to talk to him. Ugh...why was all of this so hard? She picked at the fabric of the seat, trying to think of a way to rescind her words. "I mean I'm not actively looking for a boyfriend. If it happens, it happens." That didn't sound much better, so she decided to just shut up.

"I hear you. That's why I debated coming over here when I saw you. I don't need distractions." He looked her in the eyes again. "But I do need to know you."

She melted. Right there in the middle of the Union lobby, with her stone-washed jeans and heavy jacket and pink Guess sweatshirt, she melted.

***

Lunch was magical. Well, as magical as a burger and fries at Burger King could be. The conversation flowed so easily that it felt like she'd known him forever. She continued her inquisition and learned he was an only child, his parents were both teachers and that his favorite rap group was Eric B. and Rakim, whom she'd never even heard of.

Then it was his turn to ask the questions. He was intrigued by her parents as small business owners and seemed impressed by her brothers' education and accomplishments. Then he asked about her dorm life, which sent the conversation on an entirely different level as she described her roommates. She couldn't believe she was sitting here with this total stranger gabbing like this. Her smile was wide, the laughter easy and sincere. He was funny but in a teasing way. He laughed at her jokes, too, which she found odd because she'd never considered herself funny. Before she knew it, he was reminding her that her class was about to start.

"Oh shoot..." she looked at her watch. She had five minutes. "I better go." Standing slowly, she took a deep breath and smiled at him. "Thanks for lunch, Kyle." He had insisted on paying and wouldn't take no for an answer. Almost like a real date.

"No problem." He stood, too. Stepping close to her, he shoved a hand in his jeans pocket, leaned forward and asked quietly, "Can I get your number? Or your last name, so I can look you up?"

Melting and sighing intermingled within Marisa, who – matching his quiet tone – gave him both.

"Thanks. Enjoy your class. I'll talk to you later." Reluctantly, she turned and walked away, trying not to look behind her. The temptation was too great, though, and she turned at the entryway to find him still standing at the table, watching her. She felt warm all over, smiled at him again, threw two fingers in a wave, then practically floated down the steps.

Walking back to her dorm that afternoon, she felt like she was going to burst. The smile hadn't left her face for a second all afternoon, even as the cold and blustery day turned even colder. She knew she had to get a grip before she got back to her room because she knew one of the girls would ask her what the deal was. She didn't feel comfortable talking about it with Courtney, who was her favorite roommate. And she knew for a fact that the first thing Shawnda would talk about would be sex. No one knew she was a virgin and she wasn't anxious to share. All of the other girls had experience. She'd been shocked to see Courtney's birth control pills casually flung on her desk one day. Her jaw dropped at the frank and bold way Shawnda and Janet and the other black girls talked about sex and guys' private parts. No, it was no one's business that she was still a virgin, no one's business about why she was still a virgin and no one's business that she'd just met a guy who suddenly made her think about her virginity and how soon she could lose it.

"Hey Marisa," a voice next to her called out.

Turning, she saw Trent, a white boy from Hamilton who lived on the brother floor. "Hey Trent. How's it going?"

"Good." His head was buried deep inside his collar and his eyes watered from the wind. "I guess I should have worn a hat or scarf or something today."

"Yeah, it's pretty brutal," she admitted. It was only November. What was January or February going to be like? "But we're both from west Michigan, so we're used to the lake effect snow and all that."

"True." Silence engulfed them until Trent asked, "Hey, a bunch of us are going out to the bar tonight. Wanna come?"

Surprised, she looked at him but was faced with only his profile, still buried deep into his collar. His face was turning red from the wind and his hair was practically standing straight up. "Uh...nah, I'll pass. I have an early class tomorrow."

"Me, too."

"You're already planning on skipping class?"

"I may not skip class, but it's bar night. You gotta go out, right?"

Bar night. Every Thursday. Marisa had participated with Molly and Sharon early in the fall but soon realized it was just a bunch of rowdy white guys and goofy white girls drinking to excess and hooking up later. At any rate, Thursday night was TV night. Why would she want to miss "The Cosby Show," "A Different World," "Family Ties," "Cheers" and everything else? Last week she'd watched with Jacqui in their room and they'd actually seemed to settle into a peaceful bond. She didn't know where and with whom she was going to watch tonight's shows, but there was no way bar night would be more fun than that.

"Thanks, but I'll pass."

Silence while the wind whipped barren trees into a high-pitched whistle, causing Trent to hunch his shoulders as he turned to her. "We're having a progressive on our floor tomorrow night if you want to come."

What was going on with him? She looked at him closely, trying to figure out if he was asking her to all these things because he ... liked her? She hoped not. She didn't want to be rude so she said, "Cool. That sounds fun."

He looked her way as they reached the crosswalk leading to Brody. "Great. I'll look for you. See you later!" He ran off, leaving her perplexed and more than a little unsettled. Why would she ever look at a white guy again when she'd met someone like Kyle?

He called that night. She missed it, though, because she was next door in Nikki's room with Jacqui, Shawnda and Janet watching her shows until ten. When she came back to the room, Courtney told her, "Someone named Kyle called for you."

She tried to keep her face impassive but failed miserably when she whirled around at the news. "Kyle? When?"

Courtney, who was sitting at her desk painting her nails black, turned and smiled coyly. "Around 9 or so. I didn't know where you were, otherwise I would have come and got you." Blowing on her nails, she continued, grinning. "Who is Kyle? His voice sounded so sexy!"

You're telling me, Marisa thought. Outwardly, she shrugged and disappeared into the closet for her shower caddy. "Just a guy."

"From home?"

Yeah, right, like Petersville ever had anyone who looked and sounded like *that*! "No, he goes here. He lives in Shaw."

"Oh, then you met him in class then." Courtney turned back around and Marisa didn't feel like correcting her so she didn't reply. "Do you like him?"

"I just met him, Court," she said, keeping her eyes averted as she changed into her pajamas.

"OK, but he sounded so sexy and polite."

A number of questions swirled through her head. Was she supposed to call him back? Did he leave his number? And why didn't she get his last name? She couldn't just call the operator and ask for "Kyle in Shaw Hall."

"He said he'd call you back."

"Tonight?"

"He didn't say."

He didn't call back that night. Marisa lay awake in bed, tossing and turning, daydreaming and wondering until after midnight. She tried not to second-guess her decision to go to Nikki's room to watch the shows because she didn't want to be "that girl." The one who sat by the phone and put her life on hold for some guy. But why didn't she hear the phone ring next door? Why didn't she come back in during commercials just to check in? Stop it, Marisa, she scolded herself as she thudded her pillow. He said he'd call back so he will.

The next afternoon, Marisa's thoughts turned again to football. The team was playing Purdue on Saturday, with one week remaining until the crucial game against Indiana. The excitement for the team's possible Rose Bowl berth was palatable. Unfortunately, none of the black girls on the floor were interested at all. Janet only cared about basketball, Jacqui didn't like any sports and Shawnda had already made her feelings known. "It's stupid. They spend too much money on athletes and sports here anyway."

Marisa ignored them and tried not to notice how her room filled with white girls that afternoon, all of whom – like her – had season tickets. Since the white girls were the only ones who shared her excitement, Marisa hung out with them all afternoon and into the evening for her first progressive.

She'd never seen so much beer in her life. If the point of a progressive was to have variety in each room, then these guys just didn't get the point. There was a keg in every room. Loud, red-faced white guys in every room. Giggly white girls in every room trying to figure out which one had the best-looking guys. Marisa stayed close to Molly, who was slightly less wild than either Courtney or Sharon. She nursed a red Solo cup filled with beer and pretended to drink while trying not to make a face.

The music was familiar. Heavy metal and rock. Nothing to dance to, which was fine, because no one was dancing anyway. Even if they wanted to, they couldn't because there was no space. Each room was elbow-to-elbow. It was so crowded that Marisa started to feel claustrophobic. And the smell! Sweat. Beer breath. BO. Leaning close to Molly, she yelled, "I think I'm done. You?" Nodding, Molly followed her out the door, where they were stopped by Trent coming in.

"Hey! You came!" He engulfed Marisa in a drunken hug. "Where are you going?"

"We're heading back," she yelled over the din.

"No! You guys got here!" His red-face and glazed eyes stared at her and veered way too close to hers. "I mean, you guys just got here!"

"We've been here awhile, you just didn't see us!" She continued to edge her way into the hallway. He followed them.

"Hey, Steve! Look who's here!" A tall, blonde guy in the hall turned and leered at both Molly and Marisa.

"Hey....Lookit Ebony and Ivory!" He cackled at his own joke.

Trent was either too drunk to get it or so drunk that he didn't care what his friend said. Molly and Marisa, though, glanced at each other. Molly looked embarrassed; Marisa disgusted. "I told you, Steve. Isn't Marisa the prettiest black girl you've ever seen?"

Her skin crawled as Steve looked her up and down. "Yeah, she's pretty for a black girl."

"Come on, Molly." She grabbed her friend's arm and stalked down the hall, pushing drunken students out of the way. Near the end of the hall, she saw the R.A. and the resident director heading their way, hopefully to break up the parties.

"Is that alcohol in that cup?" The R.D. asked Marisa, pointing to her red Solo cup.

"Uh . . ."

"Get rid of it." He threw over his shoulder as he continued down the hall.

Once in the lobby, neither girl said a word. Finally, Molly sighed. "Those guys...don't pay any attention to them..."

Marisa appreciated the effort, but Molly had no idea what she was feeling right now. Once again, she tried to fit in where she didn't belong. Once again, she was reminded in no uncertain terms that she did *not* belong. That she was an "other." She felt like a fool for even trying. Instead of sharing that with Molly, though, she patted her on the arm. "Forget it. Those guys were so drunk they won't even remember any of this."

"Well, I'm going to make sure Trent knows. He's a good guy. Usually."

They turned into their hallway and Marisa stopped short. There was a tall guy knocking on her open dorm door. He was wearing a brown leather jacket. It was Kyle.

"Who's that?" Molly asked. "He looks like a football player."

She bristled. "All black guys at MSU are not athletes, Molly," she lectured, conveniently forgetting that she thought he played football, too.

Molly reddened. "Sorry."

As they neared the room, Marisa felt her pulse quicken. What was he doing here? Granted, it was only nine p.m., but it was too late to go to dinner or a movie, wasn't it? Maybe he didn't even want a date. Maybe he was just stopping by to say hi. Stopping by? With Jacqui and Shawnda in the room? Great...

She stepped to the door, which he consumed with his tall, wide frame. "Kyle?"

Turning, he smiled in surprise. "Hey . . ." He spotted the cup in her hand and she saw his eyebrows raise in surprise. "How you doing?"

"Good." She tried not to look at Shawnda and Jacqui, who were in the room with wide eyes and appreciative grins. "Uh, this is Molly. She lives down the hall."

"Hi," he nodded. "Kyle."

"Oh, sorry," Marisa stumbled. Seeing him here with everyone, and especially with her holding a beer, threw her off. "You met Shawnda and Jacqui? Jacqui is one of my roommates. Shawnda lives down the hall."

"Yeah, they were telling me. I didn't know you had a quad. Nice set-up." He stepped into the room, freeing up space for her – and Molly – to come in, too. She set the cup down on her desk.

"Girl, what is that? Don't tell me you drinking beer!" Shawnda said, rising to smell the contents of the cup. "It's full! How many you had?"

"I didn't drink any beer. This is my only cup and I didn't even drink it." For some reason, she felt compelled to defend herself. "You know I don't like beer."

"I don't know why you went to that progressive, anyway. Crazy white boys over there..." Shawnda shook her head, ignored Molly, then turned her attention to Kyle. "So Kyle, how do you know my girl Marisa?"

He was peering at the pictures on her desk, particularly the one of her at the beach. "She bumped into me in the lobby, then I ran into her at the Union yesterday."

Silence. "That's it? You don't have a class together?"

"Nope."

"You live in Brody, though?"

"Nope. I live in Shaw."

Marisa felt three pairs of eyes staring at her. All three girls were wondering how on Earth she'd managed to capture the attention of this gorgeous guy merely by bumping into him. "OK. Well, you didn't come here to talk to us. Jacqui, you coming to my room to borrow that tape, right?" It was the most obvious lie in an effort to give Marisa and Kyle some privacy.

"Yeah." Rising, she and Shawnda passed by, gave Marisa knowing glances, then said their goodbyes to Kyle, while also dragging Molly out of the room. Two seconds later, Shawnda was back, closing the door in the most obvious manner ever.

Being alone with Kyle was, to say the least, unsettling. He turned and leaned against her desk. "Hi."

"Hi." She stood before him, not knowing quite where to go or how to stand or hold her hands. So she put them in her jeans pockets, not knowing how endearing that looked.

Smiling softly, he locked gazes with her. "I called you yesterday. Did your roommate tell you?"

"Yeah, she did. She said you'd call back..." She hoped it didn't sound accusatory.

"Well, I was working on a paper and then it got late, so ...I didn't want to wake everyone up..."

"That's OK." She dug her hands deeper in her pockets. "What's your last name?"

"My last name?" He chuckled. "It's Williams. Kyle Joseph Williams, to be exact. Why do you ask?"

"Well, I was going to call you back then realized I didn't have your number or your last name, so ...I couldn't."

Nodding, he didn't respond. He just kept looking at her and smiling. She suddenly didn't feel "pretty for a black girl." She just felt pretty. "I was over at a friend's house in Spartan Village and asked him to drop me off over here so I could stop by and see you."

It sounded so intimate that Marisa felt her legs turn to Jell-O. "But how are you going to get home?"

"I'll walk. No biggie. I walk a lot in Philly, so this is nothing. Just more trees."

"Oh."

Somehow the easy conversation they'd shared in the Union yesterday was gone. Now she was back to being nervous and shy and self-conscious. If only Shawnda had left the door open!

"Is that OK? I didn't mean to surprise you or anything. I know you were at a party...if you want to get back to it, I understand." He moved away from the desk and Marisa's hand shot out of her pocket and rested on his chest.

"No, no, don't go. It's fine. The party was lame. It's not really my scene." Her hand seemed incapable of moving, so he did it for her by capturing it in his.

"Good." Pulling on her hand, he drew her closer. "I'm glad."

Standing so close to him, she felt like she couldn't breathe. Was he going to kiss her? No, he just continued to hold her hand while he talked. "I came over to see you but also ... to ask you out. For tomorrow night after the game." He was caressing her hand. "And not Burger King this time."

The smile she gave was anchored by a bite on her lower lip. "That sounds nice." It actually sounded nicer than nice but she had to keep her cool. He was so freakin' sexy and so freakin' nice that she was about to melt all over again. The scent of Drakkar Noir was faint but she could still catch a whiff of it. His hand was warm, despite the cold outside and the fact that he didn't seem to wear any gloves. "Where do you want to go?"

"I have some ideas," he winked, then reached forward and drew her other hand out of her pocket to capture both in his. "I'll be here tomorrow at ... six? Is that cool?"

"Yeah, that's good." Could he hear her heart pounding? How was it possible that she was in her dorm room with this amazing guy so soon after meeting him? Raising her eyes to his, she noticed he had a dimple in his left cheek, which gave his face an adorable off-kilter look.

"Good." Locking her gaze, he dropped his smile and almost imperceptibly licked his lips. Then he shook his head, released her hands and stepped away from the desk. "OK, I should probably get out of here before . . ."

"Before what?" She asked, slightly alarmed that he didn't kiss her, but also slightly relieved. Who knew what would have happened if he had?

"Nothing." He turned away and ran his hand over his face. "So uh, I'll see you tomorrow then."

"You don't have to go, Kyle," she said quietly. She didn't know what she meant by that, but she knew she didn't want him to leave.

Turning to her, suddenly serious, he answered in an equally quiet tone. "Yes, I do."

Biting her lip, she looked at the clock on her dresser. "It's early. The Brody Break Station is still open. Want to grab some hot chocolate or something? My treat this time." Where did this forward girl come from? She didn't know, she just knew she wasn't ready to say goodbye and realized they probably needed to lighten the mood.

It worked. They sat at a table and talked for hours while the hot chocolate turned cold and the jumbo chocolate chip cookie sat uneaten. When the time came for him to walk back to his dorm, Marisa felt guilty. It was late and cold and now he had to walk home. "I wish I could call Dial-a-Ride for you."

"I'm fine. The hot chocolate warmed me up." He caught her gaze. "And the company."

She felt warm now, too. "Thanks." She paused, wanting to tell him what she was feeling. That the last two days felt like a roller coaster. "I..." Staring at him, she saw a similar expression of wonder and puzzlement mirrored on his face.

"I know." He reached out and instead of capturing her hands again, pulled her into a loose hug, his hands resting around her waist. "I know. I feel almost dizzy."

"Yeah." The intensity and instant attraction they felt was overwhelming. Was this love at first sight? Marisa always thought that concept was ridiculous – she was a wanna-be scientist, after all – but after meeting Kyle, she wasn't so sure.

"Let's just go on the ride, OK? There's no way I can get off now anyway." He rocked them back and forth.

"Me either." Looking up at him, she knew he was going to kiss her this time. And she was right. Leaning forward slowly, he met her lips softly for the briefest of seconds. It was so light and so quick that it almost felt like he'd merely breathed on her. She met his eyes, wanting more.

"Tomorrow," he said.

***

She floated through the next day as she watched the Spartans jump to an early and insurmountable lead at the football game, so Marisa left at the beginning of the fourth quarter to get ready for her date. Sharon, Molly and Charla waved at her, told her good luck, have fun and "don't do anything I wouldn't do!"

While walking back to her dorm, she slowed her steps. Now that she was away from her friends and even away from Kyle, she could think clearly. Was it possible that she was falling in love with him so soon? And was it completely irresponsible of her to be caught up with a guy mere months after starting college? Wasn't she the one who said she was here to "learn, not love"? Was she some kind of hypocrite or something? Looking up, she studied the Sparty statue standing guard near the stadium. She loved college. She loved Michigan State. Doing something stupid this early would be completely unlike her.

But there was no denying how Kyle made her feel. She was comfortable around him, which by itself was a miracle. Black guys always made her mute. She never knew how to respond to their quips, come-ons or jokes. But Kyle had none of those. He was just polite from the moment they'd met. And he made her feel special. And valuable. He listened to her. She didn't feel like he was undressing her with his eyes. Instead, she felt beautiful.

Crossing Brody Path, she slowed her steps even more. What was she doing? She should just cancel, she thought. Tears sprang to her eyes. Why was she such an idiot? Other girls could date and go to college without overanalyzing everything. What the hell was wrong with her? Kyle was gorgeous and he liked *her*! She liked *him*. Deep down, though, she knew what the issue was. She was in college. She was a grown woman with grown woman feelings. Having a boyfriend here meant having sex. Having sex meant she had to be responsible. Being responsible meant getting on birth control. Now. Before something crazy happened.

She knew where the student medical center was, but she'd never been to a gynecologist before. If she wasn't having sex and didn't have any problems with her period, then what was the point? When she was dating Barry and thought she was going to prom with him, her mother lamely tried to bring up the subject of birth control but Marisa deftly changed the subject. No way would she have ever had sex with Barry. Or any white dude, really. She'd just never imagined it. Black guys were just so much sexier.

But if she wanted to have sex with Kyle – and if she was honest with herself, she'd admit she probably did – then she'd have to tell him that she was a virgin. And she was afraid that if she did that, then his attitude toward her would change. What guy wants a virgin? That means he'd have to wait longer, be more patient, and so on and so on. Marisa had two brothers so she remembered overhearing some of their comments when they were in college, especially Matthew. He was the "wham, bam, thank you ma'am, type." Robert was nicer when he was single, but in his younger days he still got his "share of booty," as Matthew would say. And if she told Kyle, when should she tell him? Doing so too soon would be presumptuous, wouldn't it? Doing it while they were making out would be a mood kill, right?

God, she was confused. And she had no one to talk to about it. A phone call to Janine would be nice, but she was kind of like Shawnda, boy-crazy and experienced. She would just tell her to do it, make sure he wore a condom, then get birth control pills later. But Marisa knew she could never do that. No, she was too careful and too meticulous. She didn't trust Jacqui not to tell Shawnda. And Nikki would just tell her she was a fornicator and to repent for her lustful thoughts.

She snuck back into her dorm without anyone seeing her. Jacqui and Shawnda were at the mall, Courtney went home for the weekend and Charla was still at the game. Picking up the phone, she dialed the number in Illinois, wondering why she hadn't called sooner.

"Hi, Kristin?" she asked.

"Yeah? Marisa?" Kristin yelled in surprise.

"Hi!" Hearing her voice made Marisa smile. According to her letters, Kristin was loving Northwestern as much as Marisa was loving MSU. But they hadn't spoken to each other since August, when Kristin left for college.

"Oh my God, it's so good to hear your voice!" Kristin said. "How are you?"

"I'm good." She couldn't stop smiling. It really was good to hear her voice. Kristin was always the level-headed one in her high school clique and the only one she could speak to freely about Barry over the years. It stands to reason that Kristin would be the one to turn to about Kyle.

After additional pleasantries about school, homework, dorm life and Petersville, Marisa got to the point. She spilled everything about Kyle. How he made her feel, how he talked, how he looked, how scared she was, how no one knew she was a virgin, how she was scared of flunking out of school and how she was scared to go to the gynecologist.

"I hear you," Kristin was saying. "As much as we couldn't wait to go to college, we didn't think about how to deal with stuff like this, did we? Drunk roommates, birth control and all of this other stuff."

She sighed. "But at some point, we have to grow up, don't we? If you feel for him like you say you do, then you have to be prepared. You don't want to get pregnant."

"God forbid." She could just imagine the reaction from her parents, her brothers – my God, her grandmother – if she got pregnant and had to drop out of school. "You're right. I just...it's just such a grown-up thing to do. It's almost like I'm officially saying goodbye to childhood."

"You are," Kristin said reasonably. "But an alternative would be *not* to have sex with him..."

"No, no, that's probably not an option," Marisa giggled. Kristin was right. She had to go to student health and get on birth control. Time to act like other girls her age for once. "It's so crazy, though. I literally just met him. I bumped into him last month and didn't see him again until Thursday. Two days ago! How is this even possible?"

"Marisa, people here meet guys at parties and have sex with them that *night*!"

"Here, too!"

"So at least you're not like them. Kyle seems to really like you. And it sounds like the attraction is intense. You're doing the right thing."

"Thanks Kristin." She glanced at the clock. "Well, I should get going. I still have to change and fix my hair."

"OK. Have fun, OK? I can't wait to see you over Thanksgiving! I've missed you!"

If Marisa was honest with herself, she missed Kristin, too. She was always the voice of reason and it felt good to talk to someone who knew the "real" her, not the person who kept trying to fit in. She knew she didn't fit in with the white girls, but she didn't yet fit in with the black ones, either. So she floated between the two worlds, trying to convince herself that one of them would eventually fit. So far neither one had.

CHAPTER 12

Winter 1988

Opening the door to her dorm room in January, Marisa felt the loss instantly. Courtney's bed was stripped, her heavy metal posters gone. She'd dropped out of school after first term. It was probably inevitable, since she spent so much time with Jamie and barely went to class. But dang, she gave up after one term? She'd told Marisa the news on the last day of finals before Christmas break. "This just isn't for me," she said, shrugging.

"But you're so smart," Marisa protested. Even without going to class, she'd seen firsthand how quickly Courtney was able to do math and how sharp her mind was when reading her required literature.

"Maybe I'm just not ready for college yet," Courtney said while emptying her desk. For once, her face was devoid of heavy black eye makeup and her usually teased hair was pulled back in a low ponytail. "Maybe I'll try again in a year or so."

"You're leaving me alone with Charla and Jacqui, though!" Marisa had protested. While she and Jacqui had an easygoing relationship, they were definitely not close. And she couldn't stand Charla. The feeling was mutual.

"Please, you spend all your time with Kyle now anyway. And when you're not with him, you're with Molly or Sharon or Shawnda. You have so many friends here already, Marisa. You belong here. I don't."

Sighing, Marisa led her parents into the room and threw her bags on her bed. Hopefully they wouldn't get a new roommate. If not, that would at least free up some dresser and closet space. Maybe they could put Courtney's bed and desk in storage to create even more space.

Her parents didn't stay long and when she hugged and kissed them goodbye she was surprised at how easy it had gotten to watch them leave. Michigan State was her home now, not Petersville.

Kyle was due back in about two hours and Marisa couldn't wait. It had been three weeks since they'd seen each other, and she was sure their respective phone bills would cause ire from both sets of parents.

For Marisa, falling in love was unexpected, fast and intense. But it happened. By the end of their first date, actually. They'd gone to dinner, talked well into the night, rode the bus home holding hands then kissed in the shadows of the stairwell outside of her floor. She spent every spare minute of the next week either talking to him or seeing him. At the library, in his dorm, in her dorm or out and about on Grand River Avenue, eating ice cream at Melting Moments or grabbing a sandwich at Bagel Fragel. At first she thought it was just lust, but their conversations flowed so easily that she knew it was more than his looks. She not only fell in love with his personality, she fell in love with his brain. He was brilliant.

By the end of the first week, she was hooked. What's more, the feeling was mutual. For Marisa, who'd spent most of her teenage years dealing with unrequited feelings, Kyle's obvious attraction and devotion to her was mind-spinning.

She met his parents after only two weeks, when they came to campus for the pivotal game against Indiana. In typical Marisa fashion, she freaked, analyzed and freaked some more until she met them. His father was basically a carbon copy of what Kyle would look like, tall, wide with a killer smile and booming voice. He hugged her immediately then turned to his wife, "Look at this pretty girl! Kyle, you didn't waste any time, did you?"

His mother was not what she expected. Instead of the polished, sophisticated woman she'd imagined, she was instead a bohemian, back-to-Mother-Africa woman. She had long braids piled high on her head, killer cheekbones and smooth, dark skin. But it was her eyes that caught Marisa's attention. They were almond-shaped, wide and almost hazel. The combination was mesmerizing.

She learned that when Kyle referred to his parents as "teachers," he should have said "professor," at least in the case of his mother. She taught African-American Studies at Temple University, while his father was a high school chemistry teacher and football coach with a slew of successful car wash franchises on the side. She loved them instantly.

Her parents found out about Kyle when she went home for Thanksgiving. Her mother found an oversized Temple sweatshirt in her laundry basket and immediately got suspicious. But when Kyle called that night and her family hung on her every word, she knew she had to confess. Her mother looked worried and told her to make sure she kept her grades up, while her father looked pleased.

She's glowing, thought her dad as he watched his daughter across the kitchen table. He didn't think he'd see Marisa this happy again ever since that fiasco with Barry over prom. But now his baby girl was babbling on and on about Kyle, a city boy from Philly with educator parents who was majoring in physics of all things.

"What kind of job can you get with a physics degree?" Matthew asked.

"Any damn job you please, is my guess," said her father.

Yes, falling in love was intense but she had to have a clear head so she endured her first ob/gyn appointment – it was absolutely horrible – and got a prescription for birth control pills. She'd been taking them for about five weeks now but she was ready. Kyle had no idea what she'd done and she couldn't wait to surprise him.

They'd declared their love for each other just before finals and Marisa was almost dizzy from how fast she'd fallen for him. Completely and utterly. And more importantly, she trusted him. There were plenty of girls on campus who would gladly sleep with him, and if not that, then gladly give him a blow job. At least that's what Shawnda said when she'd asked her if they'd slept together yet. When she discovered the answer was no, she told Marisa she had to get on the ball – literally – or she'd lose him. "He can get some anytime he wants, but he wants you! You better go on and give him some!" Yes, why didn't she go on and do it? But it was such a big step and she'd worried that he would lose patience if she waited too long.

"Marisa, I do not care that you're a virgin," he'd said truthfully after she'd apologized for making him stop one night. "In fact, I'm kinda proud. You waited for me." Smiling, he cut off any retort she had in mind. "You did. And now I will wait for you. However long you need me to."

Remembering that day brought a smile to her face and a heat flush over her entire body. She was in love. *She* was in love. It seemed surreal.

Sitting on her bed, she sighed. She couldn't remember when she'd been this happy. She was slowly becoming more comfortable with the black girls in her dorm, she was getting good grades and she was in love. Life couldn't be better.

She was sitting in the armchair swooning over George Michael singing "I Want Your Sex" on MTV – pretty appropriate, she thought – when a soft knock sounded. Rushing to the door, she felt her heartbeat quicken. When she saw him standing there, melting snowflakes on his broad shoulders and hair, she let out a muted scream. Flinging herself into his arms, she continued to gush, "Oh my God, I've missed you! God, how I missed you!" He was laughing and trying to kiss her, but she was talking too much.

"Hey, slow down! Slow down." He set her down and followed her into the room, pulling his large suitcase behind him. Kicking the door closed with his foot, he shrugged off his coat and threw his gloves on her desk. "God, you look good." She was wearing a tight black sweater and faded Calvin Klein jeans and he felt himself instantly grow hard. It had been the longest three weeks of his life, daydreaming, fantasizing and actually aching for her. Reaching out a long arm, he pulled her close and kissed her hungrily, letting his hands roam over her back, hair and butt. Moaning, Marisa was instantly breathless. She wanted to tell him. But how? When? She had the whole thing planned in her head but now it just seemed – weird.

"Kyle?"

"Mmm?" He continued to spray kisses on her lips, cheek and neck.

"I love you."

Smiling softly, he drew her closer. "I love you, too."

"Uh, you know my roommates won't be back until tomorrow," she began.

He continued to kiss and caress her, making it difficult for her to think, let alone speak. "Mmm-hmm."

"And Nikki left for the night, so she won't be next door."

No response. His lips moved to her neck, and she closed her eyes. She had to let him know, so they could just enjoy the evening. Now.

"Kyle?"

"Yeah?"

"I ....I went to the doctor."

Stopping his caresses, he looked at her with a small frown. "Is everything OK?" He knew she couldn't be pregnant, so there's that.

"I'm fine. I went...so I could...." Get it out, Marisa. You're not the small-town girl anymore. "So I could get some birth control."

Shock registered on his face in the form of two raised eyebrows and a dropped jaw. "You what?"

"I got some birth control. In December."

"In December? You got on birth control in December?" She nodded. "But..." He was going to ask why they didn't have sex before Christmas break if she was on birth control, but he didn't. He'd promised to wait and be patient. "Is everything OK? Are you sick or anything? I know some girls hate taking it . . ." He let his words fade. This was not the way he expected the evening to go.

"No. It's fine. I feel fine," she reassured him. Watching his face, she thought he'd be happier or more excited, but he just continued to look confused.

"But...you didn't have to, you know. I would have been fine wearing a condom."

"Don't worry, you're still going to wear a condom," she giggled. "I just felt better knowing that I had it taken care of."

Nodding, he surveyed her and then glanced around the room again. Did that mean? Did she mean...? Tonight? Now? Realization dawned and he furrowed his brows. "So...?"

Biting her lip, she ran her hand up and down his arm and nodded. "I love you," she said simply.

Gulping the lump that had suddenly swelled in his throat, he whispered, "Are you sure? It's OK if you're not ready, I swear it is." But please be ready, he thought. Please! She was so fine and he didn't know if he could handle any more close encounters. Blue balls, in case he didn't know before, were a real thing.

In answer, she grabbed him around the neck and kissed him. Whispering into his lips, she reassured him, "I'm sure."

***

If Marisa thought having sex with Kyle would alleviate the desire and pent-up need within her, she was wrong. The only thing it did was make her hornier. She couldn't get enough of him. Whenever they had a free moment or a roommate-free dorm, they did it. They discovered they were in the same nutrition class, so every Tuesday and Thursday they would leave class, walk across the street to his room and steal a quickie before separating to go to their next classes. It was such a turn-on that she spent the entire class fidgeting in her seat and stealing knowing glances his way. She was surprised at how quickly her defenses and insecurities came down. Kyle delighted in teaching her everything he knew and he found a willing learner in her.

Back in her dorm, the quad was now just a triple. Courtney's spot was still free so the remaining roommates decided to turn her bed into a daybed/couch, outfitted with tons of pillows and throws. The three of them came to a peaceful détente once they realized that being roommates didn't mean you had to be best friends or hang out all the time. Jacqui hung out in Shawnda's room most nights and Charla basically just used the room to sleep. She didn't even eat in their cafeteria anymore; she was too busy hanging out with her friends across campus. So more often than not, Marisa had the room to herself, which meant Kyle was with her.

He was becoming friends with her friends, too. Shawnda continued to innocently flirt with him and say anything that came to mind, such as the time she saw them walking down the hall one Saturday afternoon to go to a basketball game and she popped her head out of her door. "Hey! Marisa, are you walking different?"

Turning, Marisa was confused. "Huh?"

With a smirk, Shawnda looked her up and down. "You're walking different. You got a little switch in your step, doncha? And I know why!" With a guffaw, she disappeared back into her room.

Molly and Sharon loved Kyle, too. Marisa could tell, though, that he was quieter and more on-guard around them and one day she asked him why.

"You're the one who's comfortable around all these white people," he said while lying on the bed-formerly-known-as-Courtney's. She was on her own bed, studying French. "Not me."

Yes, she was comfortable around them but she was slowly beginning to prefer to hang out with the black girls. But was it fair to totally turn her back on Molly and Sharon just because they were white? They were nice and cool and fun. They were her friends. So she continued to straddle both worlds, wishing sometimes that she could just meld them. Let her be the conduit between the two so everyone could just get along.

February came and with it, Black History Month. Several events took place around campus to honor the occasion, and Marisa was in her element. Stories about black history dominated the student newspaper and Marisa spent several days talking to Kyle's mother on the phone about it. The Emmons Black Student Alliance hosted a panel discussion about apartheid and South Africa and Marisa went with Shawnda, Janet, Nikki and Jacqui. Before the panel started, the Alliance reviewed a list of upcoming events they were hosting, including a spring picnic and an end-of-school-year party in June. Sitting in the crowd, Marisa scanned the faces around her and only saw three white students. The rest of them looked like her. And she didn't feel out of place. She finally – finally – felt like she belonged.

On the way back to her room, she and Jacqui ran into Sharon, heading to the bathroom with her robe on, toting her shower caddy. "Hey, where have you guys been?"

"We were at a Black History Month event on South Africa," Jacqui said.

"Oh," she said, noticing that they weren't wearing coats. "Was it here? I would have liked to hear that."

"Yeah, it was here. The Emmons Black Student Alliance put it on," Marisa explained.

Sharon suddenly pursed her lips. "The Black Student Alliance? So I wasn't allowed to go?"

Jacqui and Marisa looked at each other. "Anyone could go," Jacqui began, while Marisa chimed in, "There were a few white kids there."

Shifting her weight from one foot to another, Sharon went on. "How would you guys feel if there was a White Student Alliance?"

Stunned, Marisa didn't know what to say. But Jacqui – quiet, unassuming Jacqui – had a quick rejoinder. "We call that the MSU Student Government."

"What?"

"This campus is majority white, which means that most, if not all, of the power at this school rests with white people," Jacqui explained, trying to hold her anger in check.

"I don't have any power," Sharon insisted.

"No, but because white people are in charge, you benefit the most from those people who do have power," she responded. "Last fall, when all these girls were going crazy during Rush Week, did you ever wonder why all of the girls were white? Did you ever wonder why none of the black sororities or fraternities even have houses here?"

Sharon, whose curly hair was pulled back in a high, messy ponytail, shook her head. "See, that's what I mean. Why do we have to have black and white sororities? Anyone can rush whatever sorority they want! Why do you insist on self-segregating yourselves?"

Marisa, who didn't feel comfortable trying to answer, looked to Jacqui. In truth, she was wondering herself why the black students chose to sit in the other dining room when the "white" dining room was so much bigger. How could white people get comfortable around blacks if they never saw them? But on the flip side, she totally understood the desire to be accepted and to be around people who looked and thought like her without putting on false facades.

Shaking her head and waving her hand dismissively, Jacqui pushed past Sharon, throwing over her shoulder to Marisa, "I can't even talk to her right now. You just don't understand."

Marisa was left in the hallway watching Jacqui walk away while standing awkwardly next to Sharon. She didn't want to talk about it anymore, either, especially not in the hallway. If only she was better entrenched in the black experience, she could have a better answer for Sharon. What would Kyle's mother say right now, she wondered, and vowed to ask her the next time they talked.

"Why is she mad?" Sharon whined. "It's true, though. She only hangs out with black girls on this floor. She's never even been in my room and every time I come into yours, she pretty much ignores me. Why can't she be more like you?"

Sighing, Marisa glared at her. "Sharon, did you ever look at all the white girls on this floor and ask if *they're* self-segregating? Why is it only a thing if black people do it? You all are together all the time and no one looks twice. Explain that."

Sharon's face turned red as she thought about it. Dropping her gaze, she shrugged. "I don't know. I never thought about that before."

"Well, maybe you should," Marisa left her standing in the hallway and closed the door to her room.

After that, whenever Sharon came into the room, not only would Jacqui ignore her, she would leave. Marisa started to feel like a traitor, because she believed that the more Sharon was able to ask stupid questions, the more Marisa and Jacqui could teach her. But Jacqui wouldn't even try. She lamented the tension one night to Kyle while they were studying at the library.

"Jacqui is right," Kyle was saying. "At some point, you just get tired of explaining shit to these people. Why do we have to defend ourselves when it should be *them* trying to understand *us*?"

"That's what Sharon is doing! She's trying to understand," she insisted, but Kyle was already shaking his head.

"No, she's not. If she was, she wouldn't have started out saying that stupid shit about the White Student Alliance. Instead, she would have said, 'The Black Student Alliance? Do you think I could come to a meeting one day?' If she had, then she could have come, listened and then learned a thing or two." Kyle shook his head and continued to twirl his pencil between his fingers as he did his math homework.

"I guess you're right," she was saying. "But I still don't think she needs to leave every time Sharon comes over."

Kyle looked at her, shook his head, then sighed. "You'll learn."

Suddenly irritated at his patriarchal dismissal of her, she stared at him. "Learn what?"

Pausing before replying, he spoke quietly. "You told me about some of the stuff you went through with your friends growing up. How many more chances are you going to give them to hurt you? When will you stop giving them the benefit of the doubt? 'Cause you know they don't deserve it."

She averted her gaze, feeling stupid. He was right. But somehow she didn't find it so easy to discard friendships so quickly. Jen was a prime example. For years, she kept asking herself why she even considered Jen a friend and she never really had a good answer. Barry had broken her heart to pieces, yet she still smiled at him and spoke during a New Year's party at Tara's. Who does that? But with Sharon, she felt more optimistic. And who better to bridge the gap between her white friend and her black roommate than her?

By the next week, Jacqui was never in the room when Marisa came home. She knew she was in Shawnda's room every night, avoiding not only Sharon but Marisa as well. On Tuesday night, Marisa was doing her homework with the door open when Molly and Sharon wandered in. "Hey, is it time for '21 Jump Street'?" Molly asked, flopping down on Marisa's bed.

"Oh yeah," Marisa flipped the channel and sang along with Molly and Sharon while Holly Robinson sang the catchy theme song. This was a new episode, so the room became silent while all three watched, enthralled. When the commercials aired at the end of the first thirty minutes, Marisa thought she'd figured out the entire plot. "He's not the one who did it. He's hiding something," she said, referring to the main protagonist in the episode.

"I think you're right," Molly was saying. "I hope he gets away. He's cute."

Sharon snorted, then turned to Molly. "You like that nigger?"

The room turned cold and everything seemed to freeze in mid-air. Molly quickly hissed, "Shhh!" then gestured to Marisa, who was still frozen in her seat. Sharon, who realized what she'd done, turned beet red, covered her mouth with her hands and widened her eyes. "Oh Marisa..." It was at that exact moment that Kyle appeared in the doorway, followed closely by Shawnda, who was yammering about Chicago house music.

"Marisa, you still got that house music tape your brother made you?" she asked, then paused as she noticed Sharon's red face, Molly's eyes filling with tears and Marisa's face, which was frozen in an icy glare. Her eyes were slits, her lips a straight line and her nostrils flared. Kyle, who'd never, ever seen Marisa angry, was startled. "Baby?" He glanced around the room. "What's going on?"

His deep voice made Sharon and Molly jump. They both looked at him in something akin to terror, because there was nothing scarier than a big black man, right? They were suddenly the minority in the room and petrified that Marisa would reveal what happened right then and there. Jumping out of her chair, Sharon looked at Marisa in a silent plea. Marisa rose, too, and with the same hard look on her face, growled, "Get out." Sharon pushed past a confused Shawnda, then ran down the hall to her room. Molly, who obviously didn't know what to do, looked at Marisa with tears in her eyes. Before she could issue a lame apology, Marisa stopped her. "You get out, too."

After Molly left, Marisa slammed the door as hard as she could, clicked off the TV then started picking up her books and notebooks in a fury. "What the hell is going on?" Shawnda asked.

Marisa ignored the question. Kyle and Shawnda looked at each other, then Kyle stepped forward and took the books out of Marisa's hands. Taking her by the shoulders, he asked in the same bewildered tone as Shawnda. "What is going on? What happened? You look like you're ready to kill somebody!"

But she didn't want to tell him. Not because she was protecting Sharon but because he would say "I told you so." Shawnda would, too. Jacqui definitely would. The response from all of them would be: "That's what you get for hanging around white folks all the time." But she couldn't keep it a secret. She had to let everyone know what kind of person Sharon was.

With a shaky breath that barely concealed her fury, she spoke. "That bitch sat right here – " she pointed at the chair – "in my room, and said the word 'nigger.' "

Kyle released her in shock. Shawnda gasped and started a string of curse words. "What the fuck – ? She called you a nigger?"

"No, she was talking about a black guy on '21 Jump Street'. Molly said he was cute and then Sharon turned around and said – like I wasn't even here – 'You like that nigger'? Like I wasn't even here!" She tried to pace around, anything to release the rage building within her, but Kyle was blocking her way. She wanted to throw something. She wanted to hit something. Or someone.

"The fuck...?" Kyle said. He took her by the shoulders again. "Baby, you're shaking."

"Did you hear what I said?" she screamed. "She sat right here and said that right in front of me! In my room! Did you hear me?"

"I know, I know, I heard you," said Kyle, trying to figure out what he should do. He felt like smacking that ugly Sharon himself. Seeing Marisa so upset was shocking. She was usually such a happy, calm and chill girl. "Baby, calm down..." He reached for her.

"I'm not going to calm down!" She smacked his hand away, startling him. "This can't be fixed with a hug and a kiss. She lives right down the hall from us!"

"We oughta beat her ass," Shawnda was saying.

"For real," Marisa echoed.

"Listen," Kyle interjected, making sure he stayed at least an arm's length away from Marisa's wrath. "I get it. But that won't accomplish anything but get us all into trouble. You need to go tell your R.A."

"You damn straight I will," said Shawnda, who stomped out the door, paused and then yelled down the hall toward Sharon's room. "This ain't the end of this, you stupid ass heffa!"

Marisa didn't care if Shawnda told the whole floor. No way Sharon was going to get away with this. During Black History Month, no less!

Pacing around the room, Marisa paused near the window and put her hand on her forehead. The rage she felt was mixing with sadness and embarrassment. As Kyle said, when would she learn? Well, this was it. She was done. D-O-N-E.

Watching her, Kyle guessed what she was thinking. Their conversation in the library came back to him instantly and he was smart enough to know not to rub it in. Instead, he stayed where he was, waiting for her to tell him what she needed. She had to work these feelings out herself. As nice as the thought of a colorblind society sounded, he knew it was a ridiculous notion. No, if you were black in America, you couldn't straddle the line between the races like Marisa had been trying to do. No, you had to choose. And if you didn't, America would choose for you.

Minutes later, Shawnda came back with Jacqui in tow. "She's on her way," she said, referring to the R.A. Marisa caught Jacqui's eye and with one look, expressed her acknowledgement that she'd been right about Sharon all along. Jacqui, to her credit, just asked, "You OK?"

"No," Marisa answered honestly, then looked around the room at the other three brown faces all standing by, ready to back her up and protect her. In that instant, she knew where she belonged, where she wanted to be. She knew she couldn't totally escape white people, but now, she knew. She knew they couldn't be trusted. Ever. "But I will be."

CHAPTER 13

March 1988

It was time for Kyle to meet Marisa's parents. He agreed to go home with her for spring break on the condition that they would only stay a few days before heading to Chicago to meet Robert and Kristin and hang out with Shawnda.

They were both nervous as they neared Petersville; Marisa, because she was afraid of his reaction to the small, rural town; Kyle, because he was meeting her parents, and her mother had been less-than-thrilled with the thought of Marisa even having a boyfriend.

"You're not nervous, are you?" she asked in the car, rubbing his hand.

"Well, yeah, who wouldn't be? You're their only girl and the youngest. I'm sure they hate me already," he joked, only half-serious.

"Daddy doesn't hate you," she reassured, then let the obvious omission hang in the air. Her mother never asked about Kyle on the phone, and whenever Marisa brought him up, she would respond with some kind of sarcastic, dismissive remark. It didn't matter what her mother thought of Kyle. She loved him and he was good for her.

When they were about five miles outside of the city limits, Marisa heard Kyle curse. "Shit." Looking in the rearview mirror, he muttered, "Cop."

Swirling around, Marisa recognized the brown cruiser of the county sheriff's department. "You're not even speeding," she said.

"I know." With a big sigh, he carefully put on his blinker and pulled to the side of the road. Marisa looked out her window and recognized the house they were in front of. The high school art teacher lived there alone with about five cats. Marisa never took her class, had never really liked her, but nevertheless was grateful that she didn't appear to be home.

"Hand me the rental car agreement out of the glove compartment." Kyle was speaking slowly and quietly, with both hands still on the steering wheel while his eyes darted from the rearview mirror to the driver's side mirror.

With a concerned glance at him, she did as he asked, then watched as the cop slowly walked alongside the driver's side door, where Kyle had already rolled down the window.

"You live around here?" The officer asked, looking Kyle up and down.

"No. We're visiting her family." Kyle was speaking slowly and hadn't moved his hands from the steering wheel.

The officer glanced into the car and surveyed Marisa. She'd known the county sheriff for years because he was married to her second-grade teacher. But she didn't know this guy.

"You live around here?" He asked her sharply. Something in his tone made her snap.

"Why did you pull us over?" she asked, staring him straight in the face, where her reflection glittered in his sunglasses.

"I asked you a question. Do you live around here?" He asked again.

Marisa glanced at Kyle in indignation, but he never took his eyes off the road. "Can you tell us why you stopped us? He wasn't speeding."

The officer paused, looked at Kyle again and then glanced in the empty backseat. "License and registration."

Infuriated at being ignored, Marisa asked again, enunciating each word. "Officer, why did you stop us?" She would have gone on, but at that moment, Kyle glanced at her with big eyes and hissed. "Marisa, please. Stop."

Startled, she swallowed the rest of her sentence and bit her lip. Kyle slowly handed the officer the rental car agreement and his driver's license then immediately returned his hands to the steering wheel.

"Philadelphia? What are you doing around here?"

When Marisa would have jumped in with another sarcastic remark, she bit her lip again and let Kyle answer. "We're students at Michigan State on spring break. My girlfriend grew up here and we're going to her parents' house in Petersville." Then as an afterthought, he added, "They own Logan's Hardware on Main Street."

The officer paused, smirked, then looked at Marisa. "Let me see your ID."

Before she could stop herself, she blurted. "Why do you need to see my ID?" But then she saw Kyle's face. It was pale, his chest was heaving up and down and she could see beads of sweat on his forehead. My God, she thought. He's scared. Without another word, she retrieved her purse, pulled out her driver's license and handed it to the officer. He glanced at it, turned it over, then handed it back to her.

"I'll be back."

They waited in silence, not looking at each other, not speaking, barely breathing. Marisa watched the cop out of her mirror and felt her nostrils start to flare. She wanted to cuss him out so badly, but she knew Kyle wanted to handle it his way. But what exactly was his way? To be meek and submissive? She'd never seen him like this and it was startling.

In order to have something to do, she reached into her purse again and stuffed a stick of gum in her mouth. After a few seconds, the loud pops from her chewing amplified the silence in the car while inwardly she stewed.

"You don't have any outstanding tickets or warrants, do you?" she asked in between pops.

When he didn't answer, she turned to him and expected to find him looking irritated at her question. Instead, his expression halted her mid-pop. He looked hurt. And betrayed. She didn't know whether to apologize or tell him she was joking so she said nothing, astounded and embarrassed at the disappointed look he'd shot her.

After several long, agonizing minutes, the officer returned, shoved Kyle's paperwork at him, then told him to watch his speed.

"I'll let you slide this time," he intoned. "No ticket. But this isn't big-city Philly. Life moves a little bit slower around here."

God, could he fit the stereotypical, small-town cop any better? How many episodes of "The Dukes of Hazzard" or "The Andy Griffith Show" did he watch, anyway? She still didn't know why he'd pulled them over and she didn't care what Kyle said, she was going to find out.

"Officer...Barnes," she said slowly as she read his name tag. "I'm positive we weren't speeding. In fact, I'd told him just a few minutes ago that he was going slow because he didn't want to meet my parents. Why did you pull us over?"

Officer Barnes leaned into the window and stared at her. "Your boyfriend here was going seventy in a fifty-five."

Before she could stop herself, Marisa let out a loud laugh. "That's crazy. No way he was going that fast!"

"I clocked him at seventy. You can come in the squad car and see for yourself." The statement, although worded like an invitation, was clearly a veiled warning. Come into the squad car and maybe stay there for a ride to the station.

She wanted to ask him why he didn't give Kyle a ticket if he was really going that fast, but she locked eyes with the officer, narrowed her eyes and then slowly leaned back against the seat.

With one last warning to "take it easy," the officer walked away and sat in his car while they drove off. Almost immediately, he swung out behind them and tailed them all the way to Petersville's Main

Street. Only when Marisa instructed Kyle to turn down her street did the squad car pass them en route to Allegan, the county seat and home of the sheriff's office.

In front of her house, neither moved. She knew they couldn't go in the house in frosty silence, so she tried to lighten the mood. "Well, he was an asshole."

Kyle was still looking in his driver's side mirror, probably afraid the cop would come back. "Yeah."

"Kyle..." She put a hand on his arm. "Are you OK?"

Averting her gaze, he unbuckled and ran a hand over his mouth. "Yeah, I'm fine. Let's go."

"Wait..." She took his hand. "I'm sorry for what I said. I don't know what I was thinking..."

But he was already shaking his head. "It's fine. You just... don't know any better. It's fine."

What did that mean? Before she could ask, she noticed a face in the window and saw her mother peeking out from behind the curtains. "I guess we better go in."

***

Despite what Kyle said, it was not fine. He was not himself the rest of the night. Sure, he smiled and laughed and was courteous and polite to her parents. He came upstairs to meet her grandmother, who was sitting in bed watching a repeat of "The Waltons." He devoured her mother's lasagna and homemade garlic bread, had two helpings of pound cake and sat on the couch laughing with her parents while they all watched a VHS copy of "Hollywood Shuffle." But when he thought no one was looking, he turned somber again. His eyes fell to the floor and he sighed quietly. And during those times, he looked ... defeated.

She remembered hearing her parents talk to her brothers about the police. About how black males were always suspects, treated unfairly and incarcerated at disparate numbers. When the boys started driving, her parents hammered home how they were to respond if pulled over, and by the time Marisa began driving, she already knew the rules. But this was Petersville. They only had two cops in town and they both knew the entire Logan family well. They were regular customers of the store, their kids were in the same class as Robert and Matthew and they wouldn't harm a fly. Even when she'd ventured out of Petersville, Marisa had never really been scared of the cops. If anything, she'd been scared of getting a ticket and getting her car keys taken away. Or of being grounded. But she wasn't so scared of the cops that she wouldn't challenge them or their authority. But Kyle apparently was.

They didn't get a chance to talk that night, and she figured it was best to let him get a good night's sleep. They could talk the next day. And then she could find out what he meant when he said she didn't "know any better."

***

It wasn't until later the next night, after her parents had gone to bed and they remained in the living room watching a late March Madness game that she broached the subject.

"Kyle?" They were sitting on the couch together but not touching. He hadn't touched her once since they came home and she didn't know if it was because they were in her parents' house or because he was mad at her.

"Hmm?" His legs were stretched out in front of him with a hand resting casually on his stomach.

"What did you mean yesterday when you said, I 'don't know any better'?" She watched his face closely but he didn't even blink. "Kyle?"

"What?" He finally glanced at her, eyebrows furrowed. "What are you talking about?"

"Yesterday, after the cop pulled us over and I told you I was sorry for what I said. You said, 'you don't know any better.' What did that mean?"

He continued to search her face, not smiling. "How many cops are in this town?"

"Two. Smitty and Slim. Officer Smith and Officer Bryant, who is about six-four and as thin as a toothpick. They've been here for years." She held her breath, already knowing where the conversation was going.

Kyle was nodding. "See, that's what I meant. Your history with police is totally different from mine. Totally different from any black person I know. They're not a threat to you."

"Of course they are! I'm still black! My brothers, my father...he lectured them about it for years."

"Good for him, but it's not real until it hits home, is it? Smitty and Slim knew your brothers and they probably never did anything to make your brothers – or you – look at them in fear or dread. Am I right?"

Marisa began picking at the gold and brown afghan thrown over her legs. "Right. They're harmless."

"Exactly. And because that was your first and only introduction to police, you grew up feeling comfortable around them and actually believing that they're here to protect and serve." He swung his head around to gaze at her again. "Right?" At her nod, he continued. "That's all I meant. Your view of police is ....it's just..."

"Like a white person's?" She finished quietly for him.

Seconds ticked by while he weighed his words. "Not exactly. I mean, your father explained it to your brothers and probably to you, too, so at least you're aware. So no, not like a white person's, but not exactly like your average black person's." He watched her as she continued to pick at the afghan with her head down. Touching her hand, he leaned toward her. "You're just different. And that's not a bad thing. It's partly why I love you."

"I love you, too." Searching his face, she decided to let the matter drop. She wasn't going to ask him about his experiences with police. Not yet. She was not going to bring up how scared he'd looked and how rattled she'd been by his expression and reaction. It just wasn't the time.

By Tuesday morning, Marisa was relieved to be leaving for Chicago and she hurriedly bid her family goodbye while Kyle exchanged hugs with both her mother and grandmother, to her delight.

Five minutes into their trip, as Kyle pulled into the Shell station to fill up on gas, she turned to him. "Do you need me to drive?"

And there it was. That look again. A mixture of hurt, disappointment and betrayal. "No, I don't need you to drive." Then he got out to pump the gas.

What did she say? All she did was offer to drive. Maybe if she drove, the cops would be less likely to pull them over because of some bullshit. Why couldn't he see that? Instead of feeling sorry, she was irritated. Since when did he become so sensitive, anyway?

They didn't speak again for the next hour. Once it became obvious that he was in a mood and was not going to talk, she grabbed her heavy jacket from the backseat, rolled it into a ball and used it as a pillow. Within minutes, she was sound asleep with her back to him. When she woke, they were already in Indiana.

"We're making good time," she yawned, before realizing they weren't speaking.

"Yep. I'm assuming we won't hit traffic until we get closer to the city." The answer was polite and unemotional.

And that's how it remained, all the way to Robert's place in Hyde Park, all the way through the Museum of Science and Industry on Wednesday, all during dinner at Rosebud's with Robert and Monica on Thursday, all the way to Evanston to say hi to Kristin at Northwestern on Friday, all the way to Chatham to hang out with Shawnda and her boyfriend-dujour, Alonzo, on Friday night.

Only there, in the bungalow-filled, black neighborhood, did he start to relax. He joked with Alonzo and Shawnda, teased Marisa about her never having tasted malt liquor and seemed back to normal. When the guys ventured to the store to get beer and some snacks, Marisa turned to Shawnda, who was perched on her water bed flipping through Cosmo. She spilled the entire story, about how the cop pulled them over for no reason, how weird Kyle acted, how Marisa challenged the cop and how odd Kyle had been acting ever since.

"Girl, that's some shit," Shawnda tsk'd and threw down the magazine. "I can understand how Kyle feels, being out in the boonies with some country-ass cop staring at him and shit. Damn."

"I get it, but why is he acting like he's mad at me?"

"He probably feels like you didn't have his back, that's why."

Marisa bristled. "What? I was the one who stood up for him! I was the one who challenged that asshole, not Kyle!"

With a shake of her head, Shawnda tsk'd again. "That's my point! You were making things worse. And what was he supposed to do if something went down, except protect you? It's like you were egging the cop on, which meant you were putting Kyle in danger. What if that cop tried to pull you out of the car, frisked you, had his hands all over you? What was Kyle supposed to do? What could he do? Don't you see how that made him feel?"

With every word, Marisa lost a breath. She felt like she was sinking deeper into the water bed as the ramifications of what had happened hit her. Damn, she really didn't know any better, did she? It never occurred to her that she was putting Kyle in danger. She thought he was being too submissive and accommodating, but damn. He was just trying to survive.

"What should I do?" she asked quietly.

"Don't say anything, that's for damn sure!" Shawnda hauled her ample rear end off the bed, stood at the dresser and combed her hair with quick, hard strokes. "Black men don't want to talk about this shit. They think it makes them look weak. And he probably thinks you're already looking at him like that, asking him if you should drive. Girl, what were you thinking? You act like you didn't grow up with three black men in the house!"

"I know! I know!" Marisa held her head in her hands. Although she'd grown up with three black males, those same males had shielded her from the reality of being a black man in America. But Kyle...being by his side, being the man she loved...that was different. Now she was going to see the realities up close. And the effects on his psyche, self-esteem and emotions. "What can I do?"

Shawnda glanced at her in the mirror with a sigh. "You need to build him up. Make him feel needed, strong, brave, what have you. You need to look at him like you used to. It's bad enough that this country emasculates him, he doesn't need his girlfriend to do it, too."

When Marisa lowered her head in shame, Shawnda nudged her. "Oh, girl, come on! Don't be like that. Just go back to how you used to be, all sickening and sweet and lovey-dovey. He'll get over it soon enough, OK?

"It's not easy loving a black man, you know," Shawnda said, then smiled. "But it's definitely worth it."

CHAPTER 14

Fall 1988

Sophomore year at Michigan State and Marisa was fully embraced and ensconced in black campus life.

With Shawnda as her roommate, Jacqui and Janet two doors down, a new black R.A. next door and two black freshmen from Flint across the hall, there was no longer a need for Marisa to hang out with any white girls. Most of the girls she knew from freshman year were gone, anyway. Molly and Charla moved somewhere else on campus, and no one cared enough to find out where, and of course, Sharon didn't dare show her face around Brody anymore. Aside from the forced encounters in class, Marisa didn't talk to, socialize with or dine with any white students. Her time in the "other" dining room was over for good.

One night in late October, after attending an off-campus party with her friends and Kyle, Marisa climbed the steps to her loft bed and snuggled under the covers, still feeling the effects of the Jack Daniels she'd drank. Just when she was about to doze off, she heard Shawnda's voice.

"Marisa?"

"Yeah?"

"I have to tell you something."

Turning over to face her in the dark, she asked again. "Yeah?"

"I'm pregnant."

Raising on one elbow, Marisa strained her eyes to see if Shawnda was smiling or laughing. She had to be kidding. "What? Shawnda, that's not funny."

"I'm not laughing."

Marisa froze in the same spot, trying to figure out if she was being played for a fool. It didn't help that the liquor was dulling her senses and her reaction time. "You are not pregnant. You must think I'm an idiot."

A loud sigh from the other side of the room, then a voice that didn't even sound like Shawnda's pierced through the darkness. It was quiet and tinged with tears. "Why would I lie about this?"

Throwing back the covers, Marisa rose, clamored down the steps and turned on a lamp underneath the loft. She then climbed back up the stairs and stared at Shawnda. "Are you really pregnant?" But as soon as she saw Shawnda's face, streaked with tears, she knew she was telling the truth.

"Oh my God..." Her heart started to beat faster and she couldn't stop staring at her roommate, now sitting up herself and shaking her head.

"I was so dumb," she was saying. "You know the Pill made me sick, but I was always so careful..."

Marisa didn't know what to say. Through her buzzed haze, she recognized the feelings coursing through her as shock, numbness and – honestly – irritation. How could she have been so stupid? To Marisa, not taking the Pill was not being "so careful."

"Does Alonzo know?" she asked. Yes, he was kind of a loser with no future, but he was nice and he had a job and he seemed to really like Shawnda. Even without all that, he deserved to know he was going to be a father.

"Girl, it's not Alonzo's."

Marisa almost fell off the step. "Wait, wait..." She climbed down, told Shawnda to get down, too, and sat on the love seat. A few seconds later, she saw Shawnda's pink and white polka dot socks emerge on the steps.

Plopping wearily next to her, Shawnda put her feet on the coffee table, grabbed a green throw pillow and clutched it to her bosom.

"If it's not Alonzo's, then whose is it?" Marisa demanded, clutching the matching throw pillow to her chin. She was almost afraid to hear her answer. What if she didn't know whose baby it was? She could be a guest on Sally Jessy Raphael to find out.

"I dropped Alonzo at the end of July. No way this is his. I got with my high school boyfriend over Labor Day. Remember me telling you about him?" Marisa nodded. Darren was her boyfriend all through high school, but she broke up with him right before leaving for Michigan State because she learned that he'd tried to get with one of her friends. That didn't stop her from talking to him on the phone occasionally, writing him letters and – apparently, sleeping with him.

"This is Darren's baby?" At her nod, Marisa continued. "What did he say?"

She shook her head. "I didn't tell him."

Marisa didn't know how much more she could take. "Well, are you going to?"

"Hell no." Shawnda clutched the pillow tighter and shook her head again. "He has a girlfriend. It was just … it was nothing. He don't need to know."

"Shawnda…" Marisa put a hand on her arm. "You have to tell him! He's going to be a father!"

"No, he's not." Shawnda had yet to meet Marisa's eyes.

"What are you talking about? You said it was his baby…?"

"Yes, it is. But he's not going to be a father. I'm getting rid of it."

At that, Marisa recoiled. Abortion? She stared at Shawnda in horror. Was she serious?

She finally looked at her. "Don't give me that look. You know I can't have no baby. I'm nineteen! I'm in college! What would I look like, having a baby now?"

"Yeah, but…" Marisa was horrified at the thought. Could she really have an abortion?

"But nothing. I don't have a choice. I'm getting rid of it."

Marisa wished she'd stop using that phrase. It wasn't an "it." It was a baby. "There's always adoption. You could give the baby to someone who can't have kids. I keep hearing how newborns are hard to find."

"Who's gonna take a black baby?" Shawnda tsk'd and sighed. "It's all arranged. My appointment is Monday morning. I wasn't even gonna tell you but they said I need someone to drive me home. They won't let me take the bus or a cab by myself."

"But I don't have a car," Marisa protested.

"You can ask Kyle to borrow his. We do it all the time." True, Marisa borrowed Kyle's Bronco to drive her friends to the mall, the grocery store, the movies and to pick up takeout for dinner.

"But I have class Monday morning." She didn't know what else to say, she was still trying to wrap her mind around this entire conversation.

"You can't skip? It's not finals or nothing." Shawnda looked at her, pleading. "You're the only person I've told."

For God's sake, didn't she have anyone else at home she could trust? She had a good relationship with her big sister. Couldn't she tell her? Or her high school best friend. She would be more than supportive. "Shawnda, don't you think you need to tell Darren? And anyway, how do you even know you're pregnant? Have you actually gone to a doctor?" Before the words were out of her mouth, Shawnda was nodding.

"Yes, girl, yes. I went to the student health center last week. You didn't notice me throwing up and sleeping all the time?"

Suddenly embarrassed at how oblivious she'd been, Marisa turned away, holding her head in her hands. She wasn't ready for this. College was supposed to be fun. This was way too serious and heavy and deep to be dealing with. "Well, how far along are you? Maybe it's too late for ..."

"No, I'm about five weeks, the doctor said. Not too late."

They sat in silence for several minutes, Marisa trying to grasp the gravity of this revelation. Her roommate, one of the first black girls on the floor to reach out to her, was asking for her help and support. But could she give it? Marisa had never known anyone to have an abortion before. The concept was so far-fetched that she never gave it much thought. When she was freaking out about having sex with Kyle and the possibility of birth control, she'd never considered what she'd do if she actually did get pregnant. She'd obviously keep the baby, right? But what if she was presented with another option? Could she do it? While she wasn't exactly raised in the church, she'd gone enough times to know the commandment "thou shalt not kill." And west Michigan was a hotbed for members of the Republican Party and the conservative Christian Reformed Church. She doubted anyone could get an abortion in west Michigan even if they wanted to. Granted, she and her family were always staunch Democrats and she was looking forward to voting for Michael Dukakis in her first presidential election next month. But while she agreed with a woman's right to choose, it was always abstract before. Now it was real. And staring at her from the other side of the love seat.

"Well? Can you drive me?" Shawnda asked.

Turning to face her, Marisa took her hand. "Are you sure you want to do this?"

"I'm sure, Marisa," she said, sounding anything but.

"Well, how are you paying for this anyway? Doesn't it cost a lot of money?"

"It does. My dad sent me some money for my birthday, I had some saved up and then I pawned some jewelry to make up the rest," she said, shrugging.

"Why should you have to pawn your jewelry? Darren should help pay for it! You have to tell him!"

"No, dammit!" Shawnda got up and grabbed a tissue from her desk.

"Why not? Why do you care about his girlfriend? He obviously doesn't care about her! Why should you?"

With another swipe of her eyes, Shawnda sighed resignedly, looking like a kid herself in her pale pink pajamas. "Because he'd want to keep it."

"Oh." Well, that made it even worse, Marisa thought. How would he feel to find out later that she'd killed his child? She didn't voice that thought, though, because Shawnda looked stricken enough already. "Listen, it's late. You need some sleep." She looked tired and scared and sad. Marisa rose, gave her a long hug and sighed. "It'll be OK. We'll talk tomorrow, OK?"

"OK." Then with a lingering look, said, "Thank you, Marisa. Please don't tell anybody, OK? Not even Kyle. Promise?"

"I promise."

***

And she kept that promise, even though Kyle knew something was on her mind the next day during the game. He didn't press, and Marisa was grateful to be lost in her own thoughts.

By the time she got back to her room later that night, Shawnda was there, in the loft again, flipping through a pamphlet from the clinic. "You told Kyle, didn't you?" she asked without looking up.

"What? No, I didn't. I told you I wouldn't."

With a raised eyebrow, Shawnda continued to read. "OK. What'd you tell him about borrowing his car?"

She hesitated. "I didn't. I couldn't come up with an excuse for why I needed it when he knew I'd usually be in class."

With a frustrated sigh, Shawnda put down the pamphlet. "Girl, why are you so scary around him? He's not your daddy! Just tell him anything! Dang..."

"I know, I know, but it's his car. I usually ask for it only on weekends or at night. What possible reason could I have to borrow it on a Monday morning?"

"Don't matter. All you had to do was sweet talk him into it after y'all got through fucking." Marisa flinched. She hated it when Shawnda talked like that. She made their relationship sound so primitive. "Men will agree to anything right after, you know."

Marisa didn't respond and struggled with a way to give her a definitive yes or no. But how could she when she didn't even know yet? Before she could speak, Shawnda spoke again. "Anyway, it don't matter. The clinic called while you were gone this morning. They're changing my appointment to Tuesday afternoon."

"Oh." Her classes ended at 2 p.m. on Tuesdays, which meant it was perfectly reasonable to ask Kyle to borrow his Bronco then. She could pretend she had to go get groceries or something. "What time Tuesday?"

"Three-thirty," Shawnda flipped her pillow over and faced the wall.

"OK. I'll talk to Kyle." She waited for a response but none came.

***

But Marisa didn't talk to Kyle. She couldn't bring herself to do it on Sunday nor on Monday morning while they walked to class. She knew that the more time went by, the more she was going to be backed into a corner. Delaying was not a good option but she honestly had no idea what to do.

When she arrived home from class that afternoon, she found the lights off in her room and the blinds closed. The TV, usually tuned into Oprah Winfrey at that hour, was off. Shawnda was in bed, deep under the covers. Marisa tiptoed to the closet, hung up her coat then did a doubletake at something that caught her eye. In Shawnda's laundry basket was a pair of gray sweat pants, stained with blood.

Puzzled, she looked closer. Yep, it was definitely blood. And those were the same sweatpants Shawnda was wearing that morning when Marisa left for class. Did that mean she got her period? Was she not pregnant after all?

Looking around the darkened room, she searched for clues, such as a bottle of Tylenol for cramps, a box of tampons or some chocolate, which Shawnda ate by the ton every month during her period. She didn't find any of those, but she did spot two prescription bottles on Shawnda's desk. Inching closer, she quietly picked them both up, saw they were both prescribed to Shawnda with today's date then looked at the names of the medicines. She didn't know what either one meant, but the label on one read "Take 1 every 4-6 hours as needed for pain." The other read, "Take 2 daily with food." What on Earth? Marisa bit the inside of her mouth, speculating. Had she changed her mind about the abortion? Maybe these were prenatal vitamins?

The phone ringing made her jump. Reaching for it after the first ring so Shawnda wouldn't wake up, she answered quietly.

"Hi. May I speak to Shawnda, please?"

Well, that settled it. The official-sounding voice on the other end could only belong to someone from Planned Parenthood, she surmised. They must have been calling to confirm her appointment for the next day. She heard Shawnda stirring and held the phone out to her. "It's for you. I think it's the clinic."

She listened as Shawnda said several "uh-huh's" and "OKs" then "Eight." When she was done, she handed the receiver to Marisa and got back under the covers. "Shawnda?"

No answer.

"Why are you in your pajamas? And why are the lights off and the blinds closed?"

Still no answer.

With her heart beating faster, Marisa picked up the pills. "Shawnda, what are these for? Do you have to take these...before...?"

Still no answer.

"Listen," Marisa said, looking up at the loft at Shawnda's darkened form outlined in the shadows. "I'm heading to Kyle's now to ask him about his car for tomorrow." She knew it was too late for Shawnda to find another ride, so she basically realized she had no choice.

"Forget it," Shawnda said into the covers.

"What?"

In a louder voice, Shawnda answered. "I said forget it. It's done."

Marisa suddenly felt cold. "What do you mean, it's done?"

A pause, then: "I already went."

Marisa blinked and her legs turned to Jell-O. Leaning against Shawnda's desk, she asked in a shaky voice. "What do you mean?"

Shawnda finally turned over and looked Marisa in the eye. "I went to the clinic myself this morning. It's done."

Shaking her head with tears in her eyes, Marisa sputtered, "But...you said they wouldn't let you....how?"

Shrugging, Shawnda avoided her eyes. "I called a friend to come pick me up. I told him I had to get some blood drawn and I was too weak to take the bus."

Marisa gulped. A friend? Did Shawnda not consider her a friend? And what friend did she have with a car? "I thought you said they moved it to tomorrow? Did they move it back?"

"Girl, they never moved it. I just told you that to let you off the hook. I knew you didn't want to do it." Shawnda looked her dead in the eye. "Am I right?"

Averting her gaze, Marisa gulped. It was true. She didn't really want to do it, but felt she had to in order to preserve their friendship. Besides, she couldn't let her do something like that by herself. But that's what she ended up doing anyway. She'd taken the bus by herself, she'd sat in the waiting room by herself, she'd signed the paperwork by herself, she'd gotten prepped by herself, she went through the procedure and the recovery by herself. And all to let Marisa off the hook.

"Shawnda…" Marisa climbed up the loft steps and sat on her bed. "You didn't have to do that. You shouldn't have gone by yourself," she chided, wiping her eyes.

Her roommate waved her hand dismissively. "It's fine. I got into this mess, I had to get myself out. No need to drag you into this drama. Your life is perfect, you don't need me to bring all this darkness into it."

She'd never heard her roommate talk like that before. Sure, she teased Marisa constantly about being "happy all the time," but she didn't really think Marisa's life was perfect, did she? "My life is not perfect," she protested.

"Girl, please. You're gorgeous, you got the perfect body, white-girl hair, you got a 4.0 GPA and you got somebody like Kyle. You don't worry about money, you don't have to stand in line at the financial aid office, you don't have to defer your leftover tuition payments to next term….You have the perfect life. I shouldn't have asked you in the first place."

Marisa felt like crying. She never considered her life perfect, especially not while living in Petersville. But here, among her black friends, she was aware of being an "other." Aside from her looks, she did realize how privileged and safe her world was. Janet had told stories of drug dealers in her neighborhood, LaToya from Flint mentioned how they had to have their football and basketball games right after school because too many shootings happened at night and Jacqui told her about how she worked two jobs this summer just to return to Michigan State. Meanwhile, Marisa was redecorating, hanging out on the beach and gallivanting to Philly, D.C. and Martha's Vineyard all summer.

"And I never should have asked you to keep it a secret from Kyle," Shawnda was saying. "I know you hate to lie to him or keep secrets from him. So if you need to talk to him about it, I understand. I just don't want him looking at me funny and shit."

"Listen, are you OK? I mean...I saw some blood on your sweats..." Marisa tried to see her face in the darkened room.

"I'm fine. I got those pills there to take for pain and to ward off any infections," Shawnda's voice got fainter. "I'm just really tired. It's been a long day."

Marisa still couldn't believe she did this by herself and vowed to make it up to her. "What do you need? Are you hungry? Need some ginger ale or something?"

"Actually, yeah, that would be good. I'm not hungry but I can take those pills with some ginger ale. It's almost time for my dose."

Marisa grabbed her wallet and keys and eased out the door, locking it behind her. She greeted a few folks in the hallway coming home from class then headed straight to the vending machines. While there, she leaned a hand against the soda machine and closed her eyes. The guilt and sadness overtook her immediately and she held back a sob. What kind of a friend was she, anyway? Friendship wasn't just about having fun and talking about guys. It was about being there for each other when needed. She'd failed miserably.

Hearing footsteps behind her, she straightened and pretended to study the choices. "I thought that was you," Kyle said behind her. He had his backpack flung over his shoulder and had obviously just walked in from class. Seeing her serious and stricken face, he touched her shoulder. "What? What's wrong?"

She didn't trust herself to speak and merely shook her head. "I'll tell you later. I have to bring this ginger ale to Shawnda. Will you be in your room?" Kyle nodded, alarmed at her glistening eyes and sad face.

"OK. I'll come by after giving this to Shawnda, OK?"

Studying her face, he watched as she wiped her eyes, held the cold drink to her eyes then sniffed. "Is she sick or something?"

Marisa merely nodded then walked away, leaving a perplexed Kyle to stare at her retreating back.

Within minutes, she walked into his room and flopped on his bed. "What's going on?"

With a heavy sigh, she spilled the whole story. He listened in shock, asked no questions and continuously rubbed her back while she talked. When she was exhausted from telling the story, she stated quietly, "I'm an awful friend."

"You're not an awful friend," Kyle continued to rub her back, trying to find words to make her feel better. "Honestly, it was a hard position for you to be in. And she didn't give you much time to digest it or think about it. Don't beat yourself up. I know you wanted to help her, deep inside."

Marisa was quiet then spoke to the floor. "Did I? Or did I want to just change her mind?"

Pausing, Kyle smoothed down her hair. "I don't know. Did you try to talk her out of it?"

Recounting their conversations, she shrugged. "I think I spent most of my time trying to convince her to tell her ex-boyfriend. He had a right to know." She turned to him with big eyes. "Didn't he?"

"Of course he did!" Kyle thought about how he'd feel if Marisa was pregnant, didn't tell him and had an abortion without his knowledge. The thought made him sick. "He definitely did."

They sat lost in their own thoughts before she asked, "What do you believe, Kyle? Are you pro-choice?" They hadn't really talked about politics before, but with the upcoming election, it was definitely a timely conversation.

Kyle paused before answering slowly. "I don't think anyone without a uterus should tell someone with a uterus what to do with that uterus. So if that makes me pro-choice, then OK."

Contemplating his words, Marisa definitely agreed with him but still had unease about the reality of it. At any rate, what was done was done.

CHAPTER 15

May 1989

Black students all over the country had had enough. In March, Howard University students took over the administration building to protest the appointment of Republican Lee Atwater to its board of trustees. In April, students at Wayne State University in Detroit had their demands met after a ten-day sit-in. Even all-girl and predominantly white Sarah Lawrence had a sit-in after someone painted a racist mural on campus.

As a member of the Emmons Black Student Alliance, Marisa was well aware of the other colleges and their activism. Michigan State, she learned, was simmering as well and would undoubtedly blow soon, too.

Black students were disgruntled by a lack of action on the administration's part regarding racism on campus, appropriate representation in the provost's office and the graduation rate of African-American students. Earlier in the year, the local NAACP joined student leaders in taking their concerns to the president's office. They'd promised to keep the lines of communication open and address the concerns.

"We have yet to hear anything from the president, the provost or the board of trustees!" Bellowed one of the student leaders during a campus-wide Black Alliance meeting in late April. Marisa was there with Shawnda, Jacqui, Janet and Kyle. "Since the meeting with them, more racist incidents have occurred on this campus! A young lady in Wonders reports someone wrote 'nigger' on her eraser board on her door. Nothing was done and the perpetrator was not caught. Now that girl is living in fear in her own dorm! In her own dorm!

"And now this latest incident. We all know how much this campus loves its eccentric astronomy professor, Doc DuBerry. They trot him out everywhere to discuss space, astronomy and his latest thoughts on space shuttle travel. But have they done anything about the racist remarks he uttered in class just a few short weeks ago?"

The orator paused like a good preacher would and kept the audience in suspense. Marisa had already heard about it because she read the campus newspaper, The State News, religiously. They had covered the whole thing.

"He had the audacity –" emphasis on audacity " – to say that the reason he doesn't have more black students in his class is because they quote 'can't handle it.'" The entire crowd groaned and gasped and Marisa saw several faculty members shake their heads in disbelief. "He thinks we're stupid, y'all. He thinks we're dumb and ignorant and can't handle anything more than the very basic classes."

"He obviously don't know you two," Jacqui leaned over and whispered to Marisa and Kyle.

The student leader continued. "And what has the administration done about their star professor? Nothing! And get this, y'all. He doesn't even deny it. When asked to comment by a reporter at The State News, he doubled down. He stood by his words, people! So you know what we need to do. We need to stand up, too, and do everything we can to get this racist professor off the faculty! Down with Doc! Down with Doc!" He led them in a chant as the meeting broke up.

As they left the building, they were handed fliers for another demonstration taking place over the weekend. But if what Marisa heard was true, then their campus would be the next one for a sit-in. Details were still sketchy and shared verbally in whispers and in private conversations, but the plan was to take over the administration building sometime in the next week. All black student alliance groups were asked to spread the word so turnout would be high. Problem was, Marisa wasn't even sure if she was going to participate.

Later that evening, in her locked dorm room, she sat with Kyle, his roommate Will, Shawnda, Jacqui and Janet discussing it.

"Look, I'm down," Kyle said while perched on her desk. "The only way to get the president's attention is to do something like this. He thinks all this mess with Doc will just pass, but nah. It's only going to get bigger once we take over the building."

Shawnda and Janet were nodding, but Jacqui, Will and Marisa were uneasy. As the resident rule-follower, she was terrified of getting kicked out of school but also itching to do something daring and meaningful. "Our list of demands includes amnesty from any disciplinary actions," Kyle said in an effort to ease their minds. "Nothing will happen to you."

"But how long will we be there?" Jacqui asked.

"However long it takes."

"I don't know..." she said, biting her lip.

"I ain't going," Will said. "Shit, I got too much on the line. Y'all can go and represent for me and fight the power and all that shit, but if I don't graduate, my mama and my grandmama will kill me!" He shook his head. "Nope, I'm sitting this one out."

"Man..." Kyle rolled his eyes. "You a sucka."

"Then I'ma be a sucka with a college degree!" He stood and walked out, muttering the whole time.

"Kyle, make sure he keeps this quiet," Marisa reminded him. "We don't want the wrong people to find out about this ahead of time."

"I got you," he said, turning to a nervous Jacqui. "Well? Are you in?"

Sighing, she bit her lip again and looked around the room. "Sorry, I don't think so. I just think there are other ways to make things improve. We haven't even given the administration that much time to make it right."

"Jacqui, their timeframe has come and gone," Shawnda said heatedly. "They should have done something about this Doc mothafucker days ago! But the fact is they didn't. So now they need to pay the piper." Marisa had no idea Shawnda was so militant, but lately she'd taken to wearing black leather medallions with outlines of Africa on it and had a baseball cap in red, green and black. She'd let Marisa borrow her copy of "The Autobiography of Malcom X" and she was mesmerized. So now even Marisa had a T-shirt featuring Malcolm X with the words "By Any Means Necessary." But wearing a shirt, listening to KRS-One and Public Enemy and reading books was one thing. Putting her entire academic career on the line was another.

As Jacqui deferred joining the sit-in, Shawnda, Janet and Kyle turned to Marisa. "Well? What are you going to do?"

She looked at all three of them then looked at Jacqui. Since coming to Michigan State, she was grateful that she'd had the opportunity to taste the black experience. But she wanted the full black experience. And that meant everything. The intellectual black experience. The beougie black experience a la Martha's Vineyard. The partying black experience. The black Greek life. The musical black experience. And yes, the activist black experience. She'd been robbed of all of them her whole life and now she was like a woman dying of thirst who suddenly had acres of water fountains from which to drink. Why pick just one or two? Sample them all.

She thought back to all of the slights and comments she'd endured in Petersville. She thought of stupid Sharon and what she'd said last year. She thought about the time she'd entered Wells Hall for math class and noticed that it took her almost fifteen minutes before she even saw a non-white face. She thought about the fact that she'd only had one black professor in two years at MSU while most of her friends hadn't had any. And finally, she thought about her grandmother. Her grandmother, who'd passed away just two months earlier from a massive stroke. Marisa was still grieving and in disbelief at times that she was actually gone. She used to tell Marisa about the racism and injustice she'd endured while growing up in Kentucky. She used to tell her granddaughter to always stand up and fight. For herself, for others. In short, she taught her to never take shit from anybody.

"I'm in."

***

The sit-in lasted eight days. Janet and Shawnda caved after three nights of sleeping on a hard tile floor while Kyle and Marisa lasted the entire time. The experience was exhilarating. They sang songs, chanted, played games and called their parents to reassure them that they were fine, not in danger and not going to get kicked out of school. "I'm getting so much homework done," she told her mother, who went ballistic: "You get your ass out of there and get back to class!" Her father, though, was supportive: "Do what you feel is right. Just be careful." Both of Kyle's parents were totally down for the cause and his mother even flew in to bring them some food and give them a pep talk.

On day seven, when they knew negotiations were going in their favor and that their time in the building was ending, leaders allowed more reporters into the building, including student reporters from The State News. Marisa was leaning against a potted plant, doing her statistics homework, when a pair of Birkenstock sandals stopped in front of her. Looking up, she saw a thin white girl with long, plain brown hair smiling at her.

"My boyfriend has that same book," she said, gesturing to the statistics textbook. "He hates it. I think he's going to fail."

"Oh." Marisa grimaced. Stats was easy for her, but why brag?

"My name is Elizabeth Allen with The State News," she said as she kneeled next to Marisa. "Do you mind if I ask you a few questions?"

Marisa glanced around at the other protesters sitting nearby, students who were strangers just a week ago whom she now called friends. They watched the interaction, awaiting her response.

"What kind of questions?"

"We understand the sit-in is almost over," Elizabeth said. "What do you think will change once you get out?"

Marisa thought back to the conversations she'd had with Kristin over the past year. She was majoring in journalism at Northwestern and was working on their student newspaper. She knew what to look for with the media and how to protect yourself from being misquoted. "What's your story about exactly?"

Elizabeth seemed surprised but pleased. "It's a feature story, about why students like yourself thought campus life needed to change for black students. It's not about the list of demands or Doc DuBerry, it's more about what life is like as a black student here."

"Kind of a think piece? Or a day-in-the-life story?" Marisa asked.

"Exactly!" Elizabeth sat cross-legged on the floor. "Can you spare a few minutes?"

With a pause, Marisa considered the request. Was it fair for her to be a spokesperson for typical black MSU students? She wasn't, as Kyle and Shawnda liked to point out, a typical black student. But should that matter? She was still black.

Shrugging, she sat up straighter. "Sure."

The story ran on the front page two days after the sit-in ended. The centerpiece photo was a close-up of Marisa, talking to the reporter. The cutline read, "Marisa Logan, sophomore, packaging engineering, says black students at MSU carry an extra burden that white students do not. 'Not only are we trying to navigate college, classes and career choices, we have a fourth C: Color. The color of our skin. It impacts how professors see us, what our dorm mates think of us, what the campus police do. That kind of burden can't be contained in a backpack or in a textbook. It's too heavy.' "

THE KITCHEN ISN'T WHERE YOU COOK

Marisa was standing in the lobby of her dorm, reading it in shock. Damn. She sounded so smart and deep. The headline for the story blared: "Green and White ... and Black: What's It Like to be African-American at MSU?"

Grabbing a handful of copies, she hurried down the hallway to her room, where she read the whole story. The reporter talked to a few other students at the sit-in, but she quoted Marisa the most. The jump page had another photo of her holding hands with the rest of the protesters as they sang the black national anthem just before leaving the building. The story was well-written, fair and thought-provoking. Elizabeth did a good job, Marisa thought. In another life, they'd probably be friends. But not anymore.

On the way to class, she ran into friends from Brody, all of whom had seen the story. In statistics class, Elizabeth's boyfriend approached her and told her how much Elizabeth enjoyed talking to her. Marisa told him she was pleased with the story and to thank his girlfriend the next time he saw her.

And on and on it went. Friends she hadn't talked to since freshman year called her. Strangers stopped her and told her they recognized her from the newspaper and loved what she had to say. Professors praised her. And yes, some white students told her that her comments were completely divisive and unnecessary and "reverse-racist." But she ignored them. They essentially proved her point.

By that afternoon, as she wearily plopped down on the love seat in her room, she reflected on how weird the whole situation was. Here she was, barely two years out of Petersville, and she was the voice of the black MSU student. Was it because of how she spoke? For even though she was now immersed in black culture and didn't sound like a white girl as much, she still had that tone. Still had the vocabulary, the enthusiasm. Was that it? Or was it because she'd been able to express what she'd seen and heard from her friends over the past two years without actually experiencing it as harshly as they had? Yes, Sharon had uttered a racial slur in front of her, but it was the subtle things that drove Marisa crazy. The way professors assumed she needed extra help or was on financial aid. The way people were surprised to hear that her father owned his own business. Or how shocked they were to learn she was not from Detroit, Flint, Saginaw or Chicago. Marisa's words in the newspaper came from a place she didn't know existed. A place that had bubbled up from deep within, cultivated after years of being an outsider in both worlds. And that place was called perspective.

CHAPTER 16

Winter-Spring 1990

It pays to have connections, Marisa thought as she looked over her official internship offer.

Over the summer, while vacationing on Martha's Vineyard with Kyle's family, she met Benjamin Rice, the human resources leader for Perkins and Peterson, or P&P, one of the world's largest pharmaceutical companies. He had been intrigued by her grades, packaging engineering major and background. It helped, of course, that he had been friends with Kyle's family since he was a kid. He'd urged Marisa to apply for an internship, and when the official offer came in January of her junior year, Marisa told everyone: Her friends, her professors and even her first white friend since freshman year, Christy, from Traverse City, who was in all of her packaging classes. In their male-dominated major, they had to prove their intelligence in every class and God forbid they ever had a wrong answer because then they had to prove themselves all over again.

Christy never asked about going to Marisa's apartment, though, and while she talked about Kyle, she never introduced the two of them. To Kyle, Christy was just a friend from class. Mixing her two lives together was the last thing she wanted to do, and over time, she realized that she was reverting back to the same thing she did her freshman year: Keeping her white world and her black world totally separate.

That became harder to do during spring term when she got a phone call one Thursday evening. She was shocked to hear Tara's voice on the other line. "Tara? Hi! How are you?" For once, she was not spending the night at Kyle's and was lounging on the couch in her off-campus apartment watching "Cheers" while Shawnda and Jacqui sat at the kitchen table doing homework. She felt her roommates' eyes on her as she spoke.

She listened with a sinking heart as Tara told her how she and Jen were in East Lansing for the weekend and wouldn't she like to hang out with them and go "bar-hopping" on Friday night? "What are you doing up here, though?" Marisa asked in semi-horror. This was her spot, far away from Petersville in both distance and mindset. They couldn't ruin her utopia.

"One of Jen's friends is dating a guy up here so we just jumped in the car with her to come up and see him. He lives in a frat house so there are guys galore!" Tara gushed. Marisa felt guilty for ignoring Tara all this time. She never called her, never wrote her and hadn't seen her at home in over a year. Tara had never done anything racist or irritating to her like Jen or Barry had. Tara was just clueless. Unlike Kristin, she could never tell Tara how she was feeling about race relations because she'd think it was all one-sided and in her imagination. The last thing she wanted to do was hang out with Tara and Jen this weekend.

"Uh, well....I don't know. Let me see what Kyle has planned..." she said, rolling her eyes.

Tara left the number of the house they were staying at and Marisa pretended to write it down. Hanging up, she turned the volume back up on "Cheers" and ignored Shawnda's questions about the phone call. When a commercial came on, Marisa finally turned to her. "It was a friend from high school. She and another girl are up here for the weekend and want to hang out."

"Oh yeah? Where at?"

Marisa untangled her legs from the couch and trudged over to the table. "They want to go 'bar hopping' tomorrow night," she said, using air quotes. "And they're hanging out at some fraternity house."

"So are you going to meet up with 'em?" Shawnda asked. "You want us to come with you?"

With her mouth agape, Marisa sat at the table with a thud. "Are you kidding? No, I don't want to meet up with them. And you definitely don't want to go bar-hopping or hang out at a frat house."

"I don't know. Some of them white boys are cute," Shawnda giggled while Jacqui rolled her eyes and shook her head. Jacqui would never date a white dude. The darker the better was her mantra.

"Anyway, I'm done with those people and I'm done partying with white folks," Marisa tapped her fingers on the table.

"So why didn't you just tell her no?" Jacqui asked directly.

The truth was, Marisa didn't know why. There was some deep, internal part of her that still considered her friends from high school her friends. They'd grown up together, hung out at each other's houses, bought their first bras together, laughed, cried and matured together. Yes, they were all white and she was black, but those formative years were not so easy to turn away from. And, honestly, she'd loved almost every minute of it, except for the last two to three months of high school. If it wasn't for that damn Barry and his racist hag of a grandmother, she'd have pretty good memories of Petersville.

Tara called again the next day and left a message for Marisa. This time Kyle was with her when she got it and she had to explain the whole thing to him, too.

"We're not doing anything tonight," he said, swiping a Granny Smith apple from the kitchen and polishing it on his Polo shirt. "Why wouldn't you want to go and introduce your fine-ass boyfriend to your friends?"

"Kyle, I don't bar hop. You don't bar hop."

"We don't have to 'hop.' We can meet them at one bar early in the evening, say hi, have a couple of drinks, then leave. What are you afraid of?"

"I'm not afraid," she protested. But was she? Was she afraid of reverting back to her Petersville – that is, white – voice? Was she afraid of her friends accusing her of changing too much? "It's just not how I want to spend my time."

"And you'd rather do what tonight?" He challenged her, chomping on the apple. "We have no plans until tomorrow night. Meeting them would take maybe an hour, then you'd be done."

Opening the refrigerator door to search for some Tang, Marisa sucked her teeth. "Don't you have a step show tomorrow?"

"Yeah, so?"

"So don't you have to practice for it?"

"We practice tomorrow morning. We're good." He took the glass of Tang she offered, gulped it down in just a few swallows then looked at her. "Listen, we'll stay just long enough to say hi, chat a little, then leave. OK? Besides, I have got to meet this Jen you've told me so much about."

Later that night, she and Kyle walked hand-in-hand into Dooley's, where white students mingled outside on the sidewalk and the music from inside pulsated loudly. Inside, they surveyed the room, but to Kyle, everyone looked the same. "Do you see them?" he asked, leaning close to her ear so she could hear him.

She began to shake her head then heard a familiar laugh. Standing at the far end of the bar was Tara, her redhead bent backward as she took a shot of some kind of liquor. Standing next to her with her back to Marisa was the slim frame and blonde hair Marisa recognized as Jen's. She felt like leaving at that moment, but that's when Tara spotted her. "Marisa!" she yelled and waved, causing several heads to turn, Jen's among them. Their eyes met and neither one smiled. Jen took another sip of her drink, put it on the counter and whispered something to the other blonde girl standing with her.

Marisa nodded in their direction to let Kyle know she'd found them. They made their way around the bar where Tara jumped up and down and hugged Marisa tight. "It's so good to see you! You look amazing!" She looked Marisa up and down and despite herself,

Marisa found herself smiling and laughing. Tara always was fun to be around. "And you must be Kyle," she said, giving Marisa an approving glance before throwing her arms around him, too.

Taken aback, Kyle quickly stepped away. The last thing he needed was for some white girl to accuse him of touching her inappropriately. "Nice to meet you."

"This is Jen. Jen, look at Kyle!" Tara gushed, turning toward Jen, who finally came forward with a bored look on her face.

"Hi." Perusing Marisa up and down slowly, she spoke with a hint of surprise. "Hi Marisa. You're looking well."

"Thanks." Marisa didn't return the compliment and didn't even pretend to act glad to see her. Tara, meanwhile, tried her hardest to alleviate the tension.

"Oh, and that's Jenny. Jen's friend from Hope. Jen and Jenny! Isn't that funny?"

Jenny was also a skinny blonde who was undoubtedly Dutch as well. Marisa had been around enough of them to know exactly how to spot them. She greeted them both politely while Tara grilled Marisa on her MSU life and filled her in on Petersville gossip. While they were chatting, they heard Jenny speak to a guy who joined them. "This is a friend of Jen's from Petersville. And her boyfriend." Before she could introduce them, the guy spoke up.

"Marisa!" It was Trent, the guy from the Emmons brother floor her freshman year.

"Trent?" Marisa half-smiled and let out a laugh. After the disastrous progressive party that night, Trent had apologized to her the next time he saw her and was always friendly to her afterward but never invited her anywhere again.

"Hey!" He came forward and gave her a quick, one-armed hug since he was holding a drink in the other hand. "Oh my God, it's so good to see you! You look amazing!"

"Thanks." Trent didn't look too bad himself; he had bulked up and cut his hair so it didn't look so hound dog-ish. "Trent, this is my boyfriend, Kyle. Kyle, Trent used to live on the brother floor at Emmons freshman year."

The two guys nodded at each other, then Trent and Tara took turns monopolizing the conversation while Jen and Jenny sulked behind glasses of alcohol. "Babe, one time I invited Marisa to a progressive on our floor and I was wasted! Remember that?" he asked her. Like she could ever forget it. As she watched him closely, she figured he was probably a little wasted now, too. "Anyway, I think I tried to hit on you or something, didn't I? You were always so pretty." He smiled lopsidedly at her and shoved his hand in his pocket. Turning to Kyle, he gestured to her with his beer. "You know how many of us guys used to talk about how pretty she was? But you probably know that." Kyle frowned and glanced at Marisa to see if she was uncomfortable, but she placed a hand on his back to let him know it was OK. Jenny didn't like the way the conversation was going, either, and she interrupted quickly.

"Marisa, when are you done for the summer?" she asked with feigned interest.

"Well, we're on trimesters, so we're not done until early June." She ran her hand up and down Kyle's back while he stood stiffly with his arm around her waist.

"Oh, that's too bad. All of the summer jobs will probably be taken by then," Jenny said with a sip of her drink.

"That's OK. I already have a summer job lined up," Marisa began before Jen interrupted.

"Right, she works in her father's hardware store," Jen said with a smirk. She and Jenny gave each other a look and stifled laughs. No one else knew what was funny and Trent went so far as to ask them what they were laughing at.

"I love your dad's store," Tara said sincerely. "He's so nice and he always knows exactly what my dad needs whenever he goes in there, too."

"Yeah, he's great." But Marisa couldn't let the snide remarks pass. "Actually, Jenny, I won't be heading home this summer. I have an engineering internship with Perkins and Peterson in New Jersey. I'll be spending the summer there. You've heard of them, haven't you?"

This time it was Kyle who had to stifle a laugh. To mask his smile, he leaned over and ordered two Jack Daniels and Cokes from the bartender.

Both blonde girls bucked their eyes. "Perkins and Peterson? You mean the company that makes all those baby products?" Jen asked.

"Not just baby products. That's their consumer division. They also make several prescription drugs, including antibiotics and some drugs for diabetes. I'm sure your parents have heard of them, since they're doctors." Marisa wanted to laugh herself. The look on Jen's face was priceless. She had frozen in surprise, her glass ignored in her hand and her face pale. Well, paler than normal. "What are you doing this summer, Jen?"

She was saved from responding by Tara's and Trent's enthusiastic congratulations. As Kyle handed her a glass, he gave her a little nod of appreciation. God, that felt good. Jen didn't know what had hit her. Kyle was right. This was the perfect time to shove all of her success in Jen's face.

When a lull came in the conversation, Jen found her composure. "Well, that's great, Marisa. Good luck in New Jersey. It's so wonderful that you found a minority internship program like that."

There it was. The subtle, you-only-got-this-because-of-isms. You only got into Michigan State because of affirmation action. You only became valedictorian because Petersville never had a black one. Your dad only opened his business because of minority loan programs. Jen could never face the fact that Marisa always was and was always going to be smarter and happier and more successful than she could ever dream of being.

"This is not a minority internship program," Marisa said forcefully, while squelching the urge to throw her drink in Jen's face. "This program only hires six engineering students each summer. Six. From across the country."

Trent continued to gush over the news while Tara asked if the Petersville newspaper was going to write a story about Marisa working for such a big company. But both Jen and Jenny had had enough. "Are you ready to move on? This place is dull." In fact, Dooley's was hopping and Marisa had actually seen a few black folks come in since they'd arrived.

Sipping the last of his drink, Trent quickly acquiesced to their demands, said goodbye to Marisa, then led the two blonde girls out. Tara gave Marisa and Kyle another hug, told her to send her a postcard from Jersey, then ran out after them.

With a big sigh, Marisa leaned against Kyle, who was perched on a bar stool. "Well, that was Jen."

"Well, you didn't lie."

"No, I didn't." It was remarkable that three years out of high school and Jen was still the snooty, nasty, prejudiced bitch she was growing up. You would think she would have learned some humility and kindness from being at Hope College, a conservative, Christian school, but no.

"I loved the look on her face when you told her about your internship," Kyle said with a sip of his drink. "Imagine how jealous she's going to be when you're hired full time!"

Laughing softly, she put her arms around him. "Do you really think that's going to happen?" It would be perfect. Kyle had plans to go back East for grad school and she knew he wanted to settle near his parents in Philly, which made P&P's location an ideal spot. All she had to do was rock this internship, make more connections, then get hired after graduation next year. She wanted it, so all she had to do was make it happen.

CANDACE JOHNSON

BOOK THREE
1992-2017
"Faith the size of a mustard seed"

CHAPTER 17

Spring 1992

Tensions were high all over the country as the verdict in the trial of the police officers accused of beating Rodney King was due any day now. Marisa had been following the trial closely and felt a rage build up inside her every time she saw the officers' smug faces in court and on TV.

"I hate the way they look," she'd say to her friend Ava, a fellow black employee at P&P. Ava worked in supply chain/logistics, whose department was right next door to Marisa's. They ran into each other over the summer while waiting for the elevator, struck up a conversation and just kind of fell into an easy friendship since they were the same age and both grew up in white communities. Ava was from Fairfield, Connecticut, went to Yale and grew up in a wealthy family with both parents as doctors. Kyle didn't like her because he thought she was snooty and dismissive.

"Yeah, she does kind of look down her nose at people," Marisa admitted.

"But only at other black people, if you notice."

Yeah, Marisa noticed. Ava had no interest in hanging out with any of the other black employees, which made Marisa wonder why Ava even talked to her.

"You can't judge a person by how they look, Marisa," she said of the L.A. police officers. "You would be doing exactly what white people have done to us for years."

Yeah, yeah, yeah. Marisa had no patience for that. She couldn't wait for the verdict to come back guilty so all those cops could be sent to prison and get a taste of their own medicine.

She was sitting at her desk getting ready to leave when her boss, Josh, walked over, his face pale and his eyes big. "What?" she asked, wondering if she'd done something wrong.

"Not guilty." He whispered in shock.

"What?" Marisa's hands froze over her keyboard.

She heard Josh audibly swallow. "Those cops were found not guilty."

"No." Scooting back from her desk, Marisa shook her head dismissively. "That's not true. Where did you hear that?" Obviously his source was mistaken. Josh mostly listened to sports talk radio so if that was his source, then of course it was wrong.

"I was in Jack's office when the news came. You know he has a TV." Jack was the department vice president. "I can't believe it...The evidence was right there for everyone to see..."

Josh kept talking but Marisa couldn't hear him anymore over the roar in her head. Not guilty? Not guilty? Those bruises on Rodney King's face were, what, just make-up? Fake? Self-inflicted? She began rocking back and forth in her chair and knew she had to get away. Rising, she ignored Josh, left her department and quickly took the elevator down to the first floor, where Ben's HR office was. She had no idea if he was still here, but she knew he had a TV and if she was going to watch this coverage, it had to be with other black people.

Others had the same thought because Ben's door was open and several of her black colleagues were gathered around the TV, mouths agape and gasping.

"They gonna burn that city down!" said one younger guy in the room. Marisa felt like throwing or hitting something herself and could only imagine the helplessness and frustration the folks in that community were feeling.

"Can you blame them?" another said.

Marisa looked around the room and caught the eyes of the two lone white people in the room. One was Ben's secretary, the other was a colleague of his in HR. Both women looked like they were going to cry but Marisa felt no sympathy. White women cried if you looked at them funny. And what the hell were they crying about anyway? Their side won.

Since it was after five o'clock, the group stayed in Ben's office for a long time, lamenting and shaking their heads and yelling at the TV. After awhile, Ben – as the older voice of reason – spoke. "Listen, everyone. If anyone feels like they can't do their jobs effectively tomorrow, we have sick days for a reason. Go to a community gathering, go to a prayer vigil at your church, or just meet up with each other for support. I have a feeling this is going to get worse before it gets better."

Ben was painfully correct. The protests and burning began that night. Marisa couldn't turn away from the TV and spent hours on the phone with first her parents, then Matthew, then Shawnda and finally Kyle, who had been in class and then the lab until after nine o'clock. As usual, he sounded tired but happy. He loved his grad school coursework at Penn, probably because he was finally being challenged.

"This shit..." he began, then seemed at a loss for words. "I kind of figured this would happen as soon as they were granted the change of venue. I didn't want to get my hopes up, either, because this is so typical of this stupid-ass country."

"I know, but Kyle...there was video!" Marisa had been saying the same thing for hours, to herself and to her family and friends. "How could anyone look at that and say 'not guilty'?" She still couldn't believe it.

Walking through the hallways at work the next day, she kept her usually sunny greetings and smile in check. There was nothing to smile about today. Racist white cops essentially got cleared of assault and white America cheered. Now Los Angeles was in flames and the racial rhetoric had been ignited, too. The R&B station she listened to on the way in played nothing but empowerment music – Marvin Gaye's "What's Going On" – and spoke gravely and quietly about the

L.A. uprising and the jury verdict, calling for people to remain calm and talk out their differences. She didn't know if she actually agreed with that, though. She was mad. She was furious. She was frustrated. She could completely understand the need to lash out.

Thank God P&P had plenty of black employees, though. With them, she could quietly express her rage and frustration. Over coffee with her friends Kelli and Greg that afternoon, she noticed how all the white employees were watching them. It reminded her of how her classmates in Petersville would react every time they studied slavery or read Mark Twain. All eyes on her. In corporate America, though, seeing two or more black employees talking caused white people to freak out because they continuously watched or interrupted.

"Hi Kelli," said one woman, walking by.

"Greg! You ready for the Knicks game this weekend?" asked a tall guy standing in line.

"Hey Marisa! I love that color on you," said an older woman she knew from the regulatory department.

The three of them moved as one down the hall, away from prying eyes. "Listen, what are y'all doing tonight?" Greg asked. "We obviously can't talk here."

They made plans to meet at Kelli's townhouse, where they would order takeout, watch the news and vent.

"So guess what I heard," asked Greg as he walked in with a large pizza and beer that night. "Ben's secretary told on him."

"Karen?" Marisa liked Karen. She was always helpful and sweet and seemed to always know what was going on around the company. "Told what?"

"She was in the room yesterday, wasn't she?" Greg tossed his jacket on the kitchen table then answered his own question. "Yeah, I remember. She was standing over there crying with that other white woman. I don't know her name."

"Yeah, she was there," Marisa confirmed as she took a paper plate. "What about her, though?"

"So yesterday was impromptu, right? We just all kind of gathered in Ben's office. So Karen called the CEO's secretary yesterday to tell her that she felt 'scared' being in there with all of us."

Both Kelli and Marisa stared at him, mouths dropped open. "Why would she do that?" Marisa asked, surprised. Ben was the sweetest guy in the world and was probably the best boss, too. What reason could she possibly have for saying something like that?

"You know why, girl," said Greg, diving into the pizza by taking two slices. "She was in there yesterday with a bunch of angry black folks, got scared, then did what they do best, tattle."

As Kelli shook her head in resignation and set out some glasses, Marisa sighed. "Un-fucking-believable. If she didn't want to be in there, she could have left. No one wanted her in there anyway."

Kelli took a long swig of beer and joined Greg on the couch. "White women love to tattle. They always be telling some shit."

As Marisa got her own plate and bypassed the beer for a soda, she silently agreed. From Jen to Caitlin to Sharon to Molly, she knew firsthand the ways of white women. But still, Karen even had her fooled.

They watched CNN all evening, dissecting everything that occurred and how biased the reporting was. "Why is it 'looting' when black folks take stuff, but somehow when it's white folks it's 'finding' or 'taking'?" Kelli asked. "See, the media is half the problem. I deal with them all day and I see. There's no diversity in these newsrooms. None. No one is there to tell the other side or to check them when they get shit wrong about us."

By ten o'clock, they were emotionally drained, tired and – in the case of Kelli – a little buzzed. "So is your boyfriend coming up this weekend, Marisa?" she asked, rubbing her eyes sleepily.

"No. He's swamped. Again." She would have loved to see Kyle, if only to hug him tight and feel his reassuring warmth.

She got the chance the next weekend, when he came up after his last exam to spend two blissful weeks with her before his summer course work began. The L.A. uprising had finally died down after five days of violence, and they spent several hours reading and watching commentary on it before Marisa broached a subject that had been nagging her since the not guilty verdict.

"When was the last time you saw your cousin Nuke?"

It had taken Kyle almost six months after the police incident in Petersville for him to tell Marisa the story. Kyle and Nuke had grown up together. Nuke was his second cousin, only two years older than Kyle but a world away. While Kyle's parents were both college-educated and successful, Nuke's struggled. His mother was a grocery store cashier and his father a produce manager at the same store. With his parents working evenings and weekends, Nuke spent many nights at Kyle's house growing up. After he graduated high school, he enlisted in the Army and was stationed in South Carolina when it happened. He'd been off-duty, driving home from a club when he was stopped by police. His black Nissan fit the description of a car that sped away after a convenience store robbery and assault on the store clerk. And Nuke, being a tall black man, fit the description of the suspect. Despite his protestations – or because of them – Nuke was beaten with the officer's billy club, handcuffed and hauled to the police station, where he sat for the entire weekend. While the judge granted him bail – thanks to Kyle's parents – he remanded him to the supervision of his commanding officer at Fort Jackson, where he was essentially under house arrest. Kyle's parents paid for the best lawyer they could find, and he stressed several eyewitness accounts that Nuke was at the nightclub from 11 p.m. to 2 a.m. But it was the same nightclub that was just around the corner from the convenience store. The lawyer pointed out that Nuke had none of the stolen cash on him and no weapon – in this case, a baseball bat – when the cop arrested him. Still, the prosecutor poked holes in every alibi. Small holes, but that didn't matter. He was a black man who had the nerve to "talk back" to the cop, resist arrest and be out late in a nice car. He was convicted and sentenced to fifteen years in prison. His parents were devastated. Kyle's parents were stunned and furious. Kyle, however, was shook. If it could happen to Nuke, he reasoned, it could happen to me. And if the King verdict was any indication, the cops would get away with it.

"It's been a while," Kyle said. He was chopping tomatoes for the salad while Marisa made the pasta.

She weighed her words as she stirred the noodles. "Do you think I could meet him?" He stopped chopping and looked at her in surprise.

"What?"

"Do you think I could meet Nuke?"

He seemed at a loss for words. "Why do you want to meet Nuke?"

"He was your best friend growing up. It's obvious how much you love him. He was a big part of your life."

He turned back to the chopping block but laid down the knife. Turning down the stove burner, she stepped behind him and put her arm around his waist. "I don't know," she sighed. "Watching this whole King thing...and hearing how dirty and racist the cops were...it just made me think about him more, that's all. It's such bullshit. And you know he's not the only one convicted of a crime he didn't commit."

"Not even close," he muttered.

"You said yourself it's hard for your mother and his mother to visit. They just get so upset. So he must be lonely...Does his lawyer come up much?"

A pause, then a shrug. "I don't know."

She hugged him tighter. "I know it's hard for you, too, isn't it?"

Kyle paused, picked up the knife and began chopping again. "Every time I've visited him, I spent thirty minutes in the car afterward, crying my eyes out."

Tears sprang to Marisa's eyes at the thought of her strong, handsome and calm boyfriend crying all alone in the car over the cousin he loved so much. Resting her head on his shoulder, she spoke quietly. "And as hard as it is for you, it must be doubly hard for him. I'm sure he doesn't want you to see him in there, either."

Kyle was already shaking his head. "No, he doesn't. He was like my big brother. But every time I go, all he wants to talk about is what I'm up to, school, sports... you."

"Me?" She glanced up at him and was gratified to see a small smile on his face.

"I told him all about you. Not just in person, but in letters. I do write him a lot, you know. It's a little easier. That place...It takes all day. First getting admitted and through security, then the wait...the long-ass wait...you see wives, girlfriends, mothers, fathers...but the worst are the kids. Kids and babies in there waiting forever to see their fathers or uncles or whoever. And almost all of them black. It's horrible."

Sighing again, Marisa felt the rage building up again. This racist-ass country and its police state. Taking away someone Kyle loved for something he didn't do. Ruining his life. Ruining his military career. Destroying a family. Couldn't something be done? As she went back to the stove, a thought occurred to her. She couldn't fix the system, but she could damn sure try to help Nuke.

CHAPTER 18

Summer 1992

"I can't believe he was ever convicted," Matthew was saying as he rifled through the folder with Nuke's case history. Matthew was one month out of Georgetown Law School and spending the summer cramming for his bar exam while also interning at a local law firm. Marisa had called him a week ago to discuss Nuke's case after she remembered a story he'd told her about one of his professors. The professor started something called the Wrong Arrest Project, which aimed to overturn wrongful convictions or, at best, get cases thrown out before they even made it to court. The professor recruited students, alums, fellow professors and attorneys from around the country to volunteer. Marisa was praying that they would help Nuke.

"This has got to be the flimsiest case I've ever seen," Matthew said with a snort as he shoved himself away from the kitchen table in his apartment. Marisa had driven down for the weekend to visit and to discuss the case. Kyle knew nothing about this, but she'd discussed it with Barb, who had helped her retrieve the relevant files needed to appeal Nuke's case. "They didn't appeal back then?" Matthew asked.

"They tried, but the D.A. put such a stranglehold on it that they're still waiting. And you know how appellate judges are. They hate to overrule lower courts. But you would know more about this than me." Marisa was so proud of him and still couldn't believe he was able to stay serious and focused enough to make it through law school. He would always just be her goofy brother.

"Yeah, so many hurdles and so many variables can come into play. Well, this sounds like a perfect case for this project."

"How come you're not in the group anymore?" Marisa sipped her lemonade and looked around Matthew's apartment. Law books and papers were everywhere, but it looked ...different from the last time she'd seen him.

As Matthew explained that he was too busy studying for the bar exam to participate but that he might rejoin after he was settled in the firm, she realized what was different about his place. There was a big plant by the door and a spider plant hanging from the ceiling in the corner. Since when did Matthew care about stuff like that? And...were those throw pillows on the couch?

"Matthew..." Rising, she walked to the couch and picked up the pale orange pillow. "What is this?" She pointed to the plant. "And that?" When he didn't answer but continued to stare at her with big eyes, she continued. "What's next, curtains? I thought you didn't have time for much of anything, yet here you are decorating? What gives?"

Instead of answering, he retreated to the kitchen, where he refilled his glass of lemonade. Marisa remained in the living room, looking for more clues of a girlfriend. That was the only explanation. Matthew was finally getting serious about someone. "Who is she, Matthew?" His continued silence made her raise her eyebrow. Wow, he must really be serious about this sista, she thought. Otherwise he would have shrugged it off and changed the subject dismissively.

Sauntering to the counter, she rested her arms on the countertop as he avoided her eyes. "Well?"

"OK, I am seeing someone. She's actually the person I'm planning to give Nuke's files to. She's been in the Wrong Arrest Project for two years and really knows her stuff." He took a big gulp of his drink then refilled it again nervously as his little sister continued to stare at him with a grin.

"That's great! Where's she from? How'd you meet?"

"She's from Northern Virginia. Great Falls. It's a ritzy area. Her father owns a tech business," he began, before realizing he was babbling.

"Really? Wow. You met at Georgetown then?" Marisa held out her glass for a refill.

"Yeah. We met two years ago, became friends and then...started dating."

"When?"

"What?"

Marisa sighed. "When did you start dating? And what's her name?"

"We started dating about...maybe around...Valentine's Day."

Marisa was stunned. "Valentine's Day? You've had a girlfriend since Valentine's Day and didn't bother to tell anyone?"

"She was at graduation," he said defensively.

"Oh yeah! Your graduation! You didn't say anything then, either!" Shaking her head, she slurped her drink loudly. "I don't remember meeting anyone at graduation." She racked her brain, trying to remember all of the friends Matthew invited to his party but no one stood out. "What was her name?"

"It's Emily." Matthew said it quietly and avoided her eyes.

"Emily?" A black girl named Emily? Nah, it couldn't be... "Emily?" When she felt her stomach drop, she knew. Matthew was dating a white girl. She had to hear it from him, though, because what if she was wrong? "I've never met a black girl named Emily."

If silence could be loud, then the next five seconds were deafening as she continued to stare at him from across the counter. Finally, he looked her in the eye. "She's white."

The silence continued as she weighed his words, weighed the next words she had to say. "Is that why you didn't tell us?"

"Partly. I don't know...I told Robert, though."

Now that hurt. "You told Robert but you couldn't tell me?" Granted, they were brothers and had a bond that she would never have with either of them, but she and Matthew had become really close since he graduated from high school. Absence makes the heart grow fonder and all of that, she guessed.

"I didn't know if I could tell you or not! Ever since the sit-in, you've become Miss Fight-the-Power and a little Angela Davis wannabe. Face it, you're a militant." He said this with a raised eyebrow and a vigorous nod.

"A militant? Me? I grew up in Petersville, same as you. You act like we were raised by Black Panthers or something," she snorted. Marisa the Militant? Was he kidding?

"How many times were you interviewed by the media in East Lansing and Detroit any time something went down on campus?"

"That's because I was a member of the Diversity Task Force and the minority liaison to the student government..." Yes, after the sit-in and the story in the student newspaper, her campus activism had exploded. But she was still his sister. Nothing could change that.

"True, but I've heard how you talk about white people, Marisa. Face it. You don't approve." For all of his goofiness, teasing and outright terrorism her entire life, he faced her for the first time ever as a vulnerable grown man. And he wanted her approval.

"I..." She couldn't say it, but she couldn't hurt him, either. "I don't even know her, Matthew. Are you happy? Are you in love or something?"

With his hands his pockets, he nodded solemnly. "We are."

Trying to hide the tears that had formed, she entered the kitchen and put her glass in the dishwasher. "I can't ask for anything else but your happiness, you know. What you do is your business."

"But you don't approve. Do you?" He pinned her with a penetrating stare.

"It doesn't matter if I do or not!" She shrugged. "If you're happy, I'm happy. It's your life. And when are you going to tell Mama and Daddy? They're not going to care one way or the other."

"Daddy probably won't, but you know Mama will. She'll ask me why she sent me to Howard just for me to end up with a white girl."

THE KITCHEN ISN'T WHERE YOU COOK

Marisa was wondering the same thing, but didn't say so. God, Matthew in love with a white girl? A white girl he might "end up" with? Like as her sister-in-law? She loved Monica, Robert's wife, but mostly because she stayed out of the way, was serene and sophisticated and was a fabulous mother to their little girl, Stephanie. Marisa didn't know what she'd have in common with a rich white girl named Emily. But for now, she'd have to play nice, for that same Emily held the keys to Nuke's freedom.

***

She didn't seem like a rich, spoiled brat when Marisa and Matthew met her Saturday morning for brunch. Instead of an expensive outfit, Emily was wearing a casual yellow sundress Marisa had seen for sale at The Limited. Instead of a designer purse, she carried a large leather satchel as her briefcase. Her brownish hair sported deep red highlights and cute, thick bangs that she kept brushing out of her face.

"It's so nice to see you again, Marisa," she said in a deep, rich voice a la Kathleen Turner or Debra Winger.

"Same." Marisa sat and busily studied the menu while Matthew and Emily spoke quietly to each other. OK, this was weird. Matthew, for all of his faults, was cute. He was smart. He was a lawyer. He was funny. He could have had his pick of any of the thousands of black women around D.C., many of whom were probably Howard alums like him. He could have been part of a black power couple, raising black, powerful children. But she was supposed to bite her tongue and act like she was OK with this? Did he know what he was asking her to do? She knew white women. She'd grown up with them. She *knew* them. Better than he did, that's for sure. Did he think he needed Emily on his arm to be successful? Or to help him move up the corporate ladder? If so, then she was profoundly disappointed in him.

"So about the case..." Marisa cleared her throat after they'd placed their orders. She had no interest in small talk, didn't care to know more about Emily's background or career. Until they actually said "I do," then she was going to regard this relationship as another of Matthew's flings. So stop getting worked up about it, Marisa. Focus on Nuke.

Focus they did. Emily asked a ton of questions, most of which Marisa couldn't answer. She jotted down note after note in his file, underlined and highlighted paragraph after paragraph. Shook her head more than once, spoke in some legalese to Matthew, then turned to Marisa. "I'm going to need to speak to his lawyer for this to go any further. Is he still at this number?" She gestured to the cover page of his file.

"Yes. That's him. Do whatever you need to do. It's the most unfair thing I've ever heard. It makes me so upset to even think about ..."

"I get it," Emily said as she clicked her pen closed and put the file in her satchel. "But it's not even the worst story I've heard since I've been on this project. There are so many."

That got her attention. "How many?"

Emily stared at her and slowly shook her head. "You don't want to know."

"You mean totally innocent black men, right? Not just those with unfair or overly aggressive sentencing. Black men who definitely committed no crime – "

"Sitting in prison right now. Today. Some with life sentences. Some on death row. Our project has a backlog, there's so many."

"A backlog?" Marisa sat up straighter and looked from Matthew to Emily. "But Nuke...he's been in prison for seven years already!"

"Don't worry," Emily patted her hand and smiled. "You're Matt's sister, so we made a special exception for you."

Matt. No one ever called him Matt. Kids in Petersville tried it every now and then, but he corrected them immediately. At the name, she cut her eyes to Matthew, who narrowed his own right back as if to say, "Shut up." Instead of calling him on it, she smiled back at Emily with relief. "That's great. Thank you. I hope this works."

"I do, too. But please know that this is not a quick process. It could take a year or two before we make any progress. OK?"

Disappointed, Marisa nodded, wondering how she was going to tell Kyle...if she should tell him, lest he get his hopes up. But she knew she couldn't keep something like this a secret, especially since his parents already knew. No, she had to share the news.

***

She waited until the next weekend, when she drove from New Brunswick to his parents' house in Philly to see him. When he would have taken her to a hotel for some alone time over the weekend, she told him no, she had to stay at the house with his family so they could talk.

"Talk about what?" he asked while standing on the wide, brick porch.

"Nuke."

At that, he released his hands from her waist. "Nuke? What about him?" He looked so serious so suddenly that she regretted bringing it up without his mother around.

"He's fine. Nothing has happened to him or anything..." Peeking down the driveway, she noticed both of his parents' cars were gone. "When is your mother coming home?"

"Marisa," Kyle sat on a rocking chair, never taking his eyes off her. "What about Nuke?"

Biting her lip nervously, she leaned against the brick ledge and told him the whole story. He asked not one question and didn't interrupt at all. When she was done, he continued to stare at her. "Is this group legit?"

"Of course! It's Georgetown."

"What's their track record?"

She'd saved the best part for last. "One hundred percent. They've taken on twenty-four cases since they started and all twenty-four have resulted in freedom for the convicted."

"And their records?"

"Expunged. And in some cases, monetary damages for all the pain and suffering." But really, what amount of money could make up for seven years of a man's life? And the untold agony and likely abuse that took place in prison? As much as she wanted him out, she knew he'd never be the same.

"Babe..." Kyle stood, reached out and took her hands, shaking his head in disbelief. "I don't believe you. You did all of that? For a man you've never met?"

"It doesn't matter if we've never met. You love him. He's your family. And it was wrong! Just so wrong! That punk-ass cop and judge and D.A. and jury ruined his life! They just snatched seven years away from him, just like that." She couldn't continue because he'd drawn her in for a warm embrace.

"My God..." He whispered into her hair. "Thank you. Thank you. I had given up...I couldn't face thinking about another eight years for him...And parole was no guarantee. But now..."

Hugging him tight, she had to caution him. "Well, this won't be quick. It'll be a long process..."

"I know, but don't you see? He still has a chance. He has a chance at life. He'll never have to check that box saying he's a convicted felon. He'll be able to vote...He'll be able to go to school, get a job, whatever he wants. He's only twenty-five, for God's sake. He can still have a life!" He leaned back and searched her eyes. "All because of you."

Shaking her head, she demurred. "I'm not doing anything but bringing them the case. They're the ones doing all the work, including Emily, who is Matthew's white girlfriend, by the way!" If she expected a reaction to that news, she didn't get one. Instead, he kissed her softly and hugged her again. "I don't care who she is. If she can help Nuke, then she's OK by me."

CHAPTER 19

November 1992

Election Day. Clinton vs. Bush. Also Nuke's decision day. The State of South Carolina vs. an Innocent Black Man. In a normal world, the outcome would be a foregone conclusion. But in the post-Rodney King world, nothing was guaranteed. Nothing was a shoo-in. Nothing was certain.

Except Kyle's love for Marisa. He'd proposed to her during Homecoming weekend at Michigan State the month prior, and she was trying to balance her euphoria with her concern and worry about Nuke. Even Emily was surprised at how quickly his case moved up the list for review. But everyone who read over the transcripts, the police reports, the jury instructions – which were flawed in their own right – had the same reaction. How the hell did this kid ever get arrested, let alone convicted? If a case was ever a shoo-in, it was this one. But Marisa couldn't let herself hope, not when white people were in charge. No, she'd been burned too many times.

Work should have been a distraction, but every white face reminded her of the injustice that had befallen Nuke and everyone like him. And they couldn't understand. None of them. They didn't even think about it. They went about their peaceful, comfortable lives with none of the worries that she, Kyle, Nuke, Matthew and anyone else with black skin had to deal with. They couldn't imagine the effort it took to make small talk about their colleagues' pets or the Oscar-worthy acting job it took to listen as they bragged about their children or latest vacation in a spot that most black folks would never dare go, like Montana or Maine. So no, work didn't help.

Instead, she took her bridal magazine to the cafeteria and pored over the pages with her friend, Kelli, while nibbling on a salad and admiring the way her engagement ring sparkled with every page. Marisa had convinced Kyle to get married at the MSU Alumni

Chapel in late July, so that gave her roughly eight months to plan a wedding in Michigan while living in New Jersey.

"How many attendants are you going to have?" Kelli was asking.

"Five." Janine was her maid of honor, Shawnda, Jacqui, Janet and Kyle's cousin Keri were bridesmaids. Kristin would be the only guest from her high school. Not Tara, and definitely not Jen or Barry. For his part, Kyle had asked both Robert and Matthew to stand up for him as well as a couple of his Alpha fraternity brothers. The last slot he was saving for Nuke.

"I want him to be my best man," he told her.

Smiling, she nodded. "That would be nice." She still hadn't met him. She told Kyle she wanted to wait and hug him when he was free. Hopefully that day would be soon. They'd joined Nuke's parents and Kyle's parents at church several times over the past months, where the congregation prayed for his release. Of course, in church they called him by his given name, William.

"I can't believe his name is William Williams," Marisa said, dumbfounded.

"Yes, Lord, don't ask," said Barb, shaking her heard. "Lord knows I tried to tell his mama not to, but she obviously didn't listen. Good thing they came up with Nuke, though. That boy was so hyper, it was like a bomb went off everywhere he went."

In church, Marisa found herself tuning out the old-school pastor and instead flipping through the Bible. She'd only read it to her grandmother, never on her own. And now, with Nuke, and with her impending nuptials, church and God and Scripture were on her mind a lot. It was the last remaining black experience she still hadn't embraced. Church. Now that she was grown and on her own, it seemed like the next logical step. And even though she didn't know much about it, she knew she had faith. Faith that Nuke would be released. And she knew that God heard her when she prayed. She didn't know how she knew, but she felt ...something. Some kind of connection. So yes, having him as Kyle's best man was more than a hope. It was a definite. She was sure of it.

"Do you think I could visit your church sometime?" she asked Kelli over lunch.

The question prompted a large smile. "Are you kidding? I've been asking you to come with me for months! We can go Sunday if you want."

Returning the smile, Marisa closed her magazine. Sunday would be the perfect time to go, she thought. She could thank God for Nuke's release, which she knew was all in His hands.

***

By four o'clock, still no word from Emily or Matthew or the Wrong Arrest Project, and Marisa was getting worried. Barb and Kyle had called her at work twice already and she was sad to have no news. She wasn't going to be the first one to hear, anyway. After Nuke, his parents would be the first to know. Marisa told Barb to go over to their house and wait for word. "Once you hear, please call me."

The call came at four forty-nine, when Marisa was across the room, discussing a project with a co-worker. At the ring, she popped her head up to make sure it was her phone. Josh, her boss, was walking by her desk and she yelled, "Is that my phone?"

"Yeah. Want me to get it?" he asked.

"Yes! I'll be right there!"

By the time she skidded to her desk, Josh was already handing her the receiver. "It's someone named Emily. Is she with the new vendor we hired?"

"No, it's personal," she said, waving him away. With a shake of his head, he continued his journey, no longer interested since it wasn't work-related.

"Emily?" she whispered breathlessly.

"Marisa, we did it! He's getting out! His conviction was overturned and the case was thrown out completely!" Emily was shouting in the phone excitedly.

Closing her eyes, Marisa let the tears come. They did it. They beat the system. An innocent black man was going to get a chance at life. "Oh my God..." She breathed. "Oh my God..."

"The judges were appalled. They ripped the former D.A. to shreds, saying it was the worst case they'd ever seen and that it was a good thing the guy was dead because he shouldn't be allowed to ever step foot in a courtroom again." Marisa laughed through her tears. "And get this, they said they plan to review this cop's full arrest record to make sure there aren't others like Nuke."

That sobered her. "But you know there probably are." As excited as she was for Nuke, she knew he was just a blip in a larger community.

"I know," Emily was saying. "We can't get them all, but the longer we chip away at this institutional racism, the easier it'll be to knock this wall down."

Marisa swallowed, blew her nose then spoke softly. "Emily. Thank you. This wouldn't have happened without you." No, she didn't want her to marry her brother, but if he had to fall in love with a white girl, at least make sure it was a girl who understood. And Emily did. And she did something about it. And for that, Marisa was grateful.

***

Marisa didn't make it to Kelli's church on Sunday. Instead, she joined Kyle's family at their church, Nuke in tow. He came home Friday afternoon, to tears and sobs and shouts. Marisa stayed in Jersey until Saturday afternoon to give the family some alone time and to make sure the media cameras were gone.

THE KITCHEN ISN'T WHERE YOU COOK

When Kyle drove her over to Nuke's parents' house for dinner on Saturday, she couldn't stop fidgeting with her gloves. She was glad she'd done what she did, and she was ecstatic that Kyle was so happy, but she didn't want any undue attention. Kyle, his parents and Nuke's parents were all praising her, thanking her for what she did. The praise was so effusive that it was becoming uncomfortable. If she was white, it would be like some kind of white savior mentality. She hadn't done a thing but ask her brother for some advice. She'd suffered nothing, sacrificed nothing. In fact, Nuke was going to be the first person she'd ever met who even served time. Even her criminal cousins in Gary had never been arrested, although they probably should have been.

"Why are you so quiet?" Kyle asked. He'd been babbling on and on about how happy his family was, how muscular Nuke had gotten, how good it felt to have him home.

"I just...this isn't going to be some kind of big fuss, is it? For me?" Marisa studied his profile, so handsome in a dark blue skully cap.

"A big fuss? You mean like a party? Nah, nothing like that. It's just us, my parents, Nuke and his parents. Just dinner and dessert." Reaching out, he grabbed her hand. "Why?"

"I don't want a fuss. I didn't do anything. I just called Matthew for advice, not expecting him to have many answers at all. I didn't even know if they'd take Nuke's case. So when everyone goes on and on praising me, it just feels...weird. And undeserved. Your parents have done way more than I have. And his parents have suffered but never gave up."

"So what are you saying? They shouldn't thank you?" When she didn't answer, he squeezed her hand. "Listen, you did more than you think. You cared. For someone you never met. Do you know how many people hear stories like this and just go, 'oh, that's a shame' but never take any action? You did. You cared about him. You saw him as a human being, as a man. And you did something about it. So I'm sorry, you may not want thanks, but you're going to get it. You put the wheels in motion." His voice shook as he spoke. "You helped save his life, Marisa."

"Stop," she muttered.

"No, you stop." He squeezed her hand tightly. "We love you for this. All of us."

As they pulled into Nuke's driveway, she took a deep breath. Finally. She was going to meet the man who was the subject of so many of her prayers over the past six months.

He wasn't as tall as Kyle, but he was actually wider, if that was possible. He had light brown eyes, a wide nose and a tiny scar above his thick eyebrows. She'd expected a shaved head, but he had beautiful, close-cropped curls recently shaved into a becoming fade. The hug he gave her was heartfelt, tender and long. Swaying them both back and forth, she felt rather than heard the tears he cried. The realization made her tears flow, too. What an unfair hand he'd been dealt, she thought. All because of some racist cop.

"As far as I'm concerned, I got me a sister now." He pulled back and smiled at her through the tears. "Nice to meet you, Marisa. And thank you."

Something in his voice made her break. The tears turned into sobs and she hugged him again before turning into Kyle's embrace. The enormity of what she'd done finally hit her. No one was doing anything to help him. They'd buckled under the weight of racism and oppression and essentially accepted that his fate in life was sealed. And why? Because they'd seen it so many times before. They'd lived in it. They'd fought it and after awhile, the fight left them. Marisa, though, hadn't had to fight like they had. She had never been afraid of cops growing up, she never had any reason to doubt the judicial system until she was grown, she'd never known anyone in prison. And because they had no fight left, she picked up the sword and began swinging it. And the spoils of her victory stood in front of her.

CHAPTER 20

Summer 1998

Marisa paused the videotape and stood in front of the TV, staring at Kyle's face awash in tears. He'd cried as soon as he saw her appear for her walk down the aisle. Marisa was resplendent in an A-frame silk dress with swoop neckline and small cap sleeves dotted in delicate lace. Atop her head she wore the smallest tiara, given to her by a friend in the U.K. as a wedding present. "It was my mum's when she married her first husband, but since she hates him and has no daughters, it's just been sitting in her closet as a bad memory. She was going to throw it out but I told her I'd do it for her. So here you are."

"It's not bad luck, is it?" Marisa joked, but inside she was touched. It was beautiful and probably priceless due to its age. It was her "something old."

"You will bring it good luck," he'd said.

As she pressed play on the videotape, she watched as the tiara glowed and sparkled during her walk down the aisle. Kyle wiped his tears away and struggled to contain an outright sob while both Janine and Shawnda did the same in their pale pink bridesmaids dresses. Marisa, though, was oddly calm. She'd faltered not once, practically floated down the aisle on her father's arm and flashed the most serene smile at Kyle as she approached him.

"Wow, I can't believe it's been five years," said Kyle's deep voice behind her. Turning, she smiled at him and rested her chin on the remote in her hands. Their fifth anniversary was in just a few days and they were getting ready to leave on their anniversary trip to Hawaii, where they'd honeymooned. With any luck, she'd get pregnant on this magical trip, since the past year had produced absolutely nothing.

Everything had always come so easily for Marisa. Grades, accolades, cheerleading, track, friends, finances, career, love life. Aside from her identity crisis, she'd never really struggled at anything her entire life. To do so now, at something that was second-nature and so easy for everyone else of a certain age, made her feel inferior, ashamed and embarrassed. She was so worried about her ability to get pregnant that she'd started visiting her friend Kelli's church more often, even without her friend. There she'd pray for a baby, but seeing the babies and kids dressed in their Sunday best made the yearning even greater.

One month after the Hawaii trip, after yet another negative pregnancy test, a despondent, depressed and desperate Marisa drove into Trenton after work to attend the Juneteenth service at Kelli's church, called Trinity Revival Church. She'd told Kyle where she was going but didn't invite him to join her. This was something she had to do on her own.

The pastor was as riveting as always. He seemed to be speaking directly to her. "Only one perfect person ever walked the face of this earth and that was Jesus. You're not perfect, so stop tripping!" Marisa, who didn't know pastors could be funny, giggled. "Stop trying to be perfect! Stop trying to live up to everyone else's expectations of you! Find your identity in Christ Jesus. Not in your career. Not in your boo. Not in your material possessions! Only Jesus can give you the peace that passes all understanding. Only Jesus can fill that void inside you."

By the end of the sermon, Marisa found herself with several others at the altar, confessing her sins, asking God to forgive her and dedicating her life to Christ. She hadn't planned on it, but it just seemed such a natural thing to do. Something had been tugging at her for weeks, urging and nudging her ever since she entered the beautiful, cavernous church. The pastor's sermon about identity especially hit home. She had struggled with her identity her entire life. First as a black girl in all-white Petersville, then as a black student at Michigan State trying to walk the tightrope between black and white worlds, then as a "different" student among other black kids, then as Kyle's girlfriend, then as a black corporate career woman, then as a wife. Who was she? Who was she meant to be? Who did God plan for her to be?

"You are a child of God," Pastor Bradley said after they'd all said the sinner's prayer. "You are a child of God. You are a child of God." He pointed at each person assembled at the altar. "Welcome to your new life. You have been born again!"

With a start, Marisa realized what that meant. She was born again? Saved? Is that what she'd meant to do? Was she supposed to be a holy roller and stop drinking and stop listening to rap music now? And stop cussing?

"I know you probably wonder what that means," said Pastor Bradley. "But don't worry. We're not going to leave you alone to figure it out yourselves. If you follow the nice gentleman to your right in the blue suit, he will take you to another room to explain to you what comes next. Family, let's give God some praise for what He's done today. Glory!"

Marisa followed the line out of the sanctuary and into a small conference room where members of Trinity Revival Church explained what they'd just done, how they could come to classes at TRC every Sunday night in order to learn more about salvation, baptism, Christianity and the Bible. Marisa left to a round of hugs, warm smiles and promises to return on Sunday.

She didn't pull into her garage until after ten o'clock and she sat in her car with the ignition and radio off, listening to the silence. In that moment, she was reminded of one of her favorite books from childhood and she chuckled as she spoke aloud. "Are you there, God? It's me, Marisa." Giggling, she whispered again. "It's me. Thank you, God. And thank Grandmama for me, too."

Becoming saved brought Marisa not only peace of mind, but surprisingly, peace with white people. She learned to love her enemies, she learned about the fruits of the Spirit, including longsuffering and patience, and she learned about forgiveness. The first thing she did was forgive Barry. For years she'd harbored resentment and anger at him, but now she knew she had to let it go. She forgave Sharon for what she said their freshman year in college and realized she had to value trust over suspicion. Even when she was told in early August that she wasn't going to get promoted yet because she wasn't ready to be a "people manager," she didn't even get mad or chalk it up to racism. She figured it was all God's plan and in His timing. And that's what she started to believe regarding pregnancy. She knew she'd have a baby of her own. And as Kyle liked to tell her, "Parenting is more important than pregnancy."

CHAPTER 21

200-2011

Their baby boy, Brice, was born healthy and happy with a head full of hair in late March 2000, just two weeks before Michigan State won their second national championship in basketball. Marisa and Kyle watched the game with bursting pride while Marisa rocked and nursed Brice. He was surprised at her decision to breastfeed – neither of them knew any black women who'd done it – but was not surprised when Brice decided breast milk wasn't filling enough and they had to supplement with formula. Marisa, full of rollercoaster post-partum hormones, cried and blamed herself for not being able to fulfill her baby's needs naturally, but Kyle told her to get over it. They'd both been raised with formula and turned out fine. Their baby boy would be fine, too.

Brice's younger sister, Aria, followed three years later with no hair and a grouchy and whiny disposition. Marisa was over the moon for her son, who seemed like a male version of herself: Optimistic, sunny and smart. She had no idea where Aria got her attitude from, but she was a challenge from the very beginning. She tried not to show favoritism, but being around Brice was just so easy. As they grew older, she used to dread hearing Aria's footsteps coming down the hall for they would inevitably bring a scowl and a whine. Kyle, meanwhile, babied her all the time – despite Marisa's protests – and was the sole reason she was as spoiled as she was. His relationship with Brice, though, was not what he expected. Kyle wanted another athlete, another testosterone-fueled guy's guy. But Brice wanted nothing to do with sports. He was completely into music. He'd started singing in the church choir as a child, taught himself to play the piano at age six, and was able to play the drums and write music by the time he reached high school. Marisa was enamored and by then even Kyle was impressed.

Marisa succeeded in climbing the ranks to senior director at P&P even though she made it clear early on that her family was her top priority. She never even considered being a stay-at-home mother, though. Black women didn't have the luxury of effortlessly going back into the workforce. Thankfully, Kyle's parents and myriad of cousins and aunts came up to help whenever they needed a break and they had a cadre of support from their church family at Trinity Revival. Her father, for one, was ecstatic to finally have a grandson and he'd insisted on driving out a week before her due date just to "keep an eye on things."

Marisa had her family. She had her career. The man she loved. A relationship with God. Life couldn't get any better.

CHAPTER 22

2012-2017

After Trayvon Martin's death in 2012, Marisa watched her son with new eyes. That could have been him, she thought. Brice was growing fast. He was already taller than her and had inherited his father and grandfather's broad shoulders. But to most of America, he was a threat. She and Kyle gave him "The Talk" about how to act if approached by a police officer, and Brice, being the smart, no-nonsense boy he was, listened intently.

The aftermath of the Trayvon Martin murder, the Eric Garner murder and the unrest in Ferguson, Missouri – all because of some racist cops – tested Marisa's faith and her view of white people. The issues were unyielding, raw and consumed her on a daily basis, just like Nuke's case had done. The fact that white people insisted on giving the cops the benefit of the doubt – despite videotaped proof – at first saddened her. Then she felt the old rage build up inside her as race relations in the country only got worse. It was the same rage she felt when Barry destroyed her prom dreams. The same rage when Sharon uttered the racial slur right in front of her in college. The same rage she felt whenever Jen had said some biased, prejudiced comment to her over the years. The same rage when people at work looked at two or more black people talking with suspicion and fear. The same rage when Ben was pushed out of P&P too early and unjustly.

"White people are losing their minds," she said to her mother on the phone while watching Barack Obama get reelected in fall 2012. But even she – who knew white people better than most – couldn't have anticipated the vitriol and hatred that came his way after his election. The fact that race relations were going backwards was something she couldn't fathom. Surely God had some kind of plan, right? He was letting this happen so we could face our fears and insecurities and wash away our hatred, right?

The last thing Marisa wanted to do was to go back to hating white people. She'd been living in a nice détente for years, ever since she'd gotten saved. Her church even had several white families as members and they all got along perfectly. Yet now everything was boiling over again.

By the 2016 election, Marisa was quickly sliding into her old self. Seeing Donald Trump on TV caused her to scream and yell and – yes, cuss – at the television. Surely no one in their right mind would vote for this orange-faced fool. But as she scrolled through social media night after night, she noticed some friends posting pro-Trump messages. Tara, for one. Caitlin for another. Even her former boss, Josh, who was working in Raleigh, was a big Trump supporter. Marisa blocked them all and in doing so, vowed to cut anyone out of her life who supported him. For to support him was to support everything that had caused Marisa harm over the years. Everything that was going to cause her children harm in the years to come. And she couldn't abide by anyone who would stand by and allow such an incompetent racist to the highest office of the land.

When the election returns came in, Marisa couldn't watch the networks declare him a winner. Her entire family sat in the living room in shocked silence, dread and disbelief dotting their faces. She watched Aria, who was eager to watch the first woman president get elected, and felt her heart break. Aria's face fell with every state that was called for Trump. When Marisa went to bed, she made the kids go to bed, too.

"Hillary still has a chance, though, doesn't she, Mom?" At thirteen, Aria had stopped calling her Mommy two years ago.

"I hope so, baby. I hope so."

But it was Marisa who had to break the news to her the next morning. It was Marisa who watched her daughter's face fall in disbelief and disappointment. It was Marisa who was speechless and couldn't even turn on the TV that morning. It was Marisa who wanted to keep her children home that day, wrapped in her arms, and protected from a country that hated them so much that they would elect someone like that. South Brunswick was pretty diverse with a large Indian-American population, so Marisa was pretty confident that most of their classmates voted for Hillary, but she still feared for her kids' futures. She was sending them out into a country that applauded racist, murderous cops and maligned innocent, unarmed black boys. She was sending them into a country that thought it was OK to call the first black president and his wife every name in the book. Besides fearing for her children, Marisa was resentful. She was resentful that white people's staunch racism had propelled her out of her happy place. A place where she looked at everyone as a child of God. But she couldn't do that anymore. For no child of God would applaud what this man represented.

***

By 2017, she had blocked almost everyone from Petersville from her social media accounts except for Kristin, who was as appalled as she was at the turn of events. When her mother told her that her father had finally decided to sell the store to his longtime manager Joe and that the Petersville Chamber of Commerce was going to give her father a big banquet in his honor, she knew she had to return home. Home to a place that had overwhelmingly voted for Trump. Home to a place that she no longer loved, not anymore. And she had to do it while pretending to be happy to see everyone and while thanking them for attending her father's party and for being such great customers over the years. Could she do it?

CHAPTER 23

August 2017

The banquet for her father was being held in a meeting room of the Petersville library, a semi-new building erected in 1994, so Marisa had barely stepped foot in it. She ushered her kids into the rental SUV and refrained from taking Aria's phone away as she FaceTimed with her friend Tatiana.

"Let her be," said Kyle, with a hand on hers. "Let's just focus on your father today, OK? This is a big step."

"I'm going to see a bunch of people I don't want to see tonight," she sighed as they inched their way the few short blocks to the library. "Mama said Barry was going to be there. And Jen's parents." Jen, however, was not. She was living in a ritzy suburb of Atlanta with her two kids and her second husband, who also had two kids. Marisa couldn't picture Jen as a stepmother and instantly felt sorry for her stepchildren. Kristin was unable to come, but rumor was that Tara and her parents might show up since they were regular customers over the years thanks to their farm.

"Remember, just keep all the conversation focused on your dad," Kyle repeated. "Let's just assume that everyone here voted for Trump — "

"Which they probably did!" she interrupted while scrutinizing the long-standing Shell gas station on the corner. It hadn't changed a bit.

"OK, so let's not even try to imagine and guess whose side they're on. We know whose side they're on and you're not going to change their minds. You grew up with these people. They had the same mindset when you lived here, you just didn't know it."

He swung the SUV into the library parking lot and stopped next to Robert's Ford Flex and Matthew's Honda Pilot. Both of her brothers drove pretty boring cars, which was surprising considering they'd been obsessed with Smokey and the Bandit's TransAm and Magnum P.I.'s Ferrari growing up. They were both boring middle-aged dads now, with Robert still looking fit and trim at fifty-three despite a severe receding hairline and Matthew looking paunchy with a head of salt and pepper hair. All of their daughters were out of the house and they were both struggling with empty-nest syndrome. Marisa teased them about it, saying they were crazy and that she couldn't wait to get her kids out of the house so she could have Kyle to herself again. For even though they were now both forty-eight, their love for each other was as strong as ever. It was hard to believe that they fell in love thirty years ago and that she still loved him as much – more even – as she did when they were freshmen in college.

"Mom, I'm going to go tune up, OK?" Brice bounced out of the car, tucked his sheet music under his arm and headed inside. He was playing the piano during the dinner and would be singing a special song he'd written just for his grandfather, who was always amazed at his grandson's talent. Brice was heading into his senior year at a performing arts high school and had plans to apply to the Berklee School of Music in Massachusetts and to Juilliard in New York. Marisa was certain that he'd get into both. Aria, meanwhile, was entering the local public high school and was primarily concerned with her friends, makeup, selfies and – unfortunately – boys. The baldheaded baby had sprouted a head full of thick, shiny hair that she loved to braid, tease and curl and unfortunately had inherited Marisa's body. Unlike in Petersville, where the white boys didn't appreciate her legs and hips, the boys in South Brunswick panted after Aria, to her delight. She knew how to dress to provoke and tease and Kyle finally – finally – started to set his foot down with her because even he could tell she was getting out of hand.

They made their way inside, Kyle strolling slowly with her brothers while Marisa walked behind them with Monica and Emily,

Matthew's now-wife. It had taken her years to warm up to her and once she did, she realized they were perfect for each other. After the 2016 election, when Emily discovered that her brother and father had both voted for Trump, she vowed not to return home for a holiday or family event again. Every holiday was either spent at home, with friends or with Matthew's family. Marisa applauded her for taking such a stand.

Inside the library, the family was greeted by Mrs. Wilcox, the same librarian who had run the place when Marisa was a child. She oohed and aahed over the entire Logan family and then led them to the meeting room. Inside, Brice was tuning the piano and softly practicing his songs. Marisa looked around and smiled ruefully at the simple decorations. In the corner, though, was a display of Logan's Hardware history, photos and newspaper compilation of her father's years on Main Street.

Edging over, Marisa stood at her father's shoulder as he read through them all. "Look, that was the first write-up in the newspaper when I opened up." He pointed. "And see here, this was during the Blizzard of '78. You were just a little girl then. The entire town was buried under snow."

"I remember," Marisa said, hooking her arm through her father's. "You donated all of your plows to anyone who had a four-wheeler and you and Robert stood in the middle of a snowed-in Main Street with all of the snowmobiles, sleds and toboggans you had to help people get their groceries from the store back to their houses since they couldn't drive." Marisa had been so proud. Her father had always been a pillar of the community thanks to his big heart and easygoing spirit. She wondered, though, how he would be received today if he'd come to Petersville to open a business. Would a Trump supporter oppose his business? Would the Republican-led city council block his permits? Marisa wouldn't put anything past them.

"I know you told me before, Daddy, but with everything going on now...How did you open a business – as a black man – in the 1970s? Here, of all places? Why not Louisville or Gary?" She'd heard the story before but she needed to hear it again, if only to remind herself that not all white people were like Trump and his supporters.

"Oh, you know the story, baby girl. My Army buddy Lou and I used to be the ones to fix everything in our unit. We just had a way with tools, I guess. Anyway, we used to talk about opening up a hardware store together when we got home from Vietnam. So that's what we did. We argued for a long time about where to open it, and we did settle on Louisville, but, well, it was Kentucky. In the '70s."

"Totally racist, right?" She paused and ran a finger over a framed photo of her father receiving an award from the city council.

"You know it. Anyway, Lou grew up here and he used to tell me how the one hardware store in Petersville was always dirty and that people used to drive to Saugatuck or Holland for supplies. That didn't make any sense to us, so we started to shop for locations up here. Then we found our spot." Her father paused, cleared his throat, fished his handkerchief out of his pocket and blew his nose. "Lou was a good man. When he died...I almost called the whole thing off. I didn't think I could do it without him. And I damn sure didn't think this town would accept me the way they did. But ...when a veteran gets killed like that...by a drunk truck driver...Just think. He survived the war only to get killed right here in Petersville. So I think the town did whatever they could to honor his memory, and that included welcoming me." He smiled softly at her. "And you and your brothers. I know it didn't end the way you wanted, but you had a good life here, didn't you?"

With a soft kiss on his cheek, she hugged his arm. "I had a great life here, Daddy. Don't ever think otherwise."

As they strolled past photo after photo and news story after news story, Marisa stayed close to her dad. "Do you ever wish one of your kids would have taken over the business?" She'd asked him that question before, but now it seemed especially poignant. He was selling his business to a biracial man who mostly identified as white due to his black father being out of the picture and Marisa couldn't help but wonder if he had any regrets.

"Well, yeah, of course it would have been nice to pass this on to one of you all," he said with a pat on her hand. "But you kids had to follow your own path. I built this business not with the intention of leaving it to you all, but to give you a future. And options. Options that I never had."

By the time the cocktail hour started, Marisa had introduced her family to several of her former teachers, Caitlin, Dennis, Tara and her parents and finally, Jen's parents. They had long since retired from their medical practice and were still living in the same house in Petersville during the spring, summer and fall, but headed to the Gulf Coast of Florida during the winter.

"Jen sends you her regards," Jen's mother said unconvincingly.

"How is she?" Marisa couldn't even lie and send her return greetings because she didn't mean them.

"Oh, well," her parents exchanged glances. "It looks like it's not going to work out with Grant."

Marisa blinked. "Is that her new husband?"

"Yes. They've been married a little over a year and well, it's been hard, with his kids being so difficult, and Atlanta being so ..." Jen's mother faltered. "Hot. And crowded." Marisa knew what she wanted to say. Atlanta was so black and so urban that she could easily see someone like Jen being appalled and irritated at the city's urban flavor.

"Oh, that's too bad," Marisa said politely.

"Yes, well, she's going to move into our house in Sarasota while she...figures things out. We think the boys will be able to adjust well down there."

Marisa was already bored so she bid them goodbye and pulled Kyle away to stand next to their table. "I told you this would be torture. Remember. If they're not talking about my dad, then pull me away. Please! OK?"

Laughing, he drained his cup, then noticed a familiar face emerge in the doorway. Pointing one finger, he nudged his wife. "Look."

Turning, she locked eyes with Barry, who was standing in the doorway with a red Polo shirt and khaki slacks. His hair was darker, thinner but hardly bald. He'd gained some weight but it was evenly distributed all over his body and Marisa was oddly glad to see he didn't have a beer belly. He actually looked pretty good.

After greeting a few people on his way in, he made his way over to Marisa and Kyle.

"Marisa!" Opening his arms, he waited for her to step forward. She did, hugging him and patting his back in a friendly manner.

"Barry, how are you?" She smiled, surprised that she really was glad to see him and glad that he hadn't deteriorated into some gun-rack toting, pickup truck-driving, MAGA-hat wearing hillbilly. He actually looked like the accountant that he was. He worked for a tax firm in Holland, was married to some blonde Dutch woman from Holland and had two blonde kids, a boy and a girl. The boy was in the Army, stationed in Afghanistan while the girl was in her third year at Hope College.

He and Kyle chatted for a few minutes before Kyle excused himself to go and yell at Aria for sitting in the hallway with her headphones on while glued to her phone. "Ah, kids and their devices. It's a never-ending battle, isn't it?" He gave a laugh.

"Always a battle. Were we ever addicted to anything like this?" She crossed her arms and made a show of trying to jog her memory.

"I don't think so. You and your friends used to pass notes all the time, though. I guess that was the texting of our day." Barry swayed on the balls of his feet and shoved his hands into his pocket.

"Right. Oh, I used to be so good at passing notes without anyone seeing," she giggled. "No one would ever believe that I would do something like that."

They laughed heartily then fell silent. "Your dad is going to be missed. He's been such a stalwart in the community. Always so honest and helpful. It's going to be weird to not have a Logan's Hardware anymore."

"Oh, it'll still be Logan's Hardware. Daddy put it in the sales contract. Joe can't change the name."

"Oh good!" Barry smiled and nodded appreciatively. "That's smart. But again, that's your dad." A pause then, "He really knows how to run a business, unlike some people." Marisa didn't know who he was referring to, so she kept quiet. "He's trying to run this country the same way he ran his failed businesses. Does he want the U.S. to go bankrupt the way his companies did?"

Wait a minute. Was he talking about Trump? "Wait, so you're..." she paused because she'd promised Kyle that she wouldn't talk about politics tonight. "...talking about Trump?"

"Who else?" Barry rolled his eyes and made a "tsk" sound. "As an accountant, knowing how he ran his so-called businesses makes my head hurt. It's embarrassing. The sooner we get rid of him, the better."

Marisa couldn't believe her ears. "Wait a minute, you're not a Trump supporter?"

Barry fixed his familiar brown eyes on her. "No way. Are you?"

"Hell no!" Marisa quickly answered. "But I thought...aren't you a Republican?"

"Where'd you get that idea?" Barry folded his arms in front of his chest. "I've been a Democrat since I cast my vote for Clinton. Uh, Bill Clinton, back in 1992. I vote straight-ticket every time."

"But you live in west Michigan," she replied, still shocked. She held on to the back of her chair, she was so thrown and shocked by his admission. "That can't be easy."

"Not at all. My wife voted for him. You should have heard the arguing and yelling that went on when I found that out." A dark shadow ran over his eyes at the memory. "I mean, we have a son in the military and he can't even respect the so-called Commander in Chief because he's a dangerous moron. How could she vote to put our son in more danger?"

Marisa was speechless. The last thing she expected was to hear a litany of complaints from Barry about Trump. She looked at him again and was instantly transported back to high school, when he'd made that guy – what was his name? – apologize for using the n-word in her presence. Or when he'd told Jen to go to hell when she told him he shouldn't date her. Or how he'd ignored all of the looks whenever they went out together, even before they were dating. Maybe that type of foundational decency was harder to bury than she'd thought.

"What does your family think about you being a Democrat?" she asked. She knew his racist hag of a grandmother was long dead, but his mother was still around, living in Arizona.

"My mother and my sister have the red MAGA hats," he said ruefully. "They're among the fifty-three percent of white women who voted for that idiot. I don't have anything to say to them. I mean, they're basically hurting themselves because he doesn't care about them at all. He's just feeding them a lie."

"Barry, I gotta say, I'm shocked." Marisa set her drink down and took a seat, gesturing for him to join her at the table. "I thought for sure you and everyone here would be Trump supporters. I was dreading coming here tonight because of that."

"Oh no, are you kidding me? There's more of us than you think. But I thought you'd know better than to think I'd ever vote for his level of lunacy. And the racism! Are you kidding me? I haven't told many people this, but ...my son ..." Barry paused and she heard him gulp. "He's gay. And... he's in love with a black man."

Boy, he was really "spilling the tea," as Aria liked to say. "That must be hard for him, being in the military."

"It is. His mother hasn't come to terms with it. She's ultra-conservative, you know. She actually suggested gay-conversion therapy until I told her he'd go to that over my dead body."

"How does she feel about him being with a black man?" This should be interesting.

"She cares less about the fact that he's black but more upset that he's a man. She's convinced he's going to hell. I try to support him as much as I can. I visited them with my daughter when they were stationed in South Carolina and let him know I'm here for him whenever he needs to talk. I can't imagine how he must be feeling in this atmosphere."

"I can," Marisa said quietly.

Barry stared at her and for an instant – just an instant – she was crazy for him again. "I'll bet." They continued to stare at each other, then Barry cleared his throat and stood up. "Well, listen, I'll get back to my table. Please laugh at my jokes about your dad, OK? They're completely corny but I think you'll get most of them, since you were there for all of these stories."

"Yes, I was. And Barry, thank you for coming. And thanks for the talk."

"Anytime, Marisa." Pausing, he seemed to want to say something, glanced at the door at Kyle returning, then smiled again. "I'll see you later."

With a small wave, she watched him walk away. How different would things have been if he'd never broken her heart, she wondered? She'd thought about it over the years and always imagined different scenarios. Would they have kept dating throughout college? Or would they have broken up? Somehow she couldn't imagine introducing him to her black friends at Michigan State. And she never, ever, imagined them having sex. It was just too weird. But still, the emotional tug was strong, and if she admitted it to herself, still there.

The evening progressed with Aria scowling and looking bored, Brice enchanting everyone with his musical skills and the entire community honoring her father. Throughout the program, Marisa would casually-on-purpose turn to catch Barry's eye, and each time she did, they were already fixed on her. He was staring at her, she was sure of it. Did Kyle notice? Looking at her husband, she smiled at his expression. He had always been totally in awe of her father and seemed enthralled by the stories he was hearing. Reaching out to hold his hand, she forced herself to pay attention to the current speaker, Carole Worthington, one of the tellers at the bank that Marisa's family had frequented for as long as she could remember. But as she laughed on cue, she could feel Barry's eyes on her and wondered what he was thinking. She still looked good, even after two kids and middle age surrounding her. Yes, her hips were wider than ever and her midsection not as toned as it once was, but she was – as Kyle would say – still a dime. Monthly trips to the hairdresser kept the gray hair at bay and her face was still unlined – "black don't crack" Barb would explain – and so far glasses were still unneeded. As she crossed her legs, Kyle placed his hand on her thigh and she admired the way her legs looked in her heels. If Barry was looking, let him look, she decided.

His turn was next. As he walked to the podium, she had a sudden flashback to senior year, right before he'd kissed her that cold January evening. It was New Year's Eve and they were at a party at Dennis' house. She and her friends had been discussing the latest episodes of "Days of Our Lives" and "Guiding Light" in the living room when he'd emerged from the kitchen, striding purposely toward her just as he was striding toward the stage now.

"Marisa, let's go," he'd said, taking her by the hand and pulling her off the couch.

"What? Why? It's not even midnight yet!" She yanked her hand away, glancing in confusion at Kristin and Tara.

"Listen," he turned to her, keeping one eye trained on the kitchen door. "Just ignore those guys, OK? In fact, don't even talk to them..."

"Who?" She scanned the crowd but most of the attendees were people from her school. Just as she was about to tell Barry that she wasn't ready to leave, three guys emerged from the kitchen. She'd never seen them before and assumed they'd arrived through the back door. They had beer in their hands and were wearing West Ottawa letter jackets. And all three of them were in blackface with wigs on.

She watched as Jen sidled up to them with a smirk. "What are you supposed to be?"

"We is Buckwheat!" One of them said, mimicking the Eddie Murphy character from "Saturday Night Live." "O-tay!"

She remembered Barry and Kristin looking disgusted, Tara looking embarrassed. No one else at the party, though, seemed bothered by it and no one even looked her way. Barry had taken her elbow, led her to the hallway and quietly told her he'd take her home. She'd obliged, shaking her head and trying not to show how bothered she was by the three stupid boys at the party.

"What a bunch of idiots," he'd mumbled as he cranked up the heat in his car.

She appreciated his words but didn't feel like talking about it anymore so she'd changed the subject. Until tonight, she'd almost forgotten the whole ordeal, about how Barry had come to her rescue and had been the only guy there who thought the whole thing was out of line.

Focusing on the podium once again, she smiled as Barry recounted story after story of her father and how he'd follow him around the store as a kid, asking questions about the business and the inventory. Sometimes his stories would include anecdotes of Marisa and her family, and she laughed at the appropriate times and even caught Aria trying not to smile.

"I could go on all night," Barry was saying, one hand in his pocket casually. "But in short, here's what I know about Mr. Logan." Then he turned to Marisa's father directly. "Here's what I know about you. You were like a father to me. You taught me about honor. About kindness. About business. You showed me how to be a man. How to be a husband. How to be a father. You raised three of the best people I've ever known, and one, in particular ..." he turned, caught Marisa's eye and curved his mouth in a one-sided smile, "...was my first love."

Stunned, Marisa's mouth dropped open. His first love? Really? But he'd never told her he loved her. Was he serious? She couldn't hear the rest of his words as he wrapped up because Aria was whispering furiously at her. "Mom! Is that Barry? The one you told me about? About prom?" Her eyes were big and shocked.

Kyle shushed her and whispered to Marisa over the crowd's applause as Barry ended his speech with a big hug for her dad. "You should go up there." Glancing at him for confirmation, she kissed him then joined her brothers and mother at the podium to wait her turn to hug Barry. When she did, he held her tightly, silently, knowing how everyone in the room watched them.

"That was beautiful, Barry," she said quietly, releasing him with a teary smile.

"Thanks." Grasping her hands vigorously, he searched her eyes, causing her to take a breath. "I meant every word."

THE KITCHEN ISN'T WHERE YOU COOK

For the rest of the night, Marisa was shook. She continued to socialize but as the party wound down, she noticed that he still hadn't left. Soon he was the last non-family member remaining, talking and laughing with her brothers and Kyle about the upcoming football season. At one point she would have been right there in the middle of them, discussing it, too, but motherhood, career and church had diminished her ability to keep up with sports like she used to. Instead, she sat at a table with her legs stretched out on the chair next to her, watching everyone with her head resting on her hand. With her parents moving back to Louisville, who knew when she'd ever get back to Petersville? As it was, her parents preferred traveling to see their kids anyway. They'd spent several holidays on the East Coast with both Matthew and Marisa and they practically had a second home with Robert and Monica in Chicago's Hyde Park.

Through lazy and tired eyes, she saw Brice begin packing up his instruments while her brothers offered to help push the piano back to its original spot. Kyle was lecturing Aria about something, so that left Barry standing alone. And that's when he turned to her from across the room and slowly made his way over to her.

She watched him, as she had all night, with a wistful smile and something akin to a lump in her throat. So many years. Wasted. Wasted in anger. Wasted in resentment. Wasted in hurt. And what was the point? Deep down, he was the same old Barry. And she was the same old Marisa. Formative years are meant to form the person you eventually become. But the person you eventually become is still wrapped up in the person you were. And always will be.

"It's been so good to see you, Marisa," he said as he looked her up and down yet again. "You look beautiful as always. Your family is amazing. And your dad...I could never repay him for everything he did for me."

"Thank you, Barry. And despite everything that happened, you know you'll always be like one of the family, don't you?"

With a startled and wide smile, he bowed his head and scratched the back of his neck, touched. "I can't even tell you how much I needed to hear that. Thank you."

He continued. "You know something? I don't think I've ever had a friend like I had in you. I was an idiot to mess it up. But I'm glad we're at a point now where we can talk civilly." Walking behind her chair, he rested his hands on her shoulders and leaned forward so only she could hear him. "And I meant what I said. You were my first love." And with that, he kissed her gently on the cheek.

Smiling wistfully, she patted his hand and gazed at his tanned face, now lined with a few wrinkles. Yep, he was still the same Barry. Or as Kyle would say, the star of every childhood memory she had. And now, for the first time in thirty years, she could consider him a friend once again.

THE END

About the Author

Candace Johnson is a 2023 Hurston-Wright Fiction Fellow and a graduate of Michigan State University. "The Kitchen Isn't Where You Cook" is her first novel. She lives in the Chicago suburbs with her husband and two children.

www.ingramcontent.com/pod-product-compliance
Lightning Source LLC
Chambersburg PA
CBHW071449140726
47997CB00005B/1653